"Release me this instant," she exclaimed. She struggled hard now, fearing the import of his arousal. "You lied to me! You led me to believe you wanted to sleep, not to . . . to . . ." She could not bring herself to say it.

"Shhh, Leila, do not fight me," Guy murmured. "I have not deceived you. You have deceived yourself. Surely you know a man and woman sleep little on their wedding night. There is too much love to be shared."

"I don't love you!"

"Ah, but I love you," he said huskily. "More than life itself. That gives me plenty to share with you until the day you admit you love me, too."

"That day will never come—"

"It will!" He caressed her jaw and throat, his eyes searing hers with unflagging conviction. "It will."

Other **AVON ROMANCES**

Captive Rose

MIRIAM MINGER

AVON BOOKS ◆ NEW YORK

CAPTIVE ROSE is an original publication of Avon Books. This work has never before appeared in book form. This work is a novel. Any similarity to actual persons or events is purely coincidental.

AVON BOOKS
A division of
The Hearst Corporation
1350 Avenue of the Americas
New York, New York 10019

Copyright © 1991 by Miriam Minger
Published by arrangement with the author
Library of Congress Catalog Card Number: 90-93406
ISBN: 0-380-76311-7

Special Printing: June 1993
First Avon Books Printing: March 1991

AVON TRADEMARK REG. U.S. PAT. OFF. AND IN OTHER COUNTRIES, MARCA REGISTRADA, HECHO EN U.S.A.

Printed in the U.S.A.

RA 10 9 8 7 6 5 4 3 2

To Stephen,
*who gave me three perfect roses
and won my heart*

To lovers true, what matters dark or fair?
Or if the loved one silk or sackcloth wear,
  Or lie on down or dust, or rise to heaven?
Yea, though she sink to hell, he'll seek her there.
                    —OMAR KHAYYAM
                      (translated by E. H. Whinfield)

Prologue

Damascus, Syria
Summer, 1253

"**H**e comes, my mistress."

Majida's simple words elicited a nervous fluttering of excitement in Eve Gervais's breast. She ceased her gentle crooning and glanced at the striking Circassian odalisque, a slave woman who had been purchased from the teeming Damascus slave market on the same day as she, six months ago. Majida's lithe, broad-shouldered frame filled the narrow archway leading from Eve's private apartments.

"Is all in readiness, Majida?" Eve asked quietly, careful lest she wake the baby sleeping so peacefully in her arms. She watched as Majida crossed the shaded courtyard on strong, silent feet and knelt beside the marble couch where she was sitting.

"Yes, mistress. All is prepared."

He comes, Eve thought. Sinjar Al-Aziz. Her master. Her protector. He had spent every third night with her since she had been brought to this house; long, passionate nights she had once dreaded. Now she yearned for those nights as she yearned for him, this man who would become her husband in a week's time.

Eve felt a moment's panic, and raw guilt constricted her throat.

Forgive me, William!

"How sweetly she sleeps," Majida whispered, oblivi-

1

ous to Eve's distress. The odalisque's large gray eyes were soft as she gazed upon the baby. She reached out and lovingly caressed a plump limb. "Her skin is like the finest pearl, O my mistress," she said in hushed admiration. "White as the full moon and delicate as a dove's satin wing."

Distracted by the husky, soothing quality of Majida's voice, Eve smiled faintly as the odalisque bent her head and kissed the baby's curled fist. "You will spoil her with such talk, Majida," she said, gently reproaching her. " 'Tis a good thing Leila is only seven months old and does not yet understand your many compliments."

"Ah, she knows," Majida insisted softly, sitting back on her haunches and looking solemnly at Eve. "She hears, she smiles. She listens to her devoted Majida." The odalisque raised her hand, shielding the baby's face from the dappled late afternoon sunlight. "Leila," she intoned, "dark as night. Your ebony hair vies with the raven's gloss. Your eyes sparkle like twin amethyst jewels, fit for a sultan. Perhaps one day it might even be said your beauty rivals that of your fair mother."

"Then I will be the most fortunate of men to have a wife and a daughter blessed so richly by Allah."

Majida gasped slightly and bowed low to the floor, her indigo silk caftan splaying in shimmering folds around her. She touched her forehead to the cool paving stones as Sinjar Al-Aziz, at thirty years of age the wealthiest and most respected physician in Damascus, entered the courtyard. "O master, I have a foolish and flapping tongue—"

"Not foolish if one speaks the truth," Sinjar interrupted pleasantly as he strode toward them. "Rise now, woman, and leave us. I wish to be alone with my beloved."

As Majida scrambled to her feet, Eve's face grew warm at the stirring sight of her Arab lord.

He was so darkly handsome, his features finely etched beneath a short, carefully barbered beard, his body strong and virile beneath his flowing robes . . . a body she knew as intimately as her own. His last words were like a forbidden caress upon her skin; they burned into her mind.

"Go, Majida, and take the child," she said, her heart thundering as she felt Sinjar's gaze drift over her in a manner that never failed to unnerve and excite her. She lifted her daughter into Majida's outstretched arms. "See that my lord and I are not disturbed, yet remain close at hand in case I have need of you."

"Yes, my mistress." Hugging Leila to her chest, Majida hurried past Sinjar with her head lowered and eyes downcast, and disappeared through the archway.

A tense silence ensued, mocked by splashing fountains and sweet birdsong.

Overcome by Sinjar's presence, Eve bowed her head and stared at the small, man-made stream gurgling through the square courtyard. Lifeblood to the fruit trees and flowers blooming in colorful profusion around her, the stream was fed by the Barada, the Cool River, which flowed just beyond these thick, ivy-covered walls and supplied the water for the entire city.

Damascus. The original Garden of Eden, or so the Damascenes called their ancient home. A land of trees and rivers, fruits and birds, rising up like a verdant miracle from the desert.

A paradise.

A prison. Eve's prison . . . and Leila's. An opulent prison filled with every luxury, every comfort—even love if she would only accept it from the man who had found such favor in his Christian concubine that he had made her his favorite, and soon his third wife.

A small, plaintive sigh escaped Eve's lips. Once she was married she would be a free woman, but not so free that she could ever leave the confines of the city walls unescorted. She would still be a prisoner, trapped by tragic circumstances and a fierce, burgeoning love that was threatening to envelop her completely.

Six months ago she had wanted desperately to escape, to return with her infant daughter to the nine-year-old son she and William had left behind in England last summer when they began their pilgrimage to the Holy Land. Now she wasn't so sure she wanted to escape. She was certain

of only one thing; of the terrible guilt festering within her
like a living, breathing presence.

Eve closed her eyes tightly against the sudden tears
welling there.

Oh, William, my dearest husband, why did you have to
die? Why did you abandon me to the vile slave trader who
murdered you and then brought me here to Damascus,
selling me to this man who has the power to make me feel
again . . . make me love again? I would rather be suffering
a thousand torments than betray you in my heart. But I am
helpless against it. Please forgive me!

"Eve."

She started as Sinjar took her gently by the shoulders
and raised her up beside him. She opened her large, violet
eyes and regarded him through spiky lashes, tears tumbling down her cheeks. With infinite tenderness he cradled
her face in his hands, his thumbs caressing away the warm
wetness.

"You weep for William, yes?"

She stared into the smoldering, mahogany depths that
seemed to know her soul, and nodded.

"I weep for William . . . for what is lost," she said
truthfully, for strangely with Sinjar she had never thought
to lie. "And I weep at the remorse which is like a dagger
twisting in my heart—"

Sinjar silenced her with a finger to her lips, his gaze
burning intently into hers. "Say no more, my beloved. I
understand," he said quietly, enfolding her in his arms.
"But know this. Kismet has brought you to me, and there
is nothing that will alter what has gone before. Nothing.
You must accept your kismet, Eve. Your fate."

Eve said nothing as she buried her damp face against
his shoulder. His familiar masculine scent, tinged with
musk and sandalwood, was a compelling comfort. Her
arms crept around him, and she returned his embrace.

"I am a patient man, but I am also a jealous man,"
Sinjar continued, his arms tightening possessively. "You
lost your William ten months ago. I know you have yet to
mourn, but I will not live forever with his spirit between

us, Eve. In time, I hope you will leave him to his eternal rest and return my love.''

Eve silently cried out her anguish as Sinjar bent his head and kissed her, the demanding warmth of his lips driving William's image from her mind. She clung to him as a drowning creature would cling to a rock, unconsciously making her choice, the living over the dead.

She knew that in time, just as Sinjar had said, her guilt would ease and she would be able to voice her love. And she knew, deep in her heart, that William would wish her happiness in the new life fate had brought her.

"Come with me, my beloved," Sinjar said softly, his breath stirring her gossamer veil and the lustrous black hair curled at the base of her throat. He took her arm, and together they walked from the jasmine- and rose-scented courtyard, passing through the archway into Eve's luxurious apartments, which were set apart from the rest of the harem as befitted a favored concubine.

Now Eve led the way, taking his hand as she drew him into the salon across velvet carpets embroidered in gold and crimson.

The room was dark and cool, a welcome relief from the dry summer heat. Two window grilles looking out onto the courtyard provided soft, diffused light through elegantly carved lattices. Beautiful gilded hangings with intricate mosaic designs graced the four walls, while on three sides of the room the floor was raised several feet, forming a divan furnished with inviting brocade cushions.

Eve was pleased to see that Majida had done her job well. The low tortoise-shell table in the center of the room was set with gleaming silver plates with cream silk napkins wrapped in mother-of-pearl rings, and in the middle sat a large platter covered with plump figs, bowls of caviar, salty olives, and feta cheeses. Next to the platter was a basket of bread, the crusty, flat loaves still steaming from the harem ovens. It was a simple repast. The heavier meal would come later that evening.

While Sinjar settled himself on the tasseled pillows strewn beside the table, Eve picked up a carved crystal pitcher and poured them each a goblet of cool, citron-flavored water.

"That is work for a slave," Sinjar objected mildly, as he had done since Eve had first entered his harem. "A woman in your exalted position should have a multitude of slaves, yet you accept only one, Majida, and she is forever doting on the child instead of you."

Eve knelt on a cushion, smiling as she handed him the goblet. "I have simple needs, my lord. Simple wants. And I enjoy doing these things myself. More slaves would only disturb my privacy, which I treasure more highly than ease of living." She gave a small laugh. "As for Majida, she does dote overmuch on Leila, but she is a great help to me, and Leila adores her. It is enough."

Sinjar chuckled, shaking his turbanned head. He drank deeply from his goblet, then set it down and leaned toward her. "You, my beloved Eve, are truly a wonder," he whispered, his gaze moving slowly over her face as if memorizing its shapely contours. "My two other wives grow fat and lazy because they do not lift a finger for themselves except to bring food to their mouths, while you"—he reached out and tenderly stroked her cheek—"insist upon serving me with your own hands."

Eve closed her eyes and inclined her head, her skin tingling from his touch. She felt his smooth fingertips stray ever so slowly along the high curve of her cheekbone and down her throat, lingering at the hollow pulse point, then drift still lower. She drew in a sharp breath when he traced the firm swell of her breasts through her silken clothing.

"My touch excites you, yes?" Sinjar asked huskily, circling his palm over her taut nipples. "Your pulse betrays you, my beloved. It pants for love as a wild beast pants for water beneath the desert sun. As I pant and burn for the softness of your body. Our meal must wait."

Sinjar raised himself up suddenly and sucked hungrily at her breast despite the silken barrier, a wet and frustrating sensation that caused Eve to moan deep in her throat. How she longed to be free from her clothing and feel his lips, his flicking tongue upon her skin!

As if in answer to her wish, Eve opened her eyes to find

Sinjar kneeling in front of her. She watched, fascinated, as he reached around her narrow waist and deftly unfastened the embroidered belt securing her qumbaz, then pushed the outer garment from her shoulders. And still he suckled her. His movements were abrupt and impatient, his breathing becoming as rapid as her own. Wherever he touched her, she could feel him trembling.

It was always like this when he had not seen her for three days. Sometimes his hunger was so great he would rip the clothes from her body in his haste to possess her.

Sinjar pulled the filmy thob over her head and tossed the dress to the floor. Eve shivered as the cooler air in the salon found her naked torso. He bade her stand as he tore wildly at the silk tikkeh, the drawstring gathering together the waistline of her voluminous sirwal. It was all she could do not to collapse, her knees were so weak with desire. She leaned on his broad shoulders while he dragged the shimmering pants from her hips, his nails lightly raking her skin, and she laughed giddily when he pulled her into his lap with an exultant cry.

His need for her was so overpowering he did not bother to remove his robes. With a quick adjustment of his sirwal he freed himself and entered her, supporting the weight of their bodies on his heels.

Eve's cries of passion were silenced by his kiss. His long fingers ripped off her veil and threaded through her hair as he moved powerfully within her. Their fusion was swift and furious, their release as wild as a sudden thunderstorm breaking over the distant mountains of Lebanon. And when it was over, Sinjar drew her down beside him on the pillows, their flesh still joined.

"How you please me!" he whispered raggedly into her ear, wiping long, midnight strands from her shoulder and nuzzling her earlobe.

Eve shifted her weight, draping a slim leg over his hip and winding an arm around his neck. She played languidly with his turban, which amazingly was still atop his head. The thought made her giggle, and she hugged him impulsively. "How you please me, my lord!" she said brazenly, her eyes shining into his.

They lay entwined together until their breathing had slowed, and then for a long time afterward, simply basking in the warmth and nearness of the other.

At last, Sinjar drew himself reluctantly from her, retying his pants, and Eve covered herself with her wrinkled thob, pulling it over her head. Yet they remained close together on the pillows, sitting side by side and clasping hands.

Thinking he might be hungry, Eve picked the choicest fig from the platter and offered it to him, holding it to his lips. Sinjar smiled playfully and took the fig between his even white teeth, but he did not bite into it. He bent his head to her in a funny, familiar game, and she bit the plump fig in half, the sweet juice dripping down their chins. Sticky kisses followed, and much laughter, and they both sank back down on the pillows, embracing.

"My beautiful, wondrous Eve," Sinjar said, sifting her silken hair through his fingers. "I have found my dearest treasure in you." He kissed her soundly, then brought himself up on an elbow and gazed into her eyes. "I want to give you a gift. A marriage gift."

Eve shook her head gently, though she was touched by his offer. "No, my lord. I have riches enough. You have been more than generous with me, even adopting my daughter as your own and promising her an education that would be unheard of in my country." Her voice softened with wonderment. "I still cannot believe it, the possibility of training Leila one day to follow in your footsteps as a physician—"

"Tell me what you want, Eve." He interrupted her so firmly that she knew he would not be swayed. "And if it is within my power, I will give it. Allah has blessed me; I am a wealthy man. What can I give you? Jewels? If you wish for a sparkling diamond as large as that fig or even larger, you shall surely have it! I could build you a country villa, with fragrant rose gardens and tiled pools, and a pavilion with a gilded roof that will shine in the sun like beaten gold . . ."

Eve listened quietly as his fantastic list grew longer, her heart thudding painfully in her chest.

Dare she ask him?

There was something he could give her that was more precious than gold or silk or the rarest jewels, something they had touched upon only briefly in the past. When Sinjar had told her he wished for them to marry, he said Moslem men were allowed to take Christian women as wives, though he hoped she would one day accept his faith. She had said nothing, and had been grateful when their conversation had drifted to other topics. But now . . . did she dare?

"Th—there is something, my lord," she began hesitantly.

"Ask and it is yours, my beloved."

Eve met his gentle gaze fully, hoping against hope that he would understand and not take offense at her request. "The greatest gift you could offer me is a simple one and costs nothing, my lord, save the generosity of your heart. I . . . I want to remain a Christian"—she almost faltered as his expression hardened, but rushed on recklessly— "and I want to raise my daughter in the faith of her homeland."

There, it was said and she didn't regret it, though from the angry look flaring in his eyes, she feared he would deny her request at once. Yet no words came as his mouth drew into a thin, tight line.

She waited for long moments and Sinjar, now lying on his back and staring blindly at the muted colors on the ceiling, still said nothing. The salon was so quiet she could hear the stream rumbling outside in the courtyard and the haunting trill of a caged nightingale from a distant corner of the harem. When her hope had all but faded, he spoke.

"You have requested a hard thing of me, Eve," he said, turning his head to look at her. "A very hard thing."

"I know this, my lord."

His voice fell to a solemn whisper. "You and I . . . we shall never be together in Paradise."

"That only God may judge."

Again he was silent, and she could sense him wrestling with himself until finally he reached for her hand and gently squeezed her fingers. Her heart began to soar before he even said the words.

"You are fortunate that Islam is tolerant of other faiths, though the same cannot be said for the Christian crusaders who terrorize and rape our land and our cities. To them, we are the infidels, the unfaithful, and no better than dogs."

Eve did not respond, for she knew he spoke the truth. She kept silent, waiting.

Sinjar sighed heavily, his tone resolute. "If it is your greatest desire," he began, then paused as he searched her face.

"It is."

"Very well. Then I must grant it."

Tears of gratitude sprang to Eve's eyes and she hugged him, but he did not return her embrace. She remained undaunted, knowing he was hurt, and hugged him more fiercely, as if she would never let him go.

"I will never leave you, my lord, save in death, for today you have truly won my heart. This I promise."

Sinjar's arms wrapped around her so suddenly, clasping her tightly against his chest, that they took her breath away. He buried his face in her hair, inhaling her sweet perfume and murmuring her name over and over like a fervent prayer. She felt a hot wetness on her neck . . . his tears.

Eve smiled through her own tears as a strange lightness washed over her, releasing her. It was dizzying and wonderful, and she knew at last that she was free.

Goodbye, William. Sleep in peace, my love.

Chapter 1

Damascus, Syria
Late Summer, 1272

"**I** shall lead, mistress."

Leila inclined her head curtly in acquiescence, making no comment as Suhel opened the door and stepped outside. She lifted the opaque veil attached to her long kufiyya and tucked a corner into her headband, covering her face below the eyes, then followed the stout white eunuch into the nearly deserted street.

She hated visiting the governor's prison, even if it was to assist her father. How she wished Jamal Al-Aziz, her betrothed and Sinjar's only son by his second wife, was here in Damascus so she wouldn't have to go. But he had been summoned to Cairo to cure the caliph's family of smallpox and wouldn't be home for weeks. As her father's apprentice, she was the next likeliest choice.

A new case, Sinjar's cryptic message had read, delivered to her barely ten minutes ago just as she was beginning to relax after a long, wearying day spent caring for patients at the Hospital of Nureddine. Something highly unusual. She was to make all haste. She had to admit her curiosity was aroused, though she wished she was meeting her father anywhere but in that horrid place.

At least the walk there would be pleasant, Leila thought, much of her apprehension and weariness fading as she hurried to keep up with Suhel, who despite his bulk was maintaining a vigorous pace. It was such a beautiful summer evening, she could not help but feel exhilarated.

A balmy breeze swirled around her, lifting the embroidered edges of her veil, and she inhaled deeply, filling her lungs. The air was sweet with the scent of flowers; jasmine, oleander and her favorite, damask rose. She wore the barest hint of its fragrance at her wrists and throat, her only truly feminine indulgence when she went about her work.

She glanced up at the sky, a deepening turquoise bowl inverted above the walled city. Here and there, stars were beginning to twinkle, and the bright quarter moon was just rising over the rugged summit of Mount Kassioun. Multicolored pigeons flew high above her in ever-widening circles, searching amid the countless rooftops for a home perch. They were all familiar sights to her, yet somehow new and hauntingly different each time she beheld them.

"How I love this city," she whispered to herself, listening to the sounds of the night as they headed west along a narrow side street.

A chestnut vendor's cart rumbled past them, the wooden wheels bumping noisily on the uneven paving stones, and a donkey brayed in the distance. Laughter filtered from the houses, as did the animated drone of conversation, a baby crying, mongrel dogs barking, and everywhere the lush sound of fountains and cascading water; the stirring cacophony of life.

"This way, mistress," Suhel said over his broad shoulder, his effeminate voice intruding upon her reverie. He gestured with the lantern, the weaving light causing their shadows to bob and sway against the stucco walls. "Since I am with you," he stated pointedly, "we shall take the main streets which are faster than the rear alleys allowed to women, yes?"

Leila shot him a withering glance as an answer, but the eunuch only chuckled.

She was still piqued at him for betraying her attempt to leave the house without an escort. As long as there was daylight, she was allowed to come and go as she pleased, but since it was so near dusk, he had gone running to tell her mother. Eve, Majida, and Suhel had caught up with her just as she was about to pass through the guarded harem doors. Her mother's troubling reprimand was still fresh in her mind.

"Leila, you know women are not allowed to walk about unescorted at night," Eve had chided her. "Why must you be so willful and reckless?"

"It is not yet dark, Mother," she had objected somewhat lamely, feeling suddenly foolish and much younger than her nineteen years.

Eve waved her small, delicate hand in a dismissive gesture. "Listen well to me, my daughter. As you say, it is not dark. But you cannot expect the trappings and privileges of your profession to protect you when the hour grows late and the streets become empty. These are dangerous times, Leila. You, as a Christian, should know that well. The crusaders swarm over the land again, inciting fierce hatred and a lust for revenge that could mark any Christian as a potential target. You wear the zunnar—"

"I am not the same as them!" Leila blurted indignantly. "Any Damascene citizen would recognize that, Mother"—she tugged on the striped sash around her waist—"whether I wear this or not. The crusaders are barbarians. Wild savages who cross the sea in the name of God and piety, but who truly come to pillage and rape and destroy what they don't understand. We are civilized, Mother. We live here in peace, while those—those Christians think only of plunder and conquest."

"You speak of your own blood, Leila. Your heritage . . ." Eve's voice trailed off to a whisper, a faraway look haunting her eyes. "Ah, how can you know? I have told you so little. It is another world, another place."

"Mother," Leila said gently. Disconcerted by Eve's pensive, slightly sad expression, she felt her anger quickly fading. "Father will be waiting for me. I must go."

"Yes, you must," Eve said, her gaze finding Leila's once more. "Take Suhel with you."

Leila nodded, wanting more than anything at that moment to ease her mother's mind. For weeks Eve had seemed troubled and unusually quiet, so unlike herself, often studying Leila with a strangely wistful expression.

"I'll take ten slaves with me if it will please you," she said in an attempt to make Eve smile. She felt a sense of relief when some of the sparkle returned to her mother's lustrous eyes.

"Suhel is enough," Eve had said, leaning forward and kissing Leila's cheek. "He is stout, but he is also very strong. Go now, daughter. Your father is patient, but he will wonder what is keeping you."

As she puzzled over what could be distressing her mother, Leila's thoughts were nudged back to the present when Suhel suddenly dropped back beside her, his plump hand straying to the long, jeweled dagger hidden beneath his sleeveless coat. She followed his watchful eyes to the three Bedouin merchants approaching them on the other side of the main street, each leading a lumbering camel.

Leila bowed her head modestly until the men had passed, very much aware that they studied her curiously, their dark eyes glinting in the golden lamplight. She did not feel threatened, but in that fleeting instant she was reluctantly grateful for Suhel's company.

With the eunuch taking the lead again they walked on, passing the Great Mosque with its three graceful minarets; one of them, the Minaret of the Bride, was the oldest in Islam. At the northwest corner of the mosque stood the tomb of Saladin, the most powerful sultan of the Ayubite dynasty, who had won back Jerusalem almost a hundred years ago from the crusaders led by Richard the Lion-Hearted.

"Crusaders," Leila muttered in disgust, again recalling her mother's anxious voice. "Vile barbarians, every one."

It shamed her to think she was bred from such a treacherous and unscrupulous race. Though Eve had taught her the crusaders' language as a little girl, Leila rarely used it now, preferring to speak Arabic. Nor had her mother ever insisted she speak the foreign tongue, even when they were alone.

Eve had told her practically nothing about her true father or the strange, distant land called England. It was almost as if Eve was loath to dredge up old, probably painful memories. Which was fine with Leila. Such knowledge was of no consequence to her. Her home was here in Damascus.

All she knew of the crusaders was that every time their ships landed upon the shores of the Arab Empire, they brought discord and brutal destruction to a society of refinement, culture, and unsurpassed learning. It was enough to make her hate them all.

"We are . . . almost there, mistress," Suhel said raggedly, beginning to wheeze from exertion. The climb up the crooked street to the citadel, the fortress overlooking the city, was steep. The governor's prison was just outside the citadel's thick, honey-colored walls.

Leila's stomach knotted as they neared the forbidding flat-roofed building in anticipation of what she would find inside. She remembered the stench. The tortured screaming. The rats.

She shuddered. Yes, the rats were the worst part, but she had no choice. Her father needed her assistance.

"Thank you, Suhel," Leila said, overtaking the eunuch easily. "You may go home now. I can manage the rest of the way myself."

"I will see you there, esteemed mistress," he replied obstinately, wiping his thick neck with a sodden handkerchief. "Your beloved mother would be most displeased if I did not, yes?"

Leila clamped her mouth shut, knowing any protest would be useless. She waited until he had caught up to her, then they walked the last few paces together, stopping just outside the huge, arched entrance to the prison.

A dozen fierce-looking guards stared back at them with little expression, but when Leila introduced herself they quickly parted ranks and allowed her to pass through the tall iron gates. They knew she was the daughter and apprentice of Sinjar Al-Aziz, the private physician of Mawdud, the governor of Damascus, and of Sultan Baybars himself, whenever that great man journeyed to Damascus from the imperial city of Cairo.

Wide-eyed and nervous again, Leila glanced over her

shoulder just before she was swallowed up by a dark, inner hallway. She saw Suhel already trudging back down the hill, the lantern swaying in front of him. A silent guard steered her by the elbow into a well-lit chamber, where with a surge of relief she spied her father. His presence was so commanding, so authoritative, she could not help but be calmed by it.

"There you are, my daughter," Sinjar exclaimed, his robes swirling as he strode over to her with a grave look on his handsome face. "I have only just arrived myself from the hospital." Before she could catch her breath enough to respond, he took her arm and guided her through another set of iron gates. "Come. We must hurry."

Leila flinched when the heavy gates clanked shut behind them. She was thankful for the reassuring pressure of her father's hand on her arm and for the two well-armed guards leading the way.

As their silent group ventured deeper into the prison, they were assailed at every turn by putrid odors and pitiful moaning, like Leila's worst nightmare come to life. She could swear she heard rats squeaking and skittering in the dark, musty corners. She looked neither right nor left, hoping to spare herself any horrible images she would have a difficult time forgetting, but tormented shrieks or unintelligible gibberish occasionally drew her gaze to the prison's unfortunate inmates.

Near-skeletal figures draped in dirty rags peered from cagelike cells, hopeless, macabre shadows of what had once been strong fighting men. Leila knew that many of them were prisoners of war, but some were debtors or criminals.

Whatever their crime, most would never again see the light of day. The governor's prison was renowned for the cruelty and torture inflicted within its walls. It was a rare and fortunate man who ever walked out alive.

Tarnished brass lamps lit the high-ceilinged interior of the next cavernous room they entered. It was much cleaner than the area they had just passed through, with freshly swept floors and a few small square windows opened to the evening breeze. She knew this part of the building was where the privileged prisoners were kept.

Arched wooden doors fitted with hinged peepholes lined both sides of the room, opening into small, individual cells. All appeared empty, save for the last one on the left. Two guards flanked the yawning door, from which a swath of yellow light cut across the floor.

"He's in there," Sinjar said, releasing her arm and hurrying to the cell.

"Who?" Leila asked, following him.

"Our patient." Sinjar ducked his head and went inside, his resonant voice carrying out to her. "Good, the guards already carried in my bags. Everything we need is here. Leila, are you coming?"

She drew a deep breath as she unfastened her face veil. "Yes, father."

Please may there not be rats, she prayed.

She stepped inside, her eyes adjusting to the cell's brightness. There were at least fifteen lanterns placed around the stone walls, filling the cramped interior with light. In a far corner hot coals glowed inside a large copper brazier.

At first Leila could not see the patient for the four Mameluke soldiers flanking the foot of a wooden cot placed in the center of the cell. They were members of the governor's elite fighting corps, and their forbidding presence told her one thing. The patient was more than likely a prisoner of war.

She began to walk around the soldiers, and almost tripped over a pile of interlocking iron rings heaped on the floor. She had never seen anything like them before. She tried to pick up one end of what appeared to be a long-sleeved shirt, but the rings were so heavy she could not lift them. She drew her hand away, inhaling sharply when she saw that her fingers were covered in blood.

She thought she had cut herself, but when she wiped her hand on her qumbaz the blood was transferred to the linen garment and the pads of her fingers remained unmarred.

"My daughter, I have need of your assistance!" Sinjar snapped, startling her.

Embarrassed to have been caught dawdling, Leila rushed around the soldiers to her father's side where she stopped short, staring in openmouthed astonishment at the strapping blond giant lying unconscious upon the cot. He was so tall and huge that his heavily muscled limbs dangled off the sides.

Instinctively she noted that he was drenched in sweat, his magnificently built body wracked by tremors. Yet despite his condition, a raw power emanated from him, a vibrant life force which seemed to fill the small cell. She could almost feel his great strength in the simple rise and fall of his massive chest, and it overwhelmed her completely.

"Wh-who is he, Father?" she stammered, her gaze coming to rest upon the man's ashen face.

"A crusader knight," Sinjar said, cursing as he cut away a sweat- and blood-soaked padded vest to reveal a vicious shoulder wound. Bright red blood flowed in a steady trickle from the ugly gash, which judging from its shape and depth had been inflicted by a curved scimitar. "And soon to be a dead man, Leila, if you do not cease your gaping and help me stop this bleeding. We will have to cauterize. Prepare the irons. Now!"

Shocked into action by Sinjar's sharp command, Leila found several iron rods of various sizes in one of his bags and rushed over to place them on the glowing coals in the brazier. She watched as the long, sharpened tips grew red, then drew a protective glove over her hand and seized the first rod that was ready. She hastened back to her father's side.

"Hold his limbs," Sinjar commanded the four soldiers who quickly positioned themselves around the cot, each grabbing an arm or leg. "Tightly."

" 'Tis a good thing he's unconscious," Leila said, holding out the rod to her father. "He will feel the pain, but perhaps he will not remember it."

Sinjar nodded grimly, but he did not take the iron from her. "This time you must do it, my daughter," he di-

rected, walking to the front of the cot, where he placed
his hands on the crusader's uninjured shoulder. "I fear this
man's strength will be great, even now. I must help to hold
him down." His tone grew urgent. "Quickly, Leila, before the iron cools."

She did not waste an instant. She knew the procedure
well, having performed it many times at the hospital. With
practiced assurance, she bent over the crusader and laid
the red-hot iron on his ravaged flesh.

A wild, tortured scream rent the air, sending chills down
Leila's spine as the crusader's body arched violently upon
the cot. Her father had been right. It was all the five strong
men could do to hold him down.

As the soldiers fought to control the crusader's flailing
limbs, Leila glanced up from his shoulder.

She gasped in amazement.

The crusader's eyes were open and fixed on her face,
the astonishingly blue depths ablaze with incredible pain.
She felt a rush of pity but remained undaunted. She must
continue with the procedure if there was any hope of
staunching the flow of blood.

Leila applied the searing iron to the wound again and
again while the crusader's hideous screams echoed in the
small cell.

Soon the air reeked with the sweet, sickening smell of
singed flesh, and she swallowed against a sudden wave of
nausea, blinked several times, and then concentrated more
fully on her task. She knew the crusader would be scarred
for life, but there was nothing to be done about it. She
was grateful when his cries died away, his head lolling
back on the bloodied cot.

"Excellent, Leila. Use the smaller iron to seal the
wound completely."

She did as her father bade her, using a fresh rod, and
felt a curious mix of accomplishment, exhaustion, and relief when she finally straightened up. She smiled faintly
at her father when she saw the approval shining in his dark
eyes.

"You have done well," Sinjar said proudly. "Extremely
well. The crusader may yet have a chance." He uttered

low commands to the clearly shaken soldiers while he slathered a healing ointment on the closed wound. "Go at once, all of you. We need a large cask of cool drinking water and as many buckets of warm water as the four of you can carry. And we'll need two more cots and fresh bedding."

"But what of the prisoner, esteemed one?" asked the leader, his expression doubtful. "His Grace, Governor Mawdud, has ordered that we remain with him at all times—"

"You can plainly see my patient is no more likely to rise from this cot than a dead man is to cast off his shroud," Sinjar interrupted impatiently. "This wound is only one of his ills. Add heat exhaustion and exposure, and you may judge correctly that he will not stand for days, let alone fight. Now be quick about your tasks, or Governor Mawdud will surely hear of your refusal to assist me. It is his hope that the crusader will survive this day. The man is worth a great ransom if he lives."

So that was it, Leila thought as the soldiers respectfully bowed their turbanned heads and then quickly left the cell. No wonder her father had been summoned to attend to this man, rather than the physicians who ordinarily treated the prison's wretched inmates. His great medical skill was only called upon for special prisoners, and truly this case was most extraordinary.

With this new knowledge, the thousand questions reeling in her mind only multiplied.

She glanced at the crusader, sprawled like a sleeping giant on the cot and wearing only an odd pair of short trousers. He was still except for his breathing, his skin glistening with heavy perspiration in the lamplight, yet even now she sensed an incredible strength radiating from him.

She recalled other male patients who had braved this procedure, men who usually looked more dead than alive when the hot irons were finally withdrawn. Not so this man. He appeared indestructible.

Suddenly she doubted her father's confident words and decided the soldiers should be anxious. She would not be surprised if this crusader regained consciousness at any moment and rose up to fight them all off.

Leila felt her heart lurch when his thick, dark lashes flickered slightly, and she took a step backward, fearing he might do just that. But he did not. Inexplicably fascinated by him, she moved closer.

She was struck by the color of his long, shoulder-length hair which, now that she had a chance to study it, was more a rich brown that had been streaked by the sun than fully blond. Despite its matted appearance, it had almost a metallic sheen, like spun silver or the bright, reflective steel of fabled Damascus swords.

Leila found herself absorbed by the rugged symmetry of his features: thick, winged brows; a straight well-shaped nose that nonetheless appeared to have been broken once for the slight imperfection across the bridge; a mouth that was hard, yet sensuously curved . . .

He was quite handsome, for a barbarian.

The realization stunned her. She generally held to a far different standard of male beauty, more like Jamal's. With his dark fathomless eyes and midnight hair, her betrothed was truly the most beautiful man she had ever seen.

Until now, she amended honestly.

On second thought, this crusader could easily rival Jamal if the two were to stand side by side. He looked as she imagined the ruthless Viking warriors in her father's history books may have appeared, mighty and virile. She had always thought the Arab chroniclers had greatly exaggerated their descriptions of such men, but it was clear now that she had been wrong.

This man might have stepped from those very pages. He was well over six feet tall, probably six and a half, his massive physique a perfect match to his unequaled height. Were all crusaders like giants compared with other men?

Once again many questions flooded her mind, melding with a sense of irritation that she could become so easily engrossed in studying the crusader's masculine attributes. Yet she could not stop herself from looking at him.

How had he come to be captured? He had to be a complete fool to have ventured into Syrian lands, or perhaps his lust for plunder had overwhelmed his better judgment.

Then again, these Christian barbarians were mad in the first place to cross the seas in hopes of conquering the vast Arab Empire. How could they harbor such misguided illusions when they were outnumbered by millions, and so undeniably inferior to the men whose culture they wished to destroy?

"Leila, I will need bandages," Sinjar requested, casting a curious sideways glance in her direction.

"Yes, Father," she answered, embarrassed that she had to be reminded again of her duties.

She searched through the leather bags until she found the rolled linen, along with several vials containing the powdered medicines she judged her father would wish to administer to their valuable patient. She set everything on the edge of the cot, venturing at last to voice her nagging questions.

"Tell me, Father. Where did the soldiers capture this crusader?"

"The Lebanese border, in the foothills north of Mount Hermon," Sinjar replied, using a wine-soaked cloth to cleanse away the filth, blood, and sweat around the wound. "There were four other crusader knights in his party, a dozen men-at-arms, and several native Christians for guides, but the others were all killed in the surprise attack. This man survived only because he escaped into the hills, hiding there for many days until he was captured this afternoon. Governor Mawdud ordered that he be taken alive and held for ransom."

"But the soldiers gravely injured him," Leila said, helping her father wrap a thick bandage across the crusader's broad shoulder, underneath his arm, and up again until the wound was securely bound. " 'Tis a strange way to spare a life."

"Yes, he most likely would have died but for that padded vest he wore and his chain mail, which lessened the blow."

"Chain mail?" Leila followed her father's gaze to the

mysterious pile of iron rings lying upon the floor. At last she was able to guess their use.

"The crusader's armor," Sinjar explained, confirming her suspicion. "It covered him from head to foot, protecting him from worse injury. This man fought like an enraged lion when they finally found him, slaying three soldiers before they could bring him down with that blow to his shoulder."

Leila felt a surge of baffling excitement as she imagined the violent and bloody scene. "But why he is so valuable, Father? Is he a rich man? An important one?"

"So many questions, my daughter," Sinjar said, studying her.

Leila's cheeks burned at his perusal, a rare sensation, but she met his gaze steadily. "If we are to cure this crusader for ransoming, a most unusual case as you said yourself, Father, then surely I might know why the governor values him so."

Sinjar chuckled to himself. "You were always an inquisitive one. A very good thing in our profession." He picked up one of the opaque vials she had set upon the cot, opened it, and sniffed lightly to discern the contents. "Letters from the Mongol Ilkhan, Abaga, addressed to Lord Edward of England, were found on several of the dead men."

Leila gasped. "To Lord Edward, the English prince who arrived last year at the Christian port of Acre with his thousand crusaders?"

"Yes," Sinjar replied. "No doubt Lord Edward awaits those letters from Anatolia most impatiently." His tone grew harsh. "Fool. He does not know he waits in vain."

"Then this man must be one of his most trusted knights to undertake such a long and dangerous mission," Leila speculated. "Perhaps he is even a friend whose safe return would be much rewarded."

Sinjar nodded. "Governor Mawdud believes this crusader and his companions were personal envoys sent by Lord Edward to the Mongol dogs, who are obviously still seeking to join forces against our indomitable Sultan Baybars. It seems they have not learned from the hard lessons

of the past that one cannot defeat what one cannot count.
We are as innumerable as grains of desert sand, as strong
as the wind that shapes the dunes and causes great storms
to block out the sun. Even united against us, their efforts
are futile.'' His voice dripped with disdain. "It is a pity
the other knights were slain before the letters were found.
Governor Mawdud would have had four times the ransom
from this reckless English prince.''

Leila fell silent, pondering her father's words.

Truly, the Christian crusaders were an incomprehensi-
ble lot. Fools and madmen, all of them. No wonder her
mother had wasted few words on the life she had known
in England. Any country which bred such men must be a
very strange place indeed and hardly worth remembering—

The soldiers' sudden noisy entrance startled her. Her
thoughts flew back to the crisis at hand as the men set
brimming buckets next to the cot. Some of the water
sloshed onto the floor and soaked her open-toed sandals,
yet she gave little notice as the cell bustled with activity.

Following her father's lead and taking care to avoid the
fresh bandage, Leila took a wet sponge and began washing
the crusader to remove all sweat and grime and to cool
his feverish body. She could feel the hardness of his muscles through the sponge, and an unsettling sensation of
heat built inside her with each slow stroke upon his flesh.

Leila hoped her father didn't notice that her hand was
trembling. She forced herself to think rationally as they
discussed other scars the crusader possessed: a deep,
gougelike impression on his right thigh; an ugly eight-inch
mark over his ribs, long ago healed; numerous nicks and
scratches. Clearly he was a battle-seasoned warrior who
had already survived several serious injuries.

They bathed him from head to foot. Leila's flushed discomfort increased when they removed his short trousers,
baring his powerful body completely. Shocked by her feelings, she quickly reminded herself that she was a physician's apprentice and accustomed to such sights as a flaccid
male organ, no matter how large.

She wasn't used to the crusader's profuse body hair,

however; in Arab society such hair was considered offensive, and both men and women were ritually shaved of body hair at their baths. Her mother had adopted the custom at Sinjar's request, and Leila had never known anything different. She was as smooth as pearly satin down to her toes, and she liked it that way.

This crusader, on the other hand, was a testimony to his barbaric culture. His limbs were covered with soft downy hair, his chest thickly matted, and the dark brown thatch between his thighs was positively indecent.

It was also utterly fascinating, Leila thought with chagrin, surprised at herself. Despite her unseemly urge to watch, she modestly averted her eyes while her father cleaned that particular area.

Lastly, with the soldiers' help, they lifted the crusader from the soiled cot onto two larger ones placed side by side and made up with clean bedding and soft pillows for his head. At Sinjar's command, the hinged door covering the cell's only window was unlocked and opened to reveal thick, impenetrable iron bars. Still, it did not take long for the balmy night breeze to freshen the small room. A small square of incense was dropped into the brazier to further sweeten the air.

Leila inhaled the aromatic frankincense while she mixed powdered medications in a pestle under her father's watchful eye: equal parts of crushed plaintain seed, tamarind, and star thistle. She knew well that when combined, these ingredients would do much to arrest the crusader's fever. She carefully stirred in small amounts of water until the mixture formed a thin paste, then she poured her father's suggested dosage into a cup of cool drinking water and added a spoonful of almond oil and honey to mask the bitter taste.

"I will hold his head, Leila. Administer only a third of a drachm," Sinjar cautioned her as she knelt by the cot.

Leila's breath caught as she grasped the crusader's chin and lifted the cup to his mouth.

His skin was very warm and pliant beneath prickly dark whiskers which chafed her fingers, and she could sense from the hard line of his jaw that he was most likely a very stubborn man. As she gave him the proper dose, some of the liquid dribbled from his mouth but most he involuntarily swallowed. She wiped the corners with her head scarf, her fingers brushing his lips, and shivered at their unexpected softness.

"Good. That is enough for now," Sinjar said with satisfaction. "I will give him more medicine throughout the night which should calm his fever. He has lost a lot of blood. That is the most serious strike against him. By dawn, we should know if he will live or die."

Leila met her father's dark eyes, not surprised by his blunt statement. She knew as well as he that the physician's art was imperfect and fraught with many uncertainties. They had done all they could for their patient. Only time would decide the final outcome, yet something told her this man would survive. He was too strong not to.

"Shall I stay with you, Father?"

"No," Sinjar replied, shaking his head. "If he survives past this night, your assistance will be needed in the days to come when I am called away on other duties. I want you to go home and rest." He motioned to two of the Mameluke soldiers. "They will escort you, my daughter."

Leila handed him the cup and rose to her feet, suddenly very tired. She turned to go, but her father's hand upon her arm stopped her.

"I am very proud of you," Sinjar said simply.

"Thank you, Father."

"Your apprenticeship will soon be over. When I see such skill as you demonstrated tonight, I have no doubt you will be most worthy of our profession. Jamal is blessed to have you for his betrothed, and it pleases me that you accepted the marriage I arranged for you. Between us, the practice of Al-Aziz will be very great indeed."

Leila smiled despite her weariness. His praise never failed to send her spirits soaring, as her goal of becoming a full-fledged physician moved ever closer to reality. It was her most cherished dream.

"I owe my humble worth to the greatness of my teacher," she responded sincerely. "Good night, Father."

With a last glance at the crusader, Leila lifted her face veil and fastened it to her headband as she walked from the cell, her legs feeling slightly wooden. Her efforts of the past hour had taxed her more than usual, or perhaps she was tired simply because she had been up since dawn. She was glad the walk home was not a long one.

"This way, revered daughter of Al-Aziz," said one of the soldiers, leading the way while the other man walked a few paces behind her.

Leila clutched her kufiyya around her shoulders and silently obliged him. She kept her eyes riveted on the soldier's broad back as she followed him from the prison, not wanting to view any more wretched prisoners. Truly, she had seen and heard her fill of misery for one night.

It was enough that she could not chase the haunting image of the crusader's eyes, a blue as deep and vivid as the Mediterranean Sea, from her mind.

Chapter 2

⌒⌒⌒⌒⌒

"**W**hat has happened?" Sinjar demanded, rushing toward the grim-faced captain of the prison guard with Leila in tow. "Your message said to come in haste, nothing more. When I left my patient only a few hours ago to seek some rest at my home, he was still unconscious—"

"He is unconscious no longer, my lord Al-Aziz," the captain interrupted smoothly, bowing in greeting with his hand pressed over his heart. "That is why I sent the message. I thought you would want to see him now that he is awake. He gave us a great deal of trouble at first, but I have things well under control. Don't let his roaring trouble you. He can do no harm now. The wild animal has been tamed."

Leila sensed her father's agitation at this last statement when he proceeded across the large room, she and the captain rushing to keep up with his long strides. As they approached the crusader's cell, she could hear the enraged cries growing louder, and goosebumps prickled her skin. In a way it did sound as if a ferocious animal were caged inside.

"What happened to Governor Mawdud's soldiers?" Sinjar flung over his shoulder. "They were standing guard when I left earlier this morning."

"Our lord governor has since recalled them, O honored one, granting me full charge of your patient's security," the captain replied as they reached the cell. The two new guards snapped to attention, their wickedly curved scimitars held rigidly in front of them.

Leila's cheeks grew bright red as more incensed ranting penetrated from behind the closed door.

She had never heard such foul cursing! In one breath the crusader consigned every last one of his captors to writhe in hell's fire, and in the next he was naming all the vicious things he would do if he got his hands on a guard again. She was surprised the captain and his guards gave little notice, then she realized with a jolt that she was the only one who could understand him since he was speaking English.

"Here, see for yourself, my lord," the captain said, opening the hinged peephole. "Your patient seems remarkably improved." He inclined his head respectfully, raising his voice to be heard over the loud oaths emanating from the cell. "In my humble opinion, of course. I only presume as much because the crusader savagely attacked one of my guards before he could be subdued."

"He did not kill the man," Sinjar breathed in consternation, peering through the peephole.

"No, esteemed one. The guard lives, though he has been retired from duty until his arm mends." Contempt crept into the captain's voice. "This crusader's strength is immense. He snapped the guard's arm like a mere twig and would have easily done the same to his neck if our swords had not swayed him. It is my hope the governor's letter of ransom is delivered soon so we might be rid of this madman."

Listening incredulously to this news, Leila started as her father rounded on the man, his face livid. She had rarely seen him so angry.

"By all that is sacred, my patient is standing shackled to the wall!"

"Yes, a necessary precaution—"

"But hardly suitable to his recovery," Sinjar objected hotly. "The crusader may be fully conscious, but he is not yet out of danger. His shoulder wound could open at such rough treatment. If it putrefies the governor's ransom could well be lost."

"He is extremely dangerous, my lord," the captain countered, unwilling to back down. "If you had seen him earlier, you would agree. Loose in his cell, he will be like a tiger unleashed, ready to pounce upon and maul whoever enters, including his respected physicians. Governor Mawdud has put me in charge, and I deem it best that he remain shackled. Perhaps, if it would better please you, the prisoner could be chained to the cots. Either way, he must be restrained. I do not wish to lose any more of my men to this rabid beast."

"Perhaps we could speak with him, Father," Leila interrupted, her heart pounding. She was not surprised the crusader was already conscious. She had sensed yesterday that his strength defied that of most men.

"What are you suggesting, Leila?" came her father's agitated reply.

She rushed on, ignoring the captain's dark, menacing look. "I—I mean, allow me to speak with him in English. I doubt he understands Arabic. If the crusader knows he will be released as soon as the ransom is paid, perhaps he will restrain his fury and submit willingly to his confinement and our continued care."

Sinjar did not readily respond. He seemed to ponder her offer, a deep furrow creasing his brow. Finally, after a long moment, he nodded.

"Yes, I believe it is worth a try. Offer him a choice, Leila. If he agrees not to fight us, we will remove the shackles. You must make him understand that he will jeopardize his recovery if he refuses, and that the only alternative is for him to remain as he is now, fettered like an animal." He glanced at the captain, whose expression strongly showed his disapproval. "Open the door."

"I cannot allow this, my lord Al-Aziz. I am in command here—"

"But not for long, I can assure you, captain, if anything happens to my patient," Sinjar countered threateningly. "Governor Mawdud looks forward to the crusader's ransom with great anticipation. He is already counting the one hundred thousand dinars he expects to receive from this Lord Edward. If you are responsible for prolonging my patient's illness or, Allah protect you, causing his death, your head will roll. This I promise you." He gestured impatiently. "Open the door."

His cruel, pinched face growing sickly white, the captain hesitated for only an instant and then muttered, "Very well, very well."

As the captain signaled for one of the guards to draw back the heavy iron bolt, Sinjar took Leila's arm and drew her aside.

"My daughter, say only what is necessary to this man. I do not like that you must speak with him at all. If he questions you, translate everything to me and I will tell you how to answer him."

"Yes, Father," Leila said, feeling nervous all of a sudden. Her fingers shook as she unfastened her face veil. "I understand."

The crusader's curses exploded with fresh fury as the heavy door creaked open. The two guards proceeded first inside the cell, their scimitars lowered menacingly, followed by Sinjar and Leila. The disgruntled captain, grumbling to himself, brought up the rear.

Leila peered from behind her father, her heart leaping to her throat. If she had ever envisioned a barbarian, truly she was looking at one now. This wild-haired, wild-eyed man pulling furiously at his bonds was savagery incarnate.

Standing upright, the crusader appeared even larger to her than before and dangerously powerful, so much so that she felt terribly small and inconsequential just being in the same room with him. Despite her father's concerns she was grateful for the heavy chains at his wrists and ankles which bound his naked body to the wall. She breathed deeply in an attempt to calm her thundering pulse, but only flustered herself further when she inhaled the crusader's sweaty male scent.

"Go on, Leila," Sinjar urged, pulling her from behind him. "Talk to him."

Chagrined that she had to be encouraged to carry out her own suggestion, and telling herself she was reacting most foolishly, Leila took a few hesitant steps toward the crusader. But she stopped, her knees suddenly wobbly, when he ceased his fierce struggles and leveled his arresting blue eyes upon her.

The unswerving intensity of his gaze told her everything. He was alert, lucid, and, most unsettling of all, he seemed to recognize her.

"You . . ." the crusader rasped.

For a fleeting instant Leila could not answer, her mouth gone completely dry. She glanced uncertainly at her father over her shoulder, then back to the crusader. She swallowed and spoke, her voice husky with nervousness.

"You are a prisoner of Mawdud, governor of Damascus . . ." She paused, her face uncomfortably warm, and drew another deep breath before continuing, hoping this time her voice would resume its natural timbre. The stilted English words tumbled rustily from her tongue.

"Now that you are clearly recovering, a letter of ransom will soon be delivered to your Lord Edward in Acre. Once Governor Mawdud receives this ransom, you will be released unharmed to your people—"

"Unharmed?" the crusader spat hoarsely, his gaze burning into hers. "I don't consider torture to be child's play, wench. You wield a smoking iron as well as any sword, and inflicted as much damage upon me, I'd swear. Go to hell, and take the rest of those heathen with you!"

Leila's eyes widened and she nearly choked at his outburst. Her nervousness vanished, replaced by hot indignation. Torture? Was he mad? She had saved this bastard's life!

"What does he say?" Sinjar asked impatiently.

"This . . . this ingrate accuses me of torturing him!" she sputtered.

"Calm yourself, Leila. What did you expect? These crusaders know little of our advanced medical skill. Their own physicians are no better than butchers. Now tell him what we discussed."

Fighting to contain her fury, Leila turned back to the crusader. She kept foremost in her mind the thought that she was dealing with an ignorant barbarian. It certainly helped.

"The irons were used to close your wound," she explained tersely. "Not as torture. You would have bled to death otherwise." She nodded toward her father. "This man is Sinjar Al-Aziz, the governor's personal physician, and renowned throughout the empire. You are most fortunate that it is he who is responsible for your care while you remain in this prison."

"I see," the crusader said slowly, his tone still harsh. "And who are you?" His gaze hungrily swept her from head to toe then back again, lingering on her face.

Obviously her words had sunk in, Leila thought, growing uncomfortable again under his close scrutiny. Why was he looking at her like that? Why did she feel so funny, so unlike herself?

"Leila." Her father's voice eased her discomfiture, but only slightly. She quickly translated the crusader's question.

"Tell him only that you are my helper," Sinjar quietly instructed her, "and a slave." At her shocked expression, he whispered, "I will explain later. Go on, tell him."

She did so, almost stumbling on the words. She watched as the crusader's hard expression grew pitying, his gaze falling to the striped zunnar wrapped around her waist.

"A Christian slave," he stated bluntly.

Disconcerted even more by the strange look in the crusader's eyes, Leila was suddenly eager to be done with her increasingly unpleasant task.

"My master, Sinjar Al-Aziz, offers you a choice. If you agree to peacefully accept your temporary imprisonment and not fight against him or your guards, he will see that you are freed from those chains. If not, you must remain where you are, at the risk of your life. My fa—" She stopped, realizing what she had almost revealed. "My master believes your wound could yet cause your death, shackled as you are now. It is his wish that you live, of course, so Governor Mawdud might receive his ransom."

"How bloody charitable of him," the crusader muttered, leaning his head back against the wall. He grimaced, sweat trickling down the side of his face, and Leila had the impression he had temporarily forgotten them in his wretched misery. Clearly his wound was causing him intense pain.

"You must choose," she insisted, drawing him back into their discussion.

"So it seems I must," he replied thickly. It was obvious from his increasingly labored breathing that his earlier struggles had done him little good. He met her questioning gaze, his eyes becoming glazed and feverish. "The ransom. How do I know you are telling me the truth?"

Leila could sense he was anxious for her answer. "'Tis plain to see," she said simply. "If you were not of value to Governor Mawdud, you would already be dead."

Falling silent at her frank response, he stared out the barred window for a long moment. When he faced her again, he drew himself up despite his heavy chains, and she stepped back, startled and amazed by how small he made her feel. His huge size was only heightened by his commanding stance.

"Very well. I accept your master's offer. Better that than hang here on this blasted wall."

Relieved, Leila turned to her father. "He has agreed. He will not resist."

"Excellent," Sinjar said.

"He lies!" the captain exclaimed. "Son of a cur. Infidel! How can you believe him?"

"Ask the crusader his name," Sinjar requested, ignoring the man behind him, "so the governor may have it inscribed in the letter of ransom. Also, ask him for some small personal fact that his Lord Edward might recognize. The letter must be considered authentic."

As Leila relayed her father's words, a hint of a roguish smile touched the crusader's mouth, eliciting a strange flutter in her stomach.

"Guy de Warenne, crusader knight of the realm and lord of the Welsh Marches. And the comely wench who keeps me company in Acre is named Refaiyeh. She's got a tempting crescent-shaped birthmark, the palest pink, on the inside of her upper thigh, right below her—"

At Leila's small gasp he stopped abruptly, staring at her flushed cheeks.

"Forgive me. I almost forgot there was a lady present, and a very beautiful one at that." The crusader's gaze jumped to her father. "Tell your master"—he spat the word derisively—"that Edward will know it's I when he confirms what I've just said."

"Well, Leila?" Sinjar asked. A touch of amusement lit his eyes as she repeated the crusader's words, pointedly omitting his unexpected compliment. "Good. It is enough." He turned on the captain of the guards. "You have heard. Release my patient at once."

The man looked as if he might protest, but he kept silent, glaring at both Leila and her father. He wrestled a jangling ring of keys from the sash at his waist and threw them at the feet of the nearest guard.

"Do as my lord Al-Aziz says. Unlock the chains," the captain ordered grimly. As the guard retrieved the keys and hastened to obey, he addressed the other man. "Keep your swords at the ready while the patient receives his treatment. I will summon two more guards to assist you. When the revered Al-Aziz and his helper"—he shot a glance at Leila—"leave, bolt the door securely."

With a brusque bow of his head to Sinjar and scarcely a nod at Leila, the captain stormed from the cell.

"Clearly a man who does not recognize his place in life," Sinjar said dryly. "Most unwise." He hurried forward as the freed crusader gripped his shoulder and slumped against the wall. "Help me lift my patient to the cots!" Sinjar called out sharply to the two guards just entering.

Leila readied the bedding, plumping pillows and drawing back the blanket as the crusader was half dragged across the floor. He collapsed upon the cots, heaving a ragged sigh. His eyes met hers as she brought the blanket up to his chest.

"I need braies."

"Braies?" she asked blankly.

His dry laugh was a painful rattle in his chest. "Trousers. I'm not used to appearing unclothed before a lady—unless, of course, she is too. I'd wager you've seen more of me than many a wench I've bedded."

"I—I'll see what can be done," Leila said, shocked by his candor.

Within the harem sensuality was openly discussed, but she had never heard such a statement from a man. She wondered curiously just how many women this crusader had taken to his bed. Judging by his overwhelming masculinity and those stunning blue eyes, she guessed five score or better. No doubt his sexual prowess rivaled that of any sultan with a harem at his beck and call.

"Do not converse with him, Leila," Sinjar admonished her, frowning as he concocted a syrupy medication. "Tell him that this medicine will help to ease his pain and then say nothing more unless I give you leave to do so."

"He was asking for sirwal, 'tis all," she replied, affronted by the coldness in her father's voice. She knelt and rummaged in one of the leather bags so he might not see that she was blushing from her carnal imaginings.

She found fresh linen and ointment and busied herself with changing the crusader's bandage. All the while he watched her, even when her father administered a large dose of the syrup, but she refused to meet his eyes, concentrating very hard on her task instead.

She noted that the swelling around the wound was beginning to recede, despite the rough handling he had received and his own futile struggles. She wondered if he would remember his stay in Governor Mawdud's prison whenever he looked at the scar, and perhaps even remember her—

Whatever was she thinking? she chided herself, throwing the unused bandages into the opened bag. What did she care if this barbarian remembered her or not? She would certainly forget him!

"I'm finished," Leila said, glancing at her father as she rose to her feet.

"As am I," Sinjar responded. "Tell him he must rest and eat as much of his meals as he possibly can stomach. We will return tomorrow morning, and each morning after, to check on his recovery."

She spoke as her father bade her, the words practically running together in her haste to be gone from the cell and this man's unsettling scrutiny. Remarkably, her English was coming much easier to her now.

"Then I shall look forward to the morrow . . . Leila."

Stunned to hear her name upon the crusader's lips, uttered with a deep huskiness that she found wholly disconcerting, she could not leave the cell fast enough. She leaned against the cool wall outside, and was relieved when her father shortly followed.

Leila attached her face veil with shaking fingers and remained silent until she and her father had left the prison. A single question plagued her. She blinked in the bright midday sunshine when they first stepped outside, then proceeded along the sloping street only a short distance before she blurted, "Why a slave, Father? Why?"

Sinjar stopped and stared into her eyes, his expression deadly serious. "A necessary ploy, my daughter. If the crusader deems you are unimportant to me, he will not attempt to use you to gain his freedom. You saw how furious he was when we first entered the cell. Men such as he chafe at captivity and consider desperate acts when confinement becomes unbearable."

Leila felt a chill. "Desperate acts?"

"An improbability now—at least I hope it is so," Sinjar replied. "If the crusader believes you are only a slave, then he must also believe we would cut him down long before we came to your rescue, should he try to bargain his way to freedom by threatening your life. Such a rash move would get him nowhere." He clasped her arms so suddenly that she gasped. "But I tell you this, Leila. Governor Mawdud's ransom is lost if the crusader so much as touches you."

She was stunned by the raw vehemence in her father's voice. It was at times such as this that she realized how much he loved her, no matter that she was his adopted daughter and a Christian.

"If Jamal were home from Cairo, I would have him assist me in the days to come rather than expose you to possible harm," Sinjar continued grimly.

"But that cannot be helped, Father. The caliph needs Jamal until the smallpox has fled from his family."

"True." He pressed his lips together, thinking, then regarded her sharply. "I have decided. From now on you will attend to the crusader only when I cannot, which I hope will be rare. And when you do, I will make it clear to the captain that you must be very well guarded." He released her, the tightness in his expression easing as if his decision gave him some peace of mind. "Come, my daughter. Patients await us at the hospital."

As they walked together down the street, her father acknowledging greetings from passersby, Leila hoped that indeed her visits to the prison would be few. After hearing the crusader's wild threats and curses, she had no wish to bear the brunt of his desperate, barbarous acts.

"So they're holding you for a bloody ransom, de Warenne," Guy muttered tightly to himself, wincing at the searing fire in his shoulder as he shifted upon the rigid cots. "The wily bastards."

He rubbed his thick wrists, chafed raw from the shackles, his eyes moving from one wall to the next, then to the door, and back to the barred window. Again and again his gaze circled the small cramped cell until desperation clutched at his throat, threatening to choke him.

By the breath of God, it wasn't good enough! Whatever the amount of the ransom, he had no doubt that Edward would pay it. Yet it might be days, weeks, maybe a month or more before he was released. He would go mad long before that. He felt half mad already!

Even now he could feel the rough stone walls closing in around him, suffocating him, like the walls in that tiny prison cell eight years ago . . .

Panicking, Guy gasped for breath, feeling suddenly as if a crushing load were pressing upon his chest. He threw an arm over his eyes in an attempt to block out the dark, terrible memories, but they kept coming.

Memories of betrayal and death and utter hopelessness, of hunger so severe that he had eaten rats to stay alive, hit him with full force, so vivid, so real that he could have sworn he was once again in that same black hellhole. God help him, he had to think of something else fast before the memories completely overwhelmed him. He had to think—

"Leila!"

Guy cried out her name before he even realized it, then whispered it again and again like a powerful chant to ward off the horrible darkness. As he frantically conjured her face and lithe form in his mind, his nightmare visions gradually loosened their icy grip upon him and began to recede.

Leila.

He thought of her stunning violet eyes, her seductive rose-red lips, her breasts straining against her clothing like lush ripe fruit. The crushing load grew lighter, and he sucked in great lungfuls of air until he was able to breathe again.

Leila. His mysterious angel of mercy.

He could feel the tension ebbing from his body, thoughts of life and beauty replacing images of horror. He recalled her touch when she bandaged his shoulder, gentle yet assured; the soft, melodic sound of her voice; and the heady scent of her perfume.

It reminded him of the flowers his mother had lovingly nurtured in a walled garden in Wales. Damask roses. The bright pink blooms had burst forth every summer, scenting the castle bailey with sweet and intoxicating fragrance.

Just like Leila's. He could smell it even now, a faint whiff of her perfume emanating from the linen bandage as if her touch had left it there.

Calmer, Guy lowered his arm and wiped the sweat from his face, rational thought returning.

What cruel fate had brought her to Damascus? She must be French or English, more likely the latter, judging from her excellent command of his language.

An English rose far away from her homeland, now a Christian slave among the infidels.

It was an outrage. It made him sick. It made him even sicker to think she probably shared that Arab physician's bed. A beauty such as Leila could hardly have been spared the base indignities that were perpetrated on the female sex. No doubt she had been deflowered at a tender age by that rutting heathen!

By God, there had to be some way he could help her. Some way they could help each other, for that matter. There had to be some way they could both escape what fate had brought them. Surely she wanted to return to her own people and leave her wretched servitude behind, and he'd be damned if he was going to wait patiently in this cramped cell for a ransom.

Tomorrow he would ask for her help, he decided fiercely. Together they would devise a plan.

Chapter 3

❦

T hat evening proved balmy and clear, ushered in by a spectacular sunset that lit the western horizon like orange and crimson fire.

Now it was dark. Leila stretched languorously on the cushioned divan and gazed up at the starry heavens.

What a perfect time to relax on her mother's roof terrace. Not too warm or too windy. Only a gentle breeze played across her pale blue silk damask robe, tickling her toes and delighting her nostrils with the terrace garden's lush scents.

Leila laced her fingers together and rested her hands upon her firm breasts. She hadn't felt such peace in days. She had been so busy at the hospital and visiting her harem-bound patients scattered throughout the city that she had simply been too exhausted when she returned home to avail herself fully of the harem baths. But this afternoon had been blessedly different.

After noting the sooty smudges under her eyes, and fearing she had been working herself too hard of late, her father had insisted she leave the hospital early. He had even provided a silk-curtained litter to take her the short distance home.

A luxurious bath after a brief nap had been a balm to her senses. Ayhan and Nittia, her two personal odalisques, had first slathered her skin with an aromatic lemon paste and scraped her completely of body hair. Next they had washed her, poured silver bowlfuls of tepid water over her in the hot steam rooms, massaged her until her smooth

41

white skin had flushed pink from their pummeling, and
anointed her with her favorite rose oil.

She felt clean and fresh and satiated, her body tingling
from her scalp to the soles of her feet. The sheer physical
pleasure of her slaves' ministrations left her feeling as if
she were floating. Even her long, knee-length hair felt
charged and alive, brushed to a high gloss after being vigorously shampooed and dried, then left free to hang down
her back.

Leila coiled a perfumed tendril around her finger. As
the silken ebony threads caught the silvery moonlight, she
smiled. The glistening reflection reminded her of a poem
she had recently received from Jamal, written in praise of
her beauty. Recalling its erotic content, cloaked in flowery
verse, she was filled with anticipation.

Truly, she looked forward to the day when they would
marry. But not only for the promise of sensual delights.
There was a more important reason to consider. She would
not be allowed to practice medicine as a full-fledged physician until she was a married woman.

That was simply the way of things. All decent women
in the Arab Empire were under the protection of a man,
whether a father, husband, brother, uncle, lord, or sultan.

She would have been married already if not for her
medical studies; she had been of marriageable age since
her first monthly flow when she was fourteen. Yet her
father had insisted upon waiting until she finished her
training, believing pregnancy and children would hinder her progress.

Now that her apprenticeship would soon be completed,
that was no longer a concern. She knew it would not be
long before a date was set for the marriage. When she was
finally wed to Jamal Al-Aziz, she would have the protection she needed to fulfill her heart's ambition. Her life
would be just as she had always envisioned it. Neat. Well-
ordered. Perfect.

It didn't hurt that Jamal was everything she wanted in a
husband—kind, clever, possessing refined taste and manners. Perhaps one day she would even grow to love him,
though to her mind such affection was hardly necessary.

Their profession demanded clearheadedness, rational thought, and a firm grip on one's emotions. Love was no use to her at all. It was more important that they understand and respect each other.

And desire each other, she added, thinking again of his provocative poem. Once they were married, she would not hesitate to share his bed. There was not a more handsome man in Damascus, other than the crusader—

Leila shook her head, forcing Guy de Warenne's striking blond image from her mind.

No, she would not think of him now! It was bad enough that the barbarian's terrible curses and hungry glances had plagued her thoughts all day. She determinedly imagined Jamal instead, with his smoldering brown eyes, midnight curls, and strong, masterful hands which would someday caress her and bring her quivering body to ecstasy just as he promised in his poem.

Aroused by her wanton thoughts, Leila trailed her gaze about the dark, trellised roof terrace. She was still alone. Her two odalisques had not yet returned from the harem kitchen with the light supper of yogurt, olives, and fruit she had requested.

Slowly she drew her knees up and squeezed her slender thighs together, tightly at first, then rhythmically, eliciting a secret yearning deep inside her that made her moan and tremble.

Leila had been educated in many lovemaking techniques so that one day she might please her husband, but she had also been taught to please herself. When she married Jamal she would be sharing his attentions with his first wife and his many concubines; that, too, was simply the way of things. There would be times when he would not be able to respond to her needs, when she must look to her own fulfillment.

Her small hand crept between the embroidered folds of her robe and she touched her breast, finding the nipple warm and rigid. She ran her palm over the sensitive nub and back again, over and back, but oh so lightly, imagining what Jamal's caress would be like. She massaged her other breast, sighing with pleasure.

She could not have been more startled when the imagined caress suddenly grew rough and demanding in her mind. The huge hands she pictured stroking her body were not smooth like a physician's but callused and powerful. A warrior's hands. Blazing blue eyes swept over her, devouring her in a glance, and she could feel rock-hard muscles pressing relentlessly against her flesh. She inhaled sharply as the exquisite pressure between her thighs burned ever brighter, ever hotter . . .

A keening moan broke from her throat, and she arched upon the divan as intense pleasure engulfed her, agonizingly sweet. She held herself there, scarcely breathing, four fingers pressed hard against the moist, aching cleft of her womanhood until her climax subsided. Exhaling in a rush, she sank onto the cushions and lay there, stunned, shocked, and bewildered.

How could she have thought such a thing? It was immoral, indecent. A sin! To imagine a man other than her betrothed touching her body, caressing her . . . That barbarian, no less!

The tranquility of the evening had been spoiled. She rose in agitation, her silky hair swirling around her. As she angrily drew her robe together and tied the sash, she heard light footsteps behind her.

"I'm not in the mood for any supper," she said irritably, thinking her odalisques had returned with her meal. "Take it back."

"Indeed. And such a lovely supper it is, too."

Leila spun, her eyes widening at the sight of her mother. Swathed in peach silk from her gossamer veil to her tiny, slippered feet, Eve was holding a brass tray laden with food, a silver goblet and pitcher, and a delicate oil lantern which cast a soft golden glow upon her exquisitely beautiful face.

It never ceased to amaze Leila how youthful her mother appeared. Though Eve was forty-three years old, the two of them could easily pass as sisters. Leila was slightly taller, but other than that their lissome figures could have been shaped from the same mold.

"Nittia and Ayhan told me I would find you here, my

daughter. I dismissed them for the evening. I hope that does not displease you . . . further.''

"Of course not," Leila said, rushing forward. "Let me help you, Mother."

She took the tray and set it on the low table beside the divan. The aroma of lamb and spinach-filled pastries reached her nostrils, stirring her appetite, and her stomach grumbled noisily. It was far more substantial fare than she had expected, and it looked very tempting.

"It seems your stomach is not in agreement with your heated words," Eve said mildly, seating herself on the divan. "I would swear such a rumbling protest proves you have not eaten since this morning."

Leila sat down beside her mother, chagrined because Eve had heard her use such a petulant tone. She waited silently for the reprimand she knew was coming.

"Harshness does not suit you, Leila. 'Tis not your normal manner with your slave women, nor a just reward for their faithful service. What has provoked such a display of temper?"

Leila looked out across the moonlit rooftops, then down at the tray, anything to escape her mother's inquisitive gaze.

What could she say? That she was being tormented by lustful thoughts about the crusader? Her mother already knew of their valuable patient, but Eve hadn't yet heard that Leila had actually spoken with him earlier in the day. Oh, why couldn't she avoid the unsettling subject altogether?

"I was thinking of the crusader, 'tis all," she mumbled, opting for a version of the truth. "He regained his senses this morning and attacked a guard."

"And this has made you angry, my daughter?"

Leila sighed with convincing exasperation. "Only because Father and I worked so hard to save his life last night. His wound could have opened. He could have bled to death before we arrived, and the governor's ransom would have died with—"

"But the wound did not open, did it?" Eve interrupted her sharply.

Puzzled by her mother's tone, Leila answered, "No. It is better in fact. The swelling is almost gone."

Eve nodded as if she was not surprised by this news. "I prayed that it would be so," she said more softly. "God is with him." She fell silent and gazed into the distance.

Leila felt a tug in her breast as she watched a familiar haunted, faraway look settle over Eve's lovely face. She was about to ask her what had been bothering her these past weeks when Majida suddenly appeared at the top of the stairs leading to the terrace. The tall odalisque hurried over to the divan and bent down on one knee, taking Leila's hand in her larger one.

"Your mother has told you the wondrous news, yes?" Majida asked, her gray eyes shining with excitement. She pressed Leila's hand to her smooth cheek. "A thousand and one blessings be upon you, my young mistress!"

Leila was so surprised she could only stare from Majida, who was covering her hand with kisses, to her mother.

"Majida, please," Eve began, her voice wavering, "Leila has not . . ." She faltered, then threw up her hands, her many precious rings glittering in the moonlight. "I have not told her yet."

Majida's mouth fell open in embarrassment. She released Leila's hand and prostrated herself on the enameled tiles, her forehead resting atop Eve's slippered feet.

"Forgive me, O my mistress. Such a flapping tongue! I thought by now you would surely have shared your tidings. I waited by the stairs, impatiently counting the moments, and I could contain myself no longer. I was so happy. Ah, forgive me. I did not mean to spoil the surprise."

Eve leaned over and grasped the odalisque's broad shoulders, giving her a reassuring squeeze. " 'Tis no matter, Majida. Please stand up. I dislike it so when you do this. We can tell her together, you and I. Stand up, dearest friend—"

"Such a foolish tongue. I curse it! May it shrivel up and fall from my mouth, then I shall stomp upon it!"

"What utter nonsense. You have done nothing wrong, only given of your heart's joy. Come. Sit here by me."

With a plaintive sigh, Majida rose. She smiled apologetically at Leila as she sat on the edge of the divan.

"There. That is so much better," Eve said calmly, though she still appeared flustered. She patted the odalisque's hand. "Now. Go on, Majida. Tell Leila why you are so elated."

Leila stared at her mother, feeling for some strange reason that Eve was reluctant to share this news herself. She glanced questioningly at Majida, who was again smiling broadly.

"A date has been set for your marriage to Jamal Al-Aziz. One month hence, my young mistress, you will be a bride!"

Excitement blazed through Leila. "When was this decided?" she asked, astounded that she had been thinking of such a thing only a short while ago.

"Late this afternoon," Eve replied quietly. "Your father received a letter from Jamal at the hospital not long after you left, but since his work will stretch far into the night he sent a message requesting I give you the news. Jamal believes the caliph's family will be fully cured within a few weeks, and he has requested that the wedding preparations begin at once. He is most eager for the marriage."

Leila lowered her head, overwhelmed. Her dream had suddenly moved that much closer to becoming reality. If she was to marry so soon, that meant her apprenticeship was almost over.

"I take it you are pleased."

The sadness in her mother's voice cut through her own happiness. Leila met her eyes, a stunning likeness to her own, and was astonished to see tears trailing down Eve's alabaster cheeks. "Are you not happy for me, Mother?" she asked, perplexed.

Eve did not answer for so long that Leila grew fearful, not knowing what her mother would say.

"Jamal is a good man, the son of my beloved husband," Eve finally replied, wiping away her tears with a gossamer silk handkerchief. "If God wills it to be so . . ." Her voice trailed off and she rose to her feet, a tremulous smile on her lips. "We will talk more tomorrow, my daughter. Enjoy your supper and rest well this night. May your dreams be sweet and full of promise."

As Eve walked away, her silk garments rustling softly in the breeze, Majida jumped up from the divan to follow, but Leila caught her hand.

"Majida, please. What is troubling my mother?" Leila whispered fervently, raising her voice when Eve disappeared down the stairs. "You have served her since she came to my father's house. You know her soul. Tell me. I cannot bear to see her so distressed."

Majida's face became strangely impassive, and Leila sensed at once that the odalisque was loath to answer. She knew Majida's allegiance was first and foremost to her mother.

"Please, you must tell me," Leila insisted, almost pleading. "Have I hurt her in some way?"

"No, young mistress," Majida said solemnly, shaking her head. "You bring your mother great joy"—a faint smile stirred her lips—"ah, in truth, a bit of trouble now and then, but nothing that would so distress her heart."

"Is there unhappiness between my parents?" Leila desperately hoped this was not the case. She had seen broken hearts aplenty in the opulent harems she visited, neglected wives and forgotten concubines. Another reason to be thankful for her profession. A physician was always needed. Not so a wife.

Majida reached out and gently stroked her cheek, as if sensing her unease. "Never fear, beloved one. My master's love for my mistress is as eternal as the spring, her devotion to him like the jade oasis in the desert with its deep, life-giving pools."

"What is it, then?"

Majida drew a deep breath, and Leila could sense she was choosing her words carefully. The odalisque seemed about to speak when a small, pale-breasted pigeon alighted on a nearby trellis, distracting her. When she met Leila's gaze once more, Leila could tell from the slave woman's guarded expression that she had changed her mind.

"I must go, my young mistress," Majida said, bowing so low that the fringed ends of her veil touched the tiles. She turned and hurried away, her bare feet making no sound.

Leila had it on the tip of her tongue to call Majida back and demand an explanation for her mother's tears, but within an instant, she was alone again.

What right did Majida have to keep her mother's troubles from her? she fumed. Surely if it was something serious the odalisque would put aside her iron-clad loyalty and let Leila know what was in Eve's heart. She was her daughter, after all.

Frowning, Leila poured herself a goblet of cool white wine and took a long sip, enjoying the liquid's tart flavor. She was glad her father did not so strictly adhere to his faith's dietary regulations that he forbade wine in his home, although he himself did not drink it. She nibbled on a meat pastry, ripe olives, and sliced pomegranate, easing her hunger pains at last. Soon she felt much better, her stomach full, the wine soothing her temper.

Perhaps whatever plagued her mother was really not so serious, Leila reasoned, lying back on the divan.

Maybe it was nothing more than the normal feelings of losing one's daughter to the man she would marry. Leila would be moving to another house, another harem. She and her mother would still see each other, but not as often. That could certainly cause Eve pain, since they had always been so close.

It also seemed her mother became distressed whenever they talked about crusaders, and Leila determined then and there that she would not mention the barbarian again. It puzzled her that Eve was praying for him. She should really be praying for the guards who had to watch him instead.

Leila started as the pigeon suddenly left its vine-covered perch and flew off toward the citadel.

"Don't roost in any prison windows, little one," she

murmured under her breath. If the crusader could so easily threaten to snap a guard's neck, she could only imagine what he would do to a hapless bird who strayed too close. Probably bite off its head with his teeth!

Chapter 4

Guy stared stonily out the cell window, counting the large, square bricks in the wall next door. There were thirty-three from the flat roof to the bare ground and sixty-eight from the corner to as far as he could see toward the front of the building if he craned his neck and pressed his face against the cold iron bars. Then again, the ivy was so thick in some places that he could have miscounted—

"God's blood, has it come to this?" he shouted furiously, slamming his large fists down so hard on the window ledge that pain shot through his right shoulder. He grimaced, ignoring it.

He was surely going mad! Counting bricks to pass the time, pacing his cell, watching beetles drag bits of straw across the floor and red ants crawl up the stone walls. What next?

A familiar panic welled up inside him, cold sweat breaking out on his forehead. Desperately he grasped the bars, inhaling deep lungfuls of air to calm himself. It smelled sweet, like flowers, reminding him there was another world outside this cell, a world he hungered to be a part of once again.

Dammit to hell, where was Leila? Why hadn't she come back?

It had been almost two weeks since he had last seen her. His only visitors had been the Arab physician Sinjar Al-Aziz, and that obnoxious captain of the guards who seemed to enjoy reviling him and every Christian who had ever walked the face of the earth. What he would do to that sour-faced bastard if he ever got him alone in this cell . . .

A songbird trilled somewhere above him, and Guy looked up, blinded by the late morning sunlight. He squinted, searching the opposite roof ledge for the bird before he spied it—a white-throated nightingale.

Resting his forehead on the bars, he closed his eyes and listened to the melodic warbling, becoming more relaxed than he had been all morning. The nightingale's song swelled and surged, rich and full, almost masking the sound of rustling vines and excited whispers—

Whispers?

Guy's eyes shot open, and he stared incredulously at a ragged young boy who was expertly scaling the wall with a billowing net in his hand, his small brown feet catching splayed toeholds on the brick outcroppings. Another boy stood below, only a few feet from Guy's prison window, whispering brusque commands and gesturing at the unsuspecting nightingale.

Indignation seized him. "Leave that bird alone, you little heathen!" he roared, startling both boys, who looked from his barred window to the nightingale as it fluttered its wings and flew away.

Guy knew cursing when he heard it. He smiled wryly as the net-wielding boy colorfully vented his youthful fury upon him while clambering down the wall. He ducked just in time to avoid a handful of thrown rocks. Several stones struck the cell door, and the next thing he knew a guard had flung open the peephole.

"Silence, infidel!"

Guy sobered at the harsh command, his anger rising again like scalding bile. "You forget who is the infidel here!" he spat bitterly as the peephole was slammed shut. He turned his back to the door and leaned against the wall, rubbing his aching shoulder through the bandage.

At least he could be thankful the pain had lessened to only a fraction of what it had once been. He had no complaints as far as his injury was concerned. He was alive, which was more than he could say for the men who had accompanied him on Edward's embassy to Anatolia.

Guy squeezed his eyes shut, hearing again in his mind the dying screams of his companions. The surprise attack had come so swiftly. Most of the men were wrenched from their horses and their throats slit from ear to ear before they could utter a sound. A few others, longtime friends, died even more hideously.

He could still hear Reginald Welles calling out to him as the older knight fought off a half dozen attackers, ordering him to escape with his life, the battle lost. Guy had tried to reach him, but he was too late. He watched in horror as Reginald was split in two by a single blow from a scimitar, the severed corpse hitting the earth in a spray of blood and chain mail.

After that, Guy could remember fighting and killing his way out of the narrow ravine and then running, running . . . until he found a shallow but well-concealed cave where he could hide.

Several times in the scorching hot days that followed he heard soldiers shouting nearby, and he knew they were looking for him. Finally, famished and thirsty and unable to bear the cave's close confines any longer, he ventured out, determined to find his way on foot back to Acre. He didn't get far.

Cursing, Guy pushed away from the wall and began to pace the cell, his anger and frustration boiling hotter with each step.

It plagued him like an open, festering sore not to know if any of his companions had survived the surprise attack and were being held for ransom in this lousy prison, but there was no one he could ask. None of the guards understood English and neither did the Arab physician, who had been communicating with him in a curt sign language.

He had decided to conceal the fact that he understood some Arabic and could even speak a little, in the hope that he might glean information from any conversations he overheard. But so far, no luck.

The guards outside his cell were a taciturn lot, and when they did converse, they spoke so rapidly he was unable to grasp what they were saying. The same thing had happened between Leila and her Arab master when he was chained to the wall. God help him, if he could only speak with her again! Where the hell was she?

Guy winced as the bolt on the cell door was drawn back, the screeching sound grating on his nerves. Four guards rushed inside, their bright blades pointed at him menacingly. He knew this meant that the great physician was on his way to pay his morning call.

He was so sick of looking at that Arab's face! He always thought of Leila and what she must be suffering at his lecherous hands. Truly, if there ever was a maiden in distress, it was she.

"Where's Leila? I want to see her!" he shouted even though he knew the guards didn't understand him. He continued to pace despite their presence, feeling like a wild, restless animal stalking its cage. "I said where's Leila, damn you! Are you idiots? Leila, the Christian slave of Al-Aziz!"

Guy could scarcely believe it when she suddenly walked into the cell, followed by the captain, who had a decidedly gloating expression on his narrow face.

"Leila!" Without thinking he took a step toward her, but he immediately stopped when the guards surrounded him with their swords. He held up his hands. "Calm yourselves. I meant no harm."

He listened to the lilting timbre of Leila's voice as she quickly translated what he had said, but the guards did not relax their threatening stance. It seemed they trusted him just about as much as he trusted them, which was not at all.

"My master was called away on other duties this morning," Leila said, glancing nervously at the captain who stood beside her. "I have come in his stead to administer your treatment."

"I am glad," Guy replied, still shocked by her unexpected appearance. His eyes swept over her. "I was beginning to wonder if you were ever coming back."

God, she was beautiful! he thought, noting her look of surprise. Her dark blue linen head veil framed her oval face, emphasizing features as delicate and ethereally lovely as an angel's. Only the long, looped braid hanging well below her waist made her appear earthbound, for her hair was not blond but a glossy black, and so silky he longed to reach out and touch it.

He restrained himself, knowing he might well get his hand lopped off if he did. Instead he had to content himself with looking at her and inhaling her rose perfume. Yet why was her expression so somber? Something was wrong. He could see anxiety in her huge, violet eyes.

"The captain has just given me some grim news which I must impart to you," she said, as if reading his thoughts. "The governor's messenger who was sent to Acre over a week ago with your letter of ransom is dead."

Guy tensed. "Dead?"

Leila nodded. "Some Bedouin herdsmen found his horse wandering in the hills northeast of Acre. The messenger's body was lashed to the saddle, his throat cut. The Bedouins guessed he'd been dead for several days, judging from the stench and the look of him, exposed to the hot sun, the flies . . ." She was unable to finish, her lips pressed together. She looked slightly ill.

"When did they find him?" Guy watched as she lifted her chin resolutely, swallowing hard before she answered.

"Two days ago. The herdsmen have only arrived in Damascus within the past hour to return the body to Governor Mawdud. As you can well imagine, the governor's anger is great." She cast an agitated glance at the man next to her. "The captain was ordered to give this news to my master as soon as he arrived at the prison, but since I am here, he insisted I should tell you now rather than wait until Sinjar Al-Aziz was also present."

Guy felt an icy coldness growing in the pit of his stomach. "What about the letter of ransom—"

"It was not found on the body."

Guy absorbed this news, his mind racing. If the messenger no longer had the letter, then it must have been stolen, or lost. Surely it could not have been delivered to Edward. He and Guy were as close as brothers. Edward would never . . .

A chilling realization struck him. "The governor thinks Edward had the messenger killed, doesn't he? That it's Edward's way of saying he refuses to pay the ransom."

Leila was amazed. The crusader's perceptive response was hardly what she would have expected after the enraged shouting she had heard from him just before she had entered the cell. Hardly what she expected from looking at him, either.

He appeared even more the barbarian with his dark, heavy beard and dirty sirwal. His slightest movement screamed the strength he possessed, proof of his swift recovery since she had last seen him. She also sensed a desperation in him which made her very thankful for the guards' wary protection. She had no idea why the crusader would have been demanding to see her, but she certainly wasn't going to ask him.

"I do not presume to know the governor's mind," she replied, "but yes, so this unfortunate event could be interpreted. Yet Governor Mawdud—"

"You tell your high and mighty governor for me that Edward wouldn't leave me to rot in this stinking prison!" Guy stated fiercely. "For one thing, he's no cold-blooded killer like the butchering lot who set upon us in the Lebanon mountains. Thieves could have murdered the governor's messenger, native Christians, rival Arabs, anyone! It matters not that the letter of ransom was missing. There is no proof that Edward ever received it."

Guy's vehement words echoed in the small cell and thundered into his brain. He felt he was fast losing control. He glanced at the open door, weighing his odds.

"Ease yourself, Lord de Warenne," he heard Leila say. "If you would only allow me to finish."

His gaze riveted back on her face, and he wondered sarcastically what other good news she had to share with him. Then he chided himself, knowing she was but a slave and doing what she had been charged by the captain.

"I'm listening," he replied tightly.

"Governor Mawdud has sent another messenger to Acre within this very hour, and not alone. A full complement of Mameluke soldiers travels with this messenger to pro-

tect him. In his benevolence and wisdom, Governor Mawdud believes it is unlikely Lord Edward would so wantonly
throw away the life of one of his knights, just as you say.
He has granted your prince one more chance to pay the
ransom.''

The words ''one more chance'' sounded too damn ominous to Guy. He had no intention of waiting around to
see if anything happened to the second messenger.

Leila was here. He could finally ask her for her help.
He had no doubt she would jump at the chance to leave
Damascus with him, and he could do no less as a knight
bound by the sacred code of chivalry than see her safely
to Acre. Perhaps they might somehow manage to escape
together tonight.

''You must ask your master Al-Aziz to thank the governor for me,'' Guy said, choosing to appear grateful. Better that than show the frustration and impatience that were
eating him alive. The captain seemed positively incensed
he hadn't attacked them at this news, giving him the opportunity to force Guy into shackles again. He sensed the
bastard might still do so at the slightest provocation, which
would only thwart any attempt to escape. ''I am certain
the governor's decision will be well rewarded as soon as
Edward receives the letter of ransom,'' he added.

Leila spoke with the captain, but so fast Guy couldn't
understand what they were saying. God's bones, he should
have practiced his Arabic more diligently! Then she turned
back to him, gesturing to the cots.

''If you will sit so I may see to your wound.''

As he did so, the guards moved with him, their deadly
blades a hair's breadth from his body. But they backed off
a little when Leila uttered a few sharp words, which surprised him. She was certainly spirited for a slave. Perhaps
her position within the renowned physician's household
gave her some special status.

''What did you say to them?'' he queried as she began
to swiftly unbandage his shoulder. She was standing so
close to him that her perfume enveloped his senses,
heightened by the heat of her body. He felt an overwhelming urge to draw her into his arms, but somehow he man-

aged to restrain himself. "Maybe I could try it on the bastards when they get too close."

"Has the wound been causing you any pain?" she asked, ignoring his question. She pressed gingerly around the purplish red scar.

Guy shook his head, deciding not to waste any more time. He had no idea how long the captain would allow her to tend to him before she was escorted from the cell.

"Tell me, Leila. Have you been treating any others like me in this prison?"

Her fingers ceased their gentle prodding for the briefest moment, but she kept her head lowered, not looking at him. "No. The rest of your party perished."

Guy felt gut-twisting grief at her terse pronouncement. He shot a dark glance at the four guards and their morose commander. They were all watching him closely, their knuckles white where they clutched their swords. It was men like these who had slaughtered his friends. He swore that somehow he would avenge their deaths.

"Your wound is healing well," Leila said, relieved she was almost finished with her task. She was anxious to leave the cell. This encounter with the crusader had been most unsettling and unlike anything she had expected. Their exchange and his restrained reaction to her unpleasant news had made him seem so much more than a mindless barbarian, and she could not help but feel pity for him. Perhaps he did not realize how close he was to being executed. "I don't think you'll need bandages anymo—"

"Listen to me, Leila," he interrupted her, his tone so urgent she was compelled to meet his eyes. "I need your help."

"My help?" she parroted, the intensity of his gaze sending a jolt right through her.

"Yes. Tonight I'm going to—"

"Leila! Stand away from the crusader."

Leila whirled at the sound of her father's stern voice, so startled that she dropped a vial of ointment. The glass shattered on the slab floor. Sinjar was standing next to the captain of the guards, his white robes still rippling from his sudden entrance.

"Wh-what is the matter?"

"I have just come from the hospital. Word was brought to me there by one of Governor Mawdud's high officials."

"I know, Fa—" She clamped her mouth shut just in time. "I know, my master," she began again. "I've already told our patient that a second messenger has been sent to Acre—"

"No, he has returned," Sinjar said gravely. "Come over here, Leila. Now. There is nothing more to be done here."

Bewildered, she glanced over her shoulder at the crusader. His eyes held hers for a fleeting moment, then she quickly moved to her father's side.

"The messenger and his Mameluke escort were met on the Damascus road by one of Sultan Baybar's generals," Sinjar continued. "When the general heard where they were bound, he commanded them to return to the city."

"But why? What of the ransom?"

"There will be no ransom."

"What is this, my esteemed lord?" blurted the captain excitedly, his hand falling to the curved dagger in his belt. "No ransom?"

Sinjar shook his head slowly, a pitying expression on his face as he regarded the crusader. "The general has brought word that Lord Edward and most of his crusaders sailed from Acre three days ago, though the reason behind their sudden departure has not yet been determined. It is believed, however, that they are returning to their country across the seas. To England."

Leila gasped. If this was true, the crusader was a dead man. Sweet Jesu, who could determine kismet?

"What is it, Leila?" Guy asked, rising slowly to his feet. His expression was hard, and strain showed around his eyes. "What has happened?"

Leila's hand was trembling as she touched her father's arm. "He asks me what has happened. How shall I answer him?"

"Say nothing. In the morning his fate will become clear to him," Sinjar replied cryptically. He turned to the captain, his tone commanding as he drew a rolled parchment from his scarlet sash and handed it to him. "This was given to me by Governor Mawdud's official. Read it if you do not believe me, as I doubt you will. It is our lord governor's wish that the crusader be well treated this night. Give him good food and drink, wine if you have it. Offer him an opium pipe. It may help him through his final night upon the earth.''

The captain hastily unrolled the parchment, his shoulders visibly slumping as he read the document. "So it reads,'' he muttered. He shot a venomous glance at Guy, who was again surrounded on all sides by flashing swords, the guards preventing him from moving a muscle. "And so, regrettably, I must obey.''

Leila's heart thundered in her chest as her father pushed her none-too-gently toward the door.

"But we should tell him!'' she protested. "It would be far more cruel not to. He must have time to prepare, time to pray—''

Sinjar gave her another shove, more insistent this time. "No, there is great danger here. You will do as I tell you!''

"Leila!''

She half turned at Guy's hoarse cry, her breath stopping in her throat at what she knew was to be her last glimpse of him.

"God in heaven, it's the ransom, isn't it?'' he shouted, his blue eyes a tempest of fury and disbelief. Thin rivulets of blood trailed down his heaving chest from the razor-sharp swords holding him at bay. "It's in your face. I can see it in your face! Edward has left for England, hasn't he?''

Leila's head snapped back around as her father seized her arm and yanked her toward the door.

"Do not answer him!'' Sinjar commanded as he propelled her from the cell.

The captain of the guards hurried after them, followed at once by the guards, who backed out with their swords lowered dangerously. The door was slammed shut and bolted just as the crusader hit it with the full force of his body, pounding with his fists. Banded with wide strips of iron, the thick wooden door hardly budged.

"Leila, answer me!" he roared. "Leila? Leila!" Then came the sound of splintering wood as the cots were violently hurled against the cell walls.

"Come, my daughter," Sinjar said, noting the unshed tears swimming in Leila's eyes. "It is a harsh thing to hear when a prisoner realizes his life has become forfeit."

Leila's hands were shaking so much she could not lift her face veil. She was stunned by the depth of her emotion, and couldn't understand why she felt like weeping. Guy de Warenne's unfortunate fate was certainly none of her doing.

She jumped as a loud crash came from the cell. The crusader was beating wildly upon the door with what was left of his bed.

"By God, Leila, at least tell me what's going on! Leila!"

"So I'm to treat this raving lunatic like a prince," she heard the captain mutter sarcastically. "We'll be lucky if we can push some food through the peephole without being spit upon by that raging beast."

"He is a human being," she said almost to herself, tears running slowly down her cheeks. "Not an animal."

"Come, Leila," Sinjar insisted. "Our work here is finished."

Leila walked shakily with her father from the cavernous room, the crusader's desperate cries ringing in her ears.

Chapter 5

Seated on the hard slab floor, Guy shoved the tarnished brass tray of food with his foot. He had no appetite. He took another draft from the half-empty wine bottle, but the tangy red liquid was no balm for his burgeoning frustration. He leaned his head against the wall and closed his eyes.

If what Al-Aziz, and since then the highly amused guards, had said was true, then Edward and his fleet of ships were well across the Mediterranean Sea by now, returning home to England.

Without him.

In the long, mind-numbing hours since his outburst of rage, the guards had cracked the peephole to keep a cautious eye on him and then had left it open. Guy had never heard such animated conversation from them, and he understood just enough Arabic to make sense of what they were saying. The guards had talked of nothing else, repeating themselves so often he knew exactly what was to happen to him.

Shortly after sunrise, he was to be taken from the cell and executed before Governor Mawdud and his high officials in the prison courtyard. If he was lucky, the invincible Sultan Baybars, who was apparently in Damascus, might also be present to watch him die. What a bloody spectacle it would be.

He had heard enough gruesome stories about his father's experiences while crusading in Egypt to know that decapitation was the Arab's preferred method of execution. He imagined he could already feel the hard paving stones as he was forced to his knees. Blindfolded, his hands tied so tightly behind his back that they were numb, he could hear the executioner's sharp intake of breath as the curved scimitar was swung back, then the clean, whistling sound of steel cutting through the air—

Cursing vehemently, Guy lifted his arm and was about to dash the empty wine bottle against the opposite wall when the door suddenly creaked open and two guards entered the cell. Although both men held their swords at the ready, one also carried a lantern and the other a long, baked clay waterpipe.

What the hell was the guard doing with a hookah? He had seen such devices in Acre's brothels, though he had never tried one. He had lustily sampled the women, but smoking opium was one vice he had chosen to do without, despite the glowing praise bestowed upon the seductive practice by other crusaders.

"For me?" Guy queried sarcastically, deriving some pleasure from the guards' inability to understand him. "First food and wine—good wine at that—and now another gift. Is your great and mighty Governor Mawdud trying to ease his blasted conscience?"

The nearest guard merely grunted in response and thrust the waterpipe in his face.

Guy's first impulse was to knock the pipe aside, but a wild and desperate idea suddenly struck him. He took the pipe and dangled it between his raised knees, gesturing to the empty silver bowl set atop the airtight vessel which was partially filled with water. "Bastards. I can't smoke it if it's empty."

The same guard tossed him a square, lacquered box. Guy opened it, revealing a substance that looked like black putty and smelled of ambergris and musk. The other guard placed the lantern and some thin, wooden sticks on the floor beside him and then quickly backed away. When Guy eagerly began to pack the bowl with opium, the guards laughed scornfully and left the cell.

Guy's hand shook as he lit the waterpipe with a flaming stick. He was overwhelmed by the daring escape plan tak-

ing shape in his mind. Maybe . . . just maybe it would
work.

As he put the glazed mouthpiece between his lips and
drew on the long smoking tube, the soft whoosh of bubbling water filled the cell. He waited the barest moment
until he tasted the pungent smoke, then he quickly removed the mouthpiece and quietly exhaled what little he
had taken into his mouth. The smoke continued to curl
from the tube and drift harmlessly into the air. From where
Guy sat against the wall, he knew the guards could not
see that he wasn't inhaling.

He glanced at the cell window and was grateful it was
open to the breeze. There was a chance he might be affected by the intoxicating haze, but he hoped the effect
would only be slight.

Guy purposely made a lot of noise as he fumbled with
the lacquered opium box and the lantern, packing and re-
lighting the waterpipe several times. Finally the cell became so clouded with white smoke that the guards swore
and slammed the peephole shut.

Guy smiled grimly at their coarse, knowing laughter
and set the pipe aside, yet close enough so that he could
easily grab the long clay neck. It was obvious he had convinced them he would be no more trouble tonight. Blessed
fools. Soon it would be dark outside. When the guards
came in again to check on him, which they no doubt
would if he remained very, very quiet, he would make
his move . . .

"You are home early," Eve said, smoothing an errant
tendril loosed from Leila's braid as she sat on the marble
couch beside her. "You told me this morning you had so
many patients to see at the hospital that you didn't expect
to return until long after dark. Here it is barely dusk."

"Father sent me home," Leila replied moodily. She
continued to stare at the little stream rumbling not far
from her sandaled feet. "He was displeased with me."

"That is, indeed, a rare occurrence for a favored daughter. What could you have possibly done to displease him?"

Leila shrugged. "I'd rather not talk about it, Mother."

Indeed she did not, Leila thought as Eve sighed softly. How could she explain something that she didn't understand herself? She would never have guessed the episode with the crusader would so affect her. She had seen his face in every patient she encountered, causing her hands to tremble whenever she performed even the simplest treatment.

Eve's voice nudged her back from her unsettling reverie. "Surely it was not that serious—"

"No, though my patients might disagree. I was clumsy, 'tis all, but it's hardly worth discussing. Father will have enough to say to me when he comes home."

"As you wish." Silence settled between them for a while, then Eve patted her hand. "How is the crusader faring today? Has any word come about his ransom?"

Leila glanced at her mother in surprise. It was the first time Eve had mentioned the crusader since the night on the roof terrace. How uncanny that she should think of him now. Could Eve read her mind? "Kismet has not favored him, Mother. There will be no ransom paid for his release."

Eve's eyes grew dark with disbelief. "What do you mean, no ransom?"

"The English prince, Lord Edward, sailed from Acre three days ago. It seems he has left his crusader knight to die."

"No, this cannot be," Eve whispered, horrified. "I knew Edward as a child. He was a good boy and of a just temperament, like his father, King Henry. If Edward was aware that one of his knights languished in prison, surely he would never desert him."

Stunned by what her mother had just shared with her, Leila did not reply. Eve had never told her that she knew Lord Edward and the king of England.

"But what of the letter of ransom, Leila? The messenger left Damascus well over a week ago. Surely Edward would have received it—"

"The messenger was killed," Leila said, and quickly explained that morning's unsettling events at the prison.

Eve listened in silence until Leila finished, her face

deathly white. "Edward never received that letter of ransom. I am certain of it," she said softly, staring unseeing at the gurgling stream. "Perhaps he believes the crusader and his companions are still in Anatolia or on their way back to Acre. He cannot know the ill fortune that he has befallen—"

"Mother," Leila interrupted gently, "it no longer matters what Lord Edward knows or doesn't know. He has sailed home to England without his knight. Lord de Warenne's fate is sealed. He will be executed in the morning."

Eve's gaze grew wide as she searched Leila's face. "Did you say de Warenne?"

"Yes." Leila suddenly realized she had never told her mother the crusader's name, and judging from Eve's startled expression, neither had her father. "Guy de Warenne. Why?"

"The de Warennes are a very well-known family in England, at least they were when William and I . . ." Eve's voice trailed off and she sighed, her private thoughts clearly miles away.

"Mother . . ."

Eve started as if she had forgotten they were sitting together on the couch. "Yes . . . the de Warennes were great and loyal servants of the king. Our nearest neighbors in Wales were of that family. They had a son named Guy, about the same age as my Roger. The boys were good friends."

Leila drew in her breath, for she had rarely heard her mother mention the son born to her when she was a child-bride of fifteen.

Leila could recall asking Eve once as a little girl how she could leave her young son behind in England. Her mother had answered that it had been her duty and desire to journey with her husband to the Holy Land and that it had been best to leave Roger with a family friend. Then she had changed the subject. Leila could count on one hand the times she had heard Eve say her brother's name since then.

"How old is this crusader?" Eve asked urgently, clutching Leila's arm.

"I don't know. Twenty-seven, eight. Maybe thirty."

"Roger would be twenty-eight now, if he still lives," Eve said, growing more agitated. "Yes, this prisoner could be my son's boyhood friend."

Her mother rose so suddenly, pacing in front of the couch, that Leila became alarmed. "Mother . . . what is wrong?"

Eve didn't seem to hear her. "I must intercede for him," she said distractedly, heading toward her apartments. "I must help him."

Leila jumped to her feet and hurried after her, her heart racing. What had come over her mother? Leila had never seen her like this before.

"Help the crusader? Mother, you can't be serious. Who will listen to you? You've told me many times how deeply runs the hatred between the Christian crusaders and our people—"

"Our people?" Eve blurted, rounding on Leila. "You do not even know your own people! The crusader is one of your own blood, your own faith, and you have shown no more compassion for his plight than if he were your sworn enemy. All you have cared about was ensuring Governor Mawdud's ransom, not the precious life you saved! And now that there will be no ransom, you care naught about the terrible fate Lord de Warenne will suffer—"

"I do care!" Leila blurted before she even realized what she was saying, her shrill voice an echo in the darkening courtyard. She shrugged, trying to cover up what she had just revealed. "He . . . he may be a barbarian, but he is not an animal to be led to the slaughter."

Eve sighed heavily. "Ah, my dearest daughter, forgive me. I cannot blame you for what your eyes will not see and what your heart cannot feel. This is the only world you have ever known." She shook her head sadly. "No, it is my fault. I have shared so little with you about your homeland, your true people. There never seemed to be any point to it . . ."

Perplexed by Eve's last words, Leila reached out for her hand, but her mother turned away and walked to the archway, where she stopped and looked back to where Leila was standing.

"I will leave within the hour. If you see your father before I return, tell him I have gone to Governor Mawdud's palace . . . and tell him why. I think he will understand."

As Eve disappeared into her apartments to change into her finest garments, Leila could not help thinking that her mother's quest, although noble, was hopelessly futile.

Sultan Baybars, Supreme Lord of all the Arab Empire, was in Damascus, having arrived earlier that afternoon from Cairo. If Eve was fortunate enough to receive an audience with Governor Mawdud, she would no doubt also encounter the sultan, and then her plea would surely fall on deaf ears. Sultan Baybars had sworn publicly that he would not rest until every crusader was put to the sword or driven from the land. Now that there would be no ransom, nothing would save Guy de Warenne.

Chapter 6

Guy lay very still upon the floor when he heard the cell door scrape open, a mere half hour since he had last lit the waterpipe. He reminded himself to breathe quietly and evenly, as if asleep, which he certainly would have been if he had actually smoked the amount of opium the guards had left him.

He listened carefully, discerning three different footfalls moving toward him. There were three guards in the cell instead of two, upping the odds against him, yet he knew his lust for vengeance would see him through. The friends he had lost in the Lebanese mountains would soon receive justice.

Guy heard chuckling and lowered voices speaking directly above him, and knew the guards were looking down at him. Someone lightly kicked his leg, but he did not move, not even when the kick came harder the second time. Someone else slapped his face, and his head lolled convincingly to the side.

Thinking he was out cold, the guards laughed loudly now and began to talk among themselves, their conversation boastful and relaxed. It was his cue.

Guy seized the waterpipe next to him and swung with all his might, hitting one guard's knees as he jumped to his feet. The man buckled and Guy swung again, shattering the pipe on the stricken guard's head. The man fell heavily to the floor.

The two other guards came at him with their bare hands, for he had attacked so swiftly that they had not had time to draw their swords. Towering over them both, Guy grabbed the nearest guard by the throat and threw him against the wall. The man slumped senseless to the floor.

Unnerved by the sight of his fallen companions, the last guard uttered a short, guttural cry and made a break for the door, but he was not fast enough. Guy caught him by his belt and collar and hoisted him in the air, using the flailing man as a battering ram against the window's iron bars. Blood and brains spattered upon the ledge, and the guard crumpled into a lifeless heap below the window.

Breathing hard and fast, Guy winced at the sharp pain in his shoulder as he bent and picked up a curved scimitar. The weapon was lighter than the swords he usually wielded, but just as deadly. He took care to slit the throats of the two other guards, a ruthless but necessary precaution, then he rushed to the door, his battle-honed instincts guiding his every move.

His immediate concern was how the hell to get out of the prison without bringing the rest of the guards down upon him. He peered around the door into a large cavernous room lined with many similar cells, but as far as he could tell they were dark and empty, no other guards in sight.

Clutching the scimitar tightly with both hands, he was about to step from the cell when he heard male voices. One belonged to the captain of the guards; the two others he didn't recognize.

"Damn!" Guy muttered, backing into the cell. His hands were sweating where he held the sword, not out of fear but from the sheer exhilaration of battle pumping through him. He leaned against the wall and waited as the voices drew nearer, sweat dripping down the side of his face, the cords of his neck taut and his bare chest heaving.

The next few moments were a bright crimson blur. When two more guards rushed in the open door, followed by the alarmed captain, Guy reacted like a demon unleashed.

One guard fell instantly, clutching his abdomen as his lifeblood spilled between his splayed fingers, while the other guard fought Guy bravely before he, too, followed his compatriot into Paradise. That left the white-faced captain of the guards, who brandished his sword and circled Guy, awaiting his first move.

"Keys . . . and maybe you will live," Guy demanded in halting Arabic, pointing his sword tip at the iron ring nestled in the captain's sash. "Keys!"

Clearly astonished that Guy spoke his language, the captain shook his head fiercely. He cursed Guy to the high heavens as he continued to circle and better his stance, his scimitar flashing dangerously in the yellow lantern light.

"Then die," Guy said harshly in his own tongue, any thought of mercy vanishing as fleetingly as it had come. By all the martyred saints, he had no time for this!

He lunged at the captain so suddenly that he took the man completely off guard. With little remorse he struck him through the heart and pinned him to the wall. "For Reginald Welles, you bloody bastard." The man clutched at the blade, his face twisted in horror, on his last breath a rasping curse.

Guy didn't even blink. He had been so cursed many times before. He wrenched the iron key ring from the bloodied sash and turned from the dead man's glazed, unseeing eyes, not bothering to remove the sword. He looked at the wild sprawl of lifeless bodies around him, then down at his own bloodstained trousers.

He needed clothes.

Guy quickly stripped the guards and donned garments that were not too bloodied: a voluminous pair of ankle-length pantaloons, a tunic, an overgarment with a wide belt, and a braided shoulder mantle. The clothes were a bit small for him, but he hoped that in the dark no one would notice either that or any telltale splatters of blood. Last, he slid on a pair of short leather boots, the only thing that fit him properly, and wound a long scarf around his head, securing it with a black double-ringed cord.

He picked up another highly polished sword and looked at his reflection in the famed mirrorlike Damascus steel. With his thick, dark beard and borrowed robes he could easily pass for an Arab on the moonlit streets—if no one asked him any questions. His poor Arabic would get him into trouble the minute he opened his mouth. He needed Leila's help . . .

Clutching the precious key ring in one hand and the scimitar in the other, Guy left the cell and its silent, staring dead. He shut the door, hoping to stave off any curious guards for at least a while, and began to search for a way out of the prison. He breathed an audible sigh of relief when he spied a bolted door which appeared to face the same direction as his cell.

Guy lifted the bolt and pushed on the door, but it was locked. He began fitting key after key into the rusted keyhole, all the while keeping a cautious lookout over his shoulder. He tried another key, and then another, with still no success.

''Come on . . . come on,'' he whispered, cold sweat beading his brow. Finally one of the keys grated in the lock and the door swung open in squeaky protest. A strong breeze snatched at his robes as he stepped into the sweet freedom of the night, tense elation pulsing through his veins.

He tossed the key ring to the ground and tucked the scimitar into his belt, then shut the door and went directly to the wall he had virtually memorized during his captivity. He followed the ragged young boy's recent example and began to scale the rough-hewn surface, counting brick by brick. By the time he reached the flat roof, he was straining from exertion, his right shoulder on fire. He hoisted himself over the edge and lay down on his stomach, gasping in great lungfuls of the cool night air.

When he had caught his breath, Guy rubbed his eyes and looked out over the myriad rooftops of Damascus. The ancient city was hauntingly beautiful in the pale moonlight, but he had no time to think of that now.

He had to find Leila. She was his only way out of this godforsaken place. With her command of Arabic, surely she could get them safely through the city gates and on their way to Acre.

Guy began to crawl silently to the opposite side of the building. Even if there was the remotest possibility he might escape this city on his own, he'd be damned if he would leave without her. He could never live with himself, knowing he had left her behind in Saracen hands. To do so would be to disgrace his chivalric oath which demanded that he defend his fellow Christians against the cruelty of heretics and infidels.

And if anyone's plight had touched him, it was Leila's. He would find her and help her escape, or gladly die in the attempt.

Guy reached the other side of the roof and looked down into the narrow deserted alley below. He climbed down the wall just as before, brick by brick, until his feet touched solid ground. So far, all was well.

He walked onto a main street, his robes fluttering around his legs, and turned left, heading away from the accursed prison. He kept his head down when passersby drew close, but to his relief he was attracting no curious attention. He hurried along the dark winding street, for it was past sunset, not stopping until he came upon a bent old man who was closing up his fabric shop for the night.

Guy knew that if he said too much he would give himself away. "Sinjar Al-Aziz," he muttered gruffly, clearing his throat and coughing. He was counting on the physician being as renowned as Leila had said he was, otherwise he would never find the right house.

The old Arab studied him through dimmed eyes, then pointed down the street, uttering a string of directions that Guy barely understood. When the man finished speaking Guy nodded graciously, his heart beating hard against his chest as he continued walking eastward along the same street.

So the physician Al-Aziz was a famous man, Guy thought, amazed and encouraged when each of the three passersby he stopped next was able to direct him further along his way. No one seemed in the least bit surprised that he should be asking about him; perhaps they simply believed he was seeking some medical treatment for his feigned cough.

At last Guy came to a narrow side street with elegant one-story houses built alongside the northernmost wall of the city. He could hear rushing water beyond the walls; it sounded like a fast-flowing river. The last man he had spoken with had said the home of Al-Aziz was the fourth one from the corner. Guy would know it by the intricately carved brass plates upon the door.

He paused just past the third house and looked up and down the dark, quiet street. Good. No one was coming. He could see the polished brass door on the next house, and his heart seemed to beat all the faster. He had found it! Now, how was he going to get inside? Certainly not by the front door, where any armed guards inside might see fit to carve him into little pieces . . .

He looked up at the flat roof, carefully weighing his next move. The windowless front wall was high, but he was probably tall enough to reach the ledge if he jumped for it.

Guy did just that, grimacing at the pain that shot through his shoulder and right arm. Ignoring it, he pulled himself up, swinging his leg to the side and over the ledge. In the next instant he was hugging the roof's tiled surface, where he craned his neck and got his bearings.

From what he could tell, the house was very large and divided into two main sections, with multileveled roof terraces here and there and large, lit spaces which must open into courtyards. All he had to do now was find the harem.

He crept across the roof, listening for any light, female laughter. If this physician was so wealthy, surely he had dozens of women to pleasure him. Thinking of Leila among that number, he felt anger sweep through him, fueling his furtive search.

He kept low, sometimes stealing on his hands and knees, until he reached the first terrace. All was still and silent; no one occupied the white gazebo. He moved around it and came to a courtyard, his eyes widening at the sight of a stout, silk-clad woman reclining below on a central divan while what appeared to be slave women scurried around her bearing silver trays laden with food and drink. The richly dressed woman's tone was sharp and commanding as she clapped her hands, and Guy shuddered, frowning.

Probably a wife . . . and a most unappealing one at

that, he guessed, watching for any sign of Leila among the many slaves.

Long, tense moments passed, and still he did not see her. Growing impatient and beginning to doubt his chances of finding her, Guy crept past a trellised terrace toward the farthest corner of the house, then stopped again when the roof opened into another courtyard lit by softly glowing lanterns. He crouched there, his gaze sweeping the lush, green interior, but it was empty.

He sat back on his haunches, a hollow ache of despair welling inside him. It was an emotion that rarely afflicted him, and he didn't like it at all. Yet as he considered his next move, he couldn't seem to shake it.

Maybe Leila wasn't here. Maybe Sinjar Al-Aziz had several homes in Damascus, one for his wives and one for his concubines. He had heard stories of such practices among the small Moslem population in Acre. If that was the case, the odds of finding her were dwindling indeed, and he was fast running out of time. Surely his escape from prison would be discovered soon, if it hadn't been already. Once the alarm was raised he would never get out of the city, whether she was with him or not—

Guy froze, his breath catching at the sight of a petite, dark-haired woman entering the courtyard. Dressed in rose-colored silk, she paused by a marble couch, her head bowed, the gold embroidered edges of her translucent veil hiding her face from view. He heard her sigh, and his heart seemed to stop at the plaintive sound. Then she slowly lifted her head, revealing an exquisite profile . . .

Leila!

Guy jumped from the roof and landed as silently as a cat upon a grassy mound at one end of the courtyard. He stole up swiftly behind her, his footsteps masked by the babbling stream. The last thing he wanted her to do was scream. He caught her around the middle and pressed his hand over her mouth.

"Leila, don't fear," he whispered soothingly as she struggled against him. "It's Guy de Warenne. I've come to help you . . . to take you with me."

His voice had the desired effect, for she seemed to go

limp in his arms, and for a fleeting moment he thought she might collapse. Holding her close, he turned her around to face him, her features hidden by his towering shadow. As he removed his hand and gently tilted her chin toward the lamplight, his stomach suddenly sank into his boots.

"By all that is holy, you're not Leila!" Guy was so shocked that he released his hold on the woman and stared stupidly at her. From her glossy black hair to her tiny feet, she was a close replica of Leila, but she was older, by twice as much, though the years had not marred the ethereal loveliness of her face and delicately curved figure.

"Shhh, my lord! You will bring my husband's entire household down upon us," the woman admonished him in English, looking up at him with eyes that were without fear and glistening with unshed tears. " 'Tis truly a miracle! You are safe . . . and you are here! God has answered my prayers more abundantly than I could ever have hoped." She stepped back, her gaze sweeping over him. "You have grown into a man, a knight. The last time I saw you, you were one of Ranulf de Lusignan's young pages and could barely lift a sword."

Guy felt as if he had stumbled into a dream. Perhaps the opium had affected his brain! He was afraid that if he spoke a single word this beautiful woman, the courtyard, everything would disappear, and he would find himself in prison again, awaiting death.

"Come." The woman tugged urgently on his arm with what felt like a flesh and blood hand. "We cannot talk here. Curious eyes and flapping ears abound, always ready for mischief. Come with me, my lord. Please, we must hurry."

Strangely, Guy did not protest. He went with her to a narrow archway just off the courtyard, ducking his head as she led him into a softly lit room. He took his eyes from her for an instant, his widened gaze cautiously circling the opulent interior decorated in gold, silver, and precious stones. He had never seen such luxury!

"You are safe here, Lord de Warenne, at least for a

while," he heard the woman say, the sound of his name shattering the bewildered haze that had settled over him.

His eyes fixed on her face and he grabbed her arms, as slender and delicate as water reeds. "Are you a witch, a sorceress, or an unearthly vision? How do you know the name de Lusignan?"

"I am none of those things, I can assure you, good knight," she answered, her gossamer veil slipping from her hair as she shook her head. "You seek my daughter, Leila. She told me about you many days ago when you were first captured. I am Eve Gervais. Mayhap you remember me, though you were only a child."

Guy's hands slid from her arms and dropped to his sides. Eve Gervais. Surely he was seeing the phantom of a woman long thought dead. "Eve . . . wife to William Gervais of the Welsh Marches? You left for the Holy Land twenty years ago and—"

"Never returned," Eve finished quietly. "Yes, I am she."

Astounded, Guy searched her face, wondering how he could not have seen it. Leila's mother! The two women were as physically alike as only mother and daughter could be.

"What of William?" he asked, though he immediately sensed her answer from her fleeting expression of sorrow.

"Dead these many years." She swept a slim hand around her lavish surroundings. "I have since been blessed with another husband, Leila's adopted father. The physician, Sinjar Al-Aziz."

Guy was dumbstruck, his mind reeling.

God's blood, then Leila was no slave! She had lied to him. Why? Perhaps she was no Christian either, regardless of the zunnar around her waist, though it was clear from Eve's words that she herself practiced the true faith. Yet she was married to an infidel . . .

"Ah, there is so much I could tell you, my lord, but time is our enemy this night," Eve said urgently, breaking into his thoughts. "My son, Roger Gervais. Is he yet alive? You and he were both pages under Ranulf de Lusignan, who became Roger's guardian when we left for the Holy Land. You were friends.''

Guy felt as if a fist had just slammed into his gut. He had been so caught up in everything Eve was telling him, he had not even considered her maternal connection with Roger Gervais.

Friends? Yes, he and Roger had been friends . . . once.

That had changed eight years ago when they were forced to take sides in a barons' rebellion that threatened to tear England apart. Roger chose to ride with Simon de Montfort, earl of Leicester, the grasping Norman traitor who lusted for the English throne, while Guy fought for King Henry alongside his son, Lord Edward.

It was an irreparable rift that had ended their close friendship. After the royalists lost the Battle of Lewes, King Henry became a hostage while Edward and many of his knights, Guy among them, were imprisoned in Kenilworth Castle.

Guy felt his palms grow sweaty and a tightness gather in his chest from just thinking about Kenilworth's dungeon and the tiny windowless cell where he had been held captive for over a year. All thanks to Roger Gervais. While Guy was left to die in prison, Roger forcibly seized his lands in both Surrey and Wales. Twenty odd Gervais knights took up residence in Warenne Castle, and one even became his wife Christine's lover.

Only after Lord Edward, Guy, and several other knights who survived their long and brutal captivity escaped from Kenilworth Castle and joined royalist forces at Evesham to defeat Simon de Montfort was Guy able to win back his lands. Unfortunately Roger was not killed in the battle, but captured alive. He was banished for a time and his estate forfeited, but under the king's generous peace he, too, eventually regained his family land, which bordered hard upon Guy's.

Their friendship, however, could never be restored. Roger's traitorous betrayal ran too deep.

If anything, their hatred had intensified over the years. Both had lost knights and men-at-arms during numerous confrontations until King Henry had intervened, forbidding them to make war on each other. An uneasy truce had hung between them since then, yet the hatred had remained, ever kindled and ready to ignite at the slightest provocation.

"Your silence tells me one thing, my lord," Eve said with a tremulous voice, drawing Guy back from his grim reverie. "Roger is dead."

"No," Guy stated flatly. "He lives." At her cry of joy, at the sight of tears swimming in her eyes again, he knew he did not have the heart to tell her of her son's treachery.

"And he is well?"

"Yes," he replied, wishing a bolt of lightning would strike Roger at his castle on the Welsh border even as they spoke of him.

"Then you must take Leila to him!" Eve cried passionately, clutching Guy's arm. "She belongs in her true homeland, not here. I have prayed for a way to liberate her, but my pleas went unheard until this night. Now you have answered them. You said it yourself, Lord de Warenne. You came here to take her with you." Her voice was filled with wonderment, and now she looked at him as if she could not quite believe he was real and standing before her. "If you had come a moment later, I would have missed you. I was just about to leave for Governor Mawdud's palace to intercede for your life. But you are here—"

"You speak of liberating your daughter," Guy interjected, growing more confused as he noted the richness of Eve's garments and the glittering emerald necklace at her throat, "but you are not a slave, and neither is Leila. Yet so she led me to believe."

Eve waved her hand impatiently. "A ruse. It was her father's way of protecting her. He told me as much, fearing you might use her to escape if you knew her true station."

Guy mulled over this revelation, seeing its truth. He might have tried such a stunt indeed. Then another thought of even greater import came to him.

"When I arrived in Acre, I was told the zunnar was worn by any Christian living in Arab lands . . . a good way for us to determine friend or foe. Leila wore such a garment when she came to the prison. Was that also a ruse?''

"No!" Eve said heatedly, clearly affronted by his obvious misgivings. She stepped away from him and drew herself up proudly. "Hear me well, my lord. When William was murdered—"

"Murdered?''

"Yes, before my eyes. Bedouin slave traders. They brought me and my newborn babe to this city, and I was purchased by Sinjar Al-Aziz, who later became my husband. As a marriage gift he offered me anything I wanted, yet I asked only that I might remain a Christian and raise Leila in my faith. This he granted from his heart, though his reason told him to deny me. Since then, God has given me great happiness in my second marriage. I love my husband and will never leave him, no matter his beliefs. But I do not want such a marriage for Leila and''—Eve paused, chewing her lower lip nervously—"and neither does she.''

Guy regarded her sharply, anger bubbling deep within him. "She is to marry an infidel?''

"Yes. It has all been arranged. Leila has no choice in the matter. She . . . she is most distressed. She has told me she would do anything to escape this marriage, leave Damascus, leave the country, but there was no way until now.''

"She has seemed troubled," Guy agreed, thinking back on their encounters in his cell, "although I believed it was because of her servitude.''

"Yes, Leila does not mask her unhappiness well." Eve touched his arm, her eyes pleading with him. "Please take her away from here. I can get you both safely out of Damascus. Take her back with you to England, to her brother. She should have a Christian marriage, as is her birthright, and a home and family in her true country. She is a virgin. Roger will have no difficulty finding a suitable husband for her. I beg of you, Lord de Warenne, upon your sacred oath as a knight, if ever there was a young woman needing your aid—''

"Do not fear, my lady," Guy said resolutely. "It is as good as done." Indeed, he needed no more convincing. Leila might not be a slave as he had thought, but she was truly a maiden in dire need of rescue from a heathen marriage and a barbarian land. At that moment his own personal feelings about Roger Gervais seemed inconsequential next to her wretched plight. "I will see her safely home to your son. This I swear, and may God defend my oath."

Eve's great relief was evident on her lovely face, but before she could offer any thanks, the sound of sandaled feet crossing the courtyard made her turn pale. Her eyes darted around the room, falling upon a large, lacquered cabinet.

"Quickly, you can hide in there until all is in readiness." Running with him to the cabinet, she flung open the latticed doors and pushed him inside.

Guy banged his head as she shut the doors. He bit off the curse that jumped to his tongue, crouching because he was too tall for the cabinet. He pushed aside the silken, jasmine-scented garments hanging all around him to peer out the intricate wooden grillwork.

He watched Eve move to the archway where she met another woman, obviously a servant, who bowed to her. They conversed in hushed tones for several long moments, the slave woman glancing occasionally at the cabinet. It was clear to him that Eve had divulged his hiding place, which made him nervous. Could the slave woman be trusted?

His fears were somewhat allayed when the two women warmly embraced, more like dear friends than mistress and slave. Then Eve walked back toward the cabinet while her servant disappeared into the courtyard. As Eve drew closer, Guy could not resist calling out to her in a loud whisper, "Who was the woman?"

"Do not worry, my lord. I would trust Majida with my life . . . and I just have," Eve whispered back through the tiny diamond-shaped openings in the cabinet doors. "Everything has been arranged. She has gone to seek out a friend of mine, a special friend who will help you and

Leila leave the city. Majida is stealthy and swift. My friend should be here within the hour with his wagon.''

''A wagon?'' Guy hissed, highly skeptical of such a method. ''Surely we will be found out! I say we lower ourselves over the wall next to the house and avoid traveling through the city gates altogether.''

''And be swept into the Barada? If you survive the river's swift currents, you will find Mameluke soldiers patrolling its banks when you reach the other side. No, my lord, you must leave this to me.''

Guy groaned to himself, rolling his eyes. Never before had he entrusted his hide to a woman, but he had little choice. ''As you say.''

''Good. When Majida returns, I shall summon Leila to this very room. Then I will need your help, my lord.''

''Name it.''

''I will give you a sponge and a vial of sleeping sedative to hold in readiness until I signal you.''

''Why the devil do I need that?'' Guy asked, frowning.

''Leila must be drugged for the journey.''

''Drugged? I was under the impression she wanted to leave Damascus.''

''She does, she does,'' Eve said quickly, her voice quavering, ''but I fear the excitement will be too much for her. Better she does not know what is in store. If we do not drug her, there is always the chance she may become frightened in the wagon and inadvertently give you both away. Leila is prone to tears when she becomes upset.''

''What woman isn't?'' Guy complained under his breath.

''Forgive me, my lord. I did not hear you.''

''I said we can't have that.'' Damned if he wanted a mewling female to contend with on their journey to Acre. Better to drug her and deal with any tears later, when the danger was past. ''Very well. What do I have to do?''

''When I lift my veil over my head, which is your signal, pour the sedative over the sponge and then creep up behind her as you did to me and cover her mouth. In only a moment the drug will take effect, and she will sleep for a day or better.'' Eve drummed her slender fingers on the latticework. "Oh, yes. You must wash your hands as soon as Leila is unconscious. The fumes left on your skin are potent enough to give you a terrible headache if you inhale them."

"My thanks for the warning," Guy said, wincing at the pain in his neck and shoulders. He couldn't stay cramped up like this much longer. "When did you say your friend would get here with that wagon?"

"Soon, my lord. I am sorry about the cabinet, but I have nowhere else to hide you," she apologized, sensing his discomfort. "You are as tall and broad a man as I have ever seen, other than William." She sighed softly, then asked, "Is Roger the same?"

"Close," Guy answered tersely, then quickly changed the unsavory topic. "What of your husband, Al-Aziz? Do you expect him soon?"

"No. 'Tis a most fortunate thing. Tonight he spends with his second wife . . . though Leila did say he wished to speak with her when he returned from the hospital." She appeared momentarily concerned, then shook her head. "Ah, either way, he will not come home until very late. A great physician's life is a taxing one." She fell silent, leaning her shoulder lightly on the doors.

"What will you tell him, my lady, when he discovers Leila is missing?"

"I do not know," she replied simply, meeting his eyes through the ornamental grille. "Perhaps I will tell him the truth. It is hard to deceive one who knows your heart as if it was his very own."

"That is insane!" Guy blurted, not believing her. "You must come with us. I cannot leave you here, thinking you might be imprisoned or worse—"

"No, I have told you, my lord. My place is here with my husband. As for my fate, whatever I decide to tell him about this night . . . we are all in God's hands." A small smile curved her lips. "I must go now and get the sedative from Leila's medical supplies. Majida told me she was still in the baths. Perhaps you might try resting on one knee for a while instead of hunching over like that. I will return shortly."

Guy followed Eve's suggestion as she turned and walked gracefully from the room, her gauze-like garments shimmering in the lamplight. He leaned his head on the side of the cabinet and closed his eyes, sighing heavily.

What a strange day this had been, fraught with more unsettling surprises than he could ever have imagined when he awoke that morning. And there was every indication that the day would continue its chaotic course. Soon he would be rumbling across a city swarming with soldiers in some sort of wagon with a drugged young woman who was none other than the sister of his worst enemy and the adopted daughter of the most renowned physician in the Arab Empire!

If he had any guardian angels, he seriously hoped they were watching.

Chapter 7

Leila glanced up from her book of Persian poetry as Majida entered the room and hurried over to the divan where she was reclining on a half dozen soft pillows.

"Forgive me, O my young mistress," the odalisque said, her hand pressed over her heart. "It is growing late and I do not mean to disturb your hour of solitude, but your beloved mother has requested that I escort you to her apartments."

Surprised, Leila lowered the book to her lap. "I thought she had gone to Governor Mawdud's palace. Is something wrong? Is Mother ill?"

"No, no, dearest one, she is well, but she has changed her mind about visiting our lord governor. She merely wishes to speak with you before she retires for the night."

Leila frowned. Eve changed her mind? That was indeed odd. Once her mother decided to do something, she rarely swerved from her purpose. And why was Majida looking at her so intently, as if she were memorizing every line of her face? The odalisque's gray eyes were misty and red-rimmed as if she might have been crying, and her hands were trembling slightly. "Majida, what is troubling you?"

The odalisque started at her question and backed away, bowing. "I am tired, my young mistress, nothing more. Your devoted Majida grows older with each passing day, do not forget. Please, your mother awaits."

Leila sighed softly as she flung aside the light coverlet and rose from the divan. She left her book lying open on a cushion and marked the page with a flat brass ornament shaped like a tulip, determined that she would finish reading the lengthy poem when she returned to her room.

"If you will kindly wear this," Majida said, holding up one of Leila's plainer robes made of dark blue linen. "The air has grown cool this night, and you are hardly dressed to withstand its chill."

Leila glanced down at the clothes she was wearing, a lavender silk thob with a V-shaped collar embroidered in silver thread, and matching sirwal. The iridescent fabric was so sheer she could see her rose-pink nipples and the pearly whiteness of her skin through the lightly embroidered bodice.

"Very well, Majida, I will wear the robe," she agreed, bringing her long, beribboned braid over her shoulder and shrugging into the garment. She tied the proffered sash around her waist, adding, "Though I am only going across the courtyard."

"And shoes, my dearest Leila."

Leila stared at the odalisque. Majida hardly ever called her by her name unless she was frustrated by Leila's stubbornness, which had happened often as a child. But the odalisque hardly looked angry now. Majida seemed nervous and distressed, as if she might burst into tears at any moment. For that reason Leila slipped on the soft leather sandals laid at her feet, whereas otherwise she might have objected.

"There. Satisfied?" she asked with an indulgent smile.

Majida only nodded and left the room, leading the way as Leila followed quickly after her, growing more perplexed.

In the courtyard Leila paused briefly and looked up into the sky, drinking in the jasmine-scented air. How beautiful was the night, the heavens so black and deep, the stars like many-faceted diamonds, sparkling and twinkling. She might have stood there longer if Majida hadn't tugged impatiently on her sleeve.

"Will you make your mother wait all the more, my young mistress? Come!"

This time a sharp retort flew to Leila's tongue, but Majida disappeared into her mother's apartments before she could utter it.

Whatever was going on? she wondered, walking through the archway. As her eyes adjusted to the dim lighting, for the lanterns had been turned down to barely a flicker, she saw Eve standing in the middle of the room by a low table spread with a light evening repast. Majida was at her side.

"What is it, Mother?" she asked as Eve came to meet her, taking her hand.

"Come and sit with me, Leila," her mother answered, leading her to the far side of the table and seating her on a plump floor cushion facing the open archway. Eve knelt on the cushion directly opposite her and began pouring red wine from a silver flask, offering Leila a goblet. "Drink with me, my daughter. It has been a long and trying day for us both."

Leila stared at the goblet blankly, thoroughly confused, then back at her mother, who was lifting her gold-embroidered veil over her head. Tears had sprung to Eve's eyes, and a few trickled down her pale cheeks.

"Mother?" Leila began to rise just as she heard footfalls directly behind her. She turned her head and saw a huge, dark-robed shape at the same moment that a wet sponge was pressed over her mouth. "Mother!" she screamed, but her cry was muffled as she inhaled sickly sweet fumes and swallowed the bitter liquid oozing past her lips. Dear God, she was being drugged! But by whom? Why?

Her frantic struggles were no match for the steely arms that held her. Desperately she raked her fingernails across the large hand holding the sponge and heard a deep male voice curse loudly. The room began to swim before her eyes, and she knew she was fast losing consciousness. She stared wild-eyed at the fading figure of her mother, who was holding out her hands helplessly.

"I have done this for your sake, Leila. Always remember how much I love you," she heard like a pleading echo in her ears as the room grew dimmer and dimmer . . . fading into blackness.

"She's out," Guy said, holding Leila's slumped figure

against his chest as he tossed the sponge in the silver bowl
Majida held out to him. He laid Leila gently on two cushions he kicked together, then glanced at a shaken Eve while
he washed his hands in a larger bowl filled with sudsy
water. "Are you all right, my lady?"

"Yes," she whispered, swallowing back her tears.

Guy dried his hands and handed Majida the damp towel.
"You can still reconsider—"

"Never," Eve said, her voice growing stronger.
"Never. Majida, remain by the door and call out if you
see anyone coming. Anyone . . . Suhel, Nittia, Ayhan . . .
God forbid, my husband . . ."

"Yes, my mistress." Majida fell on her knees and kissed
Leila's forehead, murmuring in Arabic, "Sweet Leila, dark
as night. Do not forget your beloved Majida." With a
heartfelt sigh, the loyal odalisque jumped up and hurried
to the archway, rubbing her eyes with the sleeve of her
caftan. "The courtyard is empty, mistress."

"Come. This way," Eve said, gesturing to a brass-
covered door inlaid with silver. She ran ahead, pushing it
open to reveal a flight of wooden steps. "My roof terrace."

Guy scooped Leila's limp body into his arms, marveling
that she was so light. He strode to the door and up the
stairs with Eve close behind him. He cautiously stepped
onto the corner terrace, gratefully noting the vine-covered
trellises which would hide their furtive activities from pry-
ing eyes.

"Over here," Eve whispered, going to the rounded roof
ledge. "My friend is waiting below in the side alley."

As Guy peered over the ledge at the ground looming
some sixteen feet below them, he was relieved to see a
wagon pulled up beside the wall and a burly man in monk-
ish garb standing on the driver's bench, his arms outstretched. But what was that god-awful smell?

"Drop her down," Eve directed him. "Thomas will
catch her."

"Thomas?"

"My friend . . . an Englishman and a fellow Christian.
You may trust him with your life." Eve lovingly touched

Leila's cheek one last time, kissed her, then watched dry-eyed and silent while Guy carefully released her into Thomas's waiting arms.

"What's in the wagon?" Guy asked Eve as Thomas drew back the canvas and settled Leila on the planked floor next to the seat, wrapping her in what looked like a heavy, white shroud.

"Corpses."

A chill shot through Guy, the one word explaining the overpowering stench emanating from the wagon.

He laughed shortly and looked heavenward in disbelief. Now they had a pile of dead bodies to protect them if the soldiers drew too close. Perhaps their rotting friends even clutched swords in their rigid fingers!

"Trust me, my lord, you and Leila will be safe," Eve insisted softly, as if reading his mind. "I would not wantonly risk my daughter's life, nor yours. Thomas is a friar from our church in Bab Touma, the Christian quarter, and one of only two such men allowed in the city. It is his job to transport dead Christian slaves in his wagon to the cemetery several miles outside the city walls."

"But what if we're stopped along the way and the wagon searched?"

"I can assure you, Lord de Warenne, no Moslem will defile himself by touching such a cargo. Just remember to keep very still and all will be well."

Guy swallowed hard, looking from the waiting wagon to Eve. "Then it is farewell, my la—" His words died on his lips at the sound of angry male shouts carrying across the silent rooftops from the direction of the governor's prison. "I believe my absence has been discovered," he said dryly, his expression grim.

"You must go. There is no more time to waste," Eve urged, her eyes shining brightly in the moonlight. She pulled a small velvet bag from her wide sleeve and handed it to him. "Jewels . . . emeralds, diamonds, rubies. They should see you safely home to England. Guard her well, my lord. I have entrusted my heart's dearest joy to your care."

"I swear on my life that Leila will come to no harm,"

Guy vowed, stuffing the bag in his sash. As he quickly lowered himself from the roof, Thomas guided his feet so he could jump down on the wagon bench.

"Lie down beside her, my lord," Thomas directed him in a hushed voice. "I'll tell you when we get close to Bab Charki so you'll know not to make a sound."

"What is Bab Charki?" Guy asked, gritting his teeth from the terrible odor assailing him as he took his place on the hard wagon floor.

"The Gate of the Sun. It's one of the city's main gates and heavily guarded, but we'll have no problems if you hold your breath and play dead when we reach it . . . just in case the guards decide to check beneath the canvas."

"I think I can manage," Guy muttered, jerking his hand away when he accidentally touched the wrapped, bloated corpse next to him. "What are the odds that they might check?"

"Hopefully slight. We have some very ripe souls in this wagon that should keep them away."

Guy had to swallow hard after that comment. As Thomas tucked a heavy linen shroud tightly around his prone body and then over his head, he heard Eve fervently whisper above him, "God go with you."

"And with you, brave Lady Eve," he answered, the world around him growing darker still when the canvas was drawn over them and pulled taut.

The wagon jerked into motion, the iron-rimmed wheels clattering loudly when they turned from the dirt alley onto the paved side street. Guy rocked back and forth, bumping into Leila on one side and the corpse on his other, all the while breathing through his mouth and not his nose. It helped . . . a little.

Funny, he thought, beginning to believe he was living some bizarre and macabre nightmare. He hadn't even asked what was to happen once they reached the Christian cemetery. Perhaps he and Leila were to walk all the way to Acre.

After what seemed a very long time, he heard Thomas hiss to him through the canvas, "We're almost to Bab

Charki, my lord. Say a prayer the lady doesn't talk in her sleep."

Guy tensed as the wagon ground to a halt and harsh male voices surrounded them on all sides. He lay totally still as the canvas was thrown back and the men cursed, drawing in sharp, disgusted exhalations of breath. It was obvious the guards were getting a full whiff of his putrid companions.

Yet the wagon stayed put and Guy began to sweat, fearing the worst. Had Leila moved? Had he? His fingers itched to reach for his sword, but that would surely give them away.

Suddenly the canvas was tossed back over them and the wagon wheels began to creak and turn again. Overwhelmed with relief, Guy willed himself to relax.

The wagon rumbled on, bumping over countless rocks and deep ruts in the road. Guy's only clue that they were a safe distance from the Gate of the Sun came when Thomas muttered vehemently, "Damn bloody heathen, may the devil skewer them all on his fork and toss them into hell's fire!" Then the friar gave a strange laugh, between a grunt and a chuckle. "If you don't mind me saying so, my lord, me being a man of God and all."

"Not in the least," Guy replied, grateful for Thomas's levity. He felt his spirits rising despite the stench. He had seen plenty of dead men in his day, but lying this close to moldering corpses was stretching the limits of his endurance.

To get his mind off his own discomfort, he wondered how Leila was faring. Now he firmly believed he and Eve had done the right thing to drug her. No woman could have endured such a ghastly experience without being reduced to frantic tears.

"This is the place," Thomas said finally, loud enough for Guy to hear. "You can get up now, my lord."

Guy couldn't throw off the shroud and tear away the canvas fast enough. He leaped from the wagon and gasped in great breaths of fresh air. "Where are we?" he asked hoarsely, his eyes watering.

''Three miles south of Damascus, just past the cemetery. We'll have to walk the rest of the way to the camp.''

''What camp?''

''Bedouin traders. Desert nomads. They camp outside
the city, preferring their camel-hide tents to any inns Damascus has to offer. We must buy horses if you want to
reach Acre swiftly, and the Bedouins possess the finest
Arabian steeds in the land. We'll leave the lady here—''

''No. She goes with me.''

Thomas shook his head firmly as he covered his bald
scalp with a pointed hood. ''If those traders catch one
glimpse of her, no amount of precious jewelry will fend
them off, my lord. Beauty such as hers is rare and worth
a sultan's price. They'll kill us both to have her. She must
remain in the wagon. Believe me, no one will come near
the dead.'' The friar went so far as to grab Guy's arm,
insisting, ''Come. We must hurry. The guards will set out
looking for me if I don't return to Bab Charki within a
few hours.''

Guy glanced at the wagon and decided to trust Thomas's
judgment. After all, William Gervais had been murdered
by such ruthless men. Guy had no desire to share his miserable fate.

''Very well,'' he said. ''We will leave her here.''

''Most wise, my lord,'' Thomas murmured, walking
with him toward the red glow of distant campfires. ''When
we reach the Bedouin camp, keep silent. I will bargain for
the horses.''

''An easy task. My Arabic is pitiful.''

The friar chuckled, then quickly sobered. ''We will buy
two strong mounts in case one goes lame along the way.
The journey from here to Acre will take you a full day,
perhaps longer, even if you travel swiftly. You would do
well to ride directly southwest following the ancient car-
avan routes to the coast.''

Guy nodded, his hand moving to his wide sash as they
neared the first low-slung tents. ''Lady Eve gave me jewels—''

''Those are for your journey,'' Thomas interrupted, patting a pocket in his dark brown robe. ''Majida gave me

an emerald necklace when she found me at the church. It will amply cover the cost of the horses, which, knowing these traders, will be excessive.'' His voice fell. ''Here they come. No more talking, my lord.''

Guy recalled Eve's heavy necklace and surmised that was the one the friar now possessed, but his thoughts quickly turned to the danger at hand as they were approached by a dozen silent Bedouins. He followed the friar's lead and stopped, the hairs prickling on the back of his neck. It was all he could do not to reach for his sword. These desert men in their coarse sheep's wool robes were as menacing as any Arabs he had seen, their dark eyes cold and suspicious.

Brusque greetings and many words were exchanged between Thomas and the Bedouins, whose guarded expressions gradually became shrewd and calculating. Guy was amazed when large tasseled pillows were brought from the nearest tent for all of them to sit upon. He lowered himself warily, while one of the traders issued a string of sharp commands to bareheaded slaves standing nearby.

''Take nothing of the food or drink they may offer you,'' Thomas whispered in an aside, clearly distrustful of their hosts' overt hospitality.

In the next instant Guy did just that, shaking his head curtly when a tray laden with figs, dates, and honeyed almonds was held before him. The Bedouin seated next to him looked slightly affronted, but they were all distracted by the shrill neighing and snorting which filled the air and echoed from the sloping hillsides surrounding the camp.

The light from the campfires and smoking torches illuminated the wild and colorful scene as prancing Arabian horses led by barefoot slaves were paraded in front of the gesticulating and highly vocal traders. Guy watched Thomas choose two magnificent black stallions, the same ones he would have picked if it had been his decision, then the real haggling began. He guessed the deal was drawing to its conclusion when the friar rose to his feet and pulled the emerald necklace from his pocket, holding it up to the firelight.

A breathless hush fell over the traders as their eyes riveted on the glittering green stones. One by one they touched the necklace, weighing it in their callused palms, though none went so far as to take it from Thomas, who seemed to be extolling the jewels' matchless quality. At last the Bedouin who seemed to be the leader gave a signal, and the two black stallions were saddled and led forward.

"Mount one of the horses. Quickly," Thomas said, still holding on to the necklace.

Guy did so, reveling in the sensation of having a powerful animal beneath him again. He wondered fleetingly what had happened to the huge roan destrier he had brought with him from England and then left in Acre when he journeyed to Anatolia. Trained to perfection, Griffin had far surpassed any other war-horse he had ever owned. He hoped Edward had shipped the animal back to England along with the rest of his knights' destriers.

Thomas mounted the other horse, and only then did he hand over the necklace to the Bedouins' leader. As the traders clustered excitedly around their priceless acquisition, the friar jerked on the reins, veering his mount in the opposite direction. "Ride, my lord!"

Guy dug his heels into the stallion's sides and rode after the friar, his mount catching up in a few forceful strides.

"Do you think they will reconsider?" he shouted over the thunderous sound of hooves striking the earth.

"They're a crafty, avaricious lot," Thomas shouted back. "Best to get back to the wagon and then on your way!"

Guy searched the darkness and some of his tension eased when the wagon came into view. He pulled up hard on the reins and dismounted at a run, holding his breath against the horrid stench as he gathered Leila's limp body into his arms. Mumbling a quick prayer for the departed souls who had protected them, he remounted and settled her in front of him, waiting impatiently while Thomas tied the other stallion's braided reins to his saddle and handed him a blanket.

"For the lady. The night is cold," the friar said, grasping Guy's wrist. "God grant you both a safe journey."

"You have my eternal thanks, friend."

Then Thomas stepped away and Guy kicked his mount, holding Leila tightly as the stallion snorted and broke into a hard gallop, the other horse cantering five feet behind them. He glanced over his shoulder to see if the Bedouins were in pursuit, but he saw only vast darkness, the friar and his wagon already faded from view.

Guy gave out a laugh of pure exhilaration. His powerfully muscled thighs hugged the saddle, his hands sure upon the reins as he veered the charging stallion to the southwest, toward Acre and freedom.

With the wind whipping at his billowing robes and wild euphoria streaking through his veins, he had never felt so alive . . . or so protective. The heat of Leila's body was like a hot brand burning against his chest, reminding him of his sworn obligation to see her safely to England.

By all that he held true and sacred, he would not fail her!

Chapter 8

L eila's head was pounding mercilessly when she opened her eyes. She immediately threw her arm over them, crying out at the blinding sunlight that had pierced her brain. With her head now hurting all the more, she trembled with nausea and lay very still, dazedly hoping the sickness would pass.

It did not. She rolled over, her eyes squeezed shut and her hands groping at thin air, and vomited. When she was finished she lay still, dangling over the edge of something soft that smelled of musk. The heavy fragrance made her sick again, this time so wretchedly that she thought her stomach would burst from the heaving pain. With her head upside down, she felt warmth rushing to her face, but she was too weak to move.

Long, agonizing minutes dragged by before she dared open her eyes again. She did so very, very slowly.

The first thing she saw was something bright red, and she thought she had vomited blood. She screamed long and loud, the stoicism she had developed after years of medical training evaporating at the terrifying sight. Other people's blood was one thing; her own was an entirely different matter.

"May the heavens protect us, what a screeching noise you are making!" Leila heard a woman shout in Arabic as she drew a ragged breath and prepared to scream again. Two hands gripped her shoulders, hoisting her up and then

96

pushing her back upon the soft surface, but she could not see for the hair streaming over her face.

"I'm bleeding! I'm bleeding!" she cried, hot frightened tears mingling with her black tresses as she tried frantically to wipe the whole damp mass from in front of her eyes.

"No, no, you're not bleeding. Here, let me help you," the female voice said soothingly, a musk-scented palm pushing the offending hair aside. "There now, that's better."

Leila blinked through her tears at the young woman staring down at her, her forehead crinkling as she tried to place the unfamiliar face.

The woman was Arab and perhaps only a few years older than herself, with beautiful eyes rimmed with kohl, a generous red mouth, and thick black hair falling below her shoulders. Her clothes were elegant, a white linen thob and sirwal that accentuated her lovely olive complexion, yet the cut of the woman's blue brocade vest was unlike any style Leila had seen in Damascus.

After a futile moment, she gave up. She had never seen the woman before.

Leila's gaze swept the room with its tapestried walls and spare yet luxurious furnishings. It, too, was wholly unfamiliar. She had no idea where she was, nor could she remember—

"Someone drugged me . . ." she suddenly recalled in a hoarse whisper, her head aching at the effort. She had gone to her mother's apartments . . . Both Eve and Majida had acted so strangely. Then she had heard footsteps and that awful sponge had covered her mouth, reeking of opium and henbane. No wonder she felt so sick.

Leila looked down and noted she was still wearing the same lavender silk clothes, though her linen robe was missing and her hair was unbraided. She also noticed for the first time the raised bed on which she was lying, the soft mattress set atop a square wooden frame with stout corner posts, and the crimson coverlet pulled up to her waist. She touched the cool satin, her eyes darting to the side of the bed and the disgusting puddle on the carpeted floor.

Relief filled her, mixed with chagrin at her foolishness. It was the red coverlet she had seen, not her own blood. She slumped back upon the propped pillows behind her and wiped the silly tears from her face with the white linen sheet.

The woman also looked down at the carpet, frowning. She clapped her hands, and a young slave girl appeared in the room, her dark oval eyes wide and curious as she studied Leila.

"Please clean up this mess, Hayat, and stop your staring."

The slave girl bobbed her head and disappeared, returning in a moment with a basin filled with water and linen rags. Leila watched silently as the woman walked with sensuous grace to the other side of the bed and sat down while the slave girl knelt on the floor and began to scrub the soiled carpet.

"My name is Refaiyeh," the woman said, her friendly smile revealing even, white teeth.

Refaiyeh. Leila could swear she had heard that name before, but where? Her mind was still so fuzzy.

"Where am I?" she demanded shakily, trying to sit up. Another wave of queasiness forced her back upon the pillows, and she crossed her arms over her stomach. "I don't know you . . . why am I here?"

Refaiyeh did not readily answer, busying herself instead with pouring a goblet of water from a tall, crystal pitcher. She offered it to Leila, her expression kind. "Drink this. It will make you feel better. Whatever Guy drugged you with must have been very powerful. You've been asleep for almost two days counting your journey from Damascus."

"What are you saying?" Leila blurted, pushing the goblet away so roughly that water spilled onto the coverlet. Her mind spun as she stared at the spreading stain, an unsettling thought niggling at her. Had the woman said "Guy"?

Refaiyeh shrugged her slender shoulders and set the

goblet on the inlaid copper table by the bed. "You're over-wrought, Leila, which is understandable after what you've suffered—"

"How do you know my name?" Leila cried sharply, growing more alarmed. "I demand that you tell me what is going on!"

Clearly stunned by her outburst, Refaiyeh seemed at a loss to answer her. Her silver bracelets jangled as she twisted her hands in her lap. "You're safe, Leila, and in Acre—"

"So she's awake at last," a deep male voice said from the open doorway. Both women started in surprise. "Thank you for watching her, Refaiyeh. I'm sorry I was gone so long. The markets were crowded this after-noon."

"Lord de Warenne!" Leila gasped, the room snapping into sharp focus. She felt the blood drain from her face, her rampant heartbeat like thunder in her ears. What strange trick was this?

Her eyes darted over him, from the rugged contours of his clean-shaven face to his foreign clothing, a white calf-length garment emblazoned with a large red cross over a black long-sleeved tunic, hose, and black leather boots. Gone was the bearded and bare-chested prisoner dressed only in sirwal, and gone was the wild fury and desperation she had last seen in his eyes. This man ex-uded authority and confidence . . . and he was smiling at her!

Refaiyeh rose from the bed, sighing with relief. "Leila is upset, Guy," she said in heavily accented English, mov-ing toward him and placing her hand with familiarity on his forearm. She shook her head in confusion. "If not from what you had told me, I would swear she has abso-lutely no inkling of why she's here."

"The drugs, Refaiyeh," Guy said, looking at Leila's wide-eyed, stricken expression. "She'll be fine. Perhaps you might prepare a light meal for her."

"Of course." Refaiyeh turned to the slave girl, who had stopped scrubbing the carpet and was watching everything with rapt interest. "Come, Hayat."

The girl jumped to her feet and ran after her mistress, and Guy closed the door behind them. He strode across the sunlit room and stopped beside the bed, enchanted by the lovely sight Leila made with her black hair streaming around her in a silky cascade. He still could not get over the incredible length of her hair.

His dreams last night had been filled with erotic visions of Leila's lithe body wrapped in her ebony tresses. Looking at her pale, exquisite beauty now, he felt a familiar heat rising in his loins, but he quickly steeled himself against it. Such feelings were unseemly for a guardian knight, and Leila was an innocent virgin, doubly worth his protection.

Sweet Jesu, the weeks ahead would be hell, Guy thought honestly, staring at her parted lips.

It was a good thing he had Refaiyeh to ease the lust which had built inside him over the past weeks or he would have an even more difficult time once he and Leila left Acre.

"I'm glad to see you are awake," Guy said gently, noting the two spots of high color on her cheeks. "For a while I thought I might have to call a physician. I believe I poured too much of that foul-smelling liquid on the sponge."

"That was you?" Leila blurted incredulously. "In my mother's apartments?" She tensed when he nodded, a hundred questions flooding her mind, along with a glaring realization. "You escaped from the governor's prison. How?"

"You don't want to hear about it," Guy said, his expression becoming grim. "I knew something had gone wrong the moment your father mentioned England, but I didn't have a chance until—"

"My—my father?" Leila cut him off, stunned. She felt her face grow hot, not believing what he had just said. "How do you know this?"

"I know a great deal about you, Leila. I know you are not a slave, although you are Christian. And I know you were soon to marry an infidel, which your mother told me was causing you great unhappiness." The hard lines in his face eased, and his voice took on a husky, intense quality. "You no longer have to fear, my lady. That blasphemous wedding will never take place. Tomorrow a ship will take us to France, and then we'll journey from there to England. Once you are in your brother's care, he will no doubt arrange a pleasing marriage for you."

So great was Leila's shock, it took a long moment before she could even bring herself to speak.

"You are mad," she finally rasped, her thoughts spinning in horrified confusion. "My mother would never have said such a thing about my marriage to Jamal Al-Aziz. She knew I was happy . . . no, not just happy. Ecstatic!" She sat up, her whole body trembling as her voice grew shrill. "Oh, God, you killed them, didn't you? My mother and Majida. You murdered them after you drugged me!"

Now Guy looked stunned, then angry, his blue eyes darkening to steely gray. "Of course I didn't kill your mother or her slave. Those drugs have addled your reason."

"My reasoning is fine! Murderer, it is you who are mad! How else could I have come to this place . . . Acre"—she spat—"if not by foul play? How else could this be happening to me?"

"I'll tell you how," Guy said, resting his weight on his knuckles as he leaned on the bed, so close to her that Leila instinctively drew back, terrified. "I rescued you at great risk to my own life and your mother's. I have never met a woman braver than Lady Eve. It was her idea to hide us in a wagon loaded with corpses so we could safely escape Damascus, and it was her idea to drug you so you might be spared the horror of such a grisly experience. And it was her emerald necklace that bought us horses to bring us here."

"No . . . that cannot be true!"

"Not true? It's as true as I'm standing here before you, a free man instead of a headless corpse rotting in an unmarked grave. As true as the jewels Lady Eve gave me to pay for our passage to England."

Leila continued to shake her head in disbelief, which

seemed to anger him all the more. He began to shout, his handsome face livid. "By the blood of God, woman! Even now your mother might be imprisoned for the part she played to help you. She told me it was what you wanted!"

The room resounded from his thunderous outburst, each of them staring furiously at the other.

Eve would never have done this to her! Leila thought desperately. This was a nightmare. A bad dream. She dug her nails into her arms so hard she cried out in pain, glancing down at the deep imprints she had left in her skin. They were real, the pain was real, Guy de Warenne was real. Then his fantastic story must be—

"No, I don't believe you!" Leila shouted as she threw back the satin coverlet and sprang from the bed. She dashed toward the door but frantically checked her path when he began to follow her.

"Leila . . ."

"Murderer! Stay away from me!" she cried, rushing back to the bed. She grabbed the crystal pitcher from the table and upturned it like a weapon, the cold water sloshing down the side of her body and soaking her silken clothes. She scarcely felt it, so great was her rage. "You lie, you . . . you filthy barbarian! You killed my mother and kidnapped me!" She waved the pitcher threateningly. "I demand you release me at once! I want to go home . . . to Damascus!"

Guy wished there was some cold water left in that bobbing pitcher to splash on his face. He had never heard such lunatic ranting. His head was beginning to pound. What the devil was she talking about? Surely the drugs . . .

"Get back into bed before you collapse," he ordered, noting she was swaying slightly, her forehead furrowed with pain.

He also noticed her pink, puckered nipples beneath her sodden silk dress and the delicious curves of her hips and thighs where the transparent fabric clung provocatively. He stared hungrily, unable to help himself. Why did she have to be so damn lovely?

Another pounding began anew in his lower body, much different from the one in his head. He gritted his teeth, reminding himself again of his sworn duty, but it took greater effort this time to quell his burgeoning desire. There was something about sheer wet clothing molded to female flesh that could drive a man wild, and this woman's body was perfection.

Leila must have sensed his discomfort, or perhaps even seen the swelling below his sword belt, for she yanked the coverlet from the bed and held it in front of her breasts. Her gaze grew wider, angrier, and he thought for sure she was going to loft the glass pitcher right at him. He tensed, ready to dodge.

"Put down the pitcher, Leila, and get into bed," he commanded again, but she only lifted it higher. "If you don't, I swear I shall come and take it from you myself and force you into the bed!"

She blinked, her expression uncertain as she weighed his dark threat, then she spouted, "Barbarian! Come near me and I'll crack this right over your skull!!"

"Very well." Guy strode around the bed, ducking to the side just in time to avoid the hurtling pitcher which barely missed his head. It crashed to the floor behind him and shattered into a thousand glittering shards.

"Bastard! Murderer! Beast! Stay away from me!" Leila screamed, jumping onto the bed as he lunged for her. She tried to scramble across the wide mattress, but he caught her leg and no small amount of her hair, easily pulling her back. "No! Let me go!" she shouted at the top of her lungs, gasping for breath and wincing at the pain in her scalp. She tore desperately at the linen sheet, dragging it with her as he grabbed her around the waist and spun her around to face him.

She dropped the sheet and raised her clenched fists to strike him, but at the dangerous look in his eyes she was suddenly swept by terror. The crusader had murdered her mother and Majida. He could easily do the same to her. Glaring at him, she lowered her arms, their faces so near his breath fanned her flushed cheek, burning her skin.

Leila had never been this close to a man.

She could feel the warmth of his powerful body emanating through his clothes. Her nostrils flared at the scent
of him . . . sweat and sandalwood. She did not pull away,
in that spellbinding moment drawn to his heat, his smell,
as inexplicably as a moth to a searing flame.

She met his eyes, seeing in those stunning cerulean
depths a will as strong and determined as her own. Becoming flustered, she dropped her gaze to his mouth,
watching as he moistened his lips with his tongue. Unconsciously she licked her own lips, then glanced back at his
eyes as his mouth curved into the smallest of smiles. She
saw a flash of humor and something else, something that
sent shivers down her spine. It made her want to slap him.
Hard.

But before she could, he tossed her onto the mattress.
"Cover yourself."

As Guy walked to the foot of the bed, Leila grabbed
the satin spread and angrily tucked it around herself,
bringing the embroidered edge up under her chin.

"Listen well, my lady," he began in a low voice, staring into her defiant gaze. "I am no murderer. I would like
to think it is the drugs speaking through your lips, but I
am beginning to believe I have been misled. As I already
told you, your mother claimed you wanted desperately to
leave Damascus and the marriage that had been arranged
for you with an infidel. From your vicious display of temper, it seems that this is not the case."

"No, it is not!" Leila declared vehemently. "And I can
assure you that the drugs have sufficiently worn off so that
I know this is not a nightmare, though I wish it was one!
If my mother did help you, and I can't imagine why she
would have—" Leila paused, recalling like a flash Eve's
lingering melancholy, and then just as quickly brushed it
off. But before she could finish, Guy broke in, his tone
harsh.

"Your mother said it was your birthright that you should
have a Christian marriage. A home and family in your true
country, to quote her exactly. Perhaps that explains Lady
Eve's motives."

Stunned, Leila remained silent as everything suddenly became clear in her mind. Terribly clear.

It was the marriage. It had to be. Her mother did not want her to wed Jamal.

That would account for Eve's unhappiness during the past weeks, the haunted look in her eyes, her hesitation in sharing news of the wedding date, her tears. And now it accounted for Leila finding herself in this dreadful predicament. Well, she would not stand for it!

"Whatever my mother's motives, she was in error," Leila stated coldly. "I have no desire whatsoever to go to England with you or anybody else, and I certainly have no wish to allow a brother I have never known to decide my fate. Why would I possibly want to leave the country of my birth for your barbaric land? Damascus is my home. I have been very happy there. Jamal Al-Aziz is to be my husband. I demand you release me at once so I might return—"

"Your desires, wishes, and demands are of no concern to me," Guy said with little emotion. "It is to your mother's I have sworn."

"What do you mean?" Leila asked, feeling apprehension at the grim set of his jaw.

"I made a vow to Lady Eve that I would see you safely to England and your brother, Roger Gervais, and so I will."

"No," Leila breathed, her heart beginning to race. "This cannot be happening . . ."

"My oath is sacred. It cannot be undone. If, when we reach England, your brother grants that you may return to Syria, then so be it. That decision is not for me to make."

"No!" Leila cried. "You do this against my will. You are kidnapping me!"

Guy shrugged dispassionately. "Call it what you like, my lady. Tomorrow we sail for France, the first leg of our journey. I have bought you some new clothes. I will bring them to you later when you have calmed down." His gaze fell to her beautiful breasts, for the coverlet had fallen into her lap. His desire to caress her smooth flesh was overwhelming, and he decided it was best he leave. "You certainly can't travel like that. It will be hard enough protecting you from the shipboard rabble without your displaying yourself for all to see."

Leila glanced down at her sheer bodice and then back at him, feeling her cheeks grow red with fury.

"For the last time, I tell you I won't go with you—"

"And for the last time, my lady," Guy said as he strode to the door, looking at her over his broad shoulder, "I say you will!"

He left the room, slamming the door behind him so hard that she couldn't possibly misunderstand the vehemence of his words.

Leila heard a bolt slide across the door, and the finality of it proved too much for her. She looked frantically around the room, along the floor, at the sparse furnishings, searching for anything with which to pound on the door. She found it in the small copper table next to the bed.

Springing from the mattress, she seized the metal tabletop from its wooden stand, paying no heed as the crystal water goblet crashed to the floor. She ran to the locked door and began pounding wildly, screaming, "Damn you, de Warenne, let me out! I won't go with you! I won't, I won't! You can't do this to me!"

She shouted and hammered until her ears rang with the noise, but still no one came to the door. Exhaustion finally swept over her and she crumpled to the carpet, overwhelmed with despair.

Ah, how cruelly kismet had turned against her! Now she was the prisoner, the unwilling captive.

God help her, what was she going to do? Everything was slipping like desert sand through her fingers . . . her hopes, her dreams, the bright, perfect future she had envisioned as a respected physician and wife to Jamal Al-Aziz.

"No. You can't just stand by and let this barbarian ruin your life," Leila whispered to herself. "Think, Leila! Think! There must be something you can do."

She slowly raised her head and spied the two high windows covered with intricate wooden grillwork on the opposite wall above the bed. The bright sunlight outside seemed to beckon to her, a promise of freedom.

A flicker of hope kindled within her. If she could reach the windows, maybe, just maybe . . .

Chapter 9

G uy breathed in Refaiyeh's musk perfume as she slept in a state of contented satiation, her voluptuous, long-limbed body nestled against him. Though he himself was not wholly satisfied, the aching fullness in his loins had been eased. There was nothing like anger to fuel a good bout of lovemaking.

Yet Refaiyeh had nothing to do with his anger.

She had been preparing Leila's food tray when he found her in the kitchen, and she had seemed to know instantly what he wanted. After shooing Hayat outside into the walled garden, she had smiled seductively at him, and that was all the invitation Guy had needed.

He had taken her right there on the lacquered kitchen table, rocking it so violently that grapes, figs, and olives had bounced from bowls and tumbled onto the tiled floor.

Guy smiled wryly. After that, he and Refaiyeh had retired to her private bedchamber where they had rutted and sweated until she had cried out she would have nothing left for their last evening together if they did not stop.

So he had stopped, although he could have kept right on going in a vain attempt to force his unsettling encounter with Leila from his mind. It had never happened before that he took one woman in his arms but could not stop thinking about another. It was a most disconcerting preoccupation.

When he smelled Refaiyeh's musk perfume, he wished it was a far more intoxicating damask rose. When he looked into her dark eyes made liquid with desire, he saw another gaze, one of flashing amethyst filled with fury, disbelief, and spite. When he sank his body in Refaiyeh's, he imagined Leila's white, white skin, satiny smooth beneath his touch, and her glossy black hair slipping through his fingers . . .

Cursing softly, Guy rubbed his eyes as if to dispel the wanton sensory images. God's blood, their journey had yet to begin! He would make his life a living hell if he didn't stop thinking of her in this way.

Like the living hell he had made of Leila's life.

Yes, he had seen that in her stunning eyes, too, but he had sworn to take her to England, and he could not rescind his vow. A knight's oath might as well be written in blood for its inviolability.

Yet would he allow Leila to return to Damascus and this Jamal Al-Aziz even if he could forswear the vow he had made to Eve Gervais? No. A Christian woman had no place in that heathen city. It was bad enough that she considered Damascus her home, Syria her country, and England nothing more than a pagan land. Hadn't Eve told Leila anything about her true homeland? He had the distinct impression she had not.

Guy pounded his fist upon the mattress. No, he was doing the right thing. Leila would be better off in England, and he was not going to question his judgment any further!

"Ah . . . what was that?" Refaiyeh asked drowsily, raising her tousled head from his shoulder and regarding him with half-closed eyes.

"Nothing. Go back to sleep," Guy murmured, kissing her soft cheek. He lifted her limp arm from his chest and rose from the bed, covering her tenderly with the silken sheet.

Truly, he would miss Refaiyeh, he thought, drawing on his clothes and sword belt. The young widow had made his life more than bearable while he'd been in Acre; she had become a friend. When he knocked on her door late last night, dusty and spent from the long ride from Damascus and with a bedraggled Leila in his arms, she had asked no questions, just ushered them quickly into her home.

Only later, after she had made Leila comfortable, had they had a chance to talk. He had described the journey to Anatolia, then his incredible ordeal in Damascus, and she had shared what information she had gleaned from the crusaders still lingering in Acre. From her lips he had learned of King Henry's death, and that Edward had sailed home to claim the English throne. Yet even with this knowledge, Guy still did not believe Edward had left him to die in prison.

His faith had been affirmed this morning when he had spoken with Simon Renier, a grizzled crusader who had decided to stay in the Holy Land, having neither lands nor titles to entice him home. Guy had just bought passage on a ship to Marseilles using some of Eve's jewels when he felt a heavy hand clap his back.

"By the breath of God, is that you, de Warenne?"

Recognizing the voice, Guy had spun around, a grin spreading across his face when he beheld the stout, red-bearded warrior.

"Indeed it is, friend."

"And all in one piece, I see," Simon said, cuffing Guy heartily on the arm. "Where are Reginald and the others? You're the first one I've seen back. Did he decide to stay with the Mongols? I've heard their women are as wild as yellow tigers and ride naked across the steppes—"

"Reginald is dead. They're all dead," Guy said tonelessly, his throat constricted as he realized no one yet knew of his companions' fate.

"Who did this? Where?" Renier blustered, his broad freckled face mottling with rage.

After Guy grimly explained what had happened, the older knight seemed thoroughly shaken and puzzled. "Lord Edward never received any letter of ransom for you, de Warenne. If he had, he would surely have let the rest of us know. He believed all was well with your embassy to the day he sailed. He even left a message for you."

"What message?"

"He wanted you and Reginald and the other knights to

follow him back to England as soon as you returned to Acre.''

If Guy had harbored any uncertainty at all, he knew then that Edward had not deserted him.

"That was already my plan," Guy said, nodding toward the docks. "I just bought passage for two aboard that galley."

"Two?" Renier blurted, his pale, blue eyes lit with curiosity. "Will you be taking that pretty Arab wench of yours home to Warenne Castle?"

"No. Refaiyeh has chosen to stay here in Acre. Lady Leila Gervais will accompany me to England."

"Gervais?" the old warrior asked, astonished. "Does she share any blood relation with Roger—"

"His younger sister," Guy cut him off dryly. At Simon's expression of complete incredulity, he gave a short laugh. "How about a pint of ale, my friend? I'd rather tell you the story in a cool tavern than out here in the hot sun. Agreed?"

"Aye, though I imagine this tale will warrant more than a pint, de Warenne," Simon said heartily, shaking his head. "More like a half barrel!"

Refaiyeh's long drawn out sigh snapped Guy's thoughts sharply back to the present. As she smiled in her sleep, a twinge of guilt tugged at his heart.

He had done Refaiyeh a great disservice to dwell so on Leila during their lovemaking. Too bad she had turned down his offer to accompany them to England. He was very fond of her . . . as fond as he had been of any woman, including Christine, his late wife.

Guy turned away and quietly left the shadowed chamber. His inability to return his wife's love had also been a disservice, but one that could never be remedied. At least he loved Nicholas, their young son, as he had never been able to love Christine. He hoped that had been some consolation for the pain they had shared from the day they were wed until her tragic death.

Putting away such dark memories, Guy went to the kitchen and quickly finished the food tray Refaiyeh had been preparing before he had so lustily interrupted her.

Leila had more than likely calmed herself by now. Two hours had passed since he had left her room. She was probably ravenous and light-headed after not eating for several days.

When he reached her chamber, he balanced the tray in one hand and unbolted the door. He ducked slightly, as he seemed to have to do when going through most entry-ways, his gaze sweeping the silent interior. The bed was pushed away from the wall and a clothing chest moved there, empty of its contents and turned upright on one end. The grille on the window directly above the chest was opened just wide enough for a slim young woman to escape.

"Damn!" Guy shouted, setting aside the tray. Why hadn't he thought Leila might try such a stunt, and maybe even succeed? Railing at his own stupidity, he ran toward the back of the house and then out and around to the attached stable, trying to determine which direction to try first.

Acre was a bustling port city on the rocky shores of the Mediterranean, but it was only a third the size of Damascus. Given Leila's head start, she could be well into the surrounding hills if she was on horseback. Those grassy slopes and craggy hollows were swarming with Bedouin herdsmen and Mameluke spies who would recognize at once the monetary worth in helping an Arabic-speaking Christian woman return to Damascus.

Those men would have nothing to lose. If she proved to have lied about her family, they would sell her in the slave markets. If she was telling the truth, they would be rewarded in gold for her safe return. Either way, the smell of money would easily gain Leila their eager assistance.

Guy flung open the wide stable doors and was relieved to see that none of the four horses was missing. That meant she was on foot.

His mind sped as he saddled one of the sleek black stallions. First he would search the twisting city streets for any sign of her and, if that failed, he would recruit several crusaders and their men-at-arms and set out for the treacherous hills.

As Guy slapped the horse's flank with the reins and took off at a fast trot down the narrow street, pedestrians, squawking chickens, and bleating sheep scattered in all directions. He was almost at the corner when he spied Hayat racing toward him as fast as her short legs would carry her, her flapping skirt held well above her knees.

"My lord! My lord!" she cried, dodging passersby and dashing between the spindly legs of a large camel blocking the street.

Guy dismounted just as Hayat reached him, falling breathless and panting into his arms.

"The . . . pretty lady, my lord! I saw her . . . jump from the window . . . when I was in the garden. I followed her . . . those men!"

"What men, Hayat?" Guy demanded, his heart banging hard against his chest. He shook her none too gently. "Where is she?"

"Three Genoese sailors, my lord!" Hayat cried, her large brown eyes filling with tears. She began to hiccough, her small body trembling. "They caught her . . . they were laughing . . . They dragged her into a tavern—"

"Show me." Guy hoisted himself into the saddle and drew the small slave girl up in front of him. As she pointed and guided him, he rode like a maniac through the winding streets, his fury mounting. God help them, if those swine had harmed Leila he would castrate them all, stuff their bloody members in their mouths, and only then sink his sword between their ribs!

"There it is, my lord!" Hayat shouted, spying a wine tavern Guy recognized as one he had earlier frequented with other crusaders. There was a brothel on the second story, filled with many rooms and dark passages that echoed with whispers and breathless cries of carnal pleasure.

Guy deposited Hayat on the ground and jumped down from the stallion, tethering the animal just outside the tavern. "Stay here!" he ordered. The slave girl bobbed her head, gasping as he pulled his glinting sword from the scabbard at his belt and ran to the door, which suddenly swung open.

Guy had scarcely an instant to step clear before out tumbled a Genoese mariner who was holding his bleeding arm and wailing to the high heavens and numerous saints for mercy, while behind him stormed Simon Renier, clad only in braies and chausses. The stocky crusader was bellowing curses and waving his bloodied sword in one hand while he yanked a woman with streaming black hair into the street.

"Leila!" Guy breathed, recognizing her instantly.

From what he could tell she seemed unhurt, although the dark tunic she must have borrowed from the clothing chest was rent in two, exposing her filmy garments underneath. As she fought against Renier's beefy grasp, scratching and kicking him like a little wildcat, Guy caught tantalizing glimpses of creamy flesh and slender limbs, and he was filled with desire and envy. How he wished he was in Renier's place so he might tame her!

His arousing fantasy was tempered when Leila suddenly spied him and stopped cold. He could swear he saw a flicker of relief in those stormy violet eyes, but it quickly vanished and she jutted out her chin. She was such a breathless vision it was almost impossible to look away, but he did when the older knight lifted his blade over the cowering soldier.

"Renier, stay your sword!" he shouted.

"What?" Renier blustered, half turning as he noticed Guy for the first time. "Ah, de Warenne!" The half-naked crusader roughly pulled Leila in front of his protruding stomach, and caught her around the waist, his bare arm pushing up her breasts. "Is this your woman?"

His gaze moving reluctantly from those seductive swells, Guy could not suppress a grin as he saw Leila bristle. "Yes, she's mine."

"I thought as much. Here I was a-whoring when I heard a terrible ruckus next door, screeching and hollering and cursing—not your normal love play, mind you, so I decided to take a look. Sweet Mother of Mary, what should I find? Three mariners fighting over the lady here, while she huddled on a bed. I've never seen such hair and eyes! I knew at once she was the woman you described to me at the waterfront, Leila, the one you're escorting home to that traitor, Gervais.''

With a grunt, Renier pushed her toward Guy. "You would do well to keep a better eye on her, de Warenne. A pretty piece like that, alone in the streets . . ." He shook his shaggy head, sucking the blood from the deep red scratches on his forearm. "A vixen, too! You've got your hands full with that one.''

"So it seems," Guy said, grabbing Leila's arm. Still silent, she tried to pull away, but he held her firmly. He dropped his voice, his words meant for her ears alone. "I hope you enjoyed the solitude of your afternoon stroll, my lady, for it is the last time you will leave my sight until we reach England.''

Leila used her free hand to toss her tangled hair over her shoulder, his threat chilling her to the bone though she would have died before she showed it had struck home. Nor would she ever admit how glad she had been to see him a few moments ago. No, not even on her deathbed.

"It matters naught to me what you do, my lord," she sneered instead, feeling his fingers tighten cruelly around her arm. "You can go to hell for all I care.''

"What did I tell you, de Warenne?" Renier shouted, throwing his head back and laughing uproariously. "A true vixen with a viperous tongue to match! What a journey you shall have!" But his laughter suddenly ceased as he raised his sword and struck viciously at the kneeling sailor, decapitating him with one solid blow.

Sickened, Leila watched incredulously as the head rolled down the street and bumped with a dull thud into a wall.

"Barbarians. Savages," she whispered to herself in horror.

"Not barbarism at all, and certainly no less than what your adopted countrymen would have done to me," Guy disagreed harshly. "Justice." When she merely turned her face from him, he added, "If this man's punishment so grieves you, my lady, know this. He would still be alive if not for your folly.''

"You blame me for this? They attacked *me*, you . . . you lout! Not the other way around—''

"Well, fair or no, that's the last of them," Simon Renier interrupted matter-of-factly, unperturbed by the blood splatters on his hairy legs or their bickering. "If you'll excuse me, my lady." He bowed gallantly, then turned to Guy with a lusty smile. "De Warenne. I've a wench waiting for me upstairs who grows cool from my long absence."

"My thanks, Simon," Guy said, meaning it more than he could say, the idea of losing Leila like a raw pain centered over his heart. He clasped the older knight's wrist.

"It's not every day a man rescues a beautiful maiden. Just glad I was there to help." Simon bent and wiped his sword on the dead man's stained tunic, then lumbered to the door, calling out, "A good journey to you both!" The crusader's booming laughter sounded again, fading as he disappeared into the tavern.

"Hayat!"

"I'm here, Lord de Warenne," the slave girl answered, scampering from the crowd of bystanders who had gathered to watch the gruesome scene.

Leila glared back at the approving faces, Arabs and native Christians alike, disgusted by their evident love for bloodsport. She could not say she was surprised. The people in this city had mingled so much with the crusaders they could not help but be influenced by their brutal ways. To gape so at a man lying beheaded in the street—

She gasped as Guy suddenly picked her up and carried her over to the stallion, where he threw her over the broad saddle, knocking the wind from her.

"How dare you!" she sputtered, enraged. She tried to raise herself up and slide off the horse, but he forced her down again and quickly mounted behind her. He laid his hand flat on her rump, his strength easily preventing her from making another movement. When he caressed her lightly she almost choked, her face burning, wholly humiliated that he would do such a thing to her in public!

"Take your hand from me!" she sputtered indignantly, the reins flicking lightly across her back as he turned the stallion around. His thighs were as hard as steel where they pressed against her.

"Don't say another word, my lady, or I can assure you a sound slap on your delectable bottom will surely follow," Guy stated. "That should entertain these good people."

"Why . . . why you—" She bit off the colorful names she was about to call him when she saw him raise his hand over her buttocks. With a sigh of pure frustration, she dropped her head and went limp, resigning herself to the indignity of her transport. Better that than be further disgraced by this vulgar and sorry excuse for a man.

"Up with you, Hayat," Guy said, trying to keep from chuckling as he lifted the slave girl behind him. He had a good idea what Leila was thinking of him at that moment, and he knew it wasn't complimentary. Yet it didn't bother him in the least. Strangely, now that he knew she was safe, he was enjoying himself immensely. Leila was the most spirited, exasperating, spoiled, misguided, imperious, exciting, and utterly beautiful woman he had ever known.

Guy glanced down at his sullen and silent captive, and was tempted to give her pretty rump a good slap just for leading him on such a dangerous chase. As Renier had said, it seemed he had his hands full. Delightfully.

Much to Leila's seething irritation, it became clear once they returned to Refaiyeh's home that Guy meant exactly what he said about not letting her out of his sight. He began dogging her every move, crowding her until it seemed he left her no air to breathe. His constant presence overwhelmed her; his huge body seemed to fill up every space he entered. Leila was forced to eat her evening meal with him and the striking Arab woman, who didn't seem pleased with the new arrangement. After Leila had relieved herself—with Guy standing right outside the water closet's cracked door, much to her humiliation!—she was seated in the garden on a cushion and bound to an orange tree with a silken cord. He and Refaiyeh sat together on a bench in the shadows, talking and sometimes laughing.

Their conversation was too low for Leila to understand the words. Not that she cared in the least. She hadn't said a word herself since Guy had threatened to slap her. It was small revenge for the callous way he was treating her. His every attempt to coax her to talk at supper had failed miserably.

Besides, it had been days since she had eaten, and she had been too hungry to talk. The spiced meat pastries and fruited yogurt had tasted like manna from heaven, and the red wine had mercifully blunted her mental anguish and growing despondency.

Exhausted, Leila soon let her head slump to her chest, Refaiyeh's low dulcet tones and Guy's rougher, deeper voice lulling her to sleep. She did not know when he finally unbound her and lifted her into his strong arms, nor did she feel him lay her down upon the bed or see him strip out of his clothes.

It was only when she felt an incredible warmth at her back that she awoke with a start, so muddled from sleep that she did not know if she had dreamed the stirring sensation. She felt someone slide a hand along the soft undersides of her breasts, pulling her close. Abruptly, fully, awake, Leila froze.

Dear God in heaven, the crusader was sleeping with her! She never would have thought he would carry his indignities so far as this! She felt such a flush of red-hot fury that she elbowed him sharply in the ribs, flailing her limbs and struggling mightily to escape his embrace. But he merely trapped her beneath a heavy thigh.

"It's no use, my lady," Guy murmured huskily into her ear. "You cannot escape. Now go to sleep. We leave at sunrise to catch our ship for Marseilles."

It was true, she thought resignedly, going limp in his arms. Her efforts were utterly useless, like a fly fluttering its wings in a spider's web. She decided instead to goad him with her tongue, ever seeking some modicum of revenge, some way to hurt this man who was destroying her life.

"Where's your whore?" Leila hissed angrily, his treatment of her going against everything she held decent. That a man not her husband should be holding her like this! It wasn't right!

"If you mean Refaiyeh, she sleeps alone," came his

dark reply, his arm tight around her waist, robbing her of breath. "That you speak so ill of someone who has treated you kindly makes her ten times more the lady than you." He jerked her hard against his chest. "Never call her that again or you shall rue it, *my lady*," he spat.

Leila gasped for air when he slightly loosed his hold on her, embarrassed deep down in her heart that she had even said such a thing about Refaiyeh. She had sensed the woman's kindness earlier, but Guy's threat was like bone-dry kindling to her rage, and she couldn't seem to stop herself.

"Surely I could not escape in the time it would take her to spread her legs for you—"

Leila was on her back so suddenly that her head spun, his hand clamped over her mouth. She stared up at his face lowered to within inches of her own, his eyes all glitter and fire in the moonlit darkness.

"Another word, Leila, and I . . ."

She gulped, wondering wildly at his unfinished warning and the humorless chuckle that broke from his throat as he removed his hand. Before she could blink, his mouth came down hard on hers.

Completely startled, Leila flailed her hands against his massive shoulders to push him away, but it was like trying to move a mountain. His overpowering strength was as relentless as his tongue, which thrust deeply inside her mouth. She cried out at his savage assault, but their lips were so fused she heard only a whimper. Yet it became a husky moan when he explored her mouth hungrily, his tongue forcing hers to partake in a wild, serpentine dance.

New and dizzying sensations poured through Leila's body, their intimate dueling overwhelming her. She felt as if she was spiraling back into thin air, her thoughts in chaos, her limbs tingling and weak. His mouth was hot and demanding. The taste of him was incredibly exciting. Nothing in her harem training could have prepared her for this. Nothing.

She had practiced kissing with a specially trained eunuch under Majida's watchful eye. There had been no fire, no passion, only technique. She would never have guessed the difference could be so glaring, so unreal. So amazingly wonderful. Without thinking, she delved her tongue into his mouth, seeking more of his seductive sweetness . . .

Reality suddenly came crashing in around her when she heard Guy's ragged groan and felt his hand cover her breast. Realizing too late the insane folly of her wanton action and wholly shocked at herself for even doing such a thing, Leila tried futilely to twist away from him.

"No!" she cried hoarsely against his mouth, her heart hammering. "Stop!"

But he did not stop. As he deepened the kiss, his caresses grew rougher, more insistent, his thumb circling the rigid nipple straining against her silk dress. Leila arched her back, stunned by the incredible pleasure she found in his touch. She knew it was wrong that she should feel this way—Sweet Jesu, he was not her husband!—yet she could not help it. Then she heard a ripping sound, and her mounting desire became raw panic as the sheer silken barrier slipped from her body. His hand, huge and warm, slid over her bare flesh.

Terrified, Leila began to fight him in earnest, all the horrible stories she had heard about crusaders running through her mind. He was going to rape her!

She balled up her fists and beat upon his shoulders, but her frantic blows might have been those of a child for the little notice he gave them. It wasn't until he tore his mouth from hers and kissed a fiery trail down her throat that she was able to exclaim breathlessly, "No, you cannot do this! I am not a whore to be taken when and wherever you choose! I am a virgin! I demand you stop at once!"

Guy's whole body tensed, her impassioned words ringing in his ears. Breathing hard, he uttered a low curse as he lifted his lips from her silky skin.

What the hell was he doing? He had only wanted to silence her poisonous barbs, to frighten her a little into behaving, not ravage her. But her kiss had astounded him, setting his blood on fire and his loins ablaze with need. When her tongue darted boldly into his mouth . . .

Guy cursed again. He knew she was no whore, but perhaps she was no innocent either. Slowly he lifted his head and met her wide, frightened eyes.

"You don't kiss like a virgin, my lady . . . though that is what your mother claimed you to be. Is it possible your heathen betrothed has already sampled your charms?"

Indignation swept away her fear. Leila was so outraged that she could not stop the tumble of words that jumped to her tongue.

"How dare you even suggest such a thing?" she snapped, swiping strands of hair from her flushed face. "In my culture, virginity is highly prized and to be saved for the wedding night! So, too, are the sensual arts I have been taught to please my future husband, Jamal Al-Aziz. They are for him alone! It is a sin for a woman to use these arts on anyone but her husband—"

"Then you have just sinned, my lady," Guy cut in thickly, his desire only heightened by her astonishing revelation.

A virgin trained in erotic arts. No wonder her kiss had been so experienced. Intensely fascinated, he let his imagination run wild, his vow to protect her pushed to the recesses of his mind. What arts might she practice upon him if he continued his carnal assault? What further sins, beyond a kiss, might she commit?

Leila gasped, wishing she could retract her outburst when his calloused palm moved over her bare breast. She had only made the situation worse! Then he bent his head and captured an aroused nipple in his mouth, and she nearly cried out as forbidden pleasure rippled through her. It was not right that he was doing this to her! She had to stop him!

"Barbarian! Beast! I should have known you wouldn't understand!" she shouted desperately, hot tears filling her eyes. "That you would force yourself upon me proves you have no morals! No honor!"

At last her agonized protest cut through Guy's raging desire like a knife, and he raised his head from her breast.

Seeing her tears in the moonlight, he felt anger sweep through him, mixed with chagrin at his inability to control himself. By God, what was the matter with him? He was acting more like a barbarian than like her guardian knight. Steeling himself against the burning ache in his loins, he shifted onto an elbow, although he kept his other arm firmly around her waist.

"You are wrong about my honor, Leila," he sought to explain, knowing how lame it sounded in light of his callous behavior. "If I didn't possess any, I wouldn't stop now, no matter what you called me. But I am not a barbarian. In my culture, virginity is also prized. When I became a knight I pledged to protect all women, their honor, their chastity—"

"Your actions belie your words!" she flung at him, and rightfully so, he realized.

"This is true," he admitted, almost to himself. "Your beauty alone overwhelms me, but when combined with your kiss . . ."

"I can imagine you've used that excuse on many other unfortunate virgins before me," Leila replied sharply, unconvinced. She looked away, but he forced her chin back to face him.

"Do not provoke me, Leila. It was such a tone that first drew my wrath. I strongly urge you to behave, or I might lose control of myself again. Now go to sleep."

Stunned, Leila felt she was choking on the stark emotion crawling up her throat, her chest rising and falling rapidly from the strain. As Guy drew her closely against him, it was all she could do to lie there without shrieking at him.

His dark threat churned like bile in her heart. That he would threaten to use his kiss, his touch, his body as punishment reinforced the opinion she had nurtured long before she had ever beheld his face.

He was nothing but a barbarian—ruthless, coldhearted, and cruel. She hated him and all his kind.

Given time, she would show him how much.

Chapter 10

❦

It was dark in the room when Leila felt someone shake her shoulder. She yawned, her eyelids fluttering, then she snuggled deeper into the pillow.

"Go away, Nittia," she murmured, her dream luring her back into sleep. "Leave me alone . . . Oh!"

Leila sat bolt upright, dazed, her derriere smarting where someone had pinched her. She could see nothing in the blackness, but she heard breathing and a rustling movement and she suddenly remembered . . . everything. Then a light flared and an oil lamp was lit, illuminating Guy de Warenne, who was standing beside the bed and smiling down at her in a most disconcerting fashion.

"How—how dare you!" she spattered, snatching together what was left of her dress. It did little good. With him so close and staring at her like a ravenous wolf, she felt naked and vulnerable.

"How dare I indeed," he said, hooking his thumbs in his sword belt. "Forgive my errant fingers, my lady, but it was the quickest way I knew to rouse you, other than a ki—"

"So I am awake!" Leila blurted, looking away as her cheeks grew hot. "I thought we were leaving at sunrise," she said testily. "It is still dark."

"Exactly. You have one half hour to bathe and dress in your new clothes, then I will come to fetch you. At the cock's crow we will set out for the harbor."

Leila's gaze swept the shadowed chamber. "I see no bath. No clothes."

"Alas, there wasn't time to prepare enough hot water for a full bath for you." He strode around the bed to the brass-fitted chest she had used in her escape attempt and gestured to a tall pitcher and a glazed clay basin placed atop the closed lid. "Your bath, my lady," he said, pouring steaming water into the basin. "There is a sponge here, scented soap, and a towel. Everything you need—"

"And my clothes?" she queried haughtily, lifting her chin.

He merely smiled. "In the chest. While you dozed in the garden last night, Hayat replaced the contents with things you will need for our journey, things I bought for you with some of your mother's jewels." He tapped the lid. "This chest and everything in it now belong to you."

Leila offered no thanks, just glowered at him.

Guy shrugged and walked to the door. "A half hour, my lady."

"I heard you the first time."

"Good. Hayat will arrive shortly to help you dress. Before coming to this house she served an Englishwoman residing in Tyre. She knows how to garb a lady."

"And where will you be, my lord?" Leila asked archly, her mind spinning with desperate possibilities for escape. "With your Refaiyeh, bidding her farewell?"

Guy stopped and studied her, a glint of anger chasing the amusement from his eyes. "We have said our goodbyes. Refaiyeh has gone to her brother's home. You will not see her again."

"Oh," Leila said, her plans deflating at this news. She lowered her chin, watching him surlily through her thick sable lashes. " 'Tis plain you care for this woman. If so, how can you leave her . . . unless you have a wife who might object to an Arab concubine?" She bit her lip, the words out before she could stop them. She silently cursed the curiosity that had gotten the better of her.

Guy seemed momentarily amused by her question, then his expression grew hard as if he sensed some malice behind it. "In England we have no concubines, nor do I have a wife," he said flatly. "I gave Refaiyeh a choice, and she has decided to stay in Acre. Not that it is any business of yours." He glanced impatiently at the chest. "The water grows tepid, my lady. Perhaps you might occupy your mind with your own affairs."

Affronted by his churlish tone, Leila said nothing as he left the room, then muttered heatedly, "I'm not surprised Refaiyeh chose not to come with us. Any woman would be a fool to traipse after a boorish lout like you!" She *was* surprised he did not have a wife, however, and was pondering this revelation when Guy opened the door slightly.

"Just a warning, Leila. Your beautiful face is easily read, even by us boorish louts. Do not think to escape through that grille again. I'll be right outside. If I hear any suspicious noises, you can be sure the gift of privacy I've granted you this morning will be instantly forfeited." He smiled roguishly, his tone growing lighter. "Watching a woman bathe is a favorite pastime of mine, so you have been duly cautioned. Oh yes, and enjoy the hot water. We won't have such a luxury again until we reach Marseilles."

"Bastard!" Leila fumed, throwing back the coverlet as he shut the door.

She sprang from the bed and stripped out of her torn dress and sirwal, then hurried to the chest and bent over the basin, her teeth chattering in the damp morning chill. Eagerly she dipped the sponge in the hot water and sighed with pleasure as she ran it along one arm and down a firm breast.

A sound just outside the room, like a boot scraping on the floor, caused her to freeze, and she glanced fearfully over her shoulder, expecting Guy to enter the room at any moment. When he did not, she turned with relief back to the basin, but her earlier enjoyment was gone.

She bathed quickly, not even the rose-scented soap lifting her spirits. The desperation that had plagued her yesterday reappeared with a vengeance, and she began to think of what lay ahead, the future seeming like a black, yawning pit before her.

The only brightness lay in a single fervent hope within her heart that she might yet escape and return to Damascus. Until she was on that ship she would not give up trying . . . No, not even then.

Leila jumped at the soft knock on the door, the sponge hitting the floor with a squelch. "Who—who is it?" she called out, darting into a shadowed corner.

"Hayat."

"You may enter." Fearing Guy might glimpse her nakedness, Leila remained in the corner until Hayat closed the door and stepped further into the room, then she asked her in Arabic, "Is he still out there?"

"Yes, my lady—"

"Not English. Please, speak to me in your native tongue," Leila insisted, walking into the light where the slave girl could see her.

Hayat nodded solemnly, watching Leila with big, dark eyes. "If you wish, mistress. Have you finished your bath?"

"Yes." Leila sighed, sensing she would receive no help from this small slave. Hayat's admiration for Guy was written all over her young face, and the girl had practically glowed with adoration at that wretched tavern. What was it about a sword-wielding, long-haired barbarian that could set a young girl's heart to fluttering? It was beyond Leila's understanding.

"Lord de Warenne said you must dress quickly, mistress," Hayat murmured, setting the pitcher and basin on the floor and lifting the lid of the clothes chest. "The wagon will be here soon to take you to the ship."

"I'll dress as slowly as a tortoise if I please, Lord de Warenne and his ship be damned!"

Hayat gasped but kept about her work, pulling several long garments from the chest. Her voice sounded very shy as she said, "Lord de Warenne asked me to tell you that another of his favored pastimes is watching a woman dress, mistress."

Leila gasped, shocked that he would order a child to say such a thing, yet she took this latest threat to heart. She grabbed the clothes Hayat held out to her, her expression baffled as she examined them.

"What are these?" she demanded, holding up a pair of gray silk stockings.

"Hose, mistress. Please, sit upon the bed and I'll show you."

Leila reluctantly sat down and watched as the slave girl deftly drew the stockings over her legs and secured them above her knees with matching silk ties. She turned her left leg to one side and then the other, scrutinizing the strange casings. She decided she didn't like hose at all.

"I will not wear them!" Leila declared just as the door was cracked and Guy's deep voice startled her.

"Another outburst, my lady, whether in Arabic or English, and I will finish Hayat's task myself. In a few moments I will open this door, and I shall expect to see you dressed as a true English lady."

The door slammed shut again, and Leila's face turned as white as the bed sheets she had grabbed to cover herself. She released them and rose shakily, her lips drawn tightly together, saying not a word as Hayat handed her each mysterious article of clothing.

"A chainse, my lady. Your undergarment."

Leila slipped the thin linen shift over her head, her fingers touching raised embroidery as she smoothed the low rounded neckline. "Where are the sirwal?" she asked, feeling the bottom hem of the chainse brush her toes.

"No sirwal, mistress. There are no pants at all."

"Savages," Leila muttered, shocked. That she was to go about with no covering for her lower body was too indecent to consider.

"Your kirtle, my lady."

Leila felt numb as she drew on the sky-blue silk gown. Hayat's hands expertly smoothed the rippling folds which also fell to the floor, then the slave girl adjusted the long fitted sleeves and simple collar, saying in a hushed voice, "Ah, how beautiful you are, mistress. Lord de Warenne will be pleased."

Leila did not waste any breath responding to that last comment. She didn't care two whits if the crusader was pleased! What about her? She wanted to wear the clothes to which she was accustomed. She wanted her family, her home!

She watched stonily as Hayat moved behind her and wrapped a girdle embroidered with silver thread around her slender waist. The girl crossed the flat belt in back and then brought the long, tasseled silk plait attached to each end forward to below her hips, where they were knotted and left to dangle down the front of her gown.

"Your slippers, mistress," Hayat said, rushing back from the chest and setting the leather footwear on the carpet before her.

Leila slid them on, deciding the buttery soft slippers were the only comfortable thing she was wearing. She felt trussed up and smothered by her foreign garments, regardless of the silk gown's light weight.

"If you would kindly sit again, mistress, so I may brush your hair."

"I can do that myself," Leila snapped, but quickly regretted her harsh tone at the slave girl's hurt expression. None of her misfortune was this child's doing, she chided herself. "Why don't we do this?" she suggested more kindly. "After I brush my hair, you may braid it if you'd like."

Hayat bobbed her head, a small smile on her lips. She watched enrapt as Leila quickly worked through the tangles and then brushed out her long hair until it shone.

"Have you never cut it?" the slave girl asked curiously, tentatively touching a silky strand.

"No. Where I come from, a woman's hair is her glory and after marriage, her husband's pride . . ." She fell silent, swallowing hard against the rush of homesickness that threatened to bring on a useless bout of weeping. She sat heavily on the bed, handing Hayat the brush. "Here. You may braid it now."

She scarcely paid any attention as the slave girl deftly plaited her hair with nimble fingers, only noticing when Hayat ran to the chest and pulled out a square of patterned silk and a thin silver circlet that glinted in the lamplight.

"Englishwomen wear veils?" she asked, surprised, as

Hayat folded the silk and placed it over her head so that the embroidered edges fell to just below her shoulders.

"Oh, yes, and many other types of headdress besides," the girl replied, setting the silver circlet around Leila's forehead. "But the veil and fillet serve your beauty well, mistress." She stepped back and clapped her hands together. "There. A true English lady, just as Lord de Warenne wanted!"

Hayat ran so swiftly to the door that Leila was barely on her feet when the portal was flung wide. Leila held her breath as Guy slowly entered, his gaze raking her from head to foot in a manner that sent her pulse racing.

"So, my taste in women's fashion has not failed me," he said, standing with his feet spread wide and his hands on his hips. "I knew English clothing would suit you. I can almost hear the jealous buzz you will cause among the ladies when we arrive at Edward's court."

Truly, he had seen no finer figure on any woman, Guy decided, his earlier irritation at her mention of Refaiyeh all but forgotten. He stared appreciatively, marveling at how the simple lines of Leila's gown clung to each exquisite curve of her body.

His eyes lingered on her full breasts, her taunting nipples clearly visible beneath the smooth fabric, then his gaze fell to a waistline as slim and supple as a reed. The girdle wound about her body in a most enviable manner, the knot tied in the silk plaits resting against the virgin juncture of her thighs.

Guy felt such a hot rush of desire that he called out to Hayat, "Where is her surcoat?" with the intention of covering Leila from other men's eyes.

"I left it in the chest, my lord," the slave girl replied, scurrying forward to stand beside him, her face tilted upward. "It will be so warm today—"

"Please fetch it, Hayat."

The girl did as he bade her, pulling from the chest a voluminous linen garment. She carried it to Leila, who looked skeptically at Guy, her fine black eyebrows arching.

"I am to wear yet another gown?" she asked, her eyes

flashing at him. "Surely I will suffer from the heat, just as Hayat says—"

"Put it on, my lady. The added warmth will be nothing to the discomfort you would suffer if a thousand pair of eyes were devouring your charms. There will be battles aplenty over you once we reach England, without our encouraging them here in Acre."

"I would not have thought a courageous knight such as you feared any battle, let alone one caused by a woman's beauty," she said sarcastically. "Is it possible my mother has commited me to a coward?"

Guy's eyes narrowed dangerously at her. "In truth, my lady, I fear no battles but the one I wage myself. A virgin's scent is a tempting trial for any man, but I have sworn to protect, not ravage you. Have I made myself clear?"

"Perfectly," Leila said with contempt, though the effect of his words was reflected more accurately in her wildly beating heart.

She had never seen such blatant desire in a man's eyes, not even Jamal's as she saw now in Guy's. Strangely it thrilled her, which disconcerted her all the more, and she realized she was trembling, her heart pounding. It was almost as if he were touching her, caressing her, such was the scorching intensity of his gaze. She imagined he must have looked at her like that last night when he—

"The surcoat, my lady. Put it on."

His terse command broke the spell, leaving her angered and deeply embarrassed. How could her emotions betray her so easily, she, who had always prided herself on her self-control? When it came to this man, she seemed to have no restraint at all. He brought out the very worst in her.

Leila grabbed the square-necked garment and thrust it over her head, upsetting the veil and fillet, which tumbled to the floor. All the while she stared furiously at Guy, hardly aware that Hayat was guiding her arms through the sleeveless sides, slit from shoulder to hip. It wasn't until a look of slow triumph spread across Guy's face that she glanced down at herself.

The surcoat hung about her in myriad folds from the

neckline to the trailing hem, completely hiding her feminine curves. Only her arms were revealed and a bit of sky-blue silk and embroidered girdle peeking from the narrow slits.

"I can see you are satisfied," she flung at him, holding still while Hayat climbed on the bed and pulled her long braid from beneath the surcoat, then resettled the veil and circlet on her head.

Guy came forward and took her arm. "Hayat, see that everything is well packed while I escort the lady to breakfast. The wagon is loaded except for this last chest. I will send the bearers to fetch it in a few minutes."

"Yes, my lord."

The liar! Leila fumed with acute regret, stiffening at his touch. So he hadn't been outside her door the whole time after all, just checking on her now and then while loading the wagon.

Striving to remain calm, she allowed herself to be led from the room, though her irritation was heightened by her difficulty walking in so many skirts. She marveled that he would think she had any appetite at all on this darkest day of her life.

Wait. Be patient, she told herself grimly as they proceeded to the kitchen. As soon as his guard was down, she would make her move. He couldn't possibly watch her every single moment. At some point he would look away, and when he turned back, she would be gone.

When Leila stepped on board the armed galley an hour later, she knew she was going to be sick. The ship's rolling motion, even at anchor, mirrored what was happening in her stomach. If not for Guy tightly gripping her arm, she would have turned and fled right back down the gangplank.

She had already tried to flee twice, the first time when Guy was supervising the bearers who were loading the chest filled with her belongings into a wagon while she stood waiting by the door with Hayat. As soon as Guy had turned his back, she had set off at a run down the street, but she was hindered by her long, foreign clothes—truly the ugliest and most cumbersome garments she had ever seen—and he caught her easily. So much for waiting until his guard was down.

Then, during the short ride from Refaiyeh's house to the busy harbor, she had tried again, jumping from the wagon and pushing her way through the crowded market, only to find herself yanked back by her surcoat and tossed unceremoniously over Guy's shoulder. When she began shouting in Arabic for help, calling him names and even cursing at him, it had taken only a terse reminder of his threat the night before and the sensation of his hands caressing the backs of her thighs to silence her.

To make matters worse, when they had returned to the wagon, he had sat her on his knee like a naughty little girl, much to the amusement of the merchants, shoppers, and even children who pointed at her and sniggered. Her cheeks burned at their laughter, and she longed for a face veil to hide her shame. Most women in Acre wore no such veils in public, a sight that shocked her.

She had kept her head bowed all the way to the harbor, desperately wishing a magic genie would spirit her away on a flying carpet, like the unhappy damsels in Majida's fanciful stories. But when she saw the galley looming in front of them, she knew there was no hope of rescue or escape. At least not in Acre.

She had never been on a seagoing vessel, only small pleasure crafts built to glide across artificial lakes and lotus-choked pools such as the one at the sultan's grand palace in Cairo; or flat-bottomed rafts used for crossing the Euphrates and Tigris rivers on the way to Baghdad. This ship was bigger than anything she had ever seen, a hundred feet between bow and stern with two tall masts, triangular sails, and two banks of oars. It had been all she could do to climb the gangplank, she was so overwhelmed by the ship's size.

Now she clutched at her stomach, watching queasily as Guy directed their two chests aboard. He gave little notice of her standing a few feet behind him, though she sensed he knew exactly where she was. He glanced over his shoulder when she gasped.

"You look a queer shade of green, my lady. Are you going to be ill?"

Leila could only nod weakly.

"Then to the side with you." He grasped her arm and steered her to the railing, holding her head as she lost what little breakfast she had forced herself to consume earlier that morning. Coughing and sputtering, she felt so terrible she gave no heed to the coarse comments made by passengers and homeward-bound pilgrims still waiting to board.

"If it's beginning already, I fear you're going to make a pitiful traveling companion," Guy said, his hands surprisingly gentle as he wiped her mouth with a square of linen he had drawn from the leather pouch hanging from his belt.

"What are you talking about?" Leila asked, her knees shaking. She took the proffered linen, balling it in her hand.

"Seasickness. Come on, I'll take you to our cabin so you can lie down."

Leila groaned, feeling so nauseated that she didn't comment on his reference to their shared accommodations. Nor did she try to pull away from him as he again took her arm.

She remotely recalled studying seasickness in medical books. Little could be done for it except bed rest and perhaps some simple drug to calm the stomach. But her medicines were in Damascus, along with her mother, her father, Majida, Jamal, the hospital that was her second home, her patients, her hopes, her dreams . . .

Tears burned her eyes, and Leila could scarcely see as Guy led her toward the stern and what appeared to be a castlelike structure built in two tiers atop the main deck. He helped her climb the steep stairs to the top level, where he pushed open a door and led her inside a low-ceilinged cabin.

"Luxurious, isn't it?" Guy asked, clearly pleased with himself. When she did not readily reply, he added with a slight shrug, "Well, it is for a ship. This cabin belongs to the captain, but he was willing to part with it during the voyage for two ruby earrings and a diamond brooch.''

Her mother's priceless jewelry, Leila thought unhappily, wiping away her tears with the crumpled linen as she looked around her. The cabin was larger than she might have imagined. Guy had to crouch because he was so tall, but other than that the interior was roomy and comfortable.

There was a bed against a side wall—only the second such piece of furniture she had ever seen—a carved table, and two high-backed wooden objects. She assumed from the small, brocade cushions that these were meant to be sat on, but they looked extremely uncomfortable.

"Chairs," Guy said softly, studying her with a slight smile. "In England a lady of gentle breeding does not sit or sleep on the floor."

Leila ignored him, thinking the English were surely mad to prefer such hard furnishings to soft pillows and mattresses spread upon thick carpets. She noted the round Persian rug on the planked floor and the gold velvet bedspread, both of which looked threadbare, but what really drew her attention was the oriel window projecting from the cabin wall above the bed. Nearly the same length across as the headboard and equally as high, the window was fitted with thick, bumpy panes that allowed a blurred, panoramic view of Acre's harbor.

Staring in wonderment, Leila temporarily forgot her nausea. She had seen glass windows before in Sultan Baybar's palace, and of course in the small church where she and her mother worshipped in Damascus, but never would she have dreamed a window could be fitted into a ship like this one.

"It opens. Look," Guy said, taking care to keep his head down as he crossed the cabin. He lifted a latch attached to one of the lower panes, splayed his fingers upon the glass, and pushed. Sure enough, the window opened outward like a tiny door, moving on hinges fit into a wooden frame.

Leila inhaled the fresh air wafting into the cabin, the breeze smelling of fish and the sea. She smiled unconsciously, liking the pungent smell and feeling better than she had since boarding the ship.

"Sweet Jesu, I didn't think you could do it," Guy said almost under his breath, gazing at her with a strange expression on his face.

"What?" Leila asked suspiciously, sobering.

"Smile. You should do so more often, my lady. Rare beauty like yours grows even more fair with a smile upon your lips."

"Surely you jest," Leila said bitterly, looking down at her hands. "I have nothing to smile about."

"Perhaps in time you will change your mind," came his soft rejoinder, stirring the anger that was brewing within her like a sudden summer storm. "We could have a pleasant journey together, Leila, if you would set aside your vain hopes of escaping and accept my aid."

"Your aid?" she hissed, her eyes flashing with cold accusation as she met his solemn gaze. "You forget you have kidnapped me against my will, Lord de Warenne. 'Tis not help, but a crime you have committed. Everything and everyone I love is in Damascus. My life's work is there—"

"Life's work?" Guy scoffed unkindly, his temper rising as an unfamiliar pang of jealousy speared his heart. That she could possibly love an unbeliever was beyond his comprehension, and that he could be envious of such a man was equally so! "What life's work could you possibly have had but as wife to an infidel, bearing him children who would be outcasts in either world!" From the bright spots of color on her cheeks, he could see that his words had angered her all the more, but his frustration at her stubbornness was so great that he could not stop. "Oh, yes, I almost forgot. You were a physician's helper. Changing bandages and a baby's dirtied linen use much the same skills, I'd wager."

She rushed at him so suddenly that he barely caught her hand before she slapped him. He hit his head on the low rafters trying to dodge the blow. Yet the dull pain seemed like nothing compared to the sheer misery reflected in her gaze. Tears swam in her eyes, and her expression was so anguished that he was assailed by guilt. He had pushed her too far.

"Not a . . . helper," she choked, sobbing and struggling against his iron grip, her face wet with tears. "My father made me tell you that . . . to—to protect me. I was—" She drew a shuddering breath, which made his throat tighten all the more. "Damn you, de Warenne, damn you to hell! I was his apprentice! After my marriage, I would have been a physician. I would have joined my father's practice along with his son, Jamal Al-Aziz . . . my new husband. It was my dream! To be a physician was all I ever wanted . . . and now you've ruined everything!"

Guy was stunned. He had never heard of a woman physician. Women healers and midwives abounded in England, but schooled physicians were always men. His gut instinct told him she was speaking the truth—no mere helper could possess the superior medical skills she had displayed in his prison cell—yet it was so hard to believe. To him, a woman's life work consisted of caring for her husband and children and supervising a great household.

"How can this be?" he queried sharply. "I know of no female physicians—"

"In my culture they are a common thing!" she broke in hoarsely. "Do you think male physicians are allowed into a harem's guarded sanctity? No! Only a woman may enter, a woman skilled in all aspects of medicine who may treat whatever malady she encounters. It is the same in our hospitals, where female patients too ill to remain in the harem are cared for in secluded wards. Yet I was also allowed to treat men. How else could I have assisted my father in your care? And do you think I learned how to cauterize wounds by chance, a skill which saved your life? No! I have been studying for my profession since I was ten years old, and I have been an apprentice for the last four. Nine long years"—her arm wildly swept the cabin— "only to have this happen to me!"

Guy's amazement was great. Leila was so different, so far outside his own experience. She was like an exotic flower opening to the sun, the unfurling petals revealing layer upon layer, each more rare than the last. Trained in sensual arts. A female physician. He was utterly fascinated by her. Yet her life would be far different in England, and it was best that she realize that now. She must begin to prepare herself for the reality of her true homeland.

"You may have held such a position in Damascus, but that will not be possible in England," he said, knowing from her stricken expression how cruel he must sound. "When you become the mistress of your husband's castle, you must confine your medicine to the care of your family and perhaps your servants. It is the way of things."

"No! I will never accept it!" Leila cried vehemently, striking his chest with her fists. "You bastard! What a fool I was! How could I ever have pitied you? I wish I had never seen your face! I wish they had chopped off your head!"

Guy grimaced as she lent a blow to his shoulder wound, but somehow the pain seemed well deserved.

How deeply he had just hurt her, yet he never meant her any harm. He had unwittingly altered her life and her dreams because he had been convinced she would welcome his rescue.

Now there was nothing he could do but fold her in his embrace, for already he heard the captain shouting orders to his crew to man their oars. Already the ship was shuddering and creaking as it was pushed away from the dock. They were under way, their journey begun.

Guy inhaled Leila's clean rose scent, the heady fragrance heightened by her futile struggles.

His captive rose . . . and so she would remain until they reached England. For despite everything she had told him, nothing had changed. He would never let her go.

"Shhh, Leila," he whispered in her ear, holding her close though she fought him with all the strength her delicate frame possessed. She was virtually trapped in his arms, yet still she writhed furiously, desperate to be free. She must have felt the ship's movement, too, for she began to weep harder.

"I hate you! I hate you!" she shouted, her voice hoarse from sobbing.

With her cheek pressed against his chest, Guy could feel

her hot tears soaking through his tunic to his skin, her curled fists still attempting to bruise him though he held one to his lips and the other behind her back. "Listen to me, Leila," he crooned over her heartrending cries. "You must believe that what your mother did was for the best. You must look ahead, not behind. Shhh, Leila, love. Shhh . . ."

Suddenly it all proved too much for her. As Leila crumpled in his arms, Guy picked her up and gently laid her down with him on the bed. He held her tightly, whispering to her, murmuring her name . . . cradling her long after the ship had left the rocky shores of the Holy Land far behind them.

Chapter 11

It was almost two weeks into the voyage before Leila felt well enough to sit up in bed. She did so with great difficulty, gritting her teeth against the ever-present queasiness in her stomach and the woozy feeling in her head. She would have sunk back down upon the mattress if not for Guy lifting her beneath the arms until she was half-reclined upon a brace of plump pillows.

"Is that better?" he asked, taking a seat in one of the high-backed chairs that had become a permanent fixture beside the bed.

Leila turned to face him, nodding weakly. There were lines of strain and weariness around his deep blue eyes, and his handsome features were so clouded with concern that she was touched, though she would never have admitted it. Just as she would never understand how this same hardened giant of a crusader who had threatened and bullied her aboard this ship could have such gentle hands.

Strange, the workings of kismet.

Since they had sailed from Acre she had become the near helpless patient and Guy the attentive provider of care. He had scarcely left her side, nursing her through wretched bouts of seasickness that she believed had come close to ending her life, though he still contended that she was not dying, only suffering from a malaise common to many seafaring travelers.

The past days were much of a blur but for that recurring, almost comical argument, and she would have laughed if she had the strength. Instead she sighed, chagrined by her own lack of mettle. Now that she was feeling somewhat better, it was clear she had overreacted.

"Do you want another pillow?" Guy offered, misreading her reproachful sigh for one of discomfort. He started to rise, but she shook her head.

"No, these two are enough," she insisted, giving him the slightest of smiles as he sat down heavily and ran his callused fingers through his long hair.

In the bright afternoon sunlight streaming from the window above her head, she could see how the blond streaks had faded, turning his hair predominantly brown. She imagined it would easily lighten again once he spent more time out-of-doors, doing whatever English knights did to occupy themselves when they were not off crusading across the seas.

Wondering what that might be, Leila met his eyes. Her cheeks warmed as she realized he was studying her just as intently. Despite his evident fatigue, his expression was open and relaxed and his gaze curious, as if he sought to discern what she had just been thinking.

"I will have to teach you some courtly etiquette before we arrive at Westminster," he said conversationally, breaking the awkward silence. "You blush too easily, my lady. You will have every unmarried knight at court hovering around you like keen-eyed hawks sensing a gullible and most delectable prey." He gave a dry laugh. "Most likely the married ones as well."

Leila lowered her eyes, amazed that no cutting remark came to mind when his comments were so ripe for one. It seemed her sickness had lowered her guard or muddled her brain, for truly, she still felt too miserable to spar with him.

Yet she wasn't worried. Once they reached Marseilles she knew her appetite for defiance and escape would return as soon as her feet touched solid ground. Right now she was simply content to be sitting upright and feeling some semblance of her normal self.

"I would suppose, then, that my elder brother would protect me," she said guilelessly, concentrating on drawing the velvet bedspread more snugly around her waist and smoothing the prim, rounded collar of her linen nightrail.

When Guy did not reply, she looked up at him and was astonished to see that his expression had completely changed. Gone was the almost boyish ease, in its place a cold grimness. His jaw was set, and raw tension emanated from his stiffened posture. He was staring at her blindly, as if he had forgotten she was there.

"Lord de Warenne?"

Guy barely heard Leila's soft query. Her innocent statement had hit him like a stinging slap in the face.

Roger Gervais. He had been so caught up in helping Leila through her illness—a constant round of care which had left him disconcertingly intimate with his beautiful charge—he had given little thought to the treasonous bastard. He had purposely avoided thinking of him at all ever since his encounter with Lady Eve in Damascus. Now it seemed he could no longer evade the unsettling issue.

Leila had the right to know to what manner of man her welfare would soon be entrusted. Roger might have been granted the king's peace five years ago, but he was still held in low regard in England, and to Guy's own heart, there wasn't a blacker scourge breathing and prospering in the land.

"Lord de Warenne . . . don't tell me you are coming down with seasickness," he heard Leila say, her worried tone drawing him back to the present. "If we're both ill, it's going to be quite a mess in this cabin."

"No, I'm not ill," Guy answered, veiling his vivid hatred in an uncomfortable mask of impartiality.

The least he could do was supply Leila with the hard facts about her brother. Then, if she observed people shunning Roger and his shrewish wife at court, she would not be surprised.

For that was exactly where he and Leila were going— to Westminster Palace, and with as much haste as possible once their ship docked in Marseilles. Royal messengers were known to make the trip from there to London in less than ten days, and Guy was determined to match it. He did not want to miss the royal coronation.

If his calculations were correct, Edward and his vast entourage of crusaders with their one week's lead would be in Lyon by now and traveling northward. Perhaps Edward had even ridden ahead with a few chosen knights. Whenever he got to the palace, preparations for the coronation would begin at once, and every nobleman in the land would be summoned to attend, including Roger Gervais, who had not gone on crusade though some of his knights had in his place. It would be a simple matter to hand Leila over to her brother there, rather than journeying on to Wales with her.

Not that he would mind spending extra time in Leila's company, Guy thought, his gaze caressing her pale features.

Even in sickness—thankfully his prayers had been answered since the worst of it seemed to have passed—she was the loveliest woman he had ever seen. He could only hope Leila's great beauty and innocence would protect her from any ill will that might be directed at Roger. The last thing Guy wanted was for her to suffer because of her blood relationship to a traitor.

"What do you know of your brother?" he asked, fighting the familiar tightness in his chest as he broached the distasteful subject.

"Very little," Leila answered with a small shrug, looking away. "My mother rarely mentioned him . . ." She paused, her brow creasing as if she had just remembered something, when she glanced accusingly at Guy, saying with no small amount of indignation, "If you must know, she spoke of Roger on the same night you kidnapped me."

Now, from the simmering tempest in her violet eyes, Guy knew she was feeling better, and realizing how much he had missed her spirited temper, he almost smiled. But he suppressed the urge, certain it would only anger her further, and turned his thoughts once more to Roger. That certainly sapped his humor.

"And what did your mother say about him?"

Leila seemed reluctant to answer, then finally she said testily, "Actually, we were discussing the illustrious de

Warennes, loyal servants of the king, one and all. My mother got the strange notion to intercede for you with Governor Mawdud after I told her your name. She said she once knew a branch of that family in Wales whose son, Guy, was a friend of Roger's—''

''True. Roger and I were friends then, and for a long time afterward until he became a traitor to the crown eight years ago. He severed our friendship when he chose to fight in a rebellion against the king. Now we could not be further apart.''

Leila stared at him without saying a word, her lips pressed tightly together. From the turmoil reflected in her eyes, a wild tumble of disbelief and uncertainty, he sensed she was shocked. Fearing for her recent recovery, he sought to soften the harshness of his revelation.

''Your brother has since been pardoned for his part in the rebellion, like many of those who fought against King Henry, and his forfeited lands in Wales were returned to him when his banishment was lifted. I have no doubt Edward will honor his late father's peace once he is crowned king. He is a fair man.''

''Your King Henry is dead?'' Leila asked numbly.

Guy nodded. ''That is why Edward sailed in such haste from Acre. It is my hope to arrive at Westminster Palace near London in time for the coronation. You will most likely meet your brother there, and his wife, Lady Maude.''

Leila shook her head slowly, as if she did not fully comprehend what he had just told her. Guy began to wonder if he should have waited until she was fully recovered before informing her of Roger's treachery. She did not look well.

''Did you tell my mother this?'' Leila said at last in a small voice, searching his face. ''Did you tell her Roger was a traitor before you vowed to take me to him? Did you tell her that you and Roger were no longer friends, but enemies?''

''No,'' Guy admitted. ''She was so happy to hear her son was alive, I could not crush her joy.''

''Crush her joy?'' Leila parroted, her voice becoming

shrill and strained. "Crush her joy? What of mine, Lord de Warenne? Surely my mother would never have entrusted me to your care if she knew you and Roger were enemies. That is why you didn't tell her, isn't it? She would never have knowingly exposed me to danger and abuse. What mother would do such a thing to a daughter she loves? It is clear to me that your sacred vow"—Leila spat the words derisively—"was a sham used to suit your own ends!"

"My personal feelings for your brother held no sway in my decision to take you with me," Guy objected. "Your plight, at least as Lady Eve described it to me, was of far more pressing importance. All I wanted to do was help you."

Leila seemed not to hear him. She sat forward in the bed, her eyes full of fire and fury. "What are your true plans, my lord? To use me somehow against my brother . . . for revenge, perhaps, for past grievances? You purposely deceived my mother, didn't you? Perhaps you do plan to rape me and offer me to my brother as damaged goods. Ah, now there's a fine revenge! I've seen your lust. I've felt it! I've heard your many threats! Or perhaps you plan to use me as a hostage and imprison me until Roger pays my ransom. Then again, maybe you have no intention of taking me to him at all!"

"By the blood of God, woman, you are more trouble than you are worth!" Guy roared, slamming his fists on the wooden armrests as he rose from the chair. "I will listen to no more of your absurd ranting!"

Leila gasped and shrank back against the pillows, her eyes lit with fear, which only angered him further. What did she think he was, a rutting animal? A wild beast? Surely she did not think he would ever strike her.

Taking care to keep his head down, Guy stormed to the cabin door but swung around just before he reached it. "If my intent was to rape you, my lady, I would have done so already, for believe me, there have been plenty of opportunities. Yes, I desire you! I want you! I will not deny it. Your beauty would drive any man to distraction. But I do not prey upon women, as you so mistakenly believe, nor did I trick your mother. My hate for your brother runs deep, but I would never use an innocent to seek my revenge. That will come in its own good time. My only intent is to get you quickly to Edward's court and be well rid of you!''

Guy made as if to turn, then changed his mind and walked back several steps toward the bed, his eyes boring into hers. He was breathing so hard his taut chest muscles were clearly accentuated beneath his fitted tunic.

''A note of caution, my lady, especially since you are so quick to accuse. Perhaps you should concern yourself with your own desires. I, too, have felt your lust!''

''What are you saying?'' Leila snapped, her face flushed with heat and embarrassment. ''You are mad if you—you think that I could possibly want . . .''

She faltered, unable to finish and sick at heart because deep down she knew he spoke the truth. Nothing in her upbringing could have prepared her for the emotions this man aroused in her. Rage, frustration, bewilderment, hatred, and worst of all, desire—each one so acute she felt she was teetering on the brink of losing control whenever she was near him.

Even now, when she so desperately wanted to contradict him, she could not. He would surely see through her lie and expose her accursed vulnerability all the more.

''Your wanton kiss that night at Refaiyeh's gave you away, Leila. If you do not wish to encourage my unwelcome attentions again, or those of any other knight when we reach Westminster, you would do well to keep your mouth chastely closed when you're kissed!''

Before she could fling a retort, he turned on his heel and strode to the door. ''Get some rest, my lady,'' he advised darkly. ''In three days we will reach Marseilles, and then the difficult part of our journey will begin. I guarantee that our pace will be relentless.'' The planked walls shook as he slammed the door, wood dust sifting down from the raftered ceiling.

Leila yanked the velvet spread up under her chin, preparing to scream out her fury when the bed seemed to dip beneath her. She moaned as her stomach pitched and roiled, her outrage quickly vanishing as she fought the urge to retch.

It soon became clear that the ship was bucking high seas. Leila grew fearful. She felt as if the vessel were riding atop a writhing serpent. Flashes of lightning eerily illuminated the darkening cabin, portending an approaching storm.

As the bed dipped and swayed again and again, she was grateful the stout corner posts were bolted to the floor or it would have gone crashing into the walls. The sterncastle which housed the cabin began to creak ominously while tall waves dashed against the oriel window with such fury, she thought the glass might shatter. She crawled into the corner and crouched there with her knees drawn tightly to her chest, feeling terribly afraid and helpless.

Dear God, could the ship weather such ferocity? she wondered wildly, her stomach lurching as it pitched into another deep trough. Surely it would split apart and they would all perish!

Thunder exploded overhead, a great booming crash. Leila shrieked in terror and wrenched the bedspread over her head, huddling beneath the covers in total misery as nature went mad all around her. She did not hear the cabin door open, nor did she hear it slam shut over the resounding thunderclap which made the whole ship shudder.

All she knew was that one moment she was alone and the next Guy was throwing back the covers and gathering her into his arms.

She did not protest as he lay down beside her. She was so horribly frightened she sought to lose herself in the compelling comfort of his embrace. Clutching his tunic, she squeezed her eyes shut to blot out the jagged lightning. He was so big, so overwhelmingly strong. Surely he would protect her from the storm's ferocious wrath.

"Shhh, Leila, it's all right," came his fervent whisper in her ear.

She pressed her cheek to his hard, muscled chest. Hearing his steady heartbeat, she concentrated desperately on its rhythm instead of on the crashing thunder. She inhaled his warm, musky scent and felt strangely reassured.

"Hold me," she pleaded, even as his powerful arms tightened around her. Her renewed sense of security was shaken when the ship plummeted into another seemingly bottomless trough. "Please . . . don't let me go."

"Never," Guy murmured, kissing the top of her head. "We'll endure this together. Do not fear, Leila, the ship is sound. It will ride out the storm."

Holding on to him for dear life, she felt his hands gently stroking her back. It was a caress she remembered well from her long days of seasickness, tender and soothing, though she could recall little else. Huge, gentle hands and blue, blue eyes.

Leila nestled as close to him as she could, his body so warm it seemed to melt away her fear, so hard and solid she could not help but believe his words.

The storm lashed viciously at the ship until well into the night, but eventually the wind and waves subsided. Now only a light rain still pelted the window. It provided a lulling sound that Leila found comforting since she had pulled away from Guy's arms, the heat of his embrace having become too much for her.

She lay on her side with her back against the cabin wall, her arm curved beneath her head, staring at his massive form in the darkness.

The bed seemed very small with him in it. Suffocatingly small. She had not noticed before because of her illness, but she was very much aware of it now. If she barely reached out her hand she would touch him, so she was careful not to move. She did not want to touch him. She did not want to rekindle the desire that had forced her to leave the solace of his arms long before the storm had lessened its fury.

Leila knew he was awake. His breathing was irregular, and she sensed a taut alertness in him, as if he was thinking about something that would not let him sleep.

So was she. After the worst of the storm had passed, she had given a great deal of thought to what Guy had told her about Roger and why he had said nothing to her mother. She had to admit his angry outburst had convinced her he meant her no harm. He wanted to be rid of her. He had made that quite clear.

And she wanted to be rid of him.

Doubly so, now that there was this other thing between them, this troubling attraction she did not understand and did not want to contemplate. It was bad enough that his words still echoed in her ears . . . *I want you, I want you.* The memory of how his eyes had ravaged her in that moment was something she would not soon forget, and with him lying so close to her, the warmth radiating from his body was an all-too-potent reminder of his embrace.

Leila drew in her breath as a shiver raced through her, almost as if he was still holding her against his heart. With great effort she forced her mind back to another matter.

She simply could not stop wondering about what might have caused the permanent rift between Guy and her brother. What little Guy had told her just didn't make sense.

If they had been such good friends and for so long, surely the fact that they had chosen opposite sides in a rebellion couldn't have brought on this hatred, especially since Roger eventually had been pardoned by the king. If King Henry had been willing to forgive an errant knight for a lapse in judgment, why not Guy de Warenne?

Leila chewed her lower lip, debating whether to voice her query. Did she dare? Probably it would only provide another argument, as almost every discussion did. There seemed to be no middle ground between them.

After another few minutes, she could stand it no longer. Inhaling softly to bolster her courage, she raised herself up on an elbow, still taking great care not to touch him. "Lord de Warenne? Are you asleep?"

Leila's soft query was like a jolt of lightning searing through Guy.

Splendor of God. Was she daft? Of course he wasn't asleep. How could he sleep when she was lying only a heartbeat away from him, her slightest movement causing him intense physical pain?

To hold her through much of the storm had been the cruelest torture, his desire for her mounting with the screaming wind. It had been almost a relief when she had abruptly pushed away from him and retreated to the wall, but not the impassioned relief he would have far preferred. Damn if his vow wasn't becoming an impossible weight around his neck!

"No," Guy grated tightly, rising suddenly from the bed. Now that he knew she was awake, he did not trust himself to remain so close to her and not touch her. If she wanted to talk, better it be on opposite sides of the room. He dragged a chair to a far wall and sat down heavily, rubbing his hands over his face as he asked, "What is troubling you, my lady?"

At his impatient tone, Leila almost lost heart. He sounded angry, irritated. Why had he practically vaulted from the bed? Perhaps it was better she didn't ask him anything. Why did she care anyway? It was none of her business—

"You asked if I was asleep, and you can see that I am not," he said in a low, husky voice, cutting into her thoughts. "What is on your mind, Leila? Out with it."

Leila nervously wet her lips, deciding it was best to blurt out her plaguing question just as he said. If he didn't wish to answer, he wouldn't.

"Why do you hate my brother so, Lord de Warenne?"

He swore vehemently under his breath, and she winced, suspecting she should have kept her curiosity to herself. She was stunned when he answered at all.

"He wrongfully chose to follow the battle cry of a traitor, Simon de Montfort, earl of Leicester, who led the barons' rebellion against the crown."

"Barons?" she asked, confused.

"The great landowners who govern directly beneath the king."

"Are you a baron?"

"No, a Marcher lord. My cousin, John de Warenne, earl of Surrey, is a baron and my overlord. Warenne Castle, where I make my home, and the surrounding land on the Welsh frontier belong to me, as well as a large estate I inherited in Surrey. But in war I fight under the earl's banner."

"And is my brother a baron?"

"No. He is also a Marcher lord, though he claims no overlord but the king. It was the same with your father, William. Both stubbornly independent men . . . clearly a trait that runs in your family." Guy exhaled with irritation. "Enough vexing questions! Go to sleep."

Unsatisfied, Leila pressed him further. "Surely this barons' rebellion could not have caused such hatred between you and Roger . . . not if he was pardoned by the king. Yet you seek vengeance against him. Why?"

Leila sensed she had struck at the heart of the matter when she heard another graphic curse. She could feel his eyes riveted upon her in the darkness, a most unsettling sensation.

"You know little of men, my lady," Guy said harshly, a tight pressure gripping his chest. His breathing was coming harder, faster, as terrible memories filled his mind. God in heaven, why was she goading him? He felt himself being drawn closer and closer to that hellish abyss, and it was all he could do to answer steadily, "Conflicting ideals and opinions about king and country can shatter the best of friendships, leaving only bitter enemies. It is easy to hate in time of war when everything you believe in is at stake." He slammed his fist on the armrest. "No more, Leila—"

"But the rebellion was over years ago, yes?" she persisted as if she had not heard him. "And the king's forces proved the victors. You said yourself Roger was banished for a time, his lands forfeited. He was justly punished, but still you thirst for revenge. I don't understand—"

"It took over a year before the royalists finally won their victory!" Guy thundered, something snapping deep inside him. The cabin was so dark, his memories so real! He could feel the walls closing around him, and in a raw panic, words he had rarely spoken to anyone tumbled from his mouth.

"And do you know where I spent that year? In a dungeon cell so black I could have been blind, a cell so small the ceiling was barely high enough for a man to kneel upright, let alone stand!" He clenched his fists, cold sweat breaking out on his forehead. "And I wasn't alone. Oh, no! A friend shared this cell with me until he died hideously from his battle wounds. The corpse was left to rot on the dirt floor"—Guy shook his head, his throat so tight he could scarcely breathe, the stench so real he thought he might retch—"until it was gnawed down to the bone by rats. Only then did the guards drag out what little remained, the bastards! Damn them to hell's fire! They gave me so little food I was forced to eat those same rats just to stay alive—"

"Stop!" Leila cried, sickened to her very core. How she abhorred anything to do with rats! "Please stop! I don't want to hear any more! I don't know why you're telling me this gruesome story. This has nothing to do with Roger!"

"It has everything to do with Roger!" Guy exclaimed, her outburst wrenching him back to reality. He hauled himself so abruptly from the chair that it toppled with a crash to the floor. He began to pace the room in a fury. "That was my life for eleven long months, and I have no one to thank for it but your brother! It was Roger Gervais and his knights who hunted me down after the king's forces lost the Battle of Lewes, capturing me when I could have gone safely into exile. It was Roger Gervais who personally escorted me to the dungeon in Kenilworth Castle. It was Roger Gervais who shoved me into that cell with a fellow knight, leaving us both to die."

"No . . ." Leila whispered, shaking her head in horror. "I cannot believe it. How could anyone be so cruel?"

"Ah, but there's more, my lady. You asked and I shall tell you . . . everything. Roger didn't stop there. Fueled by his greed and certain that I would never again see the light of day, he seized my lands in Wales and Surrey with de Montfort's blessing, claiming them as his own. Many of his knights went to live in Warenne Castle, and one of them, Baldwin d'Eyvill, became my wife's lover. He remained so secretly, long after I escaped from Kenilworth and recovered what was mine."

"But you said you had no wife."

"True. She's dead now. Five years ago, Christine threw

herself from a tower window when she heard a false rumor that Baldwin had been killed in a tournament. She left our one-year-old son, Nicholas, without a mother.''

''You have a son?''

''Yes,'' Guy answered, stopping his relentless pacing to stand near the bed. ''At least I know that he is mine. Baldwin is swarthy while Nicholas is fair. As soon as I saw the child bawling in the midwife's bloodied arms, I knew he was my son.'' His breathing was ragged. ''Tragedy upon tragedy, though I cannot blame Roger for Christine's death. For that I blame myself. I should never have agreed to the marriage. It caused her only pain, for love never grew between us. She died in my arms, cursing me for the unhappiness she had known as my wife.''

Stunned by all he was revealing to her, Leila waited a moment before asking, ''Was your marriage arranged, then?''

She held her breath as she felt him sit heavily on the bed. With his back turned to her, she had to strain to catch his low-spoken words.

''No, but it was thrust upon me in such a way that I felt I could not refuse. Her father, Ranulf de Lusignan, trained me from a lad to be a knight. It is a common thing for a son born into nobility to serve his apprenticeship in another lord's household. Ranulf was also a great friend of your father's, and Roger became his page when your parents left for the Holy Land. He treated us as his own sons, for he had none, only a daughter by his first wife. It is a good thing he died before he saw our friendship turn to dust.''

''What happened to him?'' Leila asked, unconsciously inching across the bed.

''An accident at a tournament. Ranulf tumbled from his saddle, catching his foot in the stirrup. His destrier dragged him across the field, and he was fatally injured before anyone could rescue him.''

''How terrible!''

''Yes, hardly a fitting end for one of England's bravest knights,'' Guy said dully. ''As he lay dying he lamented that Christine was not yet married. No doubt he feared for her because she had no other family. Ranulf was twice a widower. Then he claimed it had always been his fervent hope that I inherit what had been his, the manor and castle in Surrey, and his daughter. Choking on his own blood, he demanded I swear to take Christine for my wife.''

The cabin grew very quiet, the only rustling sounds made by Leila as she slid even closer. "So you swore?" she asked, seeking to nudge Guy from his brooding silence.

"God forgive me, yes, but it wasn't for her rich dower. I had already inherited land enough from my father. I owed Ranulf so much. He had saved my life several times during my hotheaded youth. I could not refuse him.'' Guy drew a slow, deep breath. "It was the strangest thing . . .''

"What?''

"Ranulf choosing me instead of Roger. He had never before favored one of us over the other, and he had long known Roger was enamored of Christine. Yet he made me swear, not Roger.''

Leila's intuition was pricked by this latest revelation. "How long was it after Ranulf's death that your friendship with Roger faltered?"

"A year, maybe less. Christine and I wed almost immediately and she seemed content until the turmoil brewing in the land began causing constant separations between us. I think she sensed my heart was not in the match, though she told me often that she believed I would grow to love her. Sadly, she was wrong. I tried, but it could not be forced. I swore when she died that I would never marry again except for love.''

Leila felt a flush of warmth at his last words. Marrying for love. What a curious notion.

A pointed question flew to her lips, one she would never have been able to ask him if not for the enveloping darkness which lent a strange intimacy to their exchange. "Is this a common practice in your country . . . to marry for love?'' She heard him turn in the darkness and knew he was looking right at her, making her heart pound.

"No. Most marriages among the noble class are arranged. But I have learned from experience that tradition does not always serve one well. I will not make that same mistake twice.'' He fell silent, as if thinking, then asked quietly yet with a tinge of tension, ''Tell me, Leila. Was your proposed marriage to that infidel Al-Aziz an arranged match, as your mother claimed, or one of choice . . . and love?''

Leila was so startled she almost forgot to breathe. For some reason she did not want to admit her marriage was arranged, nor that she looked forward to wedding Jamal for any number of selfish reasons other than love. Instead she swiftly changed the unsettling topic.

''Lord de Warenne, you said your friendship with my brother faltered less than a year after your marriage,'' she stated in a nervous rush. ''Did it never occur to you that your differences might have taken root at Ranulf's death? Perhaps you do not know men's hearts as well as you say you do.''

Guy exhaled with exasperation before answering, ''No, it is not possible. Roger was always outspoken, yet he never objected to the marriage. And it was not he who became Christine's lover when I was in Kenilworth but one of his knights.''

''Maybe by then Roger no longer wanted what you had first taken,'' she said, her theory making such perfect sense to her that she was amazed Guy could not see it. ''Though the way he treated you after the Battle of Lewes seems to suggest some sort of revenge, yes? Perhaps it was enough for him to throw you in prison and seize your lands, as well as the estate in Surrey which might have been his if Ranulf—''

Leila gasped in surprise as Guy suddenly rose to his feet and caught the hem of her nightrail, dragging her toward him until he could grab her around the waist. In the next instant she was so locked in his embrace that she felt molded to his powerful body.

''What—what are you doing?'' she stammered, her heart thumping with fear. She could feel his hard sinewed muscles pressing into her flesh as if there was no clothing between them. ''Let me go!''

''I should have known you would side with the bastard," he grated angrily, his breath hot on her cheek. "Blood is thick, even though you have never met your beloved brother."

"I've taken no sides!" Leila objected, wriggling futilely in his arms. "Release me . . . I cannot breathe!"

She thought he might when he slightly eased his hold upon her, then he seemed to change his mind and drew her even closer, his embrace no longer cruel but overwhelmingly possessive. It frightened her all the more.

"Ah, Leila, Leila, what spell have you cast over me?" he whispered, his eyes glittering in the hazy moonlight spreading like a pale shadow across the window. "I have never shared my soul with any woman as I have with you this night."

Too shocked to speak, Leila balled her fists and pushed against his chest, but to no avail. The heat of his body scorched her breasts, her belly, and that secret place between her thighs that had never felt the thrust of a man until now as he moved his hips seductively against hers.

She gasped at the rigid swelling pressing there. She knew what it was, having learned of its power in the harem, and she thought desperately to pull away even as her hips met his instinctively, her mind and body at total odds.

Guy groaned at her movement and buried his face in her neck, his lips like hot brands upon her skin. His hands slid down her back and he lifted her thin nightrail, cupping her bare bottom to pull her even harder against him.

"Woman, you have bewitched me," he said thickly, kissing her throat. "Bewitched me . . ."

Leila trembled at the primal sensations sweeping her from head to toe, at the forbidden desire racing through her veins and warming her skin like wildfire. Her mind screamed to resist what his touch was doing to her while her body sought to meld with him, pressing even closer. The incredible yearning building inside her was so much more than anything she had ever created herself, infinitely wilder, hotter, sweeter . . .

His lips claimed hers, and all coherent thought fled. Leila eagerly opened her mouth to his carnal kiss, their panting breaths meeting and tongues entwining. As he devoured her hungrily, her arms slid around his neck. Giddy excitement swept her when his hand crept between their bodies and caressed her belly. Then his splayed fingers slid even lower, lower, one thrusting slowly into her moist softness. She arched against his hand, whimpering deep in her throat as she dug her nails into his shoulder blades.

Guy tensed, his voice no more than a ragged whisper. "Oh God, Leila, how I want you . . . Damn this vow! It has become my curse!"

Suddenly she felt him pull away from her and she was shoved back against the mattress, his hoarse cry ringing in her ears. She watched in total astonishment as he strode from the cabin, so stunned she almost burst into tears.

"Damn you, de Warenne!" she shouted after him, dazed and shaking with thwarted desire. As she yanked her nightrail over her exposed body, she gasped for breath and fought back her inexplicable urge to cry. "What are you doing to me?" she whispered brokenly. "Damn you, what are you doing to me?"

She seized a pillow, punching it again and again with her clenched fists until the feathers were flying . . . hating herself for surrendering so easily, but even more, hating him for making her want to surrender.

Chapter 12

❧❧❧

It was late afternoon four days later when the galley docked in Marseilles. One precious day had been lost to the storm, and Guy was more than anxious to disembark and be on their way.

He had every intention of hiring a wagon and journeying to Avignon that very night, where they would catch a boat in the morning that would take them up the Rhone to Lyons. It would be a hard pace for Leila, just as he had promised, but he would fix her a pallet in the back of the wagon where she could rest if she grew tired.

Guy glanced down at her, somber and silent as she walked beside him across the sun-washed deck. For the hundredth time he cursed his wretched behavior of a few nights ago.

Leila had said few words to him since he had stormed a second time from their cabin, and he couldn't blame her. For all of his talk of not ravaging her and his vow to protect her person from any danger, he had acted abominably.

He had sworn to himself from that night on that he would not so much as touch her unless she needed his assistance, no matter the longing which raged like a swirling vortex inside him whenever he was near her. It was strange and frightening and growing more intense each day, like a fire burning out of control.

God help him, he would see that they set a demon's pace to London! This baffling, fascinating, and utterly ex-

quisite woman was proving too much of a temptation for
his most chivalrous intentions.

They were almost to the gangplank when Leila hesitated, and Guy quickly decided she could probably use his
help now. Still a bit wobbly on her feet from her prolonged
seasickness, she was staring uncertainly at the steeply
sloping wooden plank.

"Take my arm, Leila," he offered gently, and was almost startled when she did. He gazed at her small white
hand resting on his forearm, marveling at the elegant del-
icacy of her fingers, then caught her eyes. But she quickly
glanced away. A shallow furrow creased her brow, and
she licked her lips nervously as she surveyed the bustling
waterfront.

Guy could well understand her apprehension. As soon
as she stepped from this ship, she would be entering a
completely foreign world from the one she had known in
Damascus.

He hoped she would not think it a nightmare. His first
few days in the Holy Land over a year ago had been difficult, but he had looked upon the experience as an adven-
ture. Perhaps she might do the same, though he doubted
it. She seemed determined to resist him and what he was
doing for her every step of the way.

"Hold on tight," he bade her, walking slowly down the
gangplank. "If I'm rushing you, just let me know."

"I'm fine," Leila insisted sharply, although she wasn't
sure. The chink of Guy's heavy chain mail was a wholly
new and ominous sound to her, and the interlocking rings
felt cold beneath her fingertips. Just touching it gave her
a sense of foreboding for what was yet to come in this
unknown land.

He was practically encased in metal, from the fitted coif
over his head to his feet, and the act of dressing himself
had been a laborious and lengthy process. As the ship had
sailed into the harbor, she had watched Guy's transfor-
mation from the tall, powerfully built man to whom she
had reluctantly grown accustomed into an even more foreboding warrior knight. Now she felt as if she hardly knew
him.

While he had dressed his demeanor had changed, his expression becoming harder, almost grim as he first attached stout hose and mailed leggings, or chausses, to his braies. After that came an undertunic and a padded jacket like the one her father had cut from him in the governor's prison—a gambeson, Guy had called it. Then he had drawn on his hauberk, a long-sleeved mailed shirt which reached to his knees, and a mailed hood that covered his ears and neck. Lastly came a white linen surcoat emblazoned with the now-familiar crimson cross and his waist belt with its sheathed sword.

He had already explained he was wearing his armor because of potential dangers they would face along the road. Thieves, vagabonds and outlaws would be much less likely to attack a fully armed knight.

That unpleasant information had sunk her morale to a new low. But she didn't hit rock bottom until he told her she would have to play the part of his wife for her own safety until they reached London. The ultimate charade!

"Careful as you step onto the dock," Guy cautioned her, his warning drawing her thoughts instantly back to the present. "Good, now stay very close to me . . . like a dutiful wife. As soon as we hire a wagon and our chests are loaded, we'll be gone from here."

"Dutiful wife, indeed," she muttered. She shot him a venomous glance which seemed to amuse him, but she did stay close to him, avoiding the crush of humanity all around her, and clutched his arm tightly.

The docks were crowded with all manner of folk, mariners and richly clad foreign merchants, barefoot urchins dashing in and out, ragged hawkers selling their wares, pilgrims and hooded clergy, and even brazen women baring their breasts and calling out lustily to disembarking passengers. Leila was so shocked she forgot her self-imposed reticence and tugged on Guy's mailed sleeve.

"Are those women—?"

"Prostitutes," Guy finished for her, a wry smile on his lips. "Incoming ships bring them a healthy trade, and from the looks of this lot"—he nodded toward some dusty pilgrims coming ashore—"they could use what these ladies have to offer."

"Ladies?" Leila scoffed. "Those women would be executed without a trial in Damascus!"

"Then it's a good thing for them they're not in Damascus," Guy quipped, waving off a russet-haired woman who was sauntering toward him.

"Are you sure now, my lord?" the woman queried skeptically in heavily accented English, flashing Guy a wide, gap-toothed smile. "That little lady doesn't look to me as if she can bear the weight of you like these lily-white thighs! Why don't you give 'em a try? I'll give you a ride you won't forget!"

"Better yet," another harlot shouted, shoving the red-haired woman aside, "you're such a fine-looking man I'll pay you for the tumble! If the rest of you is as big"—her eyes fell to his crotch and she grinned lustily—"ah, now that would be a sight to see!"

"How—how dare they!" Leila blurted, her cheeks firing as both women laughed and pushed their way back into the crowd when Guy merely smiled and shook his head.

"Ignore it," he suggested, guiding her to where a line of horse-drawn wagons were waiting for hire. "You'll find the peasants are a crude lot, but they generally mean no harm."

Crude wasn't the word for it, Leila thought, her head beginning to ache. More like vile, base, and barbaric, just as she expected. She felt as if she had been dropped into some sort of swirling hell, such was the raucous activity and babble of languages all around her.

"Wait here," Guy said, leaving her beside a stack of wine barrels before she could protest and walking toward a group of coarsely dressed man gathered by the wagons.

Leila didn't like being left alone in this motley throng, but she had the distinct feeling Guy was maintaining a watchful eye on her, which made her feel a little better. She kept her gaze trained on him, trying to ignore the curious and leering glances being cast her way from male passersby.

It shocked her that men would stare at her so openly. In Damascus, women were treated with respect, and of course in public they wore numerous veils to shield themselves from any unwelcome attentions.

Without a face veil she felt exposed and naked, and she wondered how long it would take her to become used to the fact that women here wore no such veils. She hoped she would be back in Syria soon, and wouldn't have to worry about it!

Leila watched Guy through her lowered lashes and was astonished to see the men sweep off their caps and bow their heads in deference as he approached. Was he a great man, that they would treat him so? She decided they were probably acting out of fear. Guy towered above them, the rugged breadth of his shoulders equal to that of two men. With the sunlight glinting off his polished mail, he was a formidable sight.

She surmised the transaction was completed when one of the men ran to a nearby wagon and jumped into the driver's seat, snapping his whip across the two draft horses' rumps while Guy strode back to her. She experienced a rush of pleasure in his commanding appearance, but she quickly brushed it off, angry that she would feel that way.

"The driver will load our chests and then come around to pick you up," Guy said, glad to be back by her side. He didn't like leaving her alone, even for a moment.

Leila looked lovelier than any woman had a right to, despite the gray linen tunic and matching surcoat he had insisted she wear for their journey overland to Avignon. He would see that she continued to dress plainly until they were out of France. He did not trust these foreigners, even though it was from this land that his own ancestors had sprung. In England few would dare to assault them, but here . . .

"Won't you be riding in the wagon?" she asked, glancing sideways at him.

"No." Guy nodded to the dappled gray stallion being led toward them. "If I need to fight, I want to have a good horse beneath me."

He saw a flicker of fear in her eyes, and she seemed

about to respond when she was distracted by a wild brawl that had broken out between some sailors. He paid the men no heed, studying her face instead. An overwhelming sense of protectiveness surged through him as he wondered if their journey would take any further toll upon her health. He hoped not.

Leila had lost weight during the voyage, due to her seasickness but also to the galley cook's indifferent fare. He, too, had had trouble stomaching the poorly prepared food, but he had forced himself to eat while Leila could not. Her high cheekbones were more finely etched, her eyes large and darkly violet in a face that had grown too pale. He would have to see that she ate well to restore the healthy glow she had possessed in Damascus. Thankfully he still had plenty of Lady Eve's jewels to amply provide for their needs.

"Your charette, my lady," he said when their newly hired driver halted the four-wheeled wagon in front of them and prepared to jump down from his seat. "Stay where you are, man. I'll see to my wife."

Ignoring Guy's proffered arm, Leila looked doubtfully at their roughly constructed conveyance. It was so crude compared to the silk curtained litters she knew from home; no pillows or cushions, only dank straw heaped upon the wagon floor to soften the ride. "Where am I to sit?"

"In the back with our chests," Guy replied, catching her around the waist. "Up you go."

Leila gasped as he swung her into the wagon, and was mortified by the driver's gruff chuckle of approval. From the man's reaction, it seemed to be a common thing for women to be so roughly handled. She sat down awkwardly amid the straw, wrenching the surcoat's voluminous folds around her knees.

"We have to make a few stops before we leave the city," Guy informed her as he mounted the stallion. "We need food and a pallet for you to sleep on—"

"Please, my lord, don't trouble yourself on my account," Leila interrupted irritably, sneezing at the musty straw. "This hay will serve me just as well."

"Are you sure?" Guy asked, amusement lighting his eyes.

"Quite."

"Very well, then. If you're stiff and sore tomorrow morning, you've only yourself to blame."

She did not deign to reply as the wagon rumbled into motion. Instead she lowered her head and closed her eyes to the myriad perplexing sights her mind could no longer absorb. She could feel Guy watching her for a moment, but soon he rode ahead, leaving her to her silent misery.

When Leila awoke, she had no idea where she was. She tried to rise but fell back onto something quite soft, which was a great relief to her sore muscles and aching lower back. Then she felt the rocking motion; it was not as severe as what she had suffered during the sea voyage, but a rolling sensation just the same.

"Good afternoon, my lady."

Her eyes widened at the sound of Guy's voice and she turned to the side. He was sitting in a narrow wooden berth directly across from her, dressed in a tunic, hose, and his black knee boots. An oil lamp sputtered on the rough-hewn table between them.

"Afternoon?" she queried, confused. "I thought it was night." She remembered being jostled along in that accursed wagon long past nightfall, unable to sleep for the constant bumping. Then overcome at last by sheer exhaustion, she had lain down in that smelly straw . . .

"You've been asleep since before we reached Avignon, well over thirteen hours ago by now. We're on the boat to Lyons. At the rate these oarsmen are rowing, we'll be there by sunrise tomorrow."

Still dazed, she merely sighed and stared up at the low-beamed ceiling.

She wasn't surprised she had slept so long after that grueling wagon ride. What did surprise her was that she wasn't seasick, considering they were on another boat. Perhaps because this vessel was smaller—her gaze darted about the cramped cabin—much smaller, its motion wasn't affecting her as much. Or maybe it was because they were on a river instead of the open sea. In any case, she was grateful.

She noted the shadows filling the corners and realized she would have had no idea it was afternoon if Guy hadn't told her. There was no oriel window in this tiny cabin, in fact, no luxuries at all but the incredibly soft mattress on which she was lying. Covered with clean linen, it looked brand new. She hadn't slept on anything so comfortable since leaving Refaiyeh's house.

"I bought the mattress for you in Avignon," Guy said with a half smile, reading her thoughts. "You should have heard the bedding merchant's curses when I woke him early this morning." He shrugged. "It was the least I could do to make up for the miserable ride to Lyons."

Leila smiled back, touched by his thoughtfulness. "Thank you," she murmured, quickly looking away when she saw a strange warmth flare in his eyes.

Instantly some of her good will vanished, and she resolved not to smile at him again if she could help it. She didn't want to give him the impression her attitude toward him was softening. It wasn't. Not in the least.

"How well do you ride horses, Leila?"

She glanced sharply at him. "Well enough. My father taught me. He owned some of the fastest Arabians in the empire—"

"Good. After we reach Lyons, we'll ride post rather than continue on in wagons. They're too slow."

"Post?"

"It means we'll ride hard, changing horses at inns along the way and resting only when necessary."

"But what of our chests, our clothes . . . and this new mattress?"

"We'll pack what we can in saddlebags and leave everything else behind. I'm determined to make it to London in time for Edward's coronation. It will be a great day for England, and I don't want to miss it."

"So you'll kill me to do so?" she queried, her temper rising. "You may be accustomed to spending long hours in a saddle, Lord de Warenne, but I am not. My riding was limited to short races across the desert."

"Then you can ride with me," he said with an engaging grin. "We accomplished our journey from Damascus to Acre like that, and I could do so again. Gladly. You fit quite snugly in my arms. Your added weight was no trouble at all."

Exhaling in frustration, Leila rolled onto her side with her back to him, refusing to reply. Nor did she want him to see how his suggestion, and his handsome smile, had affected her. When he looked at her with that roguish glint in his eyes, she melted inside and she knew she was blushing foolishly. His smile aroused heated memories she had no wish to remember. Damn him!

"Either way, riding separately or together, we should be in Calais within six days," he continued in a rakish tone that made her certain he had sensed her discomfort. "From there we'll take a barge to Dover, then we're only a day's ride from Westminster."

Leila's thoughts spun at this news. They were less than a week's journey from London! She would never have thought she would have so little time to effect an escape. And Guy seemed equally determined not to let her out of his sight. What was she to do?

A new thought struck her, an idea she hadn't yet considered.

Maybe it might be better to wait until she was in her brother's care. Surely Roger would listen to reason and allow her to return to Syria if he knew where her heart truly lay, no matter their mother's misguided plans for her. Probably the last thing he would want was a sister he had never known to exist as an added responsibility. From what Guy had told her, it sounded as if Roger already had enough problems. He would be more than eager to be rid of her.

She pressed her lips stubbornly together. No, that idea had merit, but it would have to serve as her very last resort. She just wasn't ready to give up yet. If the right situation arose and she could secure the remainder of the jewels her mother had given to Guy, she would be gone before he could blink.

She closed her eyes, wishing Guy would magically disappear and thus solve her miserable predicament when she heard his berth creak and his boots scrape on the floor. She jumped at the sharp pop of a stopper being pulled from a bottle.

"Care for some wine, my lady? I also have fresh baked bread, soft ripened cheese, hmmm, some roasted chicken . . ." He paused, smiling broadly at her when she peeked over her shoulder, then began to make a great show of rummaging in a large cloth sack and placing the named items on the table.

Leila's nostrils flared, the savory smell of food making her mouth water and her stomach growl noisily. She winced in embarrassment and looked back at the wall.

"I'm not hungry."

"What a pity," he said nonchalantly. "Oh well, that just leaves all the more for me. This constant traveling has given me quite an appetite. I'm surprised you don't feel the same."

Leila listened, licking her lips, as he poured himself a goblet of wine. In truth she was terribly thirsty and her stomach was so hollow it hurt. It had been a long time since she had eaten a full meal. She was just about to relent when he suddenly inhaled with great vigor, and she turned over to find him sniffing the contents of a small basket.

"What's in there?" she asked, curiosity getting the better of her.

Guy held the basket lower so she might see, his lips twitching with humor. "The baker assured me these were the sweetest confections in his shop. I believe you have something like this in the Holy Land . . . almond pastries. I also bought some apple fritters dusted with cinnamon sugar, one of my favorites. There are three of each, all baked fresh this morning."

The fragrant pastries proved too much for Leila. "May I have one?" she asked, beginning to think she would faint if she didn't eat something.

"By all means, my lady," Guy said, offering her the basket. "I purchased them especially for you."

She took a pastry and eagerly bit into it, the almond

paste the most glorious thing she had ever tasted, even sweeter than she remembered from home. She quickly finished the confection, licking her fingers, and went on to another. All the while Guy watched her with a pleased expression on his face.

"Aren't you . . . going to eat?" she asked, knowing it was ill mannered to talk with her mouth full but not caring. "Or are you just going to keep staring at me?"

He laughed, a deep burst of sound that made Leila giggle in return. It felt so wonderful to eat again and not to feel she was going to lose her meal as soon as she swallowed. Or perhaps it was the sugar making her giddy. Who could say?

Guy took a long draft of wine, thinking he could stare at her for the rest of his life. To see her smiling and laughing was like a dream come true. He wished her laughter would never end, so much so that he was afraid if he said the wrong thing or made the wrong move she would stop.

So he said nothing, only cut into the bread and offered her a thick slice with a generous slather of soft cheese on top. They ate in companionable silence until nothing but crumbs and chicken bones remained on the table and a second bottle of wine was empty.

"Is there no more?" Leila asked rather tipsily, upturning her empty goblet and giggling.

"No, my lady, the wine is gone," Guy lied, using his foot to push a bag filled with more provisions further under his berth.

"Oh."

He had to stifle a chuckle. Leila had drunk only three goblets of wine to his many, but he guessed from the pretty flush on her cheeks and her occasional hiccoughs that she had had little experience with the libation, or at least in imbibing so much of it. It looked to him as if what she could really use was some fresh air.

"Would you like to take a walk on the deck, Leila? It's going to be a lovely evening. I'm sure the sunset will be spectacular."

"Could we?" she asked, her eyes brightening with excitement as she rose eagerly from her berth. She swayed slightly. "I love sunsets."

Guy's heart seemed to leap in his chest, and he groaned inwardly, longing to crush her in his arms. God in heaven, what this woman could do to him with the simplest glance, the merest smile! It was beyond his understanding, her effect on him.

"Come with me." He took her hand, exulting in the warm pressure of her palm against his own. Keeping his head down, he led her from the cabin, through a narrow hall, then up steep stairs and out into the early autumn sunshine.

His guard went up immediately when he found that other passengers had entertained the same idea, and he was glad he was wearing his sword belt. He didn't think this assorted group of peasants and merchants traveling to Lyons would cause any trouble, but one could never be sure. He carefully steered Leila across the deck toward the portside railing where they could be alone.

"How green this country is . . . the trees, the grass . . . like an oasis," she murmured, leaning against the railing.

Guy braced his arms on both sides of her, his chest against her slender back, his chin just above her head, fearing she might stagger and fall if he did not confine her movements. Reveling in their closeness, he followed her gaze to the shoreline. "Yes, but you'll find no desert beyond those trees, nor are there any deserts in England."

The minute the words were out he regretted them, for he felt her body tense. Yet she did not turn upon him with angry eyes and biting words, as he might have expected, leading him to believe the wine had softened her temper. She only shook her head slowly.

" 'Tis so different from my home. So different."

"Tell me about your life in Damascus, Leila," Guy urged her gently, taking advantage of her relaxed mood. He yearned to know more about this exotic woman. His fascination for her was like a raging thirst that could not be slaked. "What did you do when you weren't working at the hospital or visiting your patients in the harems?"

"Oh, many things," Leila replied wistfully, staring out

over the river. She was surprised Guy would be so interested in a world he seemed to disdain. She was also disconcerted by how closely they were standing together, his body warm against her back, yet she was not inclined to move. She felt a little dizzy, a pleasant sensation. And strangely enough, she found their conversation pleasant, too. It was nice not to be shouting and disagreeing for once. "I would read or play the lute," she continued, "or practice my calligraphy—"

"Calligraphy?"

"A very beautiful form of handwriting."

"Ah, and what else?"

Leila smiled to herself. "One of my favorite pastimes is to write poetry."

"Really! Then we share a common interest. I, too, compose poetry."

Thoroughly astonished, Leila twisted slightly and looked up at him. The warmth in his startling blue eyes made her heart jump. "You do?"

"Knights do know how to read and write, my lady, though perhaps they have little time for it," Guy explained, smiling wryly. "I have been working on a book of poems for years. Many knights compose verses, especially those inspired from youth by heroic legends of the past. My education was more extensive than most, by my own choice. My passion for studying used to irritate Ranulf to no end, but he allowed it because I excelled on the training field."

Leila's curiosity was fired by these revelations.

She could hardly believe it! She would never have thought this barbarian would have a scholarly bone in his massive body, nor the sheer love of creative expression that poetry demanded. She actually felt chagrin at the blind prejudice she had nurtured. How strange that she hadn't guessed from his innate intelligence that there was much more to him than brute strength. So much more.

"What subjects did you study?" she asked, flushing as he stared into her eyes.

"Mathematics, astronomy, Latin."

"I've studied some Latin. Friar Thomas at our church in the Christian quarter of Damascus taught me."

Friar Thomas, Guy thought. The man who had helped them flee the city. Maybe Leila had already guessed the friar's connection with their escape, but he wasn't about to mention it to her now. Such information would only disrupt this enjoyable exchange. There were other questions he wanted to ask her, but he feared they, too, might anger her. Yet his curiosity could not be contained, nor the jealousy that had been gnawing at him since the night he had first kissed her.

"Who taught you the sensual arts, Leila?" His gaze fell to her lips, so red and moist, and his jealousy became acute. The image of a dark-haired, dark-eyed man caressing and kissing her body was more than he could bear. "How did you learn to kiss as you do? Surely you had a man as your teacher?"

Her eyes widened, and she gasped softly, turning back to the river as if he had insulted her. "Harems are not brothels, Lord de Warenne. No man is allowed inside save for the master of the house."

Guy stiffened. By God, was she saying that her adopted father had—

"Majida taught me."

"Majida?"

"My mother's odalisque."

"You mean the slave woman I saw in Lady Eve's apartments?"

"Yes," came her small answer, and Guy regretted again his thoughtlessness, knowing he had dredged up painful memories. He was surprised when she continued at all.

"Before Majida was sold into my father's house, she was a concubine in a harem in Constantinople. When I came of age after my first flux, she became my teacher, educating me in the ways of men and women. First we would study a book together, then she would demonstrate the technique upon a eunuch slave." She shrugged almost imperceptibly. "Then I would try."

"A eunuch?" Guy asked incredulously. "But it was my

understanding that they couldn't . . ." He stopped, not wanting to be crude.

"There are varying degrees of surgical procedures that are used upon these slaves," Leila said delicately without looking at him. "This particular eunuch still had his—"

"Enough!" Guy cut in, made extremely uncomfortable at the thought. "So while you and Majida practiced upon this eunuch, he just lay there?"

"Yes."

"Poor bastard."

"Not at all. He was well rewarded for his services."

Guy was astounded. Leila's voice was so matter-of-fact, as if this was the most commonplace occurrence, which of course it was, to her.

To him, this revelation could not have been more extraordinary, or more arousing. His body was on fire just thinking about what she must know. He was tempted to ask her exactly what techniques she had learned when she pointed excitedly to the shore.

"Oh, look over there! Swans! How beautiful they are." She glanced at him over her shoulder. "We have them, too, you know. Governor Mawdud has thirty pair at his summer palace. I saw them whenever I visited his harem. The birds were so tame I could feed them right from my hand."

How beautiful you are, Leila, Guy thought as her enchanting gaze flew back to the swans.

She swayed a bit and he caught her, but she seemed not to notice that his hands now encircled her narrow waist. Her dizziness was a bittersweet reminder that she had probably been so open with him only because of the wine. He could not help wishing that perhaps one day she might show him this part of herself again, and of her own volition—

"And when would that be?" Guy scoffed under his breath, his mood suddenly darkening. When she was under Roger's roof? Not likely. He would probably never see her again except at court events, and then she would most likely be upon the arm of her new husband. The husband Roger would choose for her.

Don't think of it! he told himself grimly, refusing to dwell on the distasteful matter. He had sworn to Lady Eve that he would escort Leila to her brother, and there his duty ended. What happened to her after that was none of his concern. She would be more than a handful for any man when her sharp tongue was not dulled by wine and her eyes snapped with contempt and mistrust instead of childlike delight. Whoever that unlucky fool might be, he was welcome to her!

Guy rested his chin atop Leila's glistening hair, listening to her comment softly on the incredible height of the trees, the fair-haired children she saw playing near the shore, the villages they passed . . . all the while knowing in his deepest heart that he was a liar.

He cared what happened to her. God, how he cared. He hadn't realized how much until now.

But it made no difference. Leila hated him, and he and Roger were sworn enemies. It was an impossible situation.

Suddenly he noticed Leila had become very quiet in his arms. He looked down at her and was not surprised to see her eyelids drooping sleepily and her head nodding forward.

He was a bastard to be pushing her so hard. It was clear her long rest had only taken the edge from her exhaustion. She needed more sleep, and this boat ride would be her last chance to do so in relative comfort. Any more stops they made after reaching Lyons would be short. A few hours' rest, a quick meal, a change of horses, and they would be back on the road.

Whether he was a bastard or not, the sooner they reached Westminster, the better. For him and for Leila.

As Guy gathered her into his arms she protested a little, but it was clear the wine had taken its toll. She was already half asleep, her small hand pressed to his heart as she nestled against him. As he walked across the deck, he passed a stout peasant woman who regarded him with a quiet smile.

''Your lady is very beautiful, my lord,'' she said, her blue eyes kind.

"Yes, she is," he agreed, the woman's words cutting him to the quick. "Very beautiful."

He carried Leila down the stairs to their cabin, where he set her gently on her berth.

"Hmmm . . . so soft," she whispered, snuggling into the mattress as he covered her with a blanket.

"Sleep well, Leila Gervais."

He debated kissing her, then reluctantly decided against it. When she demanded in the morning if he had taken advantage of her after plying her with wine—and he had no doubt she would—he wanted to be able to say he had done nothing she would find objectionable.

Guy closed the door to their cabin, threw the bolt, then sat down heavily on his own berth and pulled out the bag he had hidden from her. Bottles chinked together, and he smiled grimly. He grabbed one and pulled the stopper out with his teeth. As he stared at Leila's face, thinking of impassioned kisses they would never share and silken caresses he would never know, his body grew hard with frustrated desire.

"Here's to honor"—he took a long swig, wiping his mouth with the back of his hand—"to chivalry, may the devil take it"—he drank again, his eyes on Leila's soft lips—"and to being the biggest bloody fool for ever getting caught up in this mess!"

He threw back his head and drained the bottle.

Chapter 13

Lyons, Chalon-sur-Saone, Cercy-le-Tours, Auxerre; the
towns and cities through which they had passed
were no more than a blurred collage in Leila's mind. It
seemed she and Guy barely arrived in a town before
they set out again after snatching a few precious hours
of sleep and hiring another swift horse to take them to
their next destination. Her vehement protests in Lyons
had done little good. He had stubbornly insisted they
ride together.

"Are we almost there?" she asked for the fourth time
that hour, raising her voice to be heard over their mount's
pounding hooves.

"Provins is directly ahead," Guy answered, tightening
his grip around her waist. "Look, Leila. The city wall is
just beyond those trees. Do you see it? And there, rising
above the wall . . . church spires, roofs, and chimneys."

Leila kept one hand on the pommel while she shoved
back the hood of her cloak, which had slipped low over
her forehead. She blinked against the cool drizzle hitting
her face and strained to catch a glimpse of the approaching
town through the gathering dusk. She slumped with relief
against Guy's mailed chest when she spied the landmarks
he described.

She had had enough of this infernal pace, Guy and his
royal coronation be damned! As soon as they reached an
inn she would demand a hot meal, a hot bath and a full
night's rest, and refuse to go any further until she got
them. If need be, she would even pretend a fainting spell

to convince him to spend an entire night in one place. She was ravenous, spattered with mud, her hair unwashed since they had left the ship in Marseilles, and weary to the bone. She would stand for his bullying no longer!

"It's strange to see so many people on the road after sunset," Guy said as he drew up on the reins a few hundred feet from the city gate, slowing the lathered gelding to a trot.

Leila said nothing, amazed at the number of donkeys and horses all wending their way toward the open gate, some ridden by peasants and farmers and others by what looked to be knights and their ladies. Wagons and carts loaded with produce and other goods choked the rutted road, while a train of packhorses was surrounded by men with pikes and crossbows, no doubt a more precious cargo. Guy had to carefully thread their mount through the congested traffic.

"Hello! What goes on here?" he called out to one of the heavily armed soldiers standing guard along a wide drawbridge leading to the city gates.

"The fair of St. Ayoul, my lord. Move on if you're entering the city or else pull your mount aside so others may pass."

"Damn," Guy muttered, veering the gelding to the side of the road.

"What is it?" Leila asked, not understanding their exchange in French.

"A trade fair. If I had known, we would have bypassed Provins altogether. From the looks of this crowd, every inn will be packed with merchants and buyers. We'll have to ride on to Paris—"

"No!" Leila objected hotly, twisting to face him. "I won't go any farther, I tell you! I'm hungry and tired and my—my . . ." She faltered, embarrassed, then decided he should know exactly how she felt. "My backside is fairly blistered from this wretched saddle. I'm sure if you flash one of my mother's jewels at an innkeeper, he'll jump at the chance to provide lodging for us."

Guy smiled roguishly at her, but his eyes held concern. "Ah, then, my lady, that is entirely a different matter. We cannot have your lovely bottom so raw you won't be able to sit down at Edward's coronation feast.'' Before she could muster a tart reply, he clucked his tongue and pulled sharply on the reins. "The Provins fair it is.''

Surprised he had agreed so easily, Leila nervously averted her eyes from the deep moat as their horse clomped across the wooden drawbridge. They passed beneath the lofty gate flanked by round watchtowers, her hood sliding from her braided hair as she gazed upward in wonder. Soldiers on the other side directed them onto a main thoroughfare which opened into narrow side streets where riders and pedestrians were squeezing past each other.

She was amazed at how the city was alive with motion, noise, and color despite the persistent drizzle and growing darkness. Smoking torches burned brightly from iron brackets projecting from outer walls, while lamps and lanterns hung from hooks beside painted doors, all lending much-needed light to the bustling scene. People were everywhere, and she had never heard such a raucous clamor, even in the slave markets of Cairo.

Behind the display counters of shops opened to the main street and those of rudely constructed stalls running down the middle, merchants wearing fur-trimmed coats haggled with customers in brightly colored tunics, hose, and long, pointed shoes. Ladies laughed and talked excitedly with their escorts while holding up their cloaks and gowns to step over horse dung and garbage.

Peasants ringed jugglers and acrobats, stomping their feet and hooting with delight at the entertainers' wild antics while, nearby, whores wheedled and cajoled passersby. Dogs were howling and cats mewling from doorways, horses neighing, children shrieking. Leila started in surprise when a flock of honking geese fluttered across the road in front of them, chased by a barking mongrel.

"Easy, my lady, we'll find a place soon and escape from this racket,'' Guy said in her ear, but his words and his warm breath tickling her earlobe only increased her tension.

Guy seemed to take immense pleasure in sharing a saddle with her and he had explained in great detail the sights they had passed on their journey from Lyons—the better to acquaint her with a culture and customs that were similar to England's, he had said. In truth she had found his narrative fascinating and had slightly altered her view of the country as an uncivilized place. But it made her uneasy to be so close to him for so many hours of the day. Uneasy because she found a heady comfort in his arms and a secret delight at the warmth of his chest and hard, muscled thighs pressed against her body.

Leila shivered, but not from cold, and forced herself to concentrate on what was going on around her. Thankfully it was easy to become engrossed in the enormous variety of goods for sale, and their horse was moving slowly enough because of the crush of people that she could get a good look at everything.

They passed a line of shops where bolts of cloth—wool, silk, cotton, and linen in myriad hues—were heaped on the counters. Other shops offered furs, garments already made to wear, and leather products, while further along came stalls displaying imported luxury goods; plush carpets and ivory carvings, precious jewels, chess sets carved in ebony, and the glittering work of silversmiths and goldsmiths.

When Leila caught the aroma of ambergris and camphor, she was seized by nostalgia and an incredible longing for home, and Guy's arm around her waist filled her with despair. But she quickly shrugged off such feelings knowing they were useless. She needed to be strong and ever vigilant for opportunities for escape. So far she had been presented with none, but she hadn't given up hope.

They came upon shops selling fresh meat, and she glanced away from the bloody carcasses and plucked chickens hanging from iron hooks, finding counters on her right laden with cheese, bread, and wine and, next to them, cookshops selling hot food. Her stomach seemed to flip-flop at the savory odors, reminding her just how hungry she was. Their last meal had been hours ago. Yet they rode on, passing stalls offering items that must be weighed, salt and sugar, wax, dyestuffs, grain, medicinal herbs, and spices.

Leila perused the open baskets, easily recognizing the spices and most of the herbs, both fresh and dried. Yet some were wholly new to her; the yellow-flowered herb in the basket next to the dried red poppies was a plant she had never seen before—

Her gaze flew back to the poppies just as Guy pulled up hard on the reins beside a four-story building with a colorfully painted signboard hanging over the door. She snapped her head around, startled.

"I'm going to check in this tavern to see if they have any available lodging upstairs," he said, dismounting. To her surprise, he left her in the saddle, although his eyes held a grim warning. "Don't try anything, Leila. I'll be right inside the door. Am I understood?"

She bobbed her head, murmuring a composed affirmative despite her racing pulse, but Guy didn't seem convinced. He glanced over his shoulder at a strapping peasant loitering outside the tavern door. A quick conversation ensued and she saw the flash of a coin, then the young man strode up and Guy handed him the reins.

Her heart sank. She would never be able to ride off with this beefy peasant holding the reins. But she had an even better idea. Her budding plan was farfetched and she knew she would be playing with fire, but it might work . . .

"I'll be back in a moment," Guy said with an infuriating wink. "Sit tight."

Her indignant gaze followed him into the tavern, then settled on her smiling hired companion.

"You grin like an idiot," she said to him in Arabic. Her remark was greeted with a confused stare. "I would wager you have the brains of one, too." When the young man merely chuckled, shrugging, she added in English, "Don't mind me, I just have to stretch my legs."

With that she slid from the saddle and gestured to the spice and herb stall, which was besieged by customers, then back to the saddle. He shrugged again, and she surmised he understood his job to be to watch the horse, not her.

"Blessed simpleton," she muttered, hurrying toward the busy stall. She had to be back on that horse before Guy emerged from the tavern, or he would surely guess her purpose. He was certainly no fool.

She pressed in beside three foreign merchants who were quarreling with the spice trader and fortunately occupying his attention. Her eyes fixed on the basket of poppies directly to her left. With the quickest of movements she scooped up two handfuls of dried flowers and thrust them through the side slits of her surcoat, not allowing herself to breathe until she had strolled casually back to the horse. It was clear from the continuing argument going on behind her that her crime had not been noticed.

"Could you help me up?" she asked, gifting the peasant with a smile that sent a crimson blush from his collar to his scalp. He did so and she was well settled, the poppies tucked securely into her girdle, by the time Guy stepped out into the street.

"The taverner has kindly cleared out a room for us," he said, reaching up to draw her from the saddle. "You were right about the jewels." His gaze moved from the peasant, who looked sheepish, to Leila. "Is anything amiss? This young fellow hasn't taken any liberties with—"

"No, no, of course not," Leila cut him off irritably, shaking out her skirts as if it was the first time she had been down from the horse in hours. "He's been the perfect gentleman while you have rudely kept me waiting in this rain."

"Well, I will keep you waiting no longer, my lady, for what you have so stoically earned," Guy said, taking her arm. "We'll stay the night here and leave for Paris first thing in the morning. We've made good time so far. We can afford to ease up for one night. Our meal and some wine will be sent up soon, and they're preparing enough hot water for us to bathe."

Leila was stunned as as he led her into the brightly lit tavern. Just when it seemed he couldn't be more oblivious

of her needs, he surprised her. She would never understand him—

After tonight you won't have to, she reminded herself,
and was seized by nervous excitement as she followed him
up the stairs.

Chapter 14

T his fourth-floor room was not luxurious lodging by any means, Guy thought as he ushered Leila inside the lamplit interior, but it would be more than adequate once good order was restored.

Two serving women were hurriedly changing the linens on the large curtained bed, another was laying fresh rushes in the enclosed latrine projected out from one wall, and a younger girl was dumping fresh coals in the corner brazier. The room stunk of ale from its recently vacated occupants, but the smell could easily be remedied by some fresh air.

Guy strode to the nearest window and pushed open the wooden shutters. He inhaled deeply, then turned back into the room just as a brawny manservant rolled in two large wooden tubs and placed them near the brazier. He glanced at Leila, who was still standing near the door, and a vivid image struck him, wild and arousing.

How he wished he could see her in one of those tubs, her white skin flushed and rosy from the steam, her wet hair snaking over her beautiful breasts—

Enough! You're only torturing yourself, Guy scoffed to himself. Hell's fire would freeze over long before that ever happened.

"There you go, my lord," the manservant said, dusting off his hands. "The hot water will follow soon as the women finish here and fetch it up from the kitchen, and the same goes for the food. If there's anything else you'll be wanting, just let me know."

Guy studied the man. "Better yet, why don't you help fetch the water from the kitchen? Then my wife may have her bath all the sooner, and myself for that matter."

"But that's woman's work—"

"Do it," he commanded tersely. "The payment I gave the taverner is more than enough to ensure that my every request is well met."

The man nodded grudgingly and quit the room, followed shortly by the serving maids, who cast him grateful smiles.

Guy went to Leila's side, thinking she appeared amazingly alert for someone who claimed to be so tired, then decided she was probably just eager for her bath. He, too, could not wait to wash the sweat and filth of travel from his body. "Make yourself comfortable while I'm gone, my lady."

"Gone?"

"Only for a short while. I have to see to the horse, then I want to leave a message with the taverner. It seems two of my own knights are lodging here, quite a coincidence. Apparently many other crusaders are still in Provins, no doubt enjoying the fair before returning to England." Guy gave a short laugh. "I'm surprised Burnell and Langton rented any lodgings at all. The taverner says he's hardly seen them. I imagine they've been in every brothel—" Guy stopped himself when Leila blushed, and he quickly took another tack. "I'm sure our baths will be ready soon. You may go first, if you wish."

"I don't see why we can't bathe at the same time, my lord . . . otherwise your water will surely grow cold," she replied, her blush deepening. Wetting her lips, she glanced at the burgundy velvet bedcurtains. "We could draw those curtains and set one tub on each side of the bed for privacy."

Guy was so astonished by her suggestion that he didn't know quite what to say. He would have thought she would wish him well out of the room, even the tavern, while she bathed, but now . . . He shrugged, at a loss, and decided her suggestion made sense even if it was unexpected. He hated lukewarm baths.

"As you wish," he said simply. "I'll move the tubs now so you won't have to trouble yourself trying to explain the arrangement to the servants when they return with the water."

Leila merely nodded and stayed right where she was, her knees shaking so badly she thought she might fall if she so much as moved. She was amazed she had the nerve to suggest such a thing, but it was all part of the wild scheme racing through her mind.

Since the opiate she planned to distill from the dried poppies would have to be diluted to hide the telltale bitterness, Guy would need to consume a good amount of red wine before he would feel the drug's effect. And what better way to goad him into any angry bout of drinking than a hot bath and savory meal, all served up with a bit of seemingly innocent feminine trickery?

She had been taught much in the harem. There were myriad ways to seduce or merely to tease. Tonight she would play on Guy's admitted lust and, she hoped, bring on a drunken spree like the one in which he had indulged on the boat to Lyons.

She had seen the empty bottles strewn under his berth when she awoke the next morning, her own headache no match for the splitting one that had plagued him that entire day. There had been no need to accuse him of taking advantage of her. His misery had been enough to convince her that his sacred vow had won out again.

And so it would tonight. Guy would not dare to touch her. His vow to protect her would never allow it. He would drown his desire and frustration in wine, and she would be free.

"They'll probably fill the tubs before I get back, so don't feel you have to wait."

Leila started, so lost in her thoughts she hadn't noticed that Guy had moved to the door.

"Are you all right, Leila?"

"Yes . . . it's been such a long journey, 'tis all."

"I know. Soon it will be over." He smiled, but it quickly faded as a familiar warning lit his eyes. "The taverner told me there was only one door leading outside, the front entrance, and I won't be far from it.''

Feigning affront, she stared at him stonily, which seemed to satisfy him. Without another word he left the room, and Leila slumped against the wall, trying to collect her composure. She needed her wits about her every step of the way this night.

Guy had been gone no more than a few moments when there was a sharp knock on the door. She stood back as the manservant carried in four buckets of steaming water, while behind him came the three serving women with more buckets and some thick towels. The girl brought up the rear carrying a large, cloth-covered tray; a bag of clinking bottles slung over her plump shoulder.

Leila went to the window and waited impatiently while the buckets were emptied into the tubs and the food and drink were placed on the table near the bed, where she had already noted an earthenware pitcher and some tin cups. When she heard the door pulled shut, the servants finally gone, she spun around and flew to the table.

Her hands were shaking as she drew the poppies from her girdle and crushed them into a tin cup. Then she added some water from the pitcher. Stirring the contents with her finger, she hurried to the brazier and was relieved to see the coals were glowing bright red. She set the cup upon them, for the mixture would be useless if it did not first come to a boil and was then allowed to steep.

Her anxiety mounted as she scrutinized the contents for signs of bubbling, expecting Guy to walk into the room at any moment and discover her furtive plot.

''Please . . . please boil,'' she begged desperately, beginning to think the potent brew would not be ready before he returned.

She could not believe it when at last there came a hissing sound as the boiling liquid splashed inside the cup. Using a fold of her surcoat to cover her hand, she grabbed the small vessel just as footsteps sounded outside the door. She had barely set the cup beneath the bed and straightened up, busying herself with closing the velvet curtains, when Guy entered, carrying a pair of saddlebags. He regarded her curiously.

"I expected to find you at your bath, my lady. The servants came back downstairs almost ten minutes ago."

Leila's heart was pounding so hard she could swear he would hear it. "I—I did not feel safe. There are so many men in this tavern, and the door was unlocked. I couldn't bolt it for fear you might think I had locked it against you . . . so I decided to wait."

"Ah." Guy turned and bolted the door. His expression was somber as he faced her again, his eyes bright with an emotion she could not place. "There. You are safe. No need to hesitate any longer." Clearing his throat, he strode to the other side of the bed and pulled the curtains shut, blocking him from her view. "As for myself," she heard him say as the saddlebags hit the floor with a loud thud, followed by his hauberk, "I'm going to enjoy this bath while the water is still hot."

Leila winced as the sounds coming from beyond the curtains told her that he was swiftly undressing. Courage, courage, she reminded herself.

She heard bare footfalls and almost jumped out of her skin when Guy rounded the corner post. Her astonished gaze skipped to his braies, the only garment he was still wearing, and a scanty one at that, and back to his face again.

"Y-yes?"

"Your things, my lady." He tossed a saddlebag near her feet. "I bought you some rose-scented soap. It's what you like, isn't it?"

She gave a small nod.

"Good. You'll find it in the front of the bag."

"Thank you."

He disappeared around the bed, and Leila chewed her lower lip, becoming angry with herself. She would never succeed unless she took charge of her emotions! Everything she did from this moment on would have to seem guileless or her plan would fail.

She heard a splash and squared her shoulders, taking several deep and steadying breaths. Quickly she shed her clothing until she had on nothing but her linen chainse, which she guessed might please him because of the way the thin fabric clung to her body. Stifling a sudden twinge of apprehension, she moved to the table where a half dozen wine bottles stood, silent reminders of her plot.

"Some wine, Lord de Warenne?" she asked, and was not surprised when the sounds of his bathing ceased. No doubt he was stunned that she would even think to inquire after his needs. She hastened with a feasible explanation. "If you'd like I could bring it to you, otherwise you will have to wait until I finish my bath."

There was a long pause, then he said quietly, "As you wish."

Her heart battering against her breast, Leila opened a bottle and filled one of the pewter mugs the serving girl had left on the table. Then she knelt beside the bed and very carefully, very quietly, added some of the liquid from the tin cup, taking care that no sediment from the poppies flowed into the wine. After stirring the drink, she took a tiny sip. She detected no bitterness at all.

Leila rose and walked around the bed, biting her lips to make them lush and red. Her eyes widened as she cleared the opposite cornerpost and she gasped, her breath frozen in her throat. She was not prepared for the heart-stopping sight that greeted her.

Guy was standing in the water, his long hair slicked back from his forehead, his heavily muscled body lathered with soap. Too late she realized he was much, much too large for the tub.

Had he no sense of decency? Why hadn't he wrapped a towel around himself if he knew she would find him like this? "Your—your wine," she barely managed, her hands trembling as she offered him the brimming mug.

He took the mug, and she started as his wet fingers brushed hers. She nervously inched a few steps backward.

She had seen him naked in prison, and partially clad many times during the past weeks in their shared lodgings, but this time was different. From the smoldering heat in Guy's eyes, she knew he sensed it, too. Now that she was this close to him, she didn't dare take her eyes from his face. She was afraid of what she might see, even though it was her intent to arouse him.

"Thank you, Leila." He took a long draft, then lowered the mug. His gaze trailed slowly up her body from her bare toes to her breasts swelling against the chainse, lingered there, then moved to her parted lips.

Leila unconsciously licked them, feeling that same strange sensation of inner melting. When he stared into her eyes, his desire written plainly for her to see, she wanted to run. But her feet seemed to be rooted to the floor.

"Your bath grows cold, my lady."

Leila blinked, his husky voice releasing her. "Yes. Yes, you're right. Excuse me."

She spun and fled, her face burning, supremely grateful for the shelter of the curtains. She had anticipated his reaction to her appearance, but she had hardly expected her own flustered response. She fought to still her trembling and pressed her hands to her flushed cheeks.

Her plan was working well, almost too well. How easy it was to deceive a man! She heard Guy resume his bathing, and she quickly decided to do one last thing before she began her own ablutions.

Taking the pitcher from the table, she quietly emptied the water into the tub, then refilled it with wine. Lastly she added the opiate, pouring the remainder of the cup's steeped contents into the pitcher except for the sediment, which she tossed out the open window. Since she had no idea how she would manage to drug his wine once the curtains were opened, it was better to do so now.

Leila set the tin cup on the table and then wrenched her shift over her head. Her nipples hardened from the cool breeze wafting in the window. She eased herself into the tub, amazed that the water still held warmth. She splashed her face and throat. Rivulets trickled between her breasts. How wonderful the water felt after weeks of sponge bathing!

And how wonderful it would be when she was home again and could enjoy a proper bath under the ministrations of her odalisques, she mused, glancing down at the ebony triangle between her thighs. Those short curls were indecent, and she couldn't wait to be rid of them, but there wasn't anything to be done about it until she returned to Damascus. The way this night was progressing, that hope seemed brighter than ever.

Eagerly Leila unbraided her hair, for the moment thinking more about the pleasure of her bath than her plot of escape. Holding on to the rim, she lowered her head back in the water to wet her long, rippling tresses. Only then did she remember the soap in the saddlebag.

Rising up on her knees, Leila reached over the rim and grabbed one end of the saddlebag, dragged it toward her, and flipped it open. She fumbled for the soap, found it, and was twisting around to settle in the water once more when she cried out in pain, her scalp tingling. Some of her hair was caught between two wooden staves on the other side of the tub.

"What's wrong?" came Guy's concerned query.

"Nothing . . . I'm fine," she lied, tugging at her hair and wincing. It would not come loose!

How terribly awkward, she thought, lowering herself as far as possible into the tub even though the water was barely deep enough to cover her breasts. Now she would have to ask Guy . . .

Her lips curved into a slow smile as she realized how perfectly this clumsy situation could further her plan. If Guy saw her like this, his lust could not help but he aroused. No doubt he would loose her hair and then immediately seek solace from the pitcher of wine while she continued to bathe. If he drank it down to the dregs, and quickly, he would be out cold within the hour.

She shivered, not knowing if she did so from anxiety or excitement at the thought that she might soon escape Guy de Warenne forever. Gulping a deep breath, she called out, "My lord, could you please help me? My hair is caught in this tub and I can't move."

Guy froze, a wool towel pressed so tightly against his chest he could feel his rampant heartbeat right through it. The rhythm seemed to match exactly the thundering pulsation in his loins. He was so hard, it hurt.

He groaned, cursing under his breath. God help him, he had known that bathing together, even on opposite sides of the room, would be a bad mistake. He should never have agreed. Surely he hadn't heard her correctly.

"Lord de Warenne?"

He exhaled sharply and stepped from the tub. Now he knew he hadn't imagined her request. But still he hesitated.

Was Leila out of her mind? Could it be possible she was oblivious to her maddening effect on him? When she had brought him the wine, it was all he could do not to sweep her into the tub with him. She might as well have been standing there naked for all the covering the flimsy shift had provided her, her dark woman's hair a taunting shadow beneath the white fabric. By heaven, why was he being so sorely tested, and less than four days' journey from London?

"Lord de Warenne!"

"Damn," Guy muttered, fastening a towel securely around his hips. He knew it hid little of his turgid and increasingly uncomfortable condition, but his braies wouldn't do any better. No amount of willpower could make this erection go away. As soon as he helped her, he would have to take care of it himself.

Draining his mug, Guy decided he would rather endure a trial by ordeal—carrying a red-hot iron bar three paces or picking a stone from a vat of boiling water—then walk around this bed. If there had ever been a sure test of his self-control, it was this one.

He swallowed hard as he approached the tub. Leila's slender back was to him, and he saw the problem immediately. Somehow her wet hair had snagged in the opposite staves. He would have to walk around . . .

"What took you so long, my lord?" Leila asked, trying to keep the nervousness from her voice as she sensed him behind her. She made no move to cover herself, yet she felt extremely vulnerable as she heard him draw closer. "Do you see what has happened?"

"Yes, I can see well enough," Guy answered thickly,

his gaze raking over her as he walked around the tub. "How did you manage to do this anyway?"

"Reaching for the saddlebag. I was trying to get my soap . . ." She faltered, gasping slightly as she noticed the obvious swelling beneath the towel slung low around his hips. She quickly averted her eyes.

At least he was wearing a towel this time, she thought gratefully, though from the way he was looking at her, she wished she had one with which to cover herself, too. She decided he was aroused enough. She didn't need to help him along in that direction. She slowly crossed her arms over her breasts and drew her knees up to hide her lower body, her movements causing another sharp tug to her scalp.

"Ouch!" she exclaimed softly, sucking in her breath. "Please, my lord. It hurts."

Guy smiled grimly at her remark. Surely her pain had to be slight compared to his discomfort.

Leila was as bewitching a water nymph as he had imagined she would be, even more so. He could almost feel the devil breathing down his neck, for if there had ever been a time he was tempted to break an oath . . .

Guy clenched his teeth, attempting to concentrate on his task as he knelt and began to work at the two staves.

To his relief, her hair came free in seconds, and he rose to his feet, trying not to stare at her lithe white limbs and her glistening wet breasts, but finding it impossible. When had he ever seen another woman so fair?

"Thank you, my lord," she murmured, her eyes glittering like amethyst gems in the soft lamplight. "There is wine in that pitcher . . . perhaps you might pour yourself some while I finish my bath."

He glanced at the table, thinking he could use another drink. Anything to kill the desire in him that was threatening to rage out of control.

Guy poured himself a brimming mugful and promptly drank it; he was downing his third when he staggered slightly into the table. Several tin cups clattered to the floor, sounding strangely loud and ringing in his ears.

What was the matter with him? he wondered, setting

down the mug as he bent to pick up the cups. It usually
took much more than three glasses of wine for him to feel
any adverse effects. More like three bottles.

Guy stacked the cups together and was about to rise
when he spied something stuck to the bottom of one of
them. "The serving women didn't clean out these cups,"
he muttered with mild disgust. The encrusted matter was
a dull brownish-red color and shaped oddly like flower
petals.

What the devil? If he did not know better, he would say
it was . . .

He sniffed inside the cup, and the faint, disagreeable
smell confirmed his niggling suspicion even as he heard
Leila rise abruptly from the tub behind him, water splashing onto him. The chilling realization sweeping over him
was like a knife in his back.

"God's blood, woman, what have you done?" he
shouted, pushing against the table as he jumped to his
feet, sending the pitcher, wine bottles, tray of food, and
cups all crashing to the floor. He got no answer, for Leila
had swept up her shift and was making a wild dash across
the room.

With an enraged roar, Guy cleared the tub and caught
her in three strides. As she struggled against him, he spun
her around to face him, shaking her so hard that her head
snapped back. "You drugged the wine, didn't you? Didn't
you?"

Leila had never seen such fury, and it filled her with
fear, her knees growing so wobbly she thought for sure
she would collapse. Guy's handsome face was livid, his
eyes a thunderous blue. He looked as if he wanted to kill
her.

"Answer me! Did you drug me?"

She gulped for air, inwardly cursing her stupid care-
lessness. "Y-yes."

"With what?"

"Poppies . . . wild poppies!"

"Where did you get them? You had no money."

"The spice merchant . . . outside the tavern. I-I stole
them."

"Stole them," he echoed, his furious gaze sweeping over her trembling nude body.

Suddenly he yanked her hard against his chest and threaded his fingers through her wet hair, pulling her head back. His voice became dangerously low, his breath fanning her upturned face like a hot, wine-scented wind.

"Do you think I'm a total fool, Leila? This was all a show, wasn't it? A provocative game with very high stakes. You knew exactly what you were doing. Serving me wine so I might see you in your shift, conveniently catching your hair in the tub so I might see your beautiful wet body"—he pulled her hair tighter until she winced—"then encouraging me to drink while you finished your bath."

"No! No, you're wrong!" she whispered desperately in a vain attempt to diffuse his rage. "My hair did snag in those staves!"

Guy seemed not to hear her, only drawing her closer until her breasts were flattened cruelly against him. "How far were you planning to push me, my lady? How much farther would you have carried your teasing? Through dinner, perhaps? What would you have done, fed me with your own fingers as I've heard eastern women do in the harem? Now there's an intriguing thought. And then what? When it was time for bed, would you have taken your little game as far as necessary, knowing the drugged wine would save your precious virginity before I could take it from you?"

Leila could not answer; her throat was too constricted with shock. Her mind spun to think that he would read her initial actions so clearly, but he was wrong about the rest. So wrong! She would never have—

"I drank three mugs of wine, Leila," he grated, his deep, angry voice cutting into her racing thoughts. "How long do I have before the drug will take effect?"

"I don't know!" she blurted truthfully. "Maybe an hour, maybe less. You may not have ingested enough opiate to feel more than a slight drowsiness—"

"It is long enough," he cut her off ominously, gathering her suddenly into his arms and striding back to the tub. "Long enough."

"Long enough for what?" she rasped breathlessly, her skin puckering with goosebumps as he practically dumped her into the tepid water. While he knelt beside the tub and fished around for the soap, she scrambled as far away from him as possible, but he only dragged her back.

"Long enough to see that we carry this seductive game to the end," he said huskily, locking her directly in front of him as he leaned over her shoulders. He ran the slick bar across her hardened nipples, around and around her full breasts, then slowly slid it down the valley between them to her navel. "First, we shall finish your bath. Would you have done this for me, Leila? Soaped your smooth skin while I watched? Surely that would have goaded me into drinking more of your vicious brew."

"No!" she cried, but already heady sensations flickered through her body as he dipped the soap between her legs. She tried to squeeze them together, but he forced her knees apart, his great strength overwhelming her. "No, you cannot mean to do this! What of your vow? You swore to protect me!"

"Vows mean nothing in the face of your treachery," Guy declared, so far gone with desire that he knew he could not stop now no matter how hard he tried.

He did not want to think, to reason, to feel the terrible pain cutting into his heart at the realization of what she had been doing to him. He only wanted to play the game that she had started, before it was too late. Even now he could feel a slight dullness in his brain, the heaviness in his limbs, but he would fight against it as he was fighting against the truth of her words.

To hell with his vow! Truth. Chivalry. To hell with all of them! He wanted her. More than he had ever wanted any woman.

And he meant to have her.

Right now, that was all that mattered.

"How about this, my lady fair?" he whispered, nibbling her neck while he lathered her breasts and belly. His slippery palms slid up and down her arms and her slender legs, then along her inner thighs, his fingernails lightly grazing her tender flesh. He cupped his large hands and rinsed her, caressing the soap from her flushed skin with both rough and gentle strokes.

Leila gripped his taut, powerful biceps and futilely tried to push his arms away even as she felt her body swiftly betraying her reason. She no longer felt the coolness of the water, only the scorching heat of his touch. His hands were heavy and warm upon her, arousing unbelievable pleasure wherever they roamed. A strange tension was spreading through her body and consuming her, a throbbing ache building between her thighs.

Dear God, what was this wild madness seizing her? It was a sin, this feeling! She wanted him to stop, didn't she?

"No, you must stop," she demanded raggedly as his hands glided inward from her hips and sank lower into the junction of her thighs. He parted her legs wide, his fingers venturing into her softness, and he stroked the quivering inner folds. "Stop," she moaned. "Oh, please . . ."

"How can you want me to stop, Leila, when your body is on fire with need?" came his husky words in her ear. His fingers delved deeper, only to slide out again and again to circle the sensitive bud he found buried there. "You're so hot, like flame . . . and so tight . . ."

She jerked against his hand, his intimate touch too much, too sweet, too terrible. "Barbarian!" she cried out. "I hate you for this! Hate you!"

"Ah, woman, you may hate me, but you also desire me," Guy said hoarsely, his tongue flicking across her ear. "Your need is running wild through your blood like the drug coursing in mine. I have reason to hate you as well for what you have done to me, but I cannot. I cannot!"

Leila gasped as he rose suddenly and lifted her wet body from the tub in a cascade of glistening water. In the next instant he was straddling her on the bed, the velvet curtains hanging torn from their wooden poles because he had wrenched them so violently aside. His towel was gone, his own rampant desire alarmingly evident, hard, swollen, and poised above her belly.

"Remember this, Leila," he whispered, his eyes burning into hers with an intensity that matched the heat of his huge, heavily muscled thighs. "After tonight you will never be free of me. I swear it! Somehow . . . somehow I will have you for my—" He did not finish but swayed slightly above her, then slammed his fist down on the mattress, groaning, "No, dammit! No! Not yet!"

Through the passion which gripped her, Leila knew that the opiate was weakening him. Just as she knew when he claimed her lips in a crushing kiss that it still would not fell him in time to save her. As his tongue hungrily sought the soft, inner depths of her mouth, she thought fleetingly that she should fight him, but she couldn't. She wanted him. Be it sin or the devil taunting her, she wanted him.

Guy blanketed her with his huge, hot body, and all thought fled.

There was no more right and wrong, no past and future, only the furious onslaught of his carnal kiss, his touch, his lips, his tongue. He seemed to be everywhere at once, stroking her, caressing her, his movements urgent and wild. She gave herself up completely to the trembling desire which threatened to explode from some deep, mysterious place. She was lost to feelings and sensations her body had never known . . .

The wet, shivering wonder of Guy nuzzling at her breasts, his licking tongue and nipping teeth like sweet torture to her roused nipples. His lips pulled upon her until she was half mad with delight and she entangled her fingers in his damp hair, moaning incoherently.

The weight of him, the incredible feel of him upon her as he pressed her down into the soft mattress. His muscles rippled beneath her frantic hands, his every movement bursting with strength and power.

As his knee nudged apart her legs, his fingers slid into her again and teased the quivering bud of flesh until she was writhing and gasping beneath him. Shards of heat and ecstasy pierced her, the throbbing ache now a fire raging out of control. She scarcely knew when his fingers were replaced by a mightier presence which suddenly drove deep into her body, filling her completely.

Leila cried out, half whimper, half scream, startled by

the sharp, searing sensation where an instant before she had felt only delirious splendor.

"Shhh, love. Feel me move inside you," came Guy's throaty command. "Think only of the pleasure. The pain will soon pass. I promise you."

She gripped his back, spreading her legs as he sank into her, slowly withdrew, then sheathed himself in her tightness again and again.

"Only the pleasure, Leila . . . sweet, so hot. Do you feel it?" he whispered raggedly.

"Yes . . . yes," she moaned, the pain quickly fading as her hips began to instinctively meet his quickening thrusts. As the sensations became more intense, more overwhelming, she wound her legs around his hips, wanting more of him . . . wanting all of him.

"Ah, God, woman, you are mine!" Guy groaned vehemently, slamming his body into hers until they were both shaking with desire. "No one else shall have you!"

And in the blinding moment of glory that suddenly burst upon her, Leila believed him.

She was his as she had been no other man's, and she clung tightly to him, clutching his shoulders and gripping his taut buttocks with her legs as he shuddered and spilled his hot, surging seed deep inside her. She arched wildly to meet him, laughing and crying and certain she was dying, for such wondrous pleasure could surely not be of this earth.

"Oh God. Leila . . . Leila!"

Deliciously dazed and panting hard, she fell back on the mattress as Guy collapsed heavily on top of her. She was so full of him, she could feel his body still throbbing from his climax. It was only after what seemed an eternity, when he still did not move, that she realized with a start he was unconscious. The splendid afterglow was instantly shattered, harsh reality hitting her like a cruel slap in the face.

Assailed by guilt and anger, Leila began to struggle beneath his weight, desperately trying to extricate herself from their wild tangle of limbs and wet hair. But it soon became apparent that her efforts were useless. In his drugged stupor Guy held her as fast as any bonds, his body impaling hers.

Overcome by a tumult of emotions, Leila began to cry, great, wrenching sobs that made it all the more difficult to breathe. She had never felt such wretched helplessness or such confusion.

She had doubly lost. Her virginity was gone forever, and now there would be no escape. Not tonight.

Heaving a broken sigh, Leila touched Guy's face with trembling, tear-wet fingers.

Most unsettling of all, deep in her heart she was no longer sure she truly wanted to escape him.

Chapter 15

L oud pounding upon the door startled Guy awake and
he groaned, slowly opening his eyes as he rolled over
onto his back. He stared at the velvet canopy and rubbed
his eyes until they focused clearly.

What the devil had happened? Why did he feel so damn
lousy? His head was aching and his mouth was as dry and
scratchy as coarse wool.

Guy felt the mattress depress slightly and heard the rustling of linen sheets beside him. He turned his head to see
Leila rising stiffly from the bed without so much as a
glance in his direction. She was naked, her hair still damp
and clinging to her lovely back and buttocks . . .

Suddenly the events of the previous night came rushing
back to him and he groaned again, remorse and self-disgust
flooding him, as well as incredible relief that she had not
managed to escape. Wondering dazedly how that had been
accomplished, he watched her quickly dress herself while
the vigorous pounding continued on the door.

"God's blood, who is it?" Guy shouted, throwing his
forearm over his eyes against the bright sunlight slashing
across the rumpled bed. "Cease that infernal racket or
I'll—"

"Lord de Warenne! It's Henry Langton. Robert Burnell
is here with me, too. We just got your message from the
taverner that you were here, so we came right up. Open
the door so we can get a good look at you, man. It's been
a hell of a long time. And traveling with a new wife, no
less!"

Guy sat up in bed, trying to shake off the muddled haze still lingering in his brain.

Of course. Langton and Burnell. He had left a message for them to meet with him early this morning so that they could journey together the rest of the way to London.

"Hold a minute!" he called out, climbing from the bed. As he stood up, he grabbed a torn curtain to steady himself against a sudden wave of dizziness and waited on unsteady legs until it passed. "Damn," he muttered.

How long would it be before he was free of the drug's unpleasant aftereffects? He saw Leila glance furtively at him from the bench where she was sitting, then she lowered her lashes and quickly resumed braiding her hair, her exquisite jawline set obstinately as if she was damned and determined to ignore him.

"Those men outside the door are my own knights," he sought to explain as he snatched a towel from the floor and slung it around his hips. "Remember? I told you about them last night."

Silence.

"They'll be traveling with us to Westminster. I told the taverner you were my wife, and he has obviously informed them of that, but I'll set them straight when I introduce you."

More silence.

Guy swallowed hard, acutely aware of what she must be thinking about him. If she had hated him before, he could well imagine how much she hated him now. He wanted to try and explain what had come over him last night, but she probably didn't care to hear any explanations. Maybe an apology . . .

"Leila, I'm sorry about—"

" 'Tis done," she cut him off, meeting his eyes fully for the first time. "There is nothing more to be said about it, Lord de Warenne."

Ah, but there was more to be said about it, Guy thought, seeing the hurt and defiance reflected in her unswerving gaze. Much more.

Everything was different between them now, whether she realized it or not. He had reached a decision last night before the drug overcame him. He had almost told her then; he certainly couldn't tell her now. Not with his knights pacing restlessly outside the door. It was a delicate matter, one that would have to wait until they were not pressed for time or likely to be disturbed.

He could already imagine her indignant protests. But when she heard everything he had to say, his argument would sway her. He was certain of it. Just as he was certain he did not want to live his life without her. She had become a part of him. He could not let her go.

"You might want to do something about that bedsheet," she continued tersely, glancing behind him at the mattress. "I doubt you will want your knights to see what has recently transpired in this room, especially when they discover that I am not your wife."

Guy's eyes riveted on the bright red splotches staining the white linen.

Sharp regret shot through him for her lost innocence, and even more so because he had taken it from her in such a ruthless manner. But in the next instant he forced away his guilt and any niggling self-reproach, convinced that what had happened unexpectedly between them had freed him from an impossible dilemma.

He was in love with Leila.

He had known it since that afternoon on the Rhone, and every mile they had traveled after that had driven home his realization with astounding force. Yet he had tried to tell himself over and over that his was an impossible love. Leila hated him too much and, even if she didn't, Roger would never give his suit the time of day. Now that much at least had changed.

As soon as they reached London he would confront Roger with the bloodied sheet and demand Leila's hand in marriage. By taking her virginity, he had made his inviolable claim upon her.

A claim Roger Gervais would not be able to ignore, no matter the fierce hatred between them.

That grim truth had been his final conscious thought before the drug enveloped him last night.

He turned back to Leila and gave voice to the question

still troubling him. Could he dare to hope her hate was not so strong toward him after all?

"When I blacked out, Leila, you stayed. Why?"

Her beautiful eyes flared angrily at him, giving him a heated answer before she even spoke. "You collapsed upon me, my lord. I could barely breathe, let alone escape. If you had not done so"—she jutted her chin defiantly—"believe me, I would not be here this morning but many, many miles away."

Oddly, her bitter words did not discourage him or douse his hope. He knew there was great pain and anger behind them. If anything, they only heightened his resolve.

Once they were married, somehow he would make amends. He was determined that one day she would grow to love him as much as he loved her. She already desired him. Her unbridled response to his lovemaking had proved it once and for all. Surely such passion could lead to affection and then love. Yes, it was a start.

"Believe me, my lady," he replied with quiet certainty, "if you had fled, I would not have rested until I found you."

The air seemed to crackle with tense silence until another sharp rap came upon the door.

"My lord! How long will you leave us standing in this drafty hall? From your delay, I can guess your lady must be very beautiful indeed."

"Your impatience is as strong as ever, Langton," Guy called out, leaving Leila to glare after him while he strode around the bed and pulled another pair of braies from his saddlebag.

As he yanked on the short trousers, he glanced at the telltale bloodstains and quickly decided his knights should see them. It was best he had witnesses to counter any of Roger's expected and vehement objections. He tied the drawstring at his waist as he walked to the door.

"The bedsheet, my lord!" Leila hissed, jumping up from the bench. Her cheeks colored as Guy ignored her and flung open the door.

What could he possibly be thinking? she raged silently as two mailed knights entered the room, neither man as tall or as broad as Guy but both forbidding in their glinting armor.

She clasped her hands together tightly, mortally embarrassed. Guy hadn't even bothered to dress. It was almost as if he was flaunting her disgrace before their very eyes!

"By God, de Warenne, this is certainly a grand surprise!" the knight with long, reddish-blond hair exclaimed as he embraced Guy heartily, clapping his bare back. "We didn't expect to see you until long after Lord Edward's coronation. Are Reginald and the others in Provins as well?"

"We'll talk of that later, Henry," Guy said, greeting the other knight, a robust, swarthy man, with a firm handclasp. "Robert. From a man who is usually so serious, your grin tells me that the wenches here have been treating you well."

"Aye, my lord, well indeed. But a fighting man can stand only so much frivolity. Langton and I were planning to ride out tomorrow, but a day earlier suits me just fine."

"Lady de Warenne!" Henry said without waiting for Guy's introduction, his green eyes sparkling with good humor as he strode toward her.

This freckled knight wasn't forbidding at all now that he was up close, Leila decided, offering him a small smile because he seemed so genuinely friendly. Yet her warmth faded quickly when Guy approached with the other man close behind him. She drew herself up proudly, saying to Langton, "You have been misinformed, my lord. I am not—"

"Sir Henry Langton, Sir Robert Burnell. Allow me to introduce Lady Leila Gervais," Guy interrupted smoothly, his eyes fixed warmly on her face. "I am escorting her to her brother, Roger."

"Roger Gervais?" Henry asked, glancing uncertainly from Guy to Leila.

"Yes. Lady Leila and I became acquainted"—he put an odd stress on the word—"in the Holy Land. We're not husband and wife, as the taverner claimed. I have been saying so as a guise to protect the lady during our long journey."

"Ah. I see," Henry said, clearly confounded. Nonetheless, he bowed gallantly. "Gervais or de Warenne, my lady, it matters naught. I am most pleased to meet you."

"As am I," Robert stated, staring at her appreciatively.

Apparently his knight's frank admiration was too blatant for Guy's liking. He abruptly moved behind her and rested his hands on her shoulders, his fingers idly playing with her braid. "We have much to discuss, my lords, but first Leila and I must finish packing. We can talk further on the road to Paris."

Bristling at his nearness, yet also crazily unsettled by it, Leila fought to restrain an urge to give Guy a sharp elbow in the ribs. It was clear from the subdued expressions of the knights that they had taken full note of Guy's infuriatingly possessive stance.

"Yes. Yes, of course, my lord," Henry said in a much less effusive tone. "Lady Leila. We are honored to share your company."

Leila watched in mute horror as Henry turned to go and stopped abruptly, his broad shoulders tensing as his gaze fell on the bed. Yet he said nothing and neither did Burnell, who was also staring at the bloodied sheet. As the two men glanced at the torn curtains and the mess of food, wine, and broken pottery splattered beneath the overturned table, she lowered her eyes, wishing that the floor would simply open up beneath her and swallow her whole.

"Find us some breakfast that we can eat on the road, hire three swift horses, and meet us in front of the tavern in fifteen minutes," Guy commanded as the two knights left the room, Henry looking troubled as he shut the door behind them.

Leila could restrain herself no longer. Trembling with anger, she whirled on Guy. "Do you mind telling me why you have chosen to humiliate me in this manner? I cannot believe—"

She was stunned into breathless silence when he stroked her cheek very, very gently with his knuckle and stared into her eyes. For a dizzying moment she forgot all else but her inexplicable attraction to him, which was turning her insides into liquid cascades of warmth.

"Not now, Leila. In due time."

As he walked away she could only gape at him, feeling so flustered and furious she did not trust herself to speak. And she had been doing so well, too, until he had touched her! When he turned his back to her and began to dress, she wheeled around and went in a huff to the open window, clasping her arms tightly over her breasts.

No, you must fight these feelings! You must, you must! she charged herself. This barbarian means nothing to you. Nothing at all! Remember that!

Though painfully aware of his every movement, his every breath, she ignored him until she heard a loud ripping sound. She whirled to find him tearing the offensive bedsheet in three pieces, then folding the bloodied portion and stuffing it into his saddlebag!

"Wh—what are you doing?"

"I take it you are ready to leave?" he queried, dodging her shrill question. His eyes held a strange, disconcerting light as he perused her appearance from head to toe in a most intimate fashion, causing her to shiver. "Your saddlebag is packed?"

"Of course it is packed!" Leila blurted, her cheeks burning. "I never had a chance to pull out my nightrail, if you recall, only that . . . that cursed bar of soap!"

He gave no reply, only smiled at her as he strode around the bed and picked up the saddlebag. "Then let us go, my lady. My men await."

"No!" she cried, her racing emotions making her reckless. "I won't go until you explain why you are taking that wretched piece of linen with you. Tell me, Lord de Warenne. Is it merely a barbaric custom among English knights to keep a bloody memento of each unfortunate maiden they deflower, or is the bedsheet for some darker purpose known only to your black and treacherous heart?"

"As I said a few moments ago, all will be revealed to you in good time," Guy stated very softly, his smile gone. "Now, my lady, my shoulders can easily bear both the weight of these saddlebags and you. Make your choice and make it quick. Either walk downstairs or I shall carry you."

Suddenly fearful, Leila snapped her mouth shut. His forbidding expression told her he meant exactly what he said. Without another word she whisked her hooded cloak around her shoulders and stormed out the door.

Chapter 16

~~~∽◯◯∽~~~

"**M**y lord, may I have leave to speak frankly?" Henry asked, wiping the cold salt spray from his reddened face as another choppy wave broke against the prow of the Channel barge.

Guy did not immediately answer, his eyes trained on the distant cliffs of Dover. Stark and silent, the chalk precipices rose like welcoming sentinels beneath the cloudy autumn sky.

England. There had been a time while in that Damascus prison when he thought he would never see those familiar cliffs again. Never see Warenne Castle or his son Nicholas, or Philip, his half brother and one of his most trusted counselors. Now they were within an hour of making shore, the worst of the journey behind them. The wild exhilaration he had experienced upon boarding the barge in Calais with Leila at his side had been indescribable and it lingered still hours later.

"My lord?"

"I heard you, Langton." Guy's exhilaration was tempered by the somber note in Henry's usually animated voice. He already had a good idea what was weighing on his loyal knight's mind. "You may speak." Guy heard him take a deep breath and he took one as well, filling his lungs with the bracing sea air.

"It's about Lady Leila."

Guy tensed but did not look at him. "Go on."

"I do not presume to know your relationship with the lady, but I can see with my own eyes that it is not a con-

206

vivial one, my lord. She's barely spoken since we left Provins two days ago and when she does, her tongue is as sharp as a razor. I'm just thankful her barbs have been solely directed at you.''

"Yes, her temperament doesn't lack for spirit," Guy agreed dryly.

Henry gave a short laugh, but quickly sobered. "That's exactly my point, my lord. My mind is drawn not only to what Burnell and I saw upon the bed linen that morning at the tavern, but to the questionable disarray of your room as well.''

"And what of it?" Guy queried sharply, feeling a twinge of irritation. "I already explained that you and Burnell would both serve as my witness at court that a bedding had taken place.''

"Yes, my lord, witnesses to a bedding. But a rape?"

Guy turned on him, his eyes narrowed with anger. "You know me well, Langton. It was no rape. I have never preyed upon any woman for carnal sport. And as far as Leila is concerned, I have every intention of marrying her—''

"I believe you, my lord," Henry cut in hastily. "God knows, I never thought I'd ever see you so smitten by any one wench. I posed that harsh question only because it seems you've overlooked something very important.''

"Say it then, and have done."

"Very well. What are Lady Leila's feelings in this matter? She may have willingly shared your bed, but is she as willing to become your wife? From what I have seen, and in all honesty, my lord, from everything you have told us about her, I think not. Yet you are clearly determined to wed her. Without the lady's consent, you have nothing upon which to stake your claim and it might as well have been a rape, for so it will appear to Lord Gervais—''

"Enough!" Guy roared, not so much from anger as from exasperation. "You rattle on worse than a howling fishwife, Langton! Do you think I am an idiot? Besotted, yes. An idiot, no. I have taken all these things into consideration. I am convinced that when I present my intentions to the lady, which I plan to do this very evening and on good English soil, she will accept.''

Henry cocked a sandy eyebrow. ''You are certain of this, my lord? She looks to be a woman who does not cow easily, or persuade easily, for that matter. Perhaps this is one time when you have met a woman you cannot sway. Then what?''

Langton's skepticism gave Guy pause.

He glanced over his shoulder at the low sterncastle which held the only two cabins on the barge. Leila was in one of them, sleeping. She had been exhausted upon reaching Calais, since they had ridden post all the way from Provins. Soon he would have to wake her for the next leg of their journey, which would take them to an inn in the town of Canterbury where they would spend the night.

There he would tell her what he was planning for them. If she did not agree, he had no idea what his next move would be . . .

''See that the horses are saddled and ready to go when we dock,'' Guy stated brusquely, turning back to the windswept cliffs which were drawing ever closer. ''And wake up Burnell. He's napped long enough.''

''As you say, my lord.''

Guy listened as the knight sighed heavily and strode away. He knew full well he had not answered Henry's pointed questions and he had no intention of doing so.

When it came to Leila, he would not predict anything. Why tempt the devil by claiming to discern a heart he could not fathom?

''Have you had enough to eat, my lady? I could order more food, if you'd like. More fruited custard. More wine.''

''This was quite enough, thank you,'' Leila said somewhat stiffly, very much aware of Guy's knees brushing against her own beneath the narrow trestle table. She slid her legs demurely to one side. She was eager to escape this loud and crowded dining hall for some peace and solitude upstairs. That is, if Guy was willing to afford her any . . .

She felt a sudden rush of nervousness, but forced it away. Since she had no plans of drugging him this night, she did not see any reason why he would take the same liberties with her that he had in Provins. At least she hoped he wouldn't. Or did she? Ah, whatever was the matter with her?

Leila closed her eyes and rubbed her temples in a vain attempt to will from her mind the powerful memories and accompanying feelings over which she lately seemed to have little control.

Why was this insane yearning forever plaguing her, and in the most unseemly places? In a raftered dining hall filled with all sorts of unsavory travelers and townsfolk? Perhaps she was coming down with a fever from the constant traveling. Yes, that would certainly account for her strange sensation of warmth—

"You are tired."

Leila looked up, focusing on Guy's face. His arresting blue eyes were laced with concern, and he had about him that same air of possessive familiarity to which she was reluctantly becoming accustomed. "Yes," she admitted simply, foregoing her usual sharp remark.

"Come, then. I'll take you to our room." He rose and walked around to her side of the table, where he held out his arm.

Leila noted Henry's pained expression out of the corner of her eye when she refused Guy's offer of assistance and stood up by herself. The fair-haired knight followed Robert Burnell's somber example by staring uncomfortably into his mug of pale yellow ale.

"Good night, gentlemen," she murmured, which brought both knights jumping to their feet and mumbling good-night. To her chagrin, Guy caught her arm anyway and led her quickly from the smoky dining hall and up the creaky back stairs.

"I've lodged at this inn before. The rooms are simply furnished but quite comfortable."

Leila made no attempt to converse with him, hoping against hope that he would leave her and return to drinking ale with his knights. She felt a rapid sinking feeling, as well as a good measure of nervous unease, when he ushered her into a corner room and shut the door behind him. This was the first time they had really been alone together since Provins.

She sat down on the edge of the bed while he lit an oil lamp, the cotton wick sputtering to life and flooding the dark interior with soft golden light. Other than a low drone coming from the distant dining hall, the only other sounds were their breathing and the steady drum of rain against the closed wooden shutters. Instead of soothing her, the sounds made her more tense.

Leila noticed their saddlebags propped beneath a bench and her cloak hung to dry over a wooden hanger set in front of a glowing brazier. An early evening shower had burst upon them just as they reached Canterbury, but fortunately they had made it to the inn before anything more than their outer coats were soaked. Guy's black cloak hung on the same hanger, broad, massive, just like him—

She was startled from her random musings when Guy suddenly took a seat facing her on the bed, his back against the headboard and one long leg resting casually over the side. She didn't look at him. She was afraid to. She simply stared at her hands lying folded in her lap, but it did little good. She could swear her every pore was alive to his nearness and she could smell him, his hair and clothing slightly damp with rain and sweat, a pleasing, musky odor surrounding him.

She wondered fleetingly if he could smell her, too, then she coughed lightly and glanced at the door. She had said she was tired, hadn't she?

"We'll be arriving at Westminster by tomorrow afternoon. You know that, don't you, Leila?"

She met his steady gaze. He was watching her intently, his eyes like glittering blue fire in the lamplight. Becoming flustered, she quickly looked away.

"Yes, I believe you mentioned that this morning in Calais." She took a quick breath and rushed on, hoping to dissuade him from any long discussion. "If you don't mind, my lord, I would like to get some rest. Tomorrow promises to be a long day, what with meeting my brother and his wife if they have already arrived at the palace—''

''That is exactly what I want to talk to you about.'' Guy leaned toward her, resting his elbow on his leg. ''Leila, I have decided to ask your brother for your hand in marriage. I plan to do so as soon as we can arrange a meeting.''

Leila stared at him blankly, her thundering heartbeat the only thing which made her certain she had heard him correctly. Never in a thousand years would she have expected such a startling pronouncement. He had said all along that he could not wait to be rid of her!

''I admit this decision must seem very sudden. I could have told you in Provins, but it was too soon after . . .'' He paused, his brow furrowing, then began again. ''There was no time. I knew we would be stopping at this inn for the night so I thought it best to wait and discuss the matter here.''

''You decided . . .'' Leila said slowly, finding her voice at last. ''You decided?'' A brittle laugh broke from her throat. ''What of me, my lord? Have I no say in this matter?''

''Yes, of course you do,'' Guy replied, ''but if you would only hear me out—''

''Good. My answer is no.''

He appeared momentarily stunned, then shook his head firmly. ''No, Leila. It isn't that easy.'' He grabbed her arm as she tried to rise and hauled her back onto the bed. ''You will listen to what I have to say.''

''You're hurting me!''

Guy loosened his hold on her delicate wrist, but he did not let go. He ran his finger along the stubborn line of her jaw, forcing her chin around to face him. ''And while you're listening,'' he said softly, caressing her cheek with his thumb, ''you will look at me.''

Leila's first impulse was to wrench away again, but she was captured by the haunted expression in his eyes. Her body was suffused with heat at the raw emotion reflected there . . . not just desire but so much more.

''I love you, Leila.''

Her lips parted . . . for breath, for words? She did not know. Nothing came.

"I want you for my wife."

Sweet Mother Mary . . . He was telling the truth. She knew it. The poignant tug at her heart was her guide, her gauge.

Yet she could hardly believe it. Surely kismet had thrown some new trick in her path. It was plain the fates were not finished toying with her life, her hopes, her dreams. They were turning everything upside down and all around until she did not know where her heart truly lay!

Leila suddenly remembered something, at first more a mist than a memory, but then the words were there, floating up from the recesses of her mind . . . *I swore I would never marry again except for love.*

Guy had said them. He was saying them now. And they scared her to death. Because something deep inside her wanted to believe. Wanted to accept. Yet if she did not spurn him once and for all time, she would never see her home again.

And that was what she truly wanted, wasn't it? To return to Damascus?

"I cannot be your wife," she heard herself say in a small, distant voice. "I do not love you, Lord de Warenne. I never will."

Guy felt as if he had been stabbed with a knife, such was the wrenching pain centered over his heart. But he had expected her protests, and he was not a man to give up easily. He never had been.

"How can you say you will never love me, Leila?" he demanded huskily. "You have shared your body with me, your passion, your desire—"

"Lust does not always lead to love, my lord. You said yourself that Christine believed you would one day grow to love each other. She was wrong. Your love could not be forced. Nor can mine." She seemed to shiver, then added, "Besides, my heart has been pledged to another. As soon as I return to Damascus, Jamal Al-Aziz will become my husband."

"Is that what you truly think?" Guy exploded, releasing her arm and pushing himself from the bed. He could not believe that Arab's name had come back to haunt him! Flushed with unreasoning jealousy, he could only pace the room in frustration.

Was it possible that she truly loved this man? An infidel? Not that it mattered! She had to be mad to think she would ever be returning to Damascus.

Guy stopped abruptly and turned on her, trying to keep his voice calm. "Tell me, Leila. Do you truly believe that is going to happen?"

"Y-yes. Yes, I do," she replied, sliding back farther on the bed. "I'm sure that when my brother understands the error that our mother has made, he will gladly provide transportation for me back to Damascus. Why would he want me as an added burden, especially if I was unhappy here? It sounds as if his life is complicated enough already."

"Oh, God!" Guy exclaimed, incredulous. "Woman, are you so blind? Haven't you understood anything I've told you about your beloved brother?"

Leila felt a surge of anger at his tone. How dare he infer that she was a simpleton . . . she, who had trained under the greatest medical minds of the Arab Empire?

"I know only what you have told me, my lord," she countered with marked sarcasm. "I've heard your side of the story, but I haven't heard my brother's yet. Is it fair to draw any conclusions until Roger has had an equal chance to have his say?"

"By then it will be too late, my lady," Guy muttered. "You forget how well I know him. You don't know him at all."

Leila ignored his last words. "What do you mean . . . too late?" He was shaking his head again, and she could sense that his mood was darkening considerably, as it always seemed to do whenever he spoke of her brother.

"When Roger takes one look at you, Leila, it will be as if the cat has found the cream."

"Now you are speaking in riddles."

"This one is easy to understand," he said grimly. "Your brother paid dearly to redeem his lands and his place in society after the rebellion, perhaps too dearly. Financially, it has nearly broken him.''

"I am sorry to hear this, my lord, but what has it to do with me?''

"Everything! You will fetch a very high price in the marriage market, my lady. Perhaps not among the first-born sons of the nobility, who usually seek rich heiresses, but among others who might seek to better their station by acquiring an aristocratic wife.'' Guy's voice grew quiet as his eyes moved over her lingeringly. "Then again, there are probably those who would pay a king's ransom just to possess your beauty.''

Leila swallowed hard as that same stirring warmth flooded her body. How could he make her feel this way when she was so angry? Had she no control over her emotions any longer?

"If this is all true, my lord, then how could you bring me to this country, knowing Roger might sell me to the highest bidder? That would seem to make you as ruthless as he.''

"I don't know,'' Guy replied, dragging his fingers through his hair and sighing heavily. "Maybe I thought it would still be better than the life you had in Damascus.''

"So you became my judge just because I was a Christian woman living in a world you didn't understand and couldn't appreciate. Thank you for your kind consideration, my lord. My life is now so much better for it.''

Guy exhaled slowly in the face of her pain and bitterness, more determined than ever to make amends to her if she would only give him the chance. No matter what she said, he still believed he had done the right thing in bringing her to England. Now even more so and for entirely selfish reasons. He would not rest until she became his wife.

"Leila, it doesn't have to be that way. Spare yourself what your brother is most assuredly going to make you suffer. It is within your power to save yourself. We cannot marry without your consent. It is the law. If you agree, I will confront Roger with the bed linen I saved from the other night—"

At her sudden gasp he quickly sought to soothe her.

"It must be done. The enmity between us runs too strong for Roger to give me your hand willingly. He must know what happened in Provins. He will have no choice but to accept. There could be a child . . . our child—"

"No! I don't want to hear any more!" Leila cried, brushing past him as she fled from the bed to the window. She threw open the shutters and leaned heavily on the sill as she fought for breath.

A child. She had never even considered that possibility. Dear God, she was so confused, her reason and emotions pulling her in opposite directions. She barely noticed the cool rain pelting her face and the front of her gown, but she was very much aware when Guy came up behind her and placed his hands upon her shoulders, squeezing them and kissing the top of her hair.

"No!" She jerked away from him and spun around, her back to the wall. She felt so trapped, so over-whelmed, all she could do at that moment was cling des-perately to the plan of last resort which she had nurtured since Provins.

"I told you, Lord de Warenne. I do not wish to marry you! I want to go home, to Damascus . . . and I must trust my brother to help me accomplish this. I cannot believe he would hurt me, his own sister. Even if it was his intent to force me into a marriage, he couldn't do so without my consent. That is what you said, isn't it?"

"Ah, Leila, Leila, it's not that simple. There are many ways for unscrupulous men to gain verbal consent so they might further their own ends."

Leila suddenly grew fearful, wondering what else Guy might have in store for her. She tried to back away further, but there was nowhere else to go. "Ways you might em-ploy, my lord?" she accused.

"No," he answered firmly, his expression becoming hard. "I would never force you to become my wife."

"Then have done! Please! I have given my answer." As

her strained cry died in the room, she slumped against the wall and buried her face in her hands.

Guy was silent for what seemed a long, long moment, then he reached out and drew her slowly against him, locking her within his arms. Too exhausted to struggle, Leila closed her eyes as he threaded his fingers through her braided hair and gently tilted back her head.

"Look at me, Leila."

She did so and was stunned anew by the intensity of his emotion as he bent his head and kissed her. His lips were warm and tender, yet so undeniably possessive that when he finally pulled away she was breathless and light-headed, her mouth aching from his passionate bruising.

"Here is my answer, lady fair. Go to your brother and make your plea. If he agrees that you may return to Damascus, then God go with you. But if he threatens you with a forced marriage, know this, Leila. I will be close at hand if you need me. Perhaps then my own offer won't seem so unappealing."

Your offer is most appealing! Leila wanted to cry out as Guy suddenly released her and strode from the room, closing the door firmly behind him. *Any woman would be rich beyond measure to possess the love that shines like truth from your eyes!*

"Only it cannot be me," she murmured brokenly, turning to stare blindly out the window.

What she wanted lay far across the Mediterranean Sea in a land of rivers and trees, fruits and colored birds, where her life's work beckoned and a dark-eyed man was waiting for her, calling out her name . . .

How strange, she thought, numbly wiping the rain from her cheek.

Now that she was trying to conjure Jamal in her mind, she couldn't even remember what he looked like for the striking, blue-eyed giant of a man standing in his way.

"Order more ale," Guy said gruffly, his gaze sweeping the packed dining hall as he sat down on the bench next to Burnell. The crowd had grown more rowdy since he had left with Leila, which suited his black mood just fine.

"The lady has retired?" Henry asked, his freckled face composed into a suitable mask of discretion as he signaled to a plump bar wench.

Guy shot him a dark glance. "Yes. I'll be sharing your room tonight."

"Ah."

"Ah, what?" Guy shouted, his angry roar lost to the boisterous din. "If that implies you were right, Langton, it seems indeed that is the case. For now."

"Exactly, my lord. For now. Things can always change." Henry's lips twitched with a smile as three brimming tankards were slammed upon the table. "I suggest we make a toast—"

"Aye, a toast," Robert agreed, casting his fellow knight a telling look as if to say, *And hurry, dammit*.

"Only if it's not to chivalry," Guy muttered. "I've always supported the Magna Charta, but that clause about forbidding forced marriages should be forever stricken from the rolls. I fear I was born too late."

"Nonsense, my lord. If so, you wouldn't have met the beauteous Lady Leila. So a toast! To the women who will not be swayed . . . and to the swaying of them!"

Guy drained his tankard, his foul mood a shade lighter as he wiped his mouth with the back of his hand. Henry's jests were ably serving their purpose, something his eloquent knight had been wont to do since he had pledged himself to Guy many years ago. But all levity aside, he was now faced with a most serious problem.

Leila would soon be in a buzzing hornet's nest, and he would likely have to go to battle to get her safely out of it.

Roger was a foe he knew well. The bastard would lock her in a nunnery before he would allow her to return to Damascus. But a nun's drab habit would certainly not be the garb Roger envisioned for his sister. More likely her glorious hair would be her only gown as Roger forced her into some rich man's conjugal bed.

Guy clenched his teeth at the unsettling thought.

Roger would never get that far, he hoped. As soon as Leila realized that everything he had said about her brother was true, she would call for him. She would have nowhere else to turn. And when she did, he would be ready.

Chapter 17

"**G**od's bones, de Warenne! I'm glad you're alive and back in England."

"As am I, my lord," Guy said, sitting off to one side while a quartet of tailors hovered around the tall, athletic prince.

Edward was standing very straight in the middle of the room with his arms outstretched, looking extremely uncomfortable as the four craftsmen tucked and hemmed the red silk damask tunic and crimson mantle he would wear in tomorrow morning's coronation ceremony. Guy knew Edward enjoyed the pageantry and color of royalty, but the tailors had been busily at work for the whole hour they had been talking. It was enough for any man to bear, let alone a monarch.

"And such an incredible tale," Edward continued, doing his best to ignore the low whisperings and mutterings near to the floor. "It grieves me deeply about Reginald and the others. Good men, all of them. I'm grateful for your part in the embassy, Guy, though I wish it had proved more worthwhile, especially considering that men died in its cause. Who could have known when I sent you to Anatolia that I would not be in Acre to greet you upon your return?"

"It was not a waste, my lord, despite the unfortunate loss of life. Our close relationship with the Mongol Ilkhan will hold us in good stead should we return to the Holy Land for another crusade."

"True, though God can only know when that might be.

I have much to concern me now in Britain." As the tailors seemed to pause in their work, Edward dropped his arms with a sigh of impatience. "Are you finished, gentlemen?"

"Not quite, my lord," one of the tailors spoke up, a balding man who looked extremely harried. He bowed apologetically. "Another few moments."

"That is all I shall grant you, so make haste." Edward glanced over at Guy with a wry smile. "Hand me my wine, good knight. My throat grows parched from this tedious ordeal."

Guy laughed as he rose from the chair and brought Edward a goblet from a nearby table, but he grew serious when the prince lowered the vessel after drinking deeply. "I am honored to be a knight in your service, Edward," he said, clasping his longtime friend's arm. "Tomorrow will be a glorious day for England. A new reign. A new era."

"Yes, and I equally need men like you, Guy. Men I can trust. I'm glad the governor of Damascus, his Mameluke soldiers, and his wretched prison combined proved no match for you. What a day that must have been when you escaped!"

Guy leaned against the table and crossed his arms over his chest. "I won't soon forget it. When I heard that the governor's messenger had been killed—"

"Now that puzzles me," Edward interrupted, frowning. "Do you really think thieves could have set upon the man? I doubt it. I don't believe any Arabs would have touched him, knowing he was a royal messenger. Native Christians, maybe. But I think it more likely that there was treachery involved. Perhaps someone didn't want me to receive your letter of ransom. Every man has enemies, Guy, known or unknown. And there were always crusaders patrolling the hills around Acre, both singly and in groups. It's a possibility . . ."

"Yes," Guy agreed, "but one that can never be proven."

"Perhaps. I suggest you watch your enemies well these

next few days. Much can be betrayed by a simple glance, a misspoken word, a whisper."

"There! We have finished, my lord," the chief tailor exclaimed proudly, hauling himself to his feet. The other three craftsmen were beaming, all of them clearly pleased with their meticulous handiwork.

"It's about time," Edward declared, then softened his tone as he perused his appearance. "My thanks, gentlemen. The garments are truly splendid . . . fit for a king. But now help me out of this finery and fetch me something more comfortable to wear."

As the tailors rushed about and Edward changed, Guy moodily drank his wine.

He, too, had considered the possibility of treachery, but it seemed remote. The odds of that messenger running into men who would have wished, for whatever reason, to thwart his ransom were so slim . . .

Guy inclined his head at the light burst of feminine laughter drifting to them from a distant room, and his hand tightened around the goblet.

God, he missed Leila!

He was amazed at how easily his mind could skip to thoughts of her, despite the fact that he was surrounded by bustling activity and in the presence of the crown prince, who had granted him an audience as soon as he heard Guy was at Westminster. It felt as if it had been weeks since he had last seen her, rather than a few hours. He never would have dreamed that being in love could be such torture. Yet he would not trade it. Not for a sultan's riches.

What was she doing right now? he wondered. Where might she be . . . strolling somewhere in the palace or perhaps resting in the Gervais tent, one of many such temporary lodgings which had been set up on the palace grounds? Was she thinking of him? How was she faring now that she was under Roger's guardianship?

"Come and sit with me, Guy," Edward said, shrugging into a white surcoat embroidered with gold trefoils and taking one of the four carved chairs in front of the huge fireplace. "I want to hear more about this intriguing Lady Leila Gervais."

Guy grinned wryly as he walked over and sat down next to Edward. "You read my mind exactly, my lord," he admitted, stretching out his long legs to the low burning fire. "I was just thinking about her."

"Now that's a most serious sign." Edward raised a dark eyebrow as he regarded Guy with a curious smile. "I don't recall you dwelling overmuch on any one woman before, my lord de Warenne. Since you lost your first wife, you've broken many a fair maiden's heart here at court, and God knows how many peasant wenches have lost their maidenheads back in Wales."

"You paint me as quite the rogue, my lord."

"From the sound of it, a reformed rogue. Your half brother Philip will be in his priestly glory to know you've a mind to settle down."

Guy swirled what little wine remained in his goblet as he gazed thoughtfully into the fire. "That is my hope, though how long it will take me is entirely another matter."

"Ah, yes. You would have chosen Gervais's sister. Now there's a fine trick of fate." Edward was silent for a moment, shaking his head, then he asked quietly, "How did it go when you handed her over to Roger?"

"As I expected. It wasn't hard to find him. He and his men were practicing with the lance and shield in Tothill Fields when we rode up."

"Getting ready for the jousting, I imagine. Roger's prowess with the lance grows stronger with each passing year. No doubt he's already counting the horses and armor he will win when he unseats a record number of knights at my tournament."

Guy grunted. "He's never beaten me."

"Nor have you beaten him. It's always come to a draw. Ranulf trained you both well. I've never seen two opponents more equally matched." Edward shifted in his chair, waving for a servant to bring more wine. "Another subject altogether. Forgive me, Guy. Go on with your story."

Guy waited until their goblets were refilled, then he

continued. "Roger looked as if he were seeing a ghost when he spied me, but he quickly recovered, masking his emotions as ably as he always has. He scarcely blinked when I introduced Leila to him as his sister, though he did thank me when all was said and done, which surprised me. I think the blackguard did it for Leila's benefit. He became quite charming and most solicitous, suggesting he escort her at once to his wife Maude so she might refresh herself from the journey." Guy shrugged. "That was all. He had a palfrey brought for her, and she rode with him from the field."

Without even a backward glance, he thought to himself. That last slight had cut him deeply. She must have truly believed she was finally rid of him. Ah, Leila . . .

"Hmmm. If you would like, Guy, we could arrange to have her stay here at court as one of Eleanor's ladies-in-waiting," Edward suggested. "At least then you would see her and know that she is safe. I doubt you will be allowed near enough to Gervais's castle to catch even a glimpse of her."

"Thank you for your kind offer, my lord, but no. That would only prolong the situation. She must go with Roger to Wales. From what I saw this afternoon, I'll wager he'll be on his best behavior while at court, and if so, Leila will draw no closer to seeing him for what he really is—a coldhearted opportunist who has no thought for her welfare, only for lining his own pockets."

"Well, if there's any way I can assist you, let me know. I must honor my late father's peace, but that does not mean I suffer traitors lightly. I still remember well my days of imprisonment in Kenilworth Castle."

Both men grew silent, lost to dark memories until a commotion came at the door. They rose together as a beautiful woman was ushered into the room, her patrician features lighting with a radiant smile when she saw Guy.

"Lord de Warenne! What a wonderful surprise! I just now learned you were here at Westminster, though I'm amazed it took so long for the rumor to reach me. My ladies-in-waiting are all a-twitter that the most handsome and eligible knight in England has returned from the Holy Land.''

"Hold on to your pretty plans, my dearest wife," Edward said, planting a resounding kiss on her smiling lips. "I fear your ladies will be sobbing in their pillows this night. It seems our valiant knight de Warenne is in love."

"Lady Eleanor," Guy said, bowing deeply. He was not in the least embarrassed by his sovereigns' open affection for each other. It was well known throughout the realm that Edward was devoted to his wife, their marriage an exceedingly happy one.

"What's this? In love? Oh dear, and I thought I'd have a chance to play the matchmaker now that you are back. Who is the lucky girl?"

"Lady Leila Gervais," Guy answered with a thin smile.

"Gervais? Surely not any relation to . . .'' Eleanor's voice died away as she looked from her nodding husband to Guy. Her lively green eyes widened considerably. "Oh my," she breathed, clearly nonplussed.

"Oh my, indeed," Edward said with a short laugh. "Wait until you hear where he met this mysterious lady."

"Damascus, Syria," Guy said, playing along.

"Damascus! But how—"

"Ah, did you hear that? The trumpets are sounding for the feast," Edward cut in, looping his arm through Eleanor's. "It's about time, too. I'm ravenous. Come, my beloved wife. Our guests will be gathering, and we should be there to greet them."

As he began to sweep her along with him to the door, Eleanor laughingly protested, "But, my lord, I must hear—"

"And so you shall, my love, so you shall. Guy can regale you with his romantic tale over supper." Edward called to him over his shoulder. "You will sit at our table, de Warenne, on my lady's right hand. And if you spy your Lady Leila, you must point her out to us."

"I am honored, my lord. Indeed I will," Guy said, an eagerness to his stride as he followed them. He felt like a raw youth, such was his excitement at the prospect of seeing Leila again. She was bound to be at tonight's feast in

Westminster Hall, for it marked the official beginning of the coronation festivities.

And if there was one thing he was certain about her, it was that she was easy to read. He would be able to tell with one look at her lovely eyes exactly how she was faring.

He didn't relish the thought of Roger mistreating her, but he secretly hoped the bastard had already forgone his mock gallant behavior. The sooner Leila discerned her brother's true colors, the better.

"My only wish is for you to enjoy yourself, dear sister. A king's coronation is a rare event. We will talk of your concerns further when we return to Wales, I promise you. Come. We will be late for the feast."

Leila lifted her eyes to Roger's and was still astonished hours after their initial meeting that there was so little physical resemblance between them.

He was a handsome man, no doubt of that, tall and robust, with dark, closely cropped hair which was more brown than black, piercing steel-blue eyes, and ruggedly cut features. She could only reason that he took after the father she had never known and whom her mother had never described to her. Yet in his smile, which seemed warm enough, she could see a glimpse of Eve. It made her dreadfully homesick, and she shook her head, unconvinced by his placating words.

"I don't understand why I must journey all the way to Wales. It will only waste precious time. The matter is quite plain, my lord. I wish to return to Damascus before the change of seasons makes traveling too difficult. Surely you understand by now that my presence here in England is all a dreadful mistake."

"Oh, come now, Leila," Maude interjected, taking her arm. "You must at least visit your ancestral home before entertaining any idea of leaving us. Winter is still many weeks away. There is plenty of time to enjoy the coronation and a short side trip to Wales, surely. You have come too far to leave us so soon."

Leila glanced at the striking blond woman holding her arm, not sure if she liked her sister-in-law or not.

Maude had seemed friendly enough since she had been brought to this tent. Maude had set her servants at once to cutting down one of her own gowns to fit Leila's smaller figure, and then she had personally served her cool wine and a light repast. The source of Leila's unease wasn't something she could easily put her finger on. The older woman was doing her utmost to appear cordial. Perhaps it was as simple as that . . . ah, then again, maybe it was nothing.

"Maude is right," Roger said, the same warm smile still on his face. "It's not every day one is reunited with a long-lost sister. You're the exact image of Mother, you know. I was nine when she left with Father for the Holy Land, so I remember her well. How I've missed them, and now to discover after these many years that she is still alive and well, and that I have a beautiful sister . . ." He cleared his throat meaningfully. "Please, Leila. Let us enjoy each other's company, at least for a few short weeks."

Leila sighed, looking from Maude to Roger. She was beginning to feel she had been purposely deceived by Lord de Warenne. Her brother didn't appear the evil ogre Guy had made him out to be.

Roger's demeanor had been affable since the moment they met. Most importantly, he hadn't denied outright her request to return to Damascus, as Guy had predicted he would. He had listened patiently to everything she had to say. Guy had been dead wrong, and she felt a sudden rush of resentment that he had tried to mislead her for his own selfish purposes. Her sense of pique at that moment swayed her more to her brother's favor than anything else.

She supposed she could humor Roger, and Maude as well, since he had just virtually assured her that she could leave England in a few weeks. And she was curious to see the Gervais family's ancestral home. It would be interesting to tell Eve about it once she was back in Syria.

"Very well," she murmured, smiling faintly. "I don't see that a couple of weeks' delay will hurt."

"Excellent!" came Roger's quick reply.

"Oh, Leila, I'm so pleased," echoed Maude.

Leila missed the furtive look between them as she glanced uncertainly at her rose-colored kirtle. It was indecent how the silken fabric was molded to her slim figure, giving her the sensation that she was wearing little more than a second skin. Maude's servants had clearly misjudged her proportions. This gown was much too small for her.

"Are you sure I shouldn't wear a surcoat?" she asked, raising her head.

"Heavens, no," Maude exclaimed, "and spoil the line of the gown? You look absolutely ravishing, Leila. Especially with your hair hanging free like that with only the silver circlet as a headdress. We're so proud of your beauty, we want to show you off to everyone!"

Leila felt a niggling unease at such a gushing declaration, but she gave it no more thought as Maude whisked her from the tent. Roger followed close behind with a large retinue of knights who had been waiting outside.

The air was charged with excitement as throngs of people made their way in the gathering dusk toward Westminster Hall, the chaotic procession accompanied by much laughing and good-natured jostling. Everyone seemed to be having such a wonderful time that Leila found it difficult not to become caught up in the high-spirited tumult.

She actually felt a bit adventuresome as their party entered the brightly lit building, the men forging a path for her and Maude to the middle of the hall where they all sat down, Roger on her right and one of his knights on her left.

And why shouldn't she feel lighter of heart when it was only a matter of weeks before she would be on her way home?

Leila was amazed at how quickly the hundreds of richly dressed lords and ladies, court officials, clergy, and what looked to be wealthy merchants and their wives took their places on crude benches among the rows upon rows of white-clothed tables. Everyone was clearly eager for the feast to begin; the din of animated voices and laughter was deafening. And now that people were seated, except for a few stragglers and the scores of scrub-faced servants lining the walls, she had a good view of the raised dais at one end of the cavernous hall—

"Guy . . ." She nearly choked as she spied him seated almost at the center of the head table, and her giddy excitement evaporated.

How strange and surreal everything suddenly became. Here she was sitting beside the man Guy had taken great pains to warn her about while he was up there engrossed in conversation with one of the most beautiful women she had ever seen.

"Who . . . who is that lady?" she asked, seized by sickening jealousy. It was an emotion she had never experienced before and, oh, she didn't like it. It was wretched, horrible, and miserably overwhelming. She hadn't felt like this about Refaiyeh. Why now?

"Eleanor of Castile, wife to Edward," Roger answered. "On the morrow, she will be queen."

Leila felt her cheeks burn from embarrassment. Of course, the queen. How silly of her not to have known, and why should she care anyway? Yet, her mind intoned, thank God . . . thank God.

"That is Lord Edward beside her. The man on Lady Eleanor's right you already know, though I would that it had been any other knight who escorted you to England."

Leila heard the venom in Roger's voice and glanced at him, but he was staring at Guy, a tic working in his stubbled cheek.

She saw it then, the cold hatred reflected in her brother's hard gray-blue eyes; she had seen the same in Guy's gaze whenever he spoke of Roger. She sensed at once that there was probably much truth in what Guy had told her, and her sense of unease returned. But she shoved it away defiantly. Their mutual enmity had nothing to do with her!

"I suppose I should be thankful the bastard managed to bring you here at all," Roger muttered more to himself than to Leila.

"My lord?" she asked, puzzled by his comment, but she received no answer as they were suddenly interrupted by a manservant who stepped between them with a basin of water and clean linen towels slung over his arm. She washed her hands, then Roger did, followed by the silent, swarthy knight seated on her left, to whom she had not yet been introduced.

"Forgive me, d'Eyvill," Roger said to the bearded older man, as if reading her mind and realizing his oversight. "Leila, I'd like you to meet Sir Baldwin d'Eyvill, one of my most trusted knights."

For a moment she was so stunned she could give no reply. Baldwin d'Eyvill! He had been Christine's lover. Guy's poor, unhappy wife had killed herself over this very man. She stared at him, thinking he was attractive in a very dark, rough-hewn way, but hardly the romantic figure she had envisioned as the impetus behind such a sad and drastic act.

"Lady Leila," Baldwin said in a voice marked by deep gruffness. "I am most honored."

"Sir knight." She felt a flush crawl over her cheeks at his direct gaze, and something told her he sensed she knew all about his past indiscretion.

"D'Eyvill just returned from the Holy Land," Roger added. "A half dozen of my men went in my place to represent our family name. I had pressing matters to attend to in Wales which prevented me from joining the crusade."

Funny, Guy had never mentioned to her that any of Roger's knights had been on crusade with Lord Edward. Surely he must have known. Then she shrugged. It mattered naught to her. Offering no comment to Roger's explanation, she looked away, growing uncomfortable under Baldwin's close scrutiny.

Leila kept her hands folded in her lap as thick trenchers of day-old bread were placed before each guest to serve as plates, a strange custom she still found revolting, especially after the stale slices were soiled by various glutinous gravies. She supposed the practice had its value, however, as she had learned from Guy that the trenchers were served to the poor after meals.

Her gaze flew back to the dais, only to find Guy still

deep in conversation with Eleanor. What could they possibly be talking about for so long? But all discourse ceased, the great hall becoming hushed and amazingly silent, when a rotund bishop attired in a mitre and crimson robes stood at the head table to give the grace.

Leila bowed her head, not so much in prayer but to avoid meeting Guy's eyes. She had no idea if he had seen her, but she didn't want to take any chances. As far as she was concerned, their association was finished, and she wanted nothing more to do with him.

Tell that to your heart, Leila, came a gnawing inner voice.

Disturbed by the unbidden thought, she squeezed her eyes shut and forced herself to concentrate on the bishop's stentorian tones as he recited a lengthy prayer. After a resounding "Amen" which was repeated by a thousand voices, the boisterous din began anew until it seemed to ring from the huge rafters overhead.

Leila made a point not to look again at the dais as the feast commenced with a vengeance. Cups and mazers were filled to overflowing with wine and beer, then the first course was carried forth proudly from the palace kitchens, an array of dishes that left her bewildered. She ceased counting the varieties of roasted and heavily sauced meats that passed in front of her—beef; mutton; pork, which she had never tasted until arriving in France, since it was forbidden in Moslem households; a dressed swan, which made her sad; chicken; rabbit; and more.

"Would you like a bit of this dish, Leila?" Roger asked solicitously as a platter of spiced veal swimming in cream gravy was lowered to her eye level by a grinning servant.

"No, thank you, I've plenty already," she said, practically losing her appetite at the sight of so much food. She breathed a sigh of relief as the unappetizing platter was withdrawn.

To think there were going to be four such courses, or so Maude had told her on the way to the hall. And more elaborate banquets in the days to come. It was insane.

She had always counseled her patients in Damascus to eat moderately, one of the basic tenets of her medical

training. She could just imagine the belching and breaking
of digestive wind that would reverberate from the palace
grounds later that night. If she'd had her medicines with
her, she could have made a fortune providing simple an-
tidotes for indigestion.

Soon, Leila, soon, she assured herself, her thoughts
jumping ahead to when she would be treating her patients
again at the Hospital of Nureddine and in wealthy harems.
She was so engrossed in her daydream, staring blindly at
the food heaped high on her trencher, that she scarcely
noticed when Roger and Baldwin suddenly rose from the
table.

"What do you want, de Warenne?"

Leila started at Roger's angry voice. She plopped the
roasted pheasant leg she was holding into a puddle of
brown gravy and twisted around to find Guy standing almost directly behind her, Roger and Baldwin flanking him.
Her mouth flew open in surprise.

How could she have forgotten how truly handsome he
was? she wondered crazily. Her wide gaze quickly took in
every pleasing aspect of his appearance, from the snug fit
of his dark blue tunic across his massive chest, a heavy
gold medallion dangling around his neck, to his polished
black leather boots. Now that he was this close to her, it
seemed everyone else in the hall had fallen away, leaving
only the two of them.

"My lady," Guy greeted her, an appreciative warmth
in his eyes though his expression remained serious. But
the minute he turned back to Roger, the warmth faded.
"Lord Gervais, Lady Eleanor has requested that I accompany your sister to the dais for a personal introduction.
You need have no fear. I shall return the young lady to
your table shortly."

Leila's attention was drawn to Roger as he visibly
tensed, his scarred hand straying to his sword belt. She
glanced back at Guy, who did the same, and for the first
time she noted that they were almost matched in size,
although Roger was perhaps an inch or two shorter. She
thought fleetingly of mythic titans preparing to do battle

and was certain these two knights were their perfect embodiment here on earth.

"You forget, de Warenne. Fear is unknown to me, especially when it comes to you," Roger grated. "If my sister is to be introduced to Lady Eleanor, it is I who shall escort her to the dais. Is that understood?"

"Is there some slight problem here, my lords?"

Leila gasped as Lord Edward strolled casually into their midst.

"Lord de Warenne. Lord Gervais. You are causing a stir among my guests. They are gaping so, their food is assured to grow cold, and then how shall I ever reconcile my cooks who have slaved so long and hard over this wondrous meal? I would prefer you save this display for the tournament field, where it will be much more appreciated and proper wagers may be placed. Are we in agreement?"

"Yes, my lord," Roger muttered.

"As you say," came Guy's terse response.

"Good." Edward turned to Leila, his eyes moving over her in a manner common to all men. Not a leer, just open appreciation, much as Guy had done. "I believe my wife would like to make your acquaintance, my lady." He offered her his arm and she took it, rising dazedly from the bench. Her fingers were trembling from this unexpected attention as she settled her hand in the crook of his elbow. "Leila, isn't it?"

She nodded, nervousness bubbling up within her as she realized the hall was virtually silent, just as it had been in prayer. Except this time no one's head was bowed. The guests were all looking right at her. She was certain her hot cheeks matched the deep rose of her gown.

"A beautiful name for a most enchanting beauty." Edward shot a glance at Roger over his shoulder. "Sit down and enjoy the meal, Lord Gervais, and have your knights do the same. I trust you grant me the right to escort your fair sister?"

"Of course, my lord."

Edward didn't deign a reply. "Lead the way, de Warenne."

Leila kept her eyes focused on Guy's broad back as he

strode toward the dais, not daring to look to the left or right for fear she would find everyone still staring at her. She could not measure her relief when the clamor of conversation began building anew in the hall, but as she overheard bits and pieces along the way she soon realized that she was the topic of furtive discussion.

"Have you ever seen such hair? Like fine watered silk—"

"Aye, a man could find himself ensnared in it easy enough. I'd die for such a fate."

"I've already heard about this wench from one of Gervais's knights. He said she grew up in Damascus among the infidels . . . in a harem!"

"By God, it makes a man hard just thinking about it! All that female flesh, just lying there for the taking . . ."

Leila had never felt so mortified. Was that what these barbarians truly thought? That harems were no more than mere brothels instead of an ordered way of life for a vastly superior civilization? Close to tears, she felt a light squeeze on her arm and met Edward's eyes. They were astonishingly kind.

"Forgive any ignorant and rude remarks on the part of my guests, my lady," he said in a low voice meant for her ears alone. "Though I went to the Holy Land to strike a blow against the infidels, I came away knowing we could learn much from them. My life was once saved by your Arabic medicine, much as you saved Guy's."

She was so startled she could not speak, and she didn't have time to reply, for they had reached the front of the huge hall. In one bewildering instant she was handed over to Guy. He took her arm, the warm pressure of his hand spinning her senses as he led her up the steps and across the dais toward Lady Eleanor, who was smiling in welcome.

"How absolutely lovely," she said, rising from her chair and taking Leila's hands in her own. "Oh, Guy, I can see now why you are so anxious to w—"

"Harumph!" Edward came up behind them, clearing his throat and saying in a low-spoken aside to his wife,

"My dearest Eleanor, you must take care. Remember, things have not yet been settled . . ."

"Ah, yes, forgive me."

Leila saw Eleanor flash Guy a look of apology and caught his wry smile in return. Whatever were they talking about? What things hadn't been settled? Unless . . .

She drew herself up slightly, her flustered nervousness vanishing as indignation reared hotly at her vexing realization.

Bastard! Guy had obviously told them much about her. But had he shared everything . . . what had happened in Provins, in Canterbury? She feared so. She was also convinced from Eleanor's hasty words that they assumed the wedding was as good as done. How preposterous! They couldn't be more wrong.

She felt extremely warm all of a sudden and longed to leave the dais. But she stayed, not wanting to humiliate her brother any further by causing another scene. He had been subtly insulted by Guy and Lord Edward; she could see that now. But for what purpose she could not guess.

"It is a pleasure to meet you, my lady," she murmured, feigning a sweet and gracious tone.

"And I you, dear girl," Lady Eleanor said warmly. "I hope that in the future we will have a chance to get to know each other better."

"I would have liked that, my lady," Leila continued smoothly, her heart beating hard against her breast, "but I don't think it will be possible given the circumstances."

"What circumstances?" Guy queried, a frown appearing on his brow.

"Why, I will be leaving for Damascus at the end of the month, my lord de Warenne. My brother and I spoke this afternoon, and it has all been arranged."

Her revelation was greeted by a soft gasp from Eleanor and dead silence from Guy and Edward, who met each other's eyes.

At last it was done, Leila thought. Now that Guy knew she would be returning home, her long ordeal with him was finally over. There would be no more talk of weddings.

She hazarded another glance at Guy. His face was hard, his gaze even harder as it fell upon her, and she quickly looked away. Strangely, now that she had won she did not feel triumphant as she had imagined she would. She just felt weary and curiously unsettled, her victory like ashes in her mouth.

"If you'll excuse us," Guy said, taking her arm again, more tightly this time. He spoke over her head as if she were a naughty child. "I'll escort the lady back to her table."

"Yes, of course, my lord," Edward replied, a subdued Eleanor granting them no more than a slight nod before she turned away with a troubled expression on her face.

"You're hurting my arm!" Leila hissed as he hustled her from the dais and down the stairs, her gaze darting around the raucous hall. The second course was being passed around with much fanfare among the guests, distracting most of them from recognizing her discomfort.

"Are you always so rude to people who show you kindness?" Guy hissed back angrily. "A queen offering you her friendship, no less!"

"It was not my intention to be rude. I was only speaking the truth!"

"You are blind to the truth, Leila. You won't know it until it slaps you hard across the face, and maybe even then you won't admit it. For an intelligent woman, you are playing the fool remarkably well!"

She wanted to retort, but they were nearing her brother's table. From Roger's hard glare she imagined he hadn't taken his eyes from her since Lord Edward had led her away. Maude looked none too happy, either. There was a coldness in her eyes that chilled Leila to the bone. Strangely, it was not so much directed at Guy as at her. But why would that be?

"Take care, my love," came Guy's cryptic warning just before they reached the table. "You tread within a pit of vipers. If you allow yourself to be bitten, even I may not be able to save you, though I pray to God we're both spared such agony. Just remember what I told you in Canterbury.'' Then he raised his voice, addressing Roger. ''My lord Gervais, it seems your sister has charmed the court.''

''So I see,'' Roger said, his gaze moving slowly from Leila's flushed face to Guy's. ''So I see.''

''My lady. Enjoy the feast.''

Leila watched as Guy strode away, only turning her head when Roger touched her arm.

''Stay away from him, Leila. Suffice it to say he is my greatest enemy. That makes him yours as well.''

A shiver raced up her spine at his harsh voice, but she answered him steadily, ''I fully intend to, my lord.''

Chapter 18

It did not prove difficult to avoid Guy the next day. Leila scarcely saw him.

During the lengthy coronation ceremony she was seated in the back of the congested abbey with her brother and his wife, their poor location barely affording her a view of the glittering pomp and circumstance taking place in front of the distant altar, let alone a glimpse of Guy. Not that she was looking for him. She wasn't.

By chance she did spy him later in the long train of sumptuously dressed nobles, ladies, and knights who filed out of the cathedral after the newly crowned King Edward and Queen Eleanor. Guy stood a good head taller than anyone else around him and looked devastatingly handsome in a tunic of forest green and gold. She quickly feigned interest in the stained glass windows to her right until he had passed, her cheeks hot and her heart fluttering because she sensed he had seen her, too.

The feasting and revelry that followed the coronation was on a much grander scale than the feast of the night before, and with twice as many guests crammed into the great hall. She noted at once that Guy was not seated on the raised dais, but there were so many people still milling about when their party found a table that she had no clue as to where he might be. She tried to give him little thought after that, which for some reason proved virtually impossible.

She was astounded at the inscribed menu placed in the center of the table promising hundreds of oxen, cows, sheep, and pigs, sixteen fat boars, and thousands of capons and other poultry. But even more surprising was the aqueduct that had been erected overnight down the middle of the hall and poured forth both red and white wine for everyone to drink. The guests gathered around like greedy pigs at a trough, draining their goblets as quickly as they could fill them.

As the coronation feast progressed there was such a constant swirl of bustling servants, jesters on painted hobby horses, jugglers, acrobats, players reciting poems, harpers, and minstrels that the room soon spun around Leila in a wild kaleidoscope of color, sound, and motion. She began to feel overwhelmingly dizzy. Perhaps it was because the food was too rich, the wine too sweet, or the hall too warm. Smoking torches and acrid smelling candles were ablaze everywhere, despite the beautiful autumn afternoon outside.

"You look pale, Leila," came her brother's voice through the melee, sounding like a dull echo in her head. "Is something wrong?"

She looked at him, but his face was blurred. She tried to speak, but her tongue would not work. The last thing she remembered was Maude screaming, then blackness.

Leila's eyes fluttered open and her vision gradually focused.

Where was she? In Westminster Hall? No, surely not. It was cool here and there were no bright lights, no smelly foods, no loud music or raucous laughter, just that female voice carrying over to her . . .

"We cannot afford to return to Wales with her now and continue deceiving her while we wait for a better offer, my husband. One fainting spell does not prove a woman is breeding, but dare we risk losing everything on the chance she isn't carrying de Warenne's bastard?"

Leila tensed as she recognized the voice as Maude's. Suddenly her surroundings seemed to snap into sharp relief and she realized she was in her brother's tent.

She saw them then, sitting together at a trestle table in the corner not far from her cot. With apprehension filling her heart, she closed her eyes and lay very still, listening intently. She started when Roger brought his fist down violently on the table, then she froze again, hoping they had not seen her movement.

"I should kill Guy for this! You saw how he came running after me when I carried Leila from the hall. I've never seen such a stricken look on his face, not even for Christine. If that does not prove there has been something between them, whether Leila shares his fantasy or not—"

"All the more reason why we cannot wait, my lord. Even now he may be considering a suit for her hand. Remember what we saw at the feast last night. De Warenne had eyes for no one but her."

"Only over my corpse will he marry her."

"You know the law, husband. If Leila gives her consent, we will have no choice but to allow such a union."

"So she must never be given the chance to even entertain the thought."

"Exactly. I say we wed her to that London merchant, Wellesley, who approached you last night after the feast, and the sooner the better. Tonight, even! If Leila does prove to be breeding, he'll think it's his own brat she carries. So what if he gets a surprise eight months later. He won't dare renounce her then, but will accept the child as his own or forgo the reason he paid so dearly for her in the first place. Having a titled wife is very good for business."

Listening, Leila felt so sick she thought she might retch, Roger's assurances of the day before shattered into a thousand pieces.

Sweet Jesu, Guy had been right about him all along. What a complete fool she had been!

Roger had lied to her. He had no intention of allowing her to return to Damascus. He was going to sell her off in marriage just as Guy had said he would. Maybe tonight! And all because they thought she might be pregnant with Guy's child—

"Stay here with her, Maude. I'm going back to the hall to find Wellesley. We'll fetch a priest and have done with this marriage by sunset. God, just think of it. No more

debts to the king''—his voice grew bitter—''no more selling myself and my knights out to fight in any baron's petty
war for fear I may lose the land on which I was born. The
Gervais name will be great once again . . . and all because a soft-hearted whore in Damascus saw fit to bless
me with a sister.''

Leila was so horrified she could not breathe. Whore!
Was that what Roger thought of their mother? Hearing his
footsteps approach the cot, she went limp, praying that all
her years of observing sick patients would enable her to
feign unconsciousness.

''This wench is as much a whore as her mother, that
lover of infidels back in Damascus. How could she be
anything less? Raised in a harem . . . wanting to return to
Syria to marry some bloody heathen physician. It's almost
comical.''

''What is, my lord?'' Maude asked, walking up beside
him.

''The idea of Guy caring for this wench. Knowing him,
I wager he rutted on her the whole way to England and
now fancies himself in love with her. Yet all along she's
been saying she wants to go back to Damascus. I hope
he's suffering hell's own torments.'' His voice grew very
quiet. ''Soon he'll know exactly how it feels to have a
woman stolen right out from under him. It's been a long,
long time in coming.''

''But you have me, my lord,'' Leila heard Maude say
petulantly, accompanied by the rustling of clothing. ''You
don't need memories, not when I can do this.''

''You're right. I don't,'' Roger replied huskily a few
minutes later, groaning deep in his throat. ''Lie down.''

''Here . . . on the ground?''

''Why not?''

''But what if she should wake?''

Leila knew they were looking right at her. She continued to breathe steadily though her pulse was racing madly.

''She's out cold, Maude. Can't you see that?''

Disgusted, Leila heard his grunt as he knelt, followed
by Maude's throaty laughter as he pulled her roughly to
the ground and fell on top of her. How she wished she

could plug her ears against the crude panting and squeals of their lovemaking! From Roger's hard exhalation of breath, she knew he had quickly climaxed, and from Maude's wail of disappointment, she knew her sister-in-law had not.

"Oh, Roger, it was too soon! Too fast!"

Maude's heavy sigh and the subsequent silence told Leila even more. Roger didn't care in the least that he had not pleased her; he had probably quelled her outburst with a dark and threatening look. Leila listened as he rose to his feet and adjusted his clothing, then hoisted up his wife.

"If Leila wakes while I'm gone, see that she stays in bed. I'll speak with her when I get back."

"She'll probably protest—"

"I expect it. My answer will be the same as it would have been in Wales. When she hears what I have in store for her if she refuses, she'll give her consent to the marriage readily enough. To be locked in a convent cell is a sorry fate for any beautiful young woman, even more so when she can expect to be flogged twice daily for her sins."

As they stepped away, Leila heard Maude's tone brighten sickeningly. "Oooh, you know how much I enjoy a good paddling, my lord, and giving one as well. Perhaps tonight we might celebrate our good fortune by . . ."

Leila was glad the rest of her sister-in-law's words were lost to her as they moved outside the tent. She shuddered as she raised herself on one elbow, her gaze flitting around the shadowed interior for any means of escape.

In the harem she had heard of men like Roger, men capable of only cruel, depraved relationships with women because of some romantic slight suffered in the past. At that moment she almost pitied Maude, because for whatever reason her sister-in-law had obviously chosen to accept it. Who knew? Maybe Maude even loved Roger.

Leila barely lay down in time when Maude suddenly threw aside the flap and stepped back into the tent. Roger must have said something to appease her for she was humming, her dissatisfaction clearly vanished.

How was she ever going to get out of here? Leila wondered desperately, listening as Maude poured water into a basin and began to wash herself.

She couldn't dash out the only entrance to the tent. Several of Gervais's men-at-arms were standing guard right outside. And the tent had appeared to be securely staked down on all sides. Maybe there was the slightest chance she could squeeze under one of the tent walls, but Maude would surely sound an alarm and send Roger's men chasing after her. Yet she couldn't just lie here and wait helplessly for Roger to return with the priest and that accursed merchant.

Leila opened one eye slightly and discovered that her sister-in-law was standing about twenty feet away with her back turned. Maybe, just maybe, if she was quiet enough . . .

As Maude's singing grew louder, Leila slipped from the cot, yanking her silver tunic and chainse up around her thighs, and crawled on hands and knees to the tent wall. Glancing constantly over her shoulder, she groped along the ground, trying to find a place where she could lift the tent enough to slide beneath it. She was almost ready to give up and opt for a mad dash through the front entrance when her forearm disappeared easily under a loose section of canvas.

Holding her breath, she began to lift the tent wall just as she heard Maude gasp in surprise. She turned to find her sister-in-law hurrying toward her with pure fury on her face.

"You little bitch! Stop, I tell you!"

Her heart thumping furiously, Leila dove under the tent wall, but to her dismay, she felt Maude catch her ankle. Her sister-in-law's enraged screams filled the air.

"She's escaping! Guards! Quick, go around to the other side. Catch her! I don't think I can hold her—"

"Let go of me!" Leila shouted, giving Maude a sharp kick.

In the next instant she was free and scrambling to her feet, except now she couldn't see a thing. Her hair had fallen over her face. Swiping it away, she lunged forward and broke into a run . . . and slammed right into something very hard.

"No! Let go! Let go!" she screamed, punching her captor in the stomach with her balled fists. Her teeth fairly rattled in her jaw as she was shaken roughly, her head jerking back. She found herself staring into a pair of familiar blue eyes. Such relief swamped her that she almost collapsed. Guy!

"Stand behind me. Now!" he commanded, shoving her back several feet as five men-at-arms came tearing around the tent, brandishing their swords.

Shaking her head in horror, Leila kept backing away until she hit the taut wall of another tent and almost fell. She watched as Guy drew his sword and faced his opponents, who had stopped short and were eyeing him warily.

"Come on if you dare," he taunted harshly, shifting his feet to better his stance. The gleaming blade whistled as he sliced the air.

"We have no quarrel with you, de Warenne," spoke up one of the men. "We only want the woman."

"And I say you shall not have her. Allow us to retreat in peace or I shall strike down every last one of you."

The men-at-arms glanced at each other, clearly uncertain. Matters were not improved when Maude limped around the corner on a swollen ankle, her face twisted in anger as she shouted out shrill orders.

"Cut him down! He's only one to your five. What are you? Cowards?"

Capitalizing on their indecision, Guy stepped backward, keeping his eyes on the men-at-arms while he held out his free hand to Leila.

"Take my hand. Walk quickly and be ready to move out of the way if I tell you to. Is that understood?"

"Y-yes."

"Good." He spoke again to the five men, who were venturing a few hesitant steps closer. "Follow us and I swear you will die."

The men-at-arms immediately froze, then began to retreat, sheathing their swords.

"What are you doing? They're getting away! Stop them! Stop them!"

Maude's screams faded into the distance as Guy kept Leila moving at a brisk pace away from the tents set up around Tothill Fields and toward the towering abbey.

"You were right there, beside my brother's tent. How?" she finally asked breathlessly, hurrying beside him.

"I was worried about you and I couldn't stand wondering about it any longer. I was coming to see how you were, no matter what Roger might have to say about it." He threw her a half smile. "When I saw you clambering beneath the tent, I knew you were feeling better. Much better."

Leila felt a curious pleasure to learn that he had been concerned for her, but she forgot it when another question pressed in upon her. "Where are we going?"

"To the cathedral. To get married."

Looking up at him in disbelief, Leila tried to stop, but he jerked her along, his large hand gripping hers tightly.

"I take it you have somehow discovered the truth about your brother and his lovely wife. Is that not correct?"

"Yes, yes, it is, but that does not mean—"

Guy halted so abruptly that Leila's arm was wrenched in its socket. His smile was gone, his expression dead serious.

"What does it mean, then, my lady? You had better make up your mind very quickly, for I'm sure Maude is on her way to find Roger at this moment. Either accept my offer of marriage, or find yourself back in their custody and a victim to whatever they have planned for you. If it was enough to drive you from their tent like a frightened animal, it cannot be pleasant. Now choose. It's as simple as that."

Leila glanced fearfully toward Westminster Hall, then back at Guy. "You are forcing me as much as they!"

"Perhaps. You're wasting precious time, Leila. Choose."

"You know I hate you! I will always hate you for what you've done to me. Always!"

"We shall see."

Her heart seemed to skip a beat at his words, but she continued to glare at him, chewing her lower lip.

She could not go back to her brother. She would rather die first. Marrying Guy de Warenne was her only way out of this terrible predicament.

That doesn't mean I have given up on seeing my home again, Leila assured herself. It only means I have bought myself more time. Time to think. Time to plan.

"Very well, Lord de Warenne. I shall marry you."

Joy lit his eyes, mixed with unmistakable relief, but all he said was, "Practice those words for the priest, my love. We must hurry."

"But won't I need Roger's consent as my guardian?"

"No, thank God. The Church deems such consent unnecessary for anyone older than fifteen. Come."

The next thing Leila knew they were running beside the cathedral's massive buttressed walls and then up the marble steps and into the cool, shadowed narthex.

"You there, stop!" Guy commanded a somberly clad cleric who was preparing to exit from another door.

"Me, my lord?"

"Yes." Still holding firmly to Leila's hand, Guy rushed with her up to the startled priest. "Are there other clergy in the cathedral, or has everyone gone to the feast?"

"There are a few others, my lord. You'll find them praying near the altar."

"Excellent. I want you to take this"—he drew the heavy gold medallion over his head and handed it to the man—"to King Edward."

The priest's eyes grew wide. "The king?"

"Yes. Tell him Lord de Warenne and his new wife, Lady Leila, have sought refuge in the abbey and are waiting for him in the right transept behind the altar. Do you have that?"

"Yes, yes. The right transept."

"Good. And tell him to please hurry, or blood is sure to be spilled on his coronation day. He will understand." Guy took the man none too gently by the arm and steered him to the open door. "Now go. Run!"

The priest did just that, his brown robes billowing behind him and his sandals clattering as he flew down the steps.

"Come." Guy's strides were so long as he hurried down the wide center aisle that Leila practically had to run to keep up with him. Several priests kneeling at the altar turned their heads and peered curiously over their shoulders as they approached.

"I need one of you to perform a wedding ceremony. The rest of you must serve as our witnesses."

Panting for breath, Leila swallowed hard as the three priests glanced at one another, then seemed to rise in unison. It was clear they were taking the urgency in Guy's voice very seriously. One of them, a tall, spare man, came forward and looked closely at Guy with pale blue eyes.

"I know you, my lord. Lord de Warenne, is it not?"

"Yes, and this is Lady Leila Gervais. We have come to be married."

The priest studied Leila's flushed cheeks thoughtfully. "Have you given your consent to this marriage, my lady?" he asked pointedly, holding up his blue-veined hand as Guy almost answered for her.

Leila hesitated until she felt a very hard squeeze on her fingers. She did her best not to wince. "Yes, Father. I have consented."

"Then come forward, my children."

Guy sensed Leila's tension as he led her to the altar where they knelt before the priest. Her small hand was shaking in his. As they recited their vows, she refused to meet his eyes, but when he firmly intoned "I will," after the priest, she glanced at him. Her gaze was stubbornly defiant, but there was a curious softness to her expression that made his heart thunder in his chest. How he loved this woman!

The momentary spell was broken when the priest bid them to rise. Their union was scarcely blessed when Guy heard Roger's angry voice carrying to them from the cathedral steps.

"Come with me, Leila. Quickly," Guy urged. To the priest he said with quiet vehemence, "Hold them off for as long as you can, Father. Our lives may depend upon it.''

The astonished clergyman nodded, but before he could ask any questions, Guy had swept Leila past the altar and into the right transept. He did not stop until they reached the far, shadowed corner. Drawing his sword, he pushed her behind him, blocking her with his body as the sounds of tramping feet and chinking armor grew louder.

''Where are they?''

Roger's furious query echoed ominously from the lofty arched ceiling, causing Guy to tense. He glanced over his shoulder at Leila, huddled in the corner. Her amethyst eyes were wide and frightened; he had never seen her look so vulnerable. His beautiful, proud, and reluctant bride was trembling from head to toe.

Guy held his finger to his lips, commanding her silence as Roger's voice rang out again.

''Speak up, man! Where are they? Believe me, I would not hesitate to use my sword on a priest if I felt it necessary.''

''And I, sir, demand that you and your men sheathe your swords at once in God's house! You defile its sanctity with your armed presence and vile threats—''

''Get out of my way!''

Guy grimaced, hoping the pained cry he heard meant the priest had only been shoved to the floor and not skewered.

''Search the entire building, even the catacombs. Find them! I know they are here. My wife swore she saw them running toward the abbey.''

Guy spun, gesturing for Leila to duck behind the last wooden pew. He crouched next to her, holding his sword at the ready, scarcely breathing.

He knew it was only a matter of minutes before they were found out. That fact wouldn't have seriously concerned him if he wasn't so outnumbered. It sounded as if Roger had brought to the abbey all twenty knights who had accompanied him to the coronation, as well as his men-at-arms. Fighting all of them would be impossible, but he would at least try to hold them off until Edward arrived to put an end to the carnage.

God's blood, what a way for them to spend their first moments as man and wife! There hadn't even been time for a kiss or an embrace.

He sucked in his breath slowly and tightened his grip on his sword as two pairs of footfalls drew closer, closer . . .

"My lord Gervais! They are here—"

Guy jumped up from behind the pew and slashed at the nearest knight who had sounded the alarm. The man went down, screaming in pain as he held his bleeding arm, and the other knight soon followed, injured more severely across the stomach.

"Stay where you are, Leila. Don't move!" Guy shouted, stepping over the injured men as a dozen of Gervais's knights and men-at-arms all seemed to descend upon him at once. They halted in a tight semicircle as Guy swung his sword viciously, holding them at bay.

"You're outnumbered, de Warenne. Put down your sword," came Roger's terse command as his knights stepped back to allow him to pass. Then they closed ranks against him, a jagged line of deadly weapons aimed directly at Guy's chest. "You'd be a fool not to."

"You're the fool if you think I would ever lay down my sword, Gervais, especially at your suggestion."

Roger took a step forward, his mouth a sneer as his cold blue eyes found Leila. "So, my sister. You were not unconscious after all. I should have guessed you were accomplished enough at your healer's trade to mimic a lengthy swoon. I suppose you heard everything—"

"You don't have to answer him, Leila," Guy interrupted, stepping protectively backward. He hoped she would restrain her sharp tongue, if only not to goad Roger's rage. He was gratified when she kept silent; she was probably too frightened to speak.

"I take it we are too late to prevent a marriage."

"That you are, my lord," Guy stated derisively. "Leila gave her consent, and she is now my wife."

"Is this true, dearest sister?"

"Yes," Leila answered in a small voice, trembling as

she had never done in her life. Roger was glaring at Guy with such hatred, she seemed to be witnessing the incarnation of pure evil.

"How ill-advised. You two men, seize her!"

Leila screamed as two knights lunged at her at the same moment that Roger's sword came singing through the air, directly at Guy's throat. She saw him dodge just in time, but he fell to his knees and gasped aloud in pain, and she knew with a horrible sinking feeling that he had been struck. Then she saw no more as he was swiftly encircled.

"No! Stop it! Please don't hurt him anymore!" she shouted desperately, her anguished cries echoing through the transept. Overcome by the horror of what was happening, she struggled like a captured animal as Roger's men roughly pinioned her arms.

"Cease this madness! In the name of Edward the king!"

Through dimmed eyes, Leila saw a sudden flurry of activity as Roger and his men spun around to face two score of armed knights led by Edward, who held a jeweled dress sword high above his head. Her two captors suddenly released her and she sank to the cold floor, sobbing. She could not have been more stunned when Guy broke through the ring of his opponents and lifted her into his arms. He crushed her to him, soothing her with whispered words.

"It is all right, my love. You are safe. We are safe."

"But . . . but Roger struck you. I saw it."

"Only a slight flesh wound, Leila. Merely a scratch. A small bandage and I will be as good as new."

Leila buried her face against his shoulder, overwhelmed by incredible relief. She would never have anticipated the intensity of her emotion, and she did not understand it in the least. It was hardly what she should be feeling toward a man she had insisted she hated only a half hour before.

"Lower your weapons, all of you!" came Edward's sharp command. He gestured for his own men to surround the ashen-faced offenders, who quickly complied with the king's order. Edward began to walk slowly toward Roger, his expression grave as he took in the bloody scene before him. He stopped directly in front of him. "Explain your actions, Lord Gervais."

Leila watched her brother's wide shoulders draw back proudly, his posture unrelenting even as he faced his king.

"I was protecting what was mine, sire. Lord de Warenne has seen fit to wed my sister without first seeking my counsel in the matter. I demand that this marriage be annulled at once, before any consummation"—he spat the word—"may occur."

"How do you answer this charge, Lord de Warenne?"

"Lord Gervais's counsel was not needed, Your Majesty. The lady gave her consent, which is all that is required by law. As for consummation, this marriage has already been consummated in the eyes of God. On that day I swore that I would take this woman for my wife. So it has been done."

Leila gasped at his open admission of their carnal relations before so many men and lowered her eyes in shame.

"If proof that I have taken the lady's virginity is required, sire, I have it," he continued solemnly. "My knights, Sir Burnell and Sir Langton, serve as my witnesses that a bedding occurred."

"Virgin, my ass," Roger muttered. "Whore is more like it."

"Silence!" Edward demanded. "How dare you further desecrate this holy place with your foul profanity?" He drew a deep breath, his voice still stern when he addressed Leila, though it held a note of gentleness.

"How say you to all of this, my lady? Did you consent willingly to this marriage?"

Leila did not raise her head, the cathedral suddenly grown so quiet she could swear she heard her heart pounding in her breast like a battle drum.

"Yes." At her affirmation, Guy's arms tightened fiercely around her.

"So be it." Edward turned back to Roger. "My lord Gervais, I could banish you from my court for the havoc you have wreaked today, but I will refrain from such punishment out of respect for the occasion which has drawn us all here to Westminster. But know this. If you cause any more rash disturbances or harass Lord and Lady de Warenne in any way, I will have your hide on a spit." He glanced with disgust at the groaning, wounded men lying on the floor. "Get them out of here."

Roger and his men silently obeyed. Edward waited until they were retreating down the main aisle with the two injured knights before he spoke again.

"Your arm, de Warenne. Does it need medical attention?"

Guy looked down at Leila and wished desperately that they were alone so he could wipe the tears from her face. "No, sire. I'm sure my wife will tend to it quite ably."

"Indeed. Then let us walk back to the feast, shall we? We'll have water, ointment, and bandages brought, anything you need."

"Thank you, sire. I am in your debt."

With a thin smile on his lips, Edward drew close and settled a glinting gold medallion around Guy's neck.

"No trouble, my lord. I'd wager this added excitement has only made the occasion that much more memorable for all of us, yes?"

Guy's throat was so constricted with a hitherto unknown depth of emotion, he did not trust himself to answer. Instead he tenderly kissed the crown of Leila's head, holding her close against his heart as he followed Edward from the bloody transept.

Chapter 19

"**D**o you like the room, Leila?" Guy toyed absently with his medallion, waiting for her answer, which was long in coming.

It was all he could do not to walk over to the window and capture her in his arms, she was so bewitchingly beautiful with her ebony hair streaming like a silken waterfall down her back and her silvery tunic clinging to her body so provocatively. But he willed himself to remain seated. He was determined to move very slowly with her this evening.

It was their wedding night. The night he had not expected for days, maybe weeks. It was still hard for him to believe that Leila was actually his wife.

It was the night which would set the tone for countless others to come. He wanted it to be special for both of them . . . no small task.

Leila had been coolly distant since they had returned to the coronation feast, scarcely speaking except when spoken to, and now, hours later, she was still aloof, almost as if she were resolved to keep herself tightly in check. He could also sense her nervousness, though she was trying hard not to show it. He knew her well enough to recognize the defiant jut of her chin as a sign of stubbornness, and a good measure of apprehension.

He was glad he had managed to dissuade his knights and Eleanor's ladies-in-waiting from the traditional bedding ceremony. Having a crowd of observers cramming into their chamber, he and Leila stripped naked before them and ensconced in their nuptial bed, would have unsettled her entirely. No, he wanted to do things at his own pace and in his own way.

He would have to be endlessly patient with her and infinitely caring, no matter how she might try to goad him to anger. He wanted to please her, to make her laugh and smile as she had that afternoon on the Rhone. He wanted to make up for all the unhappiness she had known since she was unwillingly wrested from her home.

He wanted her to see that she could find happiness with him, and love, if she would only open up her heart and allow him to enter. He would relinquish everything he possessed to hear her say those three simple words: I love you. He would not give up until she did. So he had silently vowed when the priest pronounced them man and wife.

Guy sighed softly when still Leila did not reply to his earlier question. Finally he spoke.

"My cousin, the earl of Surrey, and his wife were most gracious to exchange this room for my smaller one, don't you think?"

Leila cast him a wary glance. Her breath snagged in her throat at the sight of him sitting so casually in that high-backed chair, one sinewed leg slung over the low armrest, his gold medallion reflecting the flickering candlelight as he dangled it between his fingers. Yet the tension she sensed in him belied his relaxed posture. She purposely avoided his eyes and skipped her gaze to the embroidered tapestry on the wall behind him, a colorful yet disturbing scene of a wounded unicorn surrounded by hunters and baying hounds.

Even the tapestry proved too much for her. Gripped by uneasiness, she turned back to the window and stared outside at the ink-black night.

That was exactly how she felt right now. Hunted, like that unicorn. And Guy was both the hunter aiming his arrow and the hound snapping at her heels.

Oh, why had she ever agreed to marry him? She could have wed that London merchant, stolen his money, and escaped on horseback to Dover long before it would have ever come to sharing a bedchamber. Why hadn't she had her wits about her enough in Roger's tent to think of such a plan, or when Guy demanded she choose? Fool!

"Leila, why won't you talk to me?"

She started but did not turn from the window. "I have little to say, my lord. I am very tired."

"Fair enough. Then why don't you ready yourself for bed."

She gasped softly and met his eyes. There was no guile in them, although he was looking at her quite intently, half of his handsome face masked by shadows. Could she hope he had no plans to . . . ?

"I'm tired myself," he said, swinging his leg from the armrest and kicking off his boots. "It's been a most eventful day, and tomorrow's tournament will come soon enough."

Eventful day! That was an understatement, Leila thought, watching as he stood and unfastened his sword belt, dropping it on the chair with a clanking thud, along with his medallion. When he began to strip out of his tunic, she lowered her eyes, her heart thumping, and hurried to the far side of the bed where she drew the blue damask curtains. Thank God she would at least have some privacy while she undressed.

She noted a familiar saddle bag propped against the bedpost and realized someone must have been sent to retrieve her belongings from Roger's tent. With trembling fingers she slipped out of the tunic Maude had had cut down for her and then her chainse, both of which were somewhat soiled from her escapade that afternoon. She rolled down the gauzy white stockings which were hopelessly beyond repair, with huge holes at the knees.

Anxious that Guy might come around the bed and find her naked, Leila quickly drew on her white linen nightrail. Though the fabric was thin, it was a plain, unassuming garment, and for that she was grateful. She brushed her hair and braided it loosely, then blew out the two candles on the ornately carved table against the wall, plunging her side of the room into darkness.

Her courage seemed to evaporate with the light, and she

hesitated by the table, her fingers gripping the smooth edge. The last time they had shared a bed was—

Leila inclined her head slightly at the sound of Guy climbing beneath the covers, her cheeks growing as hot as the tingling flush racing through her body. Oh dear . . . oh dear.

"Leila?"

She inhaled sharply, saying nothing.

"Leila, come to bed."

She wanted desperately to flee, but knew he would catch her easily before she even reached the door. And that game of cat and mouse might only fire his lust. Perhaps if she simply went to bed, she would find him as tired as he said he was. It *had* been a very long day.

Leila moved silently to the curtains, her hands shaking as she reached up and drew them aside. Soft, golden light from a oil lamp burning on an opposite table illuminated the bed and the reclining giant whose deep blue eyes caught and held hers.

"I was beginning to think I might have to come out and get you, my love."

Oh, why did he have to call her that? Leila wondered uncomfortably, stunned by the virile picture Guy made. Why did he have to look like any woman's wildest fantasy come to life?

Guy was leaning against a brace of pillows with the covers thrown over his hips, his skin showing dark against the white sheets. By some trick of shadow and light, the muscles banding his chest and stomach were accentuated to perfection, and his arms looked supremely powerful even at rest. His long hair was swept back from his forehead, brushing shoulders that were wide and immense, the right one marred by a long, raised scar. Below it, his massive bicep was encircled by a bandage that showed a streak of blood.

"I should look at your arm again," she said without thinking, her instinctive concern honed by years of training.

"My arm is fine, Leila. Come. The room grows cold. You will catch a chill standing there."

She saw the hand he offered her, but she nervously chose to ignore it as she swiftly climbed into the bed and lay down with her back to him. Pulling the covers up to her ear, she settled herself as close as possible to the edge of the mattress, so close, in fact, that if she moved any farther she would tumble to the floor.

Guy had to stifle the chuckle welling deep in his chest.

"If you plan on sleeping like that tonight, Leila, I would take care not to dangle your arm over the side. Lady Eleanor was telling me last night that they're having a terrible problem with mice in the palace . . . maybe even rats."

Leila rolled over, her eyes wide. "Rats?"

Guy nodded gravely, feeling that same chuckle trying to force itself from his throat. But he sobered when she seemed equally disturbed about the yawning space between them. She glanced uncertainly from the bed to him.

Sweet Jesu, why did she fear him so? Or was it more a fear of the desire he had seen smoldering in her eyes when she opened the curtains . . . desire she was still fighting?

He was gratified when she suddenly slid closer to his side of the bed, though she maintained a foot's distance between them and turned her back to him again.

"Good night, my lord."

No, my reluctant love, the time to sleep is not yet, Guy thought resolutely. He rolled onto his side and swept her against his body in one fluid motion.

Leila gasped and stiffened, but to his surprise she did not struggle. "You—you said you were tired. What are you doing?" she demanded, peering at him over her shoulder.

"Is there anything wrong with a man holding his lovely new wife?" Guy countered with a slight smile.

Leila wanted to scream out a resounding "Yes!" but instead she decided it would be best not to resist him. If she lay very still and very quiet, surely he would soon fall asleep, thinking she was doing the same. "I suppose not."

She drew in her breath sharply as his large hand slid slowly down the side of her body, stopping at her thigh. He had said holding, not caressing! But when his hand rested there, she relaxed somewhat and feigned a wide yawn for his benefit. She hoped that now that Guy was comfortable, he would leave her in peace.

Leila closed her eyes and snuggled her cheek almost defiantly into the pillow. As for herself, comfortable she was not. Every fiber of her being was alive to the heady warmth of his skin burning through her nightrail. The hard planes and contours of his body were molded against her in a most disturbing way: his chest and taut belly pressed into her back, his lean hips melded to hers, a rigid swelling against her bottom . . .

Leila's eyes flew open and she tried to lunge away from him, even as his arm clamped tightly around her waist, holding her captive.

"No! Release me this instant," she exclaimed. She struggled hard now, fearing the import of his arousal. "You lied to me! You led me to believe you wanted to sleep, not to . . . to . . ." She could not bring herself to say it.

"Shhh, Leila, do not fight me," Guy murmured, his warm breath finding a ticklish place beneath her earlobe. "I have not deceived you. You have deceived only yourself. Surely you know a man and woman sleep little on their wedding night. There is too much love to be shared."

"I don't love you!"

"Ah, but I love you," he said huskily. "More than life itself. That gives me plenty to share with you until the day you admit you love me, too."

"That day will never come—"

"It will!" Guy insisted passionately as he gently but firmly drew her chin around to face him. He caressed her jaw and throat, his eyes searing hers with unflagging conviction. "It will."

Leila gasped as his mouth came down on hers, his kiss so achingly tender that she felt it all the way to her toes. His lips were startlingly warm and he pressed lightly, as if savoring the taste of her. His tongue felt like velvet when he flicked it across her wet lips, then he parted them and probed deeper, his kiss becoming rough as he stroked her inner softness.

His kisses went on and on for long breathless moments,

growing so demanding, so irresistible she could not help but respond with equal fervor. She scarcely realized she had fallen back onto the mattress until he lifted his head. She was facing upward and staring dazedly into his eyes, her arms wrapped around his neck.

"I want to know everything about you, Leila," he said ardently, caressing her cheek. "Everything. You are a wondrous mystery to me, like that brightest star in the heavens. I want to know what makes you smile, what makes you laugh"—he seized her mouth in another deep, prolonged kiss, breathing his next words against her parted lips when he pulled away briefly—"what makes you moan and writhe in pleasure."

Leila was so dizzy from his impassioned kisses that she did not protest when his hand slipped under her nightrail and glided slowly up her leg. His touch was whisper light, his fingertips just grazing the curved line of her hip before sweeping upward across her belly to the rose-scented hollow between her breasts. She sighed aloud when he cupped a firm mound and squeezed gently.

"So you like it when I do this," Guy murmured, trailing his tongue down her throat as he ran his roughened palm across a sensitive tip, back and forth, back and forth, until she thought she might surely scream. "Tell me, Leila. Tell me if you like it. I want to know."

"Yes," she breathed, tossing her head. "Yes!"

"Then I'm sure you will enjoy this even more."

Leila's eyes grew wide as he suddenly flung back the covers and brought himself up on his knees beside her. Then taking the thin fabric of her nightrail in both his hands, he ripped it in two. As her delicately limbed body was bared to his gaze, he straddled her with strong, muscled thighs the size of her waist and bent over her breasts, flicking a taut, rosy nipple with his tongue.

"How do you like this, my beautiful love?" he asked huskily, circling first one aureole, then the other, with what felt like a wet ring of fire. His caresses were no longer gentle but fierce and possessive.

Leila could not answer, her throat was so constricted with pleasure. She had already surrendered to the sensual power he wielded over her. All she wanted now was for him to continue what he was doing to her . . . to feed the sweet madness that was escalating inside her like a fever.

As he covered a tingling nipple with his mouth, drawing upon it hungrily, incredible flashes of heated sensation surged through her, and she pressed her hands against his thighs, her fingers splaying spasmodically against skin and corded muscle. She thought fleetingly of his hard arousal so close within her reach and was tempted to caress and stroke him as she had been taught. But something deep inside her forbade the wanton impulse. A tiny inner voice told her she must hold some small part of herself back from this man who had taken everything from her.

The voice was suddenly silenced, Leila's thoughts scattering when Guy spread her legs wide and knelt between them. His lips forged a fiery path along the soft undersides of her breasts and then down her taut belly.

"I know what will please you, my lady wife," he whispered hoarsely, his tongue dipping into her navel. When she arched in delicious surprise, moaning softly, he raised his head and smiled roguishly at her, his eyes stained dark blue with passion. With a low growl of laughter, he licked a sensuous trail to the downy black hair at the juncture of her thighs.

Leila cried out as he cupped her buttocks and lifted her to his mouth, his panting breath as hot as his tongue which speared into her. She clutched the sheets, her thighs tensing in excitement, wholly overcome by his wet, thrusting assault. An intense pressure was building inside her, radiating from the tiny swollen bud where he teased her so relentlessly.

"No more, please . . . It is too much," she begged him almost incoherently, bucking and twisting. She pushed frantically at his shoulders, her nails leaving red scratches. "Please . . ."

Guy ignored her cries, pressing further into her warm, seductive fragrance. Her taste intoxicated him, exciting him beyond measure. It was all he could do to contain his own burning desire, yet he wanted to drive her to the brink of ecstasy. Only when she began to tremble uncontrollably, her moans becoming throaty whimpers, did he rise above her. Catching her wrists high above her head, he embedded himself to the hilt within her slick softness.

"Ah, Leila . . . how I have dreamed . . ."

He said no more as her hot sheath tightened inexorably around him. He began to move within her, pulling back, then straining into her again as far as he could reach. He wanted to go slowly, to prolong the sweet agony that was consuming them both, but it was impossible. His movements became bold and fierce, made all the more so as she began to writhe beneath him, her hips rising seductively to meet his every thrust. He was shaking and on fire from want of her, his own climax looming ever closer.

"Come with me, Leila . . . love," he urged, the scorching pressure in his loins like nothing he had ever felt with any other woman. "Come with me. Now!"

For a breathless instant Leila marveled that she was not torn in two by the sheer size of his pounding flesh, then in the next moment, she was being carried away with him upon a wave of such blinding rapture that time ceased for her altogether. She was oblivious to all but the wild beating of blood and heart, then a throbbing rush of wet, blazing heat, deep, deep inside her . . .

She could not say how many minutes passed before she felt Guy release her wrists and lift his weight to his elbows, but it was long enough to allow their frantic breathing to ease. She opened her eyes to find him gazing down at her, smiling tenderly.

"I take it I pleased you well, my lady," he said, brushing her swollen, love-bruised lips with a kiss that was as light as air. He moved his hips provocatively against hers, their bodies still joined as one. "I think you can guess how well you pleased me."

She did not answer, a furious blush creeping over her cheeks and spreading down her throat to her high, up-turned breasts. Seeing it, Guy chuckled. He bent his head and was about to draw a soft pink crest into his mouth when she gasped, trying to twist away from him.

"What are you doing?" she asked incredulously. "We have already—"

"Surely you don't think I have had my fill of you, my love," Guy cut in huskily, feeling himself grow hard again from her abrupt movement. God's blood, he would never have enough of her! He stroked a delicately boned shoulder, reveling in the silkiness of her skin. "Wedding nights are meant to last well into the morning. There is still much I'd like to share with you, and I believe you have things to share with me." He dragged his gaze from her puckered nipples and stared into her eyes. "Tell me more about those sensual arts you were taught in the harem, Leila. What special techniques did you learn?"

Anger swept her. How dare he expect her to share her erotic knowledge with him! To do so would be a final betrayal of Jamal and everything she held to be right and decent. When she returned to Damascus, she would still possess at least some of her innocence.

"Anything I learned in the harem was not for your benefit, Lord de Warenne," she said tartly. "Those skills are reserved for my husband."

"I am your husband, Leila."

"Not my rightful husband!" The minute the words were out she regretted them, for Guy's powerful body tensed, his eyes a dark, stormy hue.

"This afternoon you became my wife before God and man in the holiest of ceremonies," he said with quiet fury. "Your consent was witnessed by me, the priest, and King Edward. If that does not make me your rightful husband, Lady de Warenne . . ."

To her utter amazement he suddenly rolled onto his back, carrying her with him. Her hair, loosed from its braid, spilled over them like a veil of glistening black silk, and she braced her hands on his muscular, sweat-glazed chest. She could feel his heartbeat race beneath her fingertips as he seized her around the waist and began to move slowly within her, his breathing coming harder, faster, his eyes burning into hers.

"I told you that the day would come when you would admit your love for me. If that means I must also wait for you to share yourself fully with me, everything that you know, everything that you are, then so be it! But understand this, woman. You are mine!''

Leila felt her anger fading as raw excitement gripped her, his deep thrusts stoking flames of desire that she thought had been long since quenched. There was no use fighting him. His sensual power over her was far too compelling.

But that did not mean he was gaining any hold on her heart, she told herself, losing all control as he drew her roughly toward him and nuzzled her breasts. Her body might surrender, but not her soul. She would shelter it against anything he might say or do while she watched for the time when she could leave him and his futile love behind forever . . .

Her defiant thoughts fled as passion overcame her, his glittering blue eyes sending her an unmistakable challenge.

You will love me, Leila, his gaze seemed to say. *One day, you will love me!*

Guy captured her lips, kissing her with a possessive fire that drove her ever closer to flinging herself from that shimmering precipice . . .

God help her. No matter how often she assured herself otherwise, deep down she feared she already did love him.

Chapter 20

"**M**y dear girl, wake up! You must bathe and dress quickly or we'll miss the opening festivities."

Leila's eyes flickered open and she half sat up, surprised by the trio of female faces looking down at her. She recognized the plump Matilda de Warenne, countess of Surrey and wife to Guy's overlord, John, but not the two other well-dressed women.

Had she met them last night at the coronation feast? she wondered dazedly. Guy had introduced her to so many people after they had returned as husband and wife to the great hall . . .

Guy. Leila glanced at the empty space beside her and realized for the first time that she was alone in the bed.

"Of course he's gone, child. Your husband is jousting in the king's tournament today. He's been up since dawn preparing for his match."

Since dawn? Leila's cheeks grew warm. Obviously only she had fallen into an exhausted slumber after the abandoned lovemaking that carried them into the early morning hours. Her wanton thoughts scattered when she felt a friendly tug on her arm.

"Up with you now, Leila. Your husband will be most anxious to see his lovely bride seated in the royal pavilion when he rides onto the field. I know you must be bone-tired from your wedding night, but we'll surely miss . . ." Matilda paused when the two younger women standing beside her tittered, quelling them with a not-too-severe glance. "Have you met these ladies?"

Leila shook her head. "I'm not sure. Yesterday was such a blur—"

"Of course it was," the countess interjected kindly, patting her hand. "I still can't believe your brother . . . On the other hand, I suppose I can—" She stopped, clearing her throat, and gestured to the pleasant-faced woman on her left, who dropped a quick curtsy. "This is Lady Margaret Gray, and this"—she nodded to the other woman, who had very pale, pinched features that were pretty nonetheless—"is Lady Blanche de Hengham. They're both married to knights who serve my husband. In fact, their husbands are also riding in the tournament."

"It's a pleasure," Leila intoned with a small smile, remembering the expected niceties Guy had taught her on the way to London.

As the two women smiled warmly, the countess added, "I brought Blanche and Margaret along this morning because I thought you might like to sit in the pavilion with some young women your own age. Guy left me a message asking me to allow you to sleep as long as possible, and I have, but now we must hurry."

Leila gasped and hastily covered her breasts as Matilda matter-of-factly threw back the covers.

"Oh heavens, child! I possess the same equipment as you, only much more padded. Now out of bed with you and into the tub before the water grows cold."

Leila quickly obeyed her, recalling that Guy had said the countess was like a mother hen not only to her brood of seven children but also to the wives of her husband's knights. Now it was clear that she, too, was under the countess's maternal wing.

As Leila settled into the deliciously warm water, two serving women who had been waiting patiently near the door came forward to assist her. One began to bathe her with a soft sponge while the other expertly soaped her hair. Strangely, their gentle ministrations reminded her of Nittia and Ayhan, so instead of protesting she decided to enjoy it.

"Leila, which gown would you like to wear today?" came the countess's voice from the bed.

Leila squinted to keep any errant soap suds from stinging her eyes. But she forgot all about any possible discomfort when she spied the five beautiful kirtles with matching silk veils laid out upon the newly made bed. The garments made a vivid rainbow of color: royal blue, peacock, scarlet, deep lilac, and silvery peach.

"Where did they come from?" she asked, stunned.

"Your husband kept Queen Eleanor's seamstresses up most of the night making these gowns for you so they would be ready this morning," Matilda replied with a smile. "Didn't you hear him discussing what he wanted with one of the queen's ladies-in-waiting during the coronation feast?"

"No," Leila murmured.

In truth, she hadn't been paying attention to much at all last night, her mind lost to anxious thoughts of what was yet to come. How could she have known then that the wedding night she feared would prove so distressingly wonderful? Her skin puckered with goosebumps as passionate memories pressed in upon her, but the stirring images vanished when Matilda spoke again.

"Guy chose the colors, saying the more vibrant the better. He wanted to show off your beauty to its best advantage. He's very proud of you, my dear."

"Lord de Warenne sent several of his own knights to London to buy this for you," Margaret added excitedly, holding up a finely linked silver girdle inlaid with creamy pearls.

"And this," Blanche said, showing Leila a delicate silver fillet studded with glittering amethysts.

"Oh, my," Leila said softly.

"You are a lucky young woman," Matilda said, fingering the fine damask fabric of one gown. "Guy has done well for himself with what he inherited from his father and Ranulf de Lusignan. He has become a wealthy man and can well provide for your needs." She glanced pointedly at Leila. "He must love you very deeply. He adorns you like a queen. And to think you were willing to forgo all of this in hopes of returning to Damascus. I'm glad you came to your senses."

Leila caught her breath, the color draining from her face.

Guy must have told Matilda all about her, as he had told Edward and Eleanor. Either that, or the news had spread directly from their majesties to the rest of the court. She must have been the subject of some intense gossip indeed.

"It was not my intent to criticize you, Leila," Matilda said more gently. "You've had to make a very difficult adjustment to a land wholly foreign to you, and you've accommodated yourself well, I must say. One would never know you had grown up in a heathen country. I'm sure you will discover you've made the right choice in marrying Guy. He is a courageous and loyal knight. What more could any woman want?"

It was hardly a choice, Leila thought, her resentment at Guy flaring anew, though now it was strangely tempered by the passion they had shared last night. Guy might be a brave knight, but he was still a barbarian in her eyes.

She glanced at the gowns upon the bed, sighing. Would a coarse barbarian have put such care and thought into clothing his wife? That premise was being shaken with each passing day. But worst of all, the same swamping sense of unease that had plagued her until she fell asleep in Guy's arms was assailing her again.

Whatever was the matter with her? She had to admit she was utterly baffled by her emotions, and frightened by them, too. How could she possibly be falling in love with a man she hated? A man she was determined to leave as soon as she found the means?

"Please close your eyes, my lady, so I may rinse your hair," the serving maid requested.

Leila did so, leaning her head back and vainly hoping the warm water would flush from her brain any absurd notion of being in love with the man who had ruined her life as surely as the soap suds were falling from her hair. She rose from the tub, agonizing over a solution to this unexpected dilemma as the serving women buffed her dry with soft towels.

"You didn't tell us which gown, Leila."

Matilda's innocent statement startled Leila from her troubled musings and gave her an idea.

What if she could prove to Guy that their backgrounds were just too dissimilar for their marriage to succeed? Surely he would then be all too happy to allow her to go back to Damascus. It was obvious from the countess's earlier words that she had given in far too easily to the customs of this culture. Well, no more! She would show Guy and everyone else just how different she was!

"I'll wear the scarlet gown," she stated.

"Splendid. You will look absolutely lovely."

It seemed that in mere moments she was dressed, her damp tresses brushed dry and plaited down her back with silver ribbons. But when Blanche draped the short matching veil over her head, Leila snatched it from her hair.

"This will not do. Where I come from, women cloak themselves in long head scarfs and face veils out of modesty. It is indecent for a woman to flaunt her beauty to the world. If you don't mind, I will finish dressing by myself." Receiving startled looks from every woman in the room, Leila felt a twinge of guilt for spurning their kindnesses, but she quickly shrugged it off. She was determined to prove that she was no more like them than a fish to fowl.

"What are you going to do?" Matilda asked, rushing to her side as Leila grabbed a small knife from a food tray and picked up the royal-blue kirtle.

"Make myself a proper head scarf, one that reaches almost to the floor. I plan to use this scarlet veil to cover my face."

"But it's a new gown!" the countess exclaimed incredulously.

Leila lifted her chin stubbornly. "I will not leave this room without a proper kufiyya."

Glancing at Margaret and Blanche, who looked just as bewildered, Matilda shook her head and threw up her hands. "Very well, my dear. Do what you must. All I ask is that you hurry."

Leila smiled to herself as she cut the gown in two at the waist. She could hardly wait to see Guy's face.

* * *

Walking toward the covered pavilion a short while later, Leila felt smug satisfaction. She knew with amusing certainty that her choice of clothing was creating quite a stir.

No sooner had she emerged from her bedchamber, with the hastily constructed head scarf wrapped around her body like a blue silk cocoon and the scarlet veil covering her face below her eyes, when a serving woman—bearing a large tray and gaping at Leila in open-mouthed surprise—collided around a corner with a manservant carrying buckets of steaming water. The palace hall had echoed with a loud crash of crockery, high-pitched shrieking, and disgruntled male cursing, while behind her opaque veil Leila had merely smiled.

Activity had ceased in each room she and her three female companions passed: servants' brushes and brooms fell still; ladies stared aghast and whispered like buzzing bees; several knights watched her with a fascinated gleam in their eyes. It had been all she could do not to laugh aloud at the silly exclamations she overheard.

"God's teeth, will you look at that? For a moment I thought I was back in the Holy Land—on crusade! I wouldn't be surprised if next a camel crossed our path!"

"Who is she?"

"I believe Lady de Warenne, and oh, just look at the poor countess of Surrey. I've never seen Matilda's face so red! It's shocking, I tell you. Such a heathen display—shocking!"

Then, once outside the palace, Leila's exotic attire spooked a horse which tumbled its hapless rider into a bed of russet chrysanthemums. She didn't bother to stop, though Margaret rushed over to inquire after the poor man's health. Leila kept right on walking until she reached the pavilion, where she gracefully climbed the steps and followed Blanche to a bench in the second row.

Leila swept a glance across the assembled lords and ladies, who had suddenly grown silent with her appearance among them. She could see that virtually every pair of eyes was upon her. To Leila, they resembled so many gaping fish, almost as strange a sight to her as she must appear to them. With a surge of defiance, she faced front and sat down—determined not to give their astonished scrutiny a second thought. It was they who were dressed inappropriately, not she! Drawing her kufiyya more closely around her, Leila looked out across a dirt field cluttered with a half dozen long, boarded enclosures. She was amazed by the hundreds of spectators ringing the rough-hewn fence that had been constructed along the field's perimeter. The air of excitement was incredible, the crowd's roar deafening. It seemed the common folk on the field were so busy jostling one another, they had paid her little notice.

"I can hardly believe we made it here in time," the countess said, glancing with annoyance at Leila as she plopped onto the cushioned bench in the front row. She leaned toward her burly husband. "Has there been some delay, my lord?"

"Aye, there was a dispute over the pairings for today's round of jousting," John de Warenne answered in a deep voice, clearly trying but failing not to stare at Leila's veiled figure. "But the matter has been resolved. The opening pageant should start at any moment."

"What problem?" Matilda persisted. "I hope nothing serious. That would truly mar the day."

"Not serious, though it could have been. It seems Lord Gervais wanted to be paired with a certain knight even though he did not draw the man's name for today's round."

Leila had not meant to eavesdrop, but now she listened intently. She sensed Blanche and Margaret, who flanked her, were doing the same, for they had ceased chattering with their neighbors.

"Which knight, my lord husband?"

"I'll give you one guess, Matilda."

Her heart pounding, Leila knew even before Matilda's soft gasp that they were referring to Guy.

"And what happened?"

"Edward himself told Gervais that he must obey the rules of the tournament. The king said he had no doubt Roger would meet this knight on the field at some point during the next few days, seeing as they were both champions with the lance."

"The cheek of that wretched man!" Matilda blurted

heatedly. Her next words were drowned out as a rousing blare of trumpets and the beating of drums sounded from the foot of the pavilion where the heralds stood in their particolored tunics and hose.

Leila's eyes widened as a long line of knights galloped into the enclosed field on the largest horses she had ever seen. The crowd began to roar even louder as the armored riders and their mounts formed a thunderous procession just inside the fence.

There must have been at least three hundred knights, each man dressed in a calf-length surcoat over polished chain mail which blindingly reflected the sunlight, and a metal helmet that completely covered the head, with only slits to allow vision and vertical vents for breathing. Most of the helmets were flat-topped, but some had steel wings or menacing horns projecting from the crown. All the knights held twelve-foot-long lances raised to the sky, brightly colored pennons fluttering at the tips, while across their opposite shoulders were slung large triangular shields.

"How do you tell them apart?" Leila wondered aloud, searching for Guy among the knights who were slowing to a trot as they rode past the pavilion. She spied a few powerfully built men, one of whom might be Guy or her brother, but she wasn't sure because of the helmets.

"It can be quite difficult unless you're able to recognize each particular coat of arms," Margaret explained, glancing uncomfortably over her shoulder at some women behind them who were gossiping about Leila's strange attire. "Do you see how each knight has the same symbols embroidered onto his surcoat as he has painted on his shield?"

"Yes, I see them," Leila replied, proudly ignoring the women. She focused instead on the myriad colorful devices represented on the field. How would she ever find Guy? The only thing she had ever seen emblazoned on his surcoat was the crusaders' crimson cross. "The symbols are even painted on the long cloth coverings worn by the horses," she added with a touch of exasperation.

Margaret turned to the field, expertly scanning the circling knights riding two by two. "If you're looking for your husband, he is . . . there, on that huge roan stallion. His coat of arms is the fierce mythical griffin, half eagle, half lion.''

Leila followed Margaret's gaze, her heart lurching in her breast as she spied Guy at last. She could not deny she was secretly thrilled by his magnificent appearance; it unsettled her just how thrilled she was.

She took in every detail, from his winged helmet and dark blue surcoat to the matched trappings on his war-horse. She had thought him forbidding when she had first seen him in chain mail. Now, seeing him like this, astride his powerful destrier, she could understand why the cru-sader knights had always struck fear into Arab hearts. Guy looked invincible, like a god, and she could not tear her eyes away.

As he circled closer to the pavilion, her pulse raced in anticipation of his fury at her appearance. Then he was in front of her, and his deep blue eyes were fixed on her as he rode by. To her acute disappointment, she saw no an-ger, only a flicker of amusement.

At another loud blare of trumpets, the knights ceased the grand procession and turned to face the pavilion. Leila dragged her gaze from Guy's distant form in time to see King Edward rise from his chair, a radiant Eleanor at his side. An expectant hush fell over the crowd.

''I, Edward, your newly crowned king, and my beau-tiful Queen Eleanor bid you welcome!''

A huge clamor of huzzahs, swords battering upon shields, and applause filled the air, which after a few mo-ments was silenced as Edward raised his hand.

''One of these valiant knights before you will prove the champion three days from now during the final round of jousting. So without further delay, I say, let the tourna-ment begin. Those knights who have drawn the first match, come forward.''

''Oh, look! Raymond is in this match,'' Margaret ex-claimed.

The young woman watched with obvious pride as her husband rode toward the pavilion along with eleven other men while the rest of the participants left the field. But her face fell when Raymond reined in his steed beside a knight dressed all in black, from the thick plume gracing his flat-topped helm to the midnight destrier pawing restlessly beneath him. Upon the man's black shield was a gold dragon with seven writhing heads.

"Lord Gervais," Margaret murmured, suddenly subdued.

Leila felt a chill as she studied her brother, thinking he looked menacing indeed. But why would this pairing so upset Margaret? Surely her husband appeared strong enough to hold his own against Roger.

"If you've a lady in the stands," Edward spoke out again, addressing the assembled knights, "go to her now and let her bestow upon you a token of good fortune."

"What's this?" Leila asked as Raymond veered his destrier toward where they were sitting. "A token?"

" 'Tis the custom," Blanche replied. "The lady bestows upon her knight some charm to guard his person during the joust."

"What a silly notion," she declared. "No charm can protect a man from his kismet."

From the color spotting Blanche's cheeks, Leila realized she had clearly taken offense. "And what is kismet?" Blanche asked.

"Fate." Leila watched as Margaret stood and tossed to her husband a delicate white lace veil she had pulled from her sleeve. Raymond caught it, brought it gallantly to his breast, then tucked it into his dark green surcoat.

"God grant you victory, my husband," Margaret said quietly, her eyes fixed upon him as he rode back toward the king.

Leila's gaze flew to the opposite side of the pavilion where she spied Maude tying a gold veil around Roger's lowered lance. Then he, too, veered his snorting stallion back to where the other knights were waiting.

"My lords, take your places at the lists!" came a voice other than Edward's, who had retaken his seat next to Eleanor.

"That man is the master of the joust," Blanche explained stiffly, indicating the portly gentleman standing below the royal box. "He will officiate for the remainder of the tournament."

Leila's eyes followed Roger and Raymond as they rode to the second closest of the six boarded enclosures. They entered and separated, her brother galloping to one end and lowering his lance while Margaret's husband went to the opposite side. Another hush descended over the spectators as the last knights took their places. The only sounds were the nervous nickering of horses and the flapping of pennants in the light autumn breeze.

All that changed when the master of the joust suddenly dropped the gold banner he had been holding high over his head. A great cry went up from a thousand throats as the twelve knights kicked their destriers into a hard canter and rode full tilt at their opponents, shields raised and lances taking aim.

Leila winced at the loud, sickening thwacks that filled the air. Four knights hit the ground with bone-shattering force. Only the victors and two pairs of opponents remained in the saddle, Raymond and Roger and the knights in the sixth list. It seemed she had no more drawn a breath than they were riding hard at each other again.

This time Raymond fell, but he did not stumble to his feet as had the other unseated knights. He lay crumpled upon the ground until four de Warenne squires came running and carried him from the field, his limbs dangling limply between them.

"I must go to him," Margaret said distractedly, her face ashen as she rose from the bench. "I must go to him."

"Come, my lady, I'll escort you," the earl of Surrey offered tersely, glancing at his wife as he stood and took Margaret's arm. "I want to see if there has been some impropriety . . ." He did not finish, but led away the shaken young woman.

"Impropriety?" Leila asked, jarred herself by what she had just witnessed. What a brutal sport!

Matilda's expression was serious. "My husband needs to know if Lord Gray merely suffered a hard fall or if Lord Gervais failed to blunt his lance and thus injured him. We shall pray that that is not the case, especially for Margaret's and her children's sakes.''

Leila clasped her hands tightly as Blanche added, ''Men have been known to use the jousts to settle personal scores, though at the king's own tournament I cannot imagine how anyone would dare. I only hope my Hubert does not select your brother's name on the morrow if he wins his match today. Lord Gervais's skill with the lance is renowned. He has never been beaten.''

No wonder Margaret had become so distressed when she had discovered her husband's opponent, Leila thought uneasily. And Blanche's statement about settling scores would certainly explain why Roger had wanted to be paired with Guy.

If any men carried grudge upon grudge against each other, it was those two, and from what she had seen in the abbey yesterday, her marriage to Guy had only made things worse between them. It made perfect sense that Roger would want revenge against Guy for ruining all his plans. Had he decided to vent his wrath on Raymond, a de Warenne knight, since he was not paired with the opponent he truly wanted? She hoped not.

''There is only one man who shares Lord Gervais's record,'' Blanche continued, raising her voice to be heard above the blast of trumpets that signaled another match. ''Your husband. Whenever they have met in the lists, it has always been a draw.''

Pondering this news, Leila reluctantly watched the next four matches. She was relieved to see that the unseated knights usually staggered to their feet with little assistance. During the fifth match, the earl of Surrey returned to the pavilion, but without Lady Margaret.

''How is Raymond?'' Matilda gripped her husband's arm when he sat down heavily. ''He's not . . .''

''No, he lives, though he'll carry quite a knot on his head for several days,'' John replied. ''Gervais's lance struck him in the helmet, knocking him unconscious. Margaret has gone with him back to the palace. He needs rest.''

''And was the lance blunted?''

"Aye."

Grateful her brother had not done anything foolish, Leila focused her attention on the field as another set of twelve knights rode toward the pavilion. Her heart skipped a beat when she spied Guy among them, but what startled her even more was that Roger was in this group.

Matilda had also noticed. "What is this? Lord Gervais is jousting again? How can this be, my lord? Each man was to joust in only one match today."

John shook his head in disgust. "Gervais somehow managed to persuade Guy's opponent to give up his place. Probably by threat of life and limb, I'd wager."

"But can he do this? What of the rules?"

"The rules allow a replacement if consent is given by all, and Guy has consented, I think out of anger for what happened to Raymond. When Margaret and I arrived at the de Warenne tent, we found him incensed. He claims Roger did not wait for the signal the second time around, but gained a lead on Raymond which gave him an unfair advantage. I did not see this, but who can say?"

"Oh dear," Matilda said as the knights began to form into pairs in front of the royal box. "Just listen to the crowd. 'Tis the favored match they've been awaiting, and two days earlier than expected."

Matilda was right, Leila thought, her head whirling from the clamor. The throng of spectators was going wild. Some people were even jumping over the fence to get closer to the lists, but the king's men-at-arms were catching them and throwing them back. Was this melee erupting simply because Guy and Roger were both champions at the joust, or was it due to the mutual enmity they made no effort to hide? Perhaps the crowd expected more than a joust from these men. Perhaps they expected a duel to the death.

Cold fear gripped her throat at this grim realization, her thoughts running away with her.

Dear God, what if Roger's skill with the lance proved superior and Guy was killed in this match?

The next moments passed in a haze as the master of the joust confirmed the change in opponents. It was only when the knights fanned out to receive their tokens, Guy halting his destrier right in front of her, that Leila felt a more poignant emotion.

Was this the last time she would ever look into his eyes? Would she ever again feel his powerful arms around her, the warmth of his kiss?

"Leila, you're holding up the match," Blanche hissed in her ear. "Everybody is waiting. Give him your face veil."

Leila started, Blanche's words reminding her of her defiant plan. "I cannot," she murmured shakily, but loud enough for Guy to hear. "I would have nothing else with which to cover my face. I will not compromise my beliefs for this barbaric sport."

A shocked gasp went up from Blanche and the spectators surrounding her, but everyone grew still when Guy pressed his hand over his heart. His voice was muffled behind the helmet, but it clearly held humor.

"By all means, my love, save your beauty for my eyes alone. Your devotion pleases me."

That was hardly the angry response she had expected to draw for her slight, Leila thought with vexation as he dug his heels into his war-horse and thundered to the nearest list where Roger was already waiting for him.

This time the crowd did not fall silent. The cheering rose to a fever pitch as the master of the joust raised the golden banner, then dropped it.

Leila's irritation fled, her heart hammering. She had the strangest sensation that events were happening in slow motion. Paying no heed to the other jousting knights, she watched numbly as Guy and Roger bore down upon each other, lances lowered, drawing closer and closer, then the familiar thwacks rang out followed by the sound of splitting wood.

"God's bones, they've both broken their lances!" John blustered loudly.

Leila felt a tightness in her chest as Guy rode unharmed to the opposite end of the list. He sharply wheeled his war-horse and took up the new lance handed to him by his squire. How long would this madness continue? she wondered, her throat so dry she could barely swallow.

She sat on the edge of the bench as the banner was lifted and held high for what seemed an interminable moment, the master of the joust waiting for the victors and unseated knights to leave the field. Now there were only two opponents left in the lists—Roger Gervais and Guy de Warenne. All eyes were focused on them as the banner fell again.

The lances broke twice more. A fierce tension seemed to hold everyone in its grip. Leila did not think she could bear to watch anymore, and she stared blindly at her lap, listening to the master of the joust bellow above the din.

"This is the final run! If there is no clear victor, the match will be declared a draw."

"Leila, you're going to miss it," Blanche said. "Look, they're charging!"

With great reluctance, Leila lifted her head in time to wish she hadn't. Her eyes grew wide with horror as Guy was knocked violently from the saddle and landed flat on his stomach.

Several moments passed. When he did not make the slightest motion to rise, a rumbling of disbelief rose from the crowd. The favored champion was down. Maybe injured. Maybe worse. Some bystanders began to leap the fence and race toward the first list, as did mounted de Warenne knights who had been watching from the sidelines.

"No," Leila murmured, her heartbeat pounding like thunder in her ears. "No!" Guy couldn't be . . .

She rose, almost unaware she was doing so, dodging Blanche who tried to grab her arm, and hurried past stunned lords and ladies to the stairs leading to the field.

She had to reach Guy.

Nearly tripping down the steps in her haste, Leila lifted her skirts and began to run. She could hear John and Matilda calling out for her to stop, saying there were too many people and horses now on the field and she might be trampled, but their shouts were soon lost in the commotion. She did not slow her pace until she reached the congested list.

"Let me pass!" she demanded hoarsely, wrenching aside her face veil and fighting for breath as she pushed her way through the crush of knights and spectators surrounding the spot where Guy had fallen. "I'm his wife. Please, let me pass!"

She still had a ways to go when a loud cheer went up from the gathered onlookers, which was echoed by those watching from the stands. Then a deep, familiar voice said almost apologetically, "I fear Gervais got the better of me this time, my lords. That fall knocked the wind right out of me. Or perhaps it was my wedding night that proved my undoing. My beautiful wife was loath to let me sleep."

Leila froze, her face burning as male laughter rang out on all sides. She did not know if she was more relieved or angry. Here she had thought Guy was fatally wounded, and instead, he was making jokes and blaming her for his mishap!

"Why, your wife is right here, Lord de Warenne," shouted a tall knight standing next to her.

As the men in front of her began to step aside, forming a narrow path, Leila groaned inwardly, any hopes of retreating before Guy spied her vanishing into thin air. Now he would see for himself just how concerned she had been, for why else would she have run out onto the field?

Love had propelled her. She could no longer deny it to herself, troubling though the realization was. She had never felt such heartrending anguish as when she had thought he might be dead. Yet she couldn't let Guy guess the truth. It would only foster his hope for something that could never be.

Nothing had changed. She was as determined to leave him as ever, as determined to prove to him the impossibility of their marriage. She simply could not allow her emotions to override her will to return home to Syria. Her lifelong dream was in Damascus; everything for which she had worked so long and so hard was in Damascus. She would not forsake it. She had to think of another reason for her presence on the field, and fast—

"Leila."

Even as her name upon his lips filled her with joy, Leila resolutely hardened her heart against him. She had to. How else could she win the fierce battle that waged in her soul, this unsettling new love vying for dominion over the life in Damascus that she had vowed to reclaim.

As Guy approached her with a slight limp, his helmet held under one arm, she thought of how he had mercilessly wrenched her from everything she knew and loved, and felt a little stronger. Just a little.

"What are you doing here, my love? The tournament field is no place for a woman."

"I-I thought you might be wounded," she replied, steeling herself against the frank warmth of his gaze, "so I came as quickly as I could." When a pleased smile spread over his sweat-streaked face, she knew she had given him the wrong impression, but he spoke before she could continue.

"I am touched by your concern, Leila."

With difficulty she feigned a nonchalant tone. " 'Tis no more than any physician would do for an injured man, unless you have forgotten that medicine was my life's work long before I became your unwilling wife."

"I have not forgotten," Guy replied tersely, his smile fading. His voice fell to a harsh whisper. "Wearing veils and refusing to grant tokens is one thing, Leila, but if it is now your plan to play the shrew, then I suggest you save your barbs for our bedchamber. It is bad enough that I lost a joust to your brother. I will not be humiliated by my wife before my fellow knights. Is that clear?"

Leila nodded, stung by his words, but before she could reply, Guy muttered under his breath, "Speak of the devil."

She turned and was surprised to see Roger riding up to them, his helmet off, an inscrutable expression on his face. He reined in his lathered war-horse only a few feet away and surveyed them both coldly.

"What a touching sight you made, my sister, dashing out onto the field to reach your fallen husband. Too bad you did not find yourself a widow."

"Don't overestimate your skill, Gervais," Guy said. "Good fortune might have played into your hands today, but there will be other matches in which you might just as easily find yourself the one eating dirt."

"Is that a challenge, de Warenne? If so, I accept. I would like nothing more than to have another go at ramming my lance down your throat. I'll see that the opponent I draw on the morrow yields his place to you."

"Done."

Roger bowed his head mockingly as he gathered the reins. "Lady de Warenne."

"This is madness," Leila cried, watching her brother ride away in a spew of dust. She turned back to Guy, not believing what she had just heard. "Surely you can see he wants to kill you. My brother wants vengeance."

"As do I," Guy muttered, his gaze still following Roger's retreating figure. "And what better place than at the king's tournament, where revenge may be hidden under the guise of lawful sport. Your brother at least has the right idea there. I say, may the better man win."

Leila shivered at the bitter venom in his voice. Try as she might, she could not suppress her deep concern for him. Nor could she bear the thought that Guy might be killed because of her.

"But Roger defeated you once, my lord. What makes you think it won't happen again, and this time to his satisfaction?"

"Enough!" Guy demanded, his eyes clouded with hurt and anger as he fastened them upon her. "As you already pointed out to me, I will not flatter myself to think you might truly care about my welfare. You fear my death only because of how it may affect you, isn't that right, Leila?"

She wanted to answer yes, but she couldn't. It was not the truth. Not anymore. Nor could she say no for fear of giving away her feelings. So she kept silent, letting him think the worst.

"And after last night I thought . . ." Guy did not finish, but scanned the knights who stood off to the side. "Langton!"

"My lord?" Henry asked, striding over.

"Escort Lady de Warenne back to the pavilion. I believe the crowd grows anxious for the next match." He said no more, only turned away and walked toward his destrier.

The trumpets sounded, but Leila barely heard them. She stared after Guy, overwhelmed by the hurtful tangle their lives had become.

Who could say what cruel trick kismet would play upon them tomorrow when he and Roger met once more in the lists? Whatever the outcome, the sooner she managed to leave this country the better.

Chapter 21

"**A**ny trouble tonight, Robert?" Guy asked his solemn-faced knight as he approached the door to his bedchamber. He acknowledged with a nod the two men-at-arms standing at Burnell's side.

"No, my lord. Your lady has been as quiet as a mouse, and we've had no unwelcome visitors come this way."

"Good. The ale and wine are still running freely in the hall, but take care you're all able to ride at dawn."

"Aye, that we will, my lord."

Guy waited until the three men had disappeared down the shadowed hall before he lifted the latch and entered the silent, dimly lit bedchamber.

It was very late, and he barred the door carefully so as not to wake Leila. Accompanied by an escort which had also served as her personal guard while he remained in the great hall, she had retired from the post-tournament feast hours ago, pleading a headache, which he was also now suffering. The plentiful red wine he had consumed since losing the joust to Roger had done much to soothe his foul mood, but had left his head pounding .

At least he could be thankful that there would be no tournament for him tomorrow, Guy thought, pulling off his boots. After propping them by the door, he crossed the floor quietly, very much aware of his unsteady gait.

"Damn lucky thing, too," he muttered under his breath, berating himself for drinking so much. He doubted he would have been at his best, a disadvantage Roger would have seized upon with glee. But there would be no more jousting tomorrow for any of the Marcher lords, including that bastard Gervais.

An exhausted messenger had arrived from Wales only an hour past with an important missive for Edward. Despite the ample number of men who had been left behind to govern the region during the coronation festivities, the restless Welsh were harrying English castles and the surrounding villages with a vengeance. Anticipating a possible rebellion, Edward had ordered all Marcher lords to return home at once and see to their castles' defenses.

Guy had already told his men to be prepared to leave for Warenne Castle at dawn. Most of the disturbances were centered in northern Wales, but he didn't want to take any chances. Not with his young son at risk. He was glad to be leaving anyway. It was time Leila saw her new home.

As he drew back the bedcurtains, soft light from a single oil lantern spilled across the bed. It was empty, the mattress practically stripped but for a single linen sheet.

Suddenly he felt stone cold sober.

By God, had Leila fled? His gaze swept the shadows. No, it wasn't possible. Burnell had been outside the door all evening, and this room was on the third floor of the palace, which ruled out the windows. Then where the hell was she?

He tensed when he heard a slight rustling coming from the other side of the bed. Rounding it in a rush, he tripped when his foot became entangled in cloth, and he caught the corner post just in time to keep from falling. He was astonished to find Leila sleeping on the floor on a mound of bedcovers and pillows.

A smile twitched at Guy's lips. What defiant game was this? The day had already been full of such curious surprises. It appeared that she was fast asleep, one delicate hand tucked under her softly rounded chin, yet he sensed she was only pretending. Her breathing was a bit too regular, and her other hand was wound into a small fist that was curled rather tightly for slumber.

Would she flail at him, he wondered, if he so much as made a move toward her? He could hardly blame her if

she did. He hadn't exactly behaved the chivalrous gentleman after his unfortunate match with Roger.

His smile gone, Guy moved to the foot of the bed and
stripped off his clothes, throwing them on a chair with a
good amount of self-disgust.

What had happened to his firm resolve to be patient and
caring with her, no matter how she goaded him? Leila had
certainly vexed him this afternoon out on the jousting field,
and how had he reacted? Like a belligerent ass.

What had he expected anyway? That one night of lovemaking would miraculously change her mind about him?
Even if it had made some small difference, he had probably destroyed any progress he had achieved with his angry accusation. And even if she had been somewhat
concerned for him, he had been so incensed after that
strained encounter with Roger that he would have missed
entirely any caring intent behind her words.

The devil take it, there was nothing like losing a jousting match to one's mortal enemy to bring out the worst in
a man, Guy thought dryly. He went to the table and snuffed
out the lamp, plunging the room into darkness.

He had acted like a brash, hotheaded youth in the first
place by even agreeing to the change in opponents. He did
not doubt his prowess with the lance, but his lack of
sleep—not that it hadn't been worth it!—the night before
had hardly put him in good stead to take on Gervais. In
the morning he would undoubtedly see a wealth of ugly
bruises to attest to his foolhardiness.

Guy walked back around the bed, wincing at his sore
muscles.

From now on in any of his dealings with that bastard,
cold reason would rule. Either that, or Leila would become a very beautiful widow—hardly a thought he rel-
ished. He would have to watch his back once they were in
Wales. Roger probably had just such a grim scenario in
mind, though he would be a fool to act upon it. King
Henry had forbidden them to make war on each other, and
the decree still stood under Edward.

Entranced by the lush rose scent of Leila's perfume
drifting to him from the floor, Guy forced away his un-

pleasant thoughts as he gently picked her up. He knew she was awake when her slender body tensed in his arms.

"I don't know what game you've been playing all day, my love, but I will not have my wife sleeping on the floor like some beggar."

Her guise of sleep discovered, Leila wriggled against his bare chest, her heart racing. "I play no game!"

"No?" he asked, depositing her on the bed. The pillows and velvet spread quickly followed, then Guy climbed in beside her, hauling the covers to his waist. She attempted to slide away from him but he easily caught her, gathering her close.

"Then what do you call wearing veils in the manner of eastern women? After you left the feast tonight, Matilda was beside herself as she told me how you ruined one of your new gowns to make a head scarf, and Lady Blanche expounded upon your rudeness. You refused me a token during the tournament, called people gluttons at supper, and lectured them to partake of a more moderate diet. Then you demanded that the servants bring you pillows to sit upon and olives, dates, and yogurt"—Guy raised himself on his elbow—"none of which would they likely find in the king's kitchens. And now I find you sleeping on the floor. Need I remind you, Leila, that you are not in Damascus anymore?"

"No, you do not need to remind me!" Leila snapped, overwhelmed by the heat of his body pressed against her.

"Then what are you trying to prove? I would almost swear you are purposely seeking to humiliate me—" He stopped when Leila gasped. "That's it, isn't it?" he demanded softly.

"I don't know what you're talking about," she countered, astounded that he would so easily read her intentions. "I am only being myself. I may have English blood in my veins, but I will not play the part of a proper English lady."

"Nor do I want you to," Guy said, running his finger along her stubborn jaw. "You cannot humiliate me, Leila, for I love everything about you that is different. And you may have shocked the court today, but most people realize that you come from a foreign land. Nevertheless, I can see that I have forced our customs and clothing upon you too rapidly. In time, I believe you'll grow to accept them, but if it pleases you now to wear your veils, then do so.''

His words took Leila completely by surprise. She would never have expected such understanding from him. No wonder her attempts to embarrass him had only amused him. That is why she had finally feigned a headache and left the feast early, her frustration at the failure of her plan becoming so great that she was afraid she would lose her temper and give herself away.

And to think she had believed her actions would hasten her return to Damascus and thus free herself from her perplexing emotions! She couldn't have been more wrong. Now she would have to think of another plan.

"Perhaps one night I might even try your custom of sleeping upon cushions,'' he continued, curling his arm around her waist. "But not tonight. We must rise before dawn, only a few hours away, and it is important that we get a good rest, something I don't think sleeping on the floor will allow, at least not for me.''

"Why must I also rise at dawn, my lord?'' she asked, confused. "I know you must prepare for the tournament—''

"I won't be riding in the tournament tomorrow, nor will any Marcher lords. Edward has ordered us back to Wales. There is trouble among the Welshmen that must be subdued.''

Leila's relief was immediate, and she breathed a silent prayer of thanks. But in the next instant she thought of Wales, and how much farther she would have to go to escape this man whose love threatened to capture her heart. Even his simple embrace was almost too much for her reeling senses.

"I'm sorry I became so angry with you today, my love,'' Guy said. "I fear my rage at your brother together with losing the jousting match spilled over—''

"Don't let it trouble you,'' Leila interrupted, surprised by the gentleness in her voice. In truth, she was deeply touched by his apology, but she didn't want to talk any more about a day that had proved more disconcerting than she would have imagined. "After everything you told me about Roger, I can imagine how you must have felt." She quickly changed the subject. "How far is it to Warenne Castle?"

Guy hugged her more closely, wondering from her tone if perhaps he had been wrong after all about her seeming lack of concern for him. Maybe she did care about him, if only a little.

Now that he thought about it, their exchange on the jousting field reminded him of the times when Leila had hotly denied she desired him on the galley to Marseilles. That had proved to be untrue. Maybe she had done the same thing today, claiming she had run onto the field with a physician's intention to heal when in fact she had been concerned for his well-being. It was possible. Then could he dare to hope she was eager to journey with him to Wales?

"It will probably take us three days, maybe longer if the weather turns bad," Guy murmured against her silky hair. "I had hoped to visit my estate in Surrey first, but that will have to wait for another time. Edward has commanded that we make all haste." He kissed her nape tenderly, an intense hunger flaring in his loins at the sweet taste of her skin. "I've already sent Henry Langton and two other knights on their way to alert Philip that we'll arrive before the week is out," he added softly. "I want everything to be perfect for you."

"Philip?"

Guy suddenly realized he had never mentioned him to Leila.

"Philip D'Arcy, my half brother. An only son from my mother's first marriage. He's a priest. I left him in charge of my estate in Wales and gave him guardianship over my son while I went on crusade." Guy smiled, imagining Philip's expression when he discovered his wayward younger brother had taken a wife, something Philip had strongly encouraged for a long time. "Philip can be a bit staid, but I think you'll like him. You have something in common. He's also a healer."

Leila found it difficult to absorb this news when Guy

was hugging her so tightly. A shiver rocked her from her scalp to her toes when he kissed that same sensitive spot on her nape.

"Three days is a long journey, my lord. We should get some sleep. As you said, dawn will arrive soon." She bit her lower lip to hold back her acute regret. Try as she might, she could not suppress the desire ripping through her body.

"Yes, we should get some sleep. Good night, my love."

Leila said nothing, her blood pounding in her veins. The sensual tension in the air was so palpable she swore she could almost taste it.

The next thing she knew she was flat on her back and gasping aloud. She could not see Guy in the dark, but she knew his face was very close, his breath like a hot flame upon her lips.

"To hell with sleeping," he growled huskily, his mouth seizing hers.

Five long days after leaving Westminster, they approached Warenne Castle in County Gwent just as the late afternoon sun was beginning to settle behind the rugged mountains soaring to the west.

Riding up the hill toward the imposing gatehouse on her dappled-gray palfrey, Leila did not think she had ever felt so tired. The weather had proved their enemy during much of the journey, the heavy rain and mud-clogged roads slowing their progress considerably. Yet they had pressed on, Guy clearly anxious to reach his home. Only short respites for sleep in rustic village inns had broken their relentless pace.

Thankfully the day had turned sunny about an hour ago, affording Leila a much different view of the rolling countryside than that of a land cloaked in dense mist and gray gloom. They had passed many small farms and prosperous hamlets since then, which Guy had informed her were all under his domain. His words had been confirmed when his tenants, both English and Welsh, had rushed from their modest wattle and daub homes to greet them. It seemed everyone knew Lord de Warenne was coming home from the crusade.

The clear skies had also granted her a first far-off glimpse of Warenne Castle, situated on the summit of a hill overlooking the River Usk. Now as they made their final ascent, the high stone walls looming closer and closer seemed like prison walls to Leila.

"Look. It's Nicholas, up there on the battlements," Guy cried out, his excited voice breaking into her somber thoughts. "And that's Philip beside him."

Shielding her eyes from the sun, Leila spied the darkly clad priest and a small, fair-haired boy looking down at them from the huge round wall tower at the right corner of the fortress. Yet they were still too far away for her to make out their faces. She glanced at Guy, riding alongside her, his roan destrier dwarfing her mare. "How old did you say your son is, my lord?"

"Six," he replied, still gazing at the tower. "I wonder if he even remembers me. I haven't seen him for almost two years."

Leila had no answer for him. She had had little personal dealings with children, except as patients, and she certainly did not feel qualified to gauge this young boy's mind. She did feel compassion for Guy, however. It must have been hard for him to be away from his son for such a long time.

"I'm glad you decided to abandon your extra veils," he added, smiling at her. "It is a shame to hide such beauty as you possess, my love. I'm sure you will win everyone's heart when they see you."

Leila blushed at his compliment and tried to ignore its unsettling effect on her. She had left off her veils only because her plan to embarrass him had failed. If he was merely amused by her foreign garb, what point was there in wearing it?

She remained silent as they came at last to the gatehouse and passed beneath the raised portcullis. Looking up at the menacingly sharp spikes, she wondered how she would ever manage to escape past this heavy wooden grille bounded with iron.

The journey had allowed her plenty of time to think about her new plan, which depended entirely on gathering enough funds to get her back to Damascus. She already had the silver girdle and fillet Guy had given her, and he had promised her a ring that had once belonged to his mother, but she doubted that would be enough. She hoped she could manage to steal some coins here and there. Her plan was devious and cruel, but what else could she do?

They passed through yet another gate, this one hinged and made of thick timber also reinforced with iron, but Leila took heart, noting a smaller door cut into one side. At least this gate might not prove difficult to pass through.

Then they were inside the fortress, and a swarm of people was rushing forward to greet them: men-at-arms and knights who had stayed behind to guard the castle during Guy's absence, beaming servants, officials of the surrounding villages and their wives, and even some well-dressed ladies, whom Leila assumed were married to returning de Warenne knights, along with their children. Guy had already told her there would probably be a celebratory feast in their honor that night, but she didn't know how she would manage it, being so weary. Perhaps if she could first rest—

She started when Guy's hands encircled her narrow waist and he lifted her to the ground. He began to introduce her to people, but the names and faces became a blur in her mind. She simply smiled, growing all the more disconcerted by the pressure of Guy's fingers entwined with hers. He hadn't touched her since early that morning, when he had awakened her with a kiss and . . .

Leila's face grew so warm she was grateful for the brisk autumn breeze blowing across the huge courtyard. She was about to ask Guy if the rest of the introductions might wait until later when he suddenly halted, the crowd of well-wishers around them parting as a little boy dashed forward with outstretched arms.

"Nicholas!" Guy exclaimed, releasing Leila's hand as he bent down on one knee and caught the child in his embrace. Just as quickly the boy pulled away, his eyes wide as he surveyed his father solemnly.

"I'm going to be a brave and fearsome knight and wear armor just like you when I grow up, aren't I, Papa?"

Guy seemed about to laugh, then he quickly sobered and answered just as seriously, "Yes, you are, my son. Just like me."

"And I may have a war-horse like Griffin?"

"Bigger, I'd warrant!" Guy answered playfully, swooping Nicholas into his arms as he stood up. "Why, you've nearly grown into a man since I've been away. Just look at you!"

Stepping back a bit, Leila could tell Guy deeply loved his child and was elated that Nicholas had so readily come to him. She wondered what had become of Philip, then she spied a priest wending his way toward them through the crowd.

She was interested to note that the older man resembled Guy no more than she did her own brother, for Philip was shorter by a head and very spare, his hair nearly gray and clipped close to his skull. Yet there was some slight similarity in the spacing of his features and in the square set of his jaw. His gray eyes were shrewd and intelligent, his expression reserved, until Guy clasped his arm heartily. Then the priestly demeanor gave way to a half smile that nevertheless conveyed his affection.

"You look none the worse for your travels, my brother," Philip said, the deep timbre of his voice similar to Guy's. "I must admit I became anxious when I heard from Henry about your imprisonment in Damascus, but I can see now that you are as fit as ever. Welcome home."

"My thanks, Philip. As I fully expected, my estate seems to have prospered under your care, and Nicholas here . . ."

Guy gave his son another fierce hug, but the boy seemed impatient to be let down, his inquisitive eyes fastened upon Leila. As soon as his small feet touched the ground, he trotted over and looked up at her.

"Sir Langton told me my new mother was a most beautiful lady," he said, innocently appraising her features. "I think it is you."

Leila felt a catch in her throat and decided this handsome child's mother must also have been very beautiful. She had never seen a more striking combination of white-blond hair and blue, blue eyes; Nicholas bore the features of his father, but they were softened and refined, his legacy from Christine.

A rush of pity swept her for the long dead woman who had tried in vain to win Guy's love . . . a love he had now given to her, but which she could not accept. How strange and mysterious were the forces that drove men's and women's hearts!

"The lad already has his father's eye for beauty," Leila heard Guy say proudly, much to the appreciation of the crowd still gathered around them. She met his gaze as he reached out and clasped her hand. "Yes, Nicholas, this is your new mother, Lady Leila de Warenne," he answered for her. "But you must ask her yourself what she wishes to be called." Guy leaned over and whispered in her ear, "We don't want to make her uncomfortable."

His fair head tilted back, Nicholas looked questioningly from his towering father back to Leila, who swallowed with embarrassment.

Oh dear. She hadn't expected this dilemma. She certainly didn't want to drag Nicholas into their difficulties, or raise the child's expectations. Then again, maybe he wouldn't like her and would find it no great loss when she was gone. She could hope so. It surely wasn't her intention to hurt an innocent child . . .

Unable to reach a decision, Leila bent down and took the boy's small hands in her own, asking gently, "What would you like to call me, Nicholas?"

He pondered her question for a moment, studying her so solemnly that she almost felt as if he could see straight into her soul. Strangely enough, it pained her when he answered, "Lady Leila, if you please."

"Then Lady Leila it shall be," she replied, forcing a smile as she rose to her feet.

"And I would like to do the same, if I may," Philip added. He stepped forward, appraising her not as a man might, but as if weighing whether she would be a friend or foe. "Welcome, my lady. Henry has told me a great deal about you."

Wondering what that might be and unsettled by his odd scrutiny, Leila answered softly, "Of course. That would be fine—"

"Did Langton tell you my wife is a trained physician?" Guy cut in, regarding her with pride. "She studied for years. I'd wager she knows more than any other healer in Britain. It was her skill that saved my life, Philip. Perhaps she might be able to show you a thing or two."

Leila was amazed. The only time she and Guy had discussed her profession, he had told her she would never be able to practice her medicine in England as she had in Damascus. Now he was boasting of her skill! Was this some kind of taunt? Sweet Jesu, she would never understand this man!

"Yes, Henry informed me of your . . . profession," Philip answered stiffly, resentment darkening his eyes.

Squeals of joy behind them shattered the awkward moment. They all turned to see wives and children running to greet the de Warenne knights who had brought up the rear of their cavalcade and were just now riding through the gates with the last of the packhorses. Nicholas scurried off to join the fray.

"More crusaders come home again," Guy said with a hearty laugh, clearly enjoying the ruckus. He turned back to Philip. "I take it a feast has been prepared?"

"The cooks have been at their spits since Henry brought us the news of your return. In an hour's time, all will be ready." Philip glanced at Leila. "Perhaps until then, my lady, you might like to rest."

She offered him a weary smile, which was not returned. "Thank you. That sounds wonderful."

"Come. I'll show you to our room," Guy began, only to be interrupted by Philip.

"Forgive me, Guy, but there are pressing matters we must discuss. The Welsh rebels . . ." He did not have to finish as Guy shook his head knowingly. "Enid will see that Lady Leila has everything she needs." Philip gestured to a buxom, middle-aged serving woman who hastened forward.

"Aye, Father D'Arcy?"

"Please escort Lady de Warenne to the lord's chamber."

"Gladly. If you'll come this way, my lady."

Anxious to be gone from the crowd, however well-meaning, Leila quietly excused herself and began to follow Enid. As she passed in front of Guy, she felt his hand lightly brush her arm.

"I'll wake you in an hour, my love."

She did not respond or even turn her head, just kept walking, his endearment stabbing into her heart.

Those two words had become a constant reminder of what she could never be to him, yet what was this pain that always swiftly followed the thought? And why, dear God, was it becoming worse with each passing day?

As Guy quietly entered their bedchamber on the top floor of the round stone keep, he knew at once that Leila was fast asleep. There was no sound, not even a stir coming from the canopied bed that dominated the large, semi-circular room.

How exhausted she must be, Guy thought, pulling aside the linen curtains so he might gaze upon her. Studying her face, he was immediately flooded with concern.

Her cheeks were so pale. Dammit, he had pushed her too hard. What she needed was a good night's rest, not a long and boisterous feast. There would be time enough for her to become acquainted with her new home. He would show her around the castle tomorrow.

Tenderly Guy pulled the soft fur coverlet up over her bare shoulder, deciding against kissing her slightly parted lips for fear of waking her. He closed the curtains and left the room, descending the spiral stone steps with a secretive smile.

Yes, he could wait one more day to reveal his surprise.

After much wrestling with himself, love had finally overwhelmed his objections. He had found the perfect way to make amends for some of the heartache he had caused her. The perfect way to give her back her dream.

Chapter 22

When Leila awoke, she knew it was morning for the bright sunlight peeking through the closed curtains and the sweet sound of birdsong. She was alone in the huge bed, her only clue that Guy had slept with her the indentation in his pillow. She was surprised but grateful that he had allowed her to sleep through the welcoming feast. She felt much better now. Wondering with a nervous rush of excitement if he might still be in the room, she sat up and tentatively drew back a curtain.

"So you're awake at last, my lady," came a cheerful voice, startling her.

"Enid," Leila breathed, her eyes darting around what she could see of the sunlit chamber. "Is Lord de Warenne . . . ?"

"Your husband and a good three dozen knights and men-at-arms rode out a few hours ago," the serving woman replied, her lively tone sobering as she tied back the dark blue curtains with tasseled cords. "Ah, the times are not good, my lady. Word came early this morning that one of the neighboring villages was raided during the night. 'Tis the first time the rebels have struck so close." Enid shook her dark head. "I share the Welsh blood of the men who committed the crime but not their hate of the English. My family has served the de Warennes for generations, and we're proud of it."

Leila felt a moment's fear for Guy, but she pushed it away. If there was one thing she had learned about her husband, it was that he was more than capable of taking care of himself in dangerous situations. She recalled wondering how knights occupied themselves, and now it seemed she had gotten her answer: by keeping the peace for the king and protecting what was theirs.

"Did he say when he might be back?"

"No, but if they manage to catch the wily scoundrels, mayhap by midafternoon. If not . . ." Enid shrugged, her plain face becoming almost pretty as she smiled reassuringly. "Don't trouble yourself about it, my lady. Your lord will come home soon enough. And until he does, Father D'Arcy asked me to tell you that he'd be honored to show you the castle in your husband's stead."

Leila frowned. The idea of spending a good portion of the day in Philip's austere company did not sound exactly pleasant, especially after his strained greeting, but it might be better than sitting in this bedchamber with nothing to do. And it certainly wouldn't hurt to learn the layout of Warenne Castle.

"Very well," she murmured, throwing back the covers and climbing from the bed with ten times more energy than she had when she sank into it yesterday afternoon.

While Leila dressed, Enid chatted about the feast; the delicious dishes that had been served, the speeches, the toasts, the spirited entertainment, the drunken brawl among some men-at-arms. Though irksome, the diverting patter freed Leila from dwelling overmuch upon Guy. Yet whenever he was not with her, he was always in the back of her mind, a troubling fact to which she had reluctantly grown accustomed in the long weeks she had known him.

Would it be the same when she left him? Leila wondered, as Enid expertly braided her long tresses. Foolish thought! She knew she would never forget him. How could she?

Oh, enough! She didn't want to think about it anymore and was glad when Enid finally finished her hair. After donning a veil and fillet, she practically flew out the door and down the spiral stairs as if she meant to escape her feelings.

"My lady, Father D'Arcy has a small office on the first floor of the keep," Enid called out after her. "If he's not there, you'll find him in the chapel."

Leila was breathless when she reached the last step, her head spinning from going round and round so quickly. Steadying herself, she knocked on the nearest door, but there was no answer. She tried two more times before a male voice called out for her to enter.

Suddenly a bit nervous, though she didn't understand why, Leila opened the creaking door. It took an instant for her eyes to adjust to the dimmer light. While her bed-chamber had several glazed windows, this room had only a very small one placed high up near the ceiling; the interior was lit with candles and oil lamps.

"Good morning, Lady Leila," Philip said, rising from a stool set before a slanted desk. His smile was restrained, and his eyes held little welcome. "I take it you slept well?"

She closed the door behind her and faced him again. "Yes, thank you. I'm sorry I missed the feast."

"No matter. Everyone understood how tired you were after your long journey. Have you eaten yet?"

"No, but I'm not really hungry."

"Nonsense," Philip objected. "Guy was telling me last night that you were too pale, and I agree. A robust diet is essential to good health." He gestured to a table laden with several trays of food. "Please. Sit down."

Remembering the flash of resentment she had seen in his eyes yesterday, Leila bit her tongue, deciding not to correct his highly inaccurate view of nutrition. What was the sense in it anyway? She wanted no trouble with this man. She had seen plenty of ugly rivalries between Arab physicians and knew what a sensitive issue medicine could be between those who held different beliefs.

From Philip's simple statement about diet, she already discerned that their approaches to healing were worlds apart. Her father had claimed many times that western physicians were like blindfolded men stumbling around in the dark, often no better than butchers. Philip would no doubt only scoff at anything she had to say. It was better to humor him.

Leila pulled out a bench and sat down, then waited silently while Philip filled her trencher with what looked like leftovers from the feast. He picked up an earthenware pitcher.

"Wine?"

She nodded, wondering why he hadn't fixed himself some food.

"Go ahead. I've already eaten," he urged, as if sensing her thoughts. After handing her a filled goblet, he went back to his desk. "If you'll excuse me a moment, I have to finish this last entry in the household accounts."

Leila picked at the food, opting for a chunk of fresh baked bread and some crumbly cheese over the distasteful morass of meat and gravy set before her. She could not help wondering how Philip managed to stay so lean yet advocate such a diet. Perhaps he kept so busy managing Guy's estate that he had little time to put his belief into practice, she surmised, listening to the scratch of the quill on paper as she sipped her wine.

Unable to eat any more, she twisted on the bench, her gaze moving around the room. She spied with great interest a row of carefully dusted books on a low cupboard. They were the first ones she had seen since Damascus; she had almost begun to believe manuscripts didn't exist in these western lands.

"May I look at your books?" she asked, trying to hold her eagerness in check.

"Only a few of them are mine, some medical texts approved by the Church. The rest of the collection belongs to Guy. I doubt he would mind if you looked at it. I've kept his books in here while he was away, but I'm sure he'll soon be moving them back to his private solar."

So Guy truly was a scholar, Leila thought as Philip went to the cupboard and selected a thick volume.

"My brother has always had a great fondness for heroic epics. Chretien de Troyes's romance of knighthood, highlighting the adventures of Lancelot and Percival." He pointed from book to book. "The Song of Roland, the poems of Bertrand de Born, various chronicles of history . . ." He paused, glancing at Leila as he added stiffly, "I heard much from Guy last night about how learned you are. Do you read French?"

"No, I don't."

"A pity. Most of these texts are written in either that language or in English. Do you—?"

"My mother taught me only to speak English, not to read or write it," Leila interrupted him quietly. "There had been no need . . ." She went no further, swallowing uncomfortably.

"Well, I'm sure Guy would be more than happy to teach you," Philip said, returning the book to its place on the cupboard. "As mistress of Warenne Castle, you will need a good command of our language to perform your many duties. I'm sure he will ask you to take over some of the household accounts."

What an intriguing notion, Leila thought—Guy teaching her to read and write. Then she felt a sudden rush of regret. Of course it would never happen. She would probably be gone long before the first lesson could ever begin.

"What of your medical texts?" she queried, hoping a change of topic would ease her darkening mood. "Are they also in English?"

She was surprised to see Philip visibly tense. "They're in Latin."

Leila brightened. "I've studied Latin. Could I look at them—"

"For what purpose, my lady?" Philip cut her off sharply. "You will certainly not need the knowledge contained in those books. I am the healer here at Warenne Castle, not you. I suggest you content yourself with your wifely duties from now on." His severe black robes fluttered as he walked in agitation to the door. "Come. I think it is time that we began our tour of the castle. Guy asked me to cover as much ground as possible so you might feel more at home in your new surroundings. Shall we go?"

Stunned by his vehement outburst, Leila rose from the bench and followed him from the room.

So that was why Philip had been so cold toward her, she thought incredulously, waiting in the dim hallway as he locked the door and pocketed the key. He felt threatened by her knowledge of medicine! Why else would he have scrutinized her so strangely when they first met, as if he had already decided he disliked her?

"I'll show you the great hall first," he said tersely, leading the way as they left the keep. "This vast courtyard is what we call the bailey . . ."

Leila scarcely heard him, her thoughts reeling.

It was very clear to her now that Philip was escorting her around the castle only because Guy had asked him to. She also suspected that any civility he had displayed to her yesterday had been wholly for Guy's benefit. She had seen that the two men were close. Philip probably did not want to give his brother the impression that anything was amiss.

Sweet Jesu, how she wished she could tell him outright that he had nothing to fear from her! One day soon she hoped to be gone from this place.

But she kept silent. Otherwise, Philip would surely tell Guy, and then where would that leave her?

A few hours later Leila longed to return to the solitude of her bedchamber. She would never have imagined her tour could prove so taxing; she doubted she would ever remember all the minute details Philip had told her about daily life in a castle.

She had seen countless rooms and buildings; the timbered great hall with its cellars, pantries, buttery, and musician's gallery; the vaulted chapel; the kitchens; the scullery; the servants' quarters; a barracks for mercenary knights; a smithy; a laundry; stables; barns; a brewery; on and on. The only respite had come when they visited the walled garden just outside the kitchen.

She had lingered there among the barren fruit trees and last herbs of the season, feeling bittersweet delight and longing when she spied rose bushes in one corner from which still hung a few fragrant blooms. She had recognized the bright pink flowers at once.

Damask roses. Just like the ones growing in the courtyard she had shared with her mother. Wondering how her favorite flower had ever come to be planted in this faraway garden, Leila was almost glad when Philip urged her to move on with him to the last site on their tour, the row of storehouses at the far end of the bailey.

Now she leaned with gratitude against some sacks of grain just inside the open door, listening with half an ear as Philip droned on about the contents of the building.

"Our foodstuffs are stored in here, staples such as peas and beans, onions, salted meat and fish—"

"There you are. The castle guard said I would find you in one of these storehouses."

Both she and Philip turned in surprise to find Guy silhouetted in the low door frame, his shoulders hunched and his head down to accommodate him.

As he stepped inside and straightened to his full height, Leila was overwhelmed by the sight of him. He was so massive, his slightest movement revealed such power. She never ceased to be amazed by how he could fill a room with his commanding presence. As his gaze raked her, she felt a dizzying warmth sluice through her veins, which increased tenfold when he took her hand in his large one. It frightened her to realize how much she had missed him.

Philip broke the charged silence. "You're back early, Guy. Did you catch any of the culprits?"

"Unfortunately, no. We searched the woods surrounding the village and found many hoofprints in the mud, but the tracks disappeared when we came to the river," he replied grimly. "We'll find them, though, and they'll pay. I'll not suffer these raids upon my land."

"And the village?"

"Four houses were torched, but no one was killed. The bastards tied up the peasants and got away with horses and livestock. Not much else. It couldn't have been more than ten or fifteen men, perhaps a renegade band that broke off from the bulk of the rebels harassing the Marcher lords to the north." Guy's voice became tinged with impatience, and he gently squeezed Leila's hand. "We can discuss this later, Philip. Has my wife seen the last storehouse yet?"

"No." Philip looked confused. "I hadn't planned to show her that one. There's nothing in it, remember? Before you left this morning you ordered that it be emptied and swept clean, and so it has been done. Have you decided upon its use?''

''A week ago, on my wedding day,'' Guy said mysteriously. He glanced at Leila, a sly twinkle in his eye. ''I have a surprise for you, my love. Come.'' Looping his arm around her waist, he called out to his half brother as he guided her through the door, ''I'd like you to accompany us, Philip. As steward of my estate, you need to know what I have planned. There will be some expenditures involved.''

Wondering crazily what Guy was up to, Leila blinked at the bright sunshine, for the interior of the storehouse had been very dark. She practically had to run as he hurried her past four similar buildings, only slowing when they reached a smaller storehouse set off by itself. She saw over her shoulder that Philip was not far behind them, his expression grave.

''We kept saddles and harnesses in here until this morning,'' Guy explained as he pushed open the door, ''so it will probably smell like leather and horses for a while.'' Once inside, he released Leila and hastily pushed open the wooden shutters on both sides of the room, flooding the empty interior with fresh air and sunlight.

''What is all this about?'' Philip asked doubtfully, standing on the threshold.

Guy took Leila's hands and drew her into the middle of the room. ''A gift for my beautiful, beloved wife,'' he answered, gazing into her eyes. ''It doesn't look like much now, but it will soon. Leila, what do you think of your new hospital?''

She was dumbstruck, her heart thumping wildly. Had she heard him right or was he merely toying with her? No, she could tell from his expression that he meant exactly what he had said.

''Hospital?'' she finally managed, tears dimming her vision. They began to spill down her cheeks when Guy nodded firmly.

''Most married women of rank are content to oversee their husband's household as they've been taught to do since childhood, but I know that would never make you happy. And I want you to be happy, Leila,'' he said fervently, his touch gentle as he cradled her face and wiped away her tears. ''I want you to see that your dream can be fulfilled here at Warenne Castle. With me.''

Incredibly moved, Leila lowered her wet lashes, afraid of what he would see in her eyes.

She had never known a moment of such weakness. She was so ready to surrender to him, to admit the love she held imprisoned in her heart . . . but something would not let her. Fear, obstinacy? Some lingering resentment against him for altering her life so drastically? She could not say.

Perhaps she had told herself so many times since the day of the tournament that their love could never be that she had actually come to believe it. They were from two different worlds. How could they possibly find happiness together? Kismet should never, never have thrown them into each other's arms!

''The afternoon we married,'' Guy was saying, ''I sent some of my men to scour the markets in London for rare herbs and spices, even cautery irons and other surgical tools. If need be, I'll send them back for whatever else you might require,'' he continued, unaware of the furious turmoil raging inside her. ''And if there are any special medicines you want, I plan to send messengers twice a year to Marseilles to meet the trading ships from the Holy Land. Tomorrow you'll find twenty beds in this room, and I've already picked three able servants to help you. I don't want you working yourself too hard, my love. And Philip will be there to help you, too''—he glanced up at his half brother—''won't you?''

''Never!''

Guy stiffened and his hands slid from her face. As he moved slightly away from her, she did not turn around. She did not need to see Philip to know how incensed he was. She had heard it in his voice.

''Tell me I misunderstood you, my brother.''

''No. You heard me well. I cannot and will not condone this . . . this hospital''—Philip spat—''either as a healer or as a priest. It is blasphemy!''

Guy's reply was slow in coming, as if he could not

believe what his brother had just said. Finally he replied, "I have always valued and trusted your counsel, but in this matter you have overstepped yourself. Explain your charge, and quickly."

"So I will, for I can no longer remain silent!" Philip blurted. "Christian or no, this wife you have brought among us is a heretic! Her beliefs are not ours! She grew up among infidels, and from everything I have been told about her, she has clearly been influenced by their evil ways. Yet I might have been able to forgive all of this if she renounced her heathen past and her profession, and became a proper mistress to this household. The preposterous idea you now propose has made that impossible!"

"Why?" Guy shouted.

"You already know the answer, but your love for this woman has blinded you to it," Philip accused him, clearly undaunted by his brother's explosive outburst. "To allow your wife to practice her questionable skills is a direct challenge to the Church. If your tenants or knights become injured or ill, they come to me or go to the monastery infirmary in Abergavenny where care is advocated, not a cure. Sickness is from God, to be healed by divine intervention, not by medicines and surgery—"

"It was not divine intervention that saved my life in Damascus," Guy cut him off harshly. "It was Leila and her adopted father. If not for their knowledge and medicines, as well as Leila's skill with the hot irons with which she sealed my wound, I would not be alive today!"

Leila started when Guy touched her arm, saying with a quietness that belied the boiling anger in his eyes, "Leave us. I will not have you hear any more of this ranting. But do not fear, my love. You shall have your hospital."

Her throat was so painfully constricted she did not attempt a reply. Rushing past Philip without so much as a glance, she fled the storehouse. She ignored the puzzled looks of servants, knights, and men-at-arms alike as she hurried toward the keep, scalding tears tumbling down her face.

Why had her mother done this to her? Why? Leila raged,

desperately needing someone to blame for the terrible pain that was ripping her apart.

Renounce her past? Renounce her profession? How could she? It would be the same as tearing out her soul. Surely Eve knew she would never live peaceably in this world. How had her mother ever believed she would find happiness here?

Entering the keep and running up the stone steps, her footfalls echoing in her ears, Leila cursed Eve.

Slamming the bedchamber door behind her, she cursed Guy.

Throwing herself on the bed, she cursed the impossible love that had crept like a thief into her heart.

Guy found her in their room a half hour later, standing as still as a statue before the window which overlooked the winding River Usk.

"Leila?"

She did not turn or answer. He saw her shoulders stiffen, and his heart went out to her. By God, if he had anticipated Philip's outburst, he would never have shared his plans with his brother. To think she had heard all those horrible accusations . . .

Guy walked to the window, but he did not touch her. She looked so vulnerable, like fragile glass that might shatter on contact.

"Leila," he said softly, gazing at her profile. "The matter has been settled. You will hear no more dissent from Philip. I want you to try and forget everything he said. Your hospital will be ready tomorrow."

Unblinking, she stared down at the river.

"We reached an agreement, he and I," Guy continued, wondering if she was even listening. "If Philip keeps his objections to himself, he will remain my steward. I believe he values his position too highly to trouble you again." He waited for a reply. None came. "Leila, did you hear me?"

Silence reigned for a long, long moment, but finally her lips parted.

"Those roses in the garden," she murmured, her low

voice almost a whisper. She did not turn her head, but he saw a tear trickle down her cheek. "Damask roses."

Sighing, Guy knew now that her mind was not on Philip. "What of them, my love?" he asked, pressing her gently.

"How . . . ?"

Understanding flooded him. "My father brought them back from the Holy Land as a gift for my mother. He was also a crusader knight."

Another tear slid slowly down her cheek. "They're so far from home."

A tightness gripped his throat, her deep hurt becoming his own. Folding her in his arms, he, too, gazed out unseeing at the river. He could say nothing, he was so choked by emotion.

Philip's words had done their damage. He sensed, deep in his heart, that he and Leila would have to start all over again. At that moment, she was as far from him in spirit as if she were across the Mediterranean Sea, half a world away.

Chapter 23

⁓⦾⦿⦾⁓

"**M**ay I roll those bandages, Lady Leila?" Nicholas asked, eagerly eyeing the new pile of linen strips atop the table. He pointed with pride at the clumsily rolled bundles he had stacked in a lopsided pyramid. "See, I finished the ones you gave me."

"So you did," Leila replied with an indulgent smile, handing him the strips she had just cut from a large bolt of white fabric. "And what a fine job, too. I don't know how I'd get all my work done without you, Nicholas de Warenne."

As the little boy giggled and plunged happily into his new task, Leila found herself watching him for a moment.

Truly, what would she have done these past four weeks without Nicholas? He had become her constant companion during the long days she had spent in her hospital, his lively chatter and enthusiasm the tonic she needed to keep her mind off her troubles.

She glanced ruefully around the room lit with late morning sunshine, at the clean-swept floors, whitewashed walls, and tidily made beds.

Her empty hospital.

Few patients had come through her door, and so far none had required an overnight stay. There had been some children with scraped knees and cuts, knights who had drunk too much the night before, a first-time mother still two months from childbirth who had come in with the usual fears and worries, a serving woman with cramps, but not much else. And all of these people had been closely associated with Warenne Castle. She had seen no tenants from the surrounding villages and farms. Not one.

Sighing softly, Leila gazed at Nicholas again. It was funny how he had opted to spend much of his time with her rather than shooting a bow and arrow with his friends, chatting with the castle guard, or playing with his hunting dogs or pet hawk, all things he had said he liked to do. She had to admit she was becoming quite fond of him, which concerned her.

These last weeks had not changed her mind about anything. She still clung fiercely to her plan of escape. She had managed to add some coins to her hidden cache, a portion of the money Guy had given her to spend when traveling merchants and their caravans visited the castle, and now she had his late mother's ring as well. Yet altogether it still wasn't nearly enough to pay her way back to Damascus.

She glanced at the wide, filigreed gold band on the third finger of her left hand. Three bloodred rubies glinted like crimson fire in the sunlight filtering through the glazed window.

Guy had given it to her on the same day he had told her about the hospital. Now every time she looked at the ring, she felt a terrible guilt, but there was nothing to be done about it. She was determined to leave him, which meant she was determined to leave Nicholas, too. This empty room was only one small proof that love could not overcome the fact that she didn't belong here, that she would never be accepted.

Leila threw the child a small smile when he looked up to find her studying him. He grinned and fell back to his work, his small fingers fumbling with a strip as he tried to roll it carefully.

Guy must have looked a lot like Nicholas when he was young, she thought absently, with a light dusting of freckles across his nose and a shock of fair hair that continually fell over his brow. As Nicholas swiped it away, his face scrunched in avid concentration, she almost hated herself for the scheme she nurtured. Yet she could not send Nicholas away, though she knew it was selfish of her to spend so much time with him. The child would probably be hurt when one day she mysteriously disappeared.

Leila was besieged by a now-familiar heartache. She did not even want to think about how Guy would feel.

He had been twice as solicitous of her since that awful scene with Philip, and there had been many times during their nights together when she had questioned the plan that drove her. It was so easy to fear she was making a terrible mistake when she was sated and flushed from passion, his whispers of love lulling her to sleep.

She was glad she hardly saw him in the daytime. That would have made things twice as difficult.

Thankfully Guy had been kept busy dealing with the Welsh insurgents—most of whom had already been caught and punished, their rebellion crushed—and training his knights so they might be ever ready for warfare. Yet though their paths rarely crossed except in the evening, memories of his fervent night whispers haunted her every waking moment, branded as they were upon her heart.

Leila could not suppress a sigh as she touched the glittering ring. Being in love with a man she was desperate to leave was the cruelest torture.

"All done!" Nicholas chirped, shattering her melancholy reverie. He looked at the bare table in front of her. "Aren't you going to cut any more?"

Leila gave a small laugh which sounded hollow to her ears. "I guess I don't work as fast as you." Setting her cutting knife and the bolt of linen on the table, she rose from her stool and fetched his fur-lined jacket from a peg near the door. "I have a better idea, Nicholas. Why don't you run to the kitchen and tell the cook to send some hot cider and honey rolls to the hospital? We've both worked so hard this morning, I'd say we deserve a treat to tide us over until the midday meal. What do you think?"

Nicholas bobbed his head, hardly able to stand still as Leila helped him into his jacket. He ran to the door, calling out to her over his shoulder, "If you cut more bandages, Lady Leila, don't roll them. I want to do it when I get back!" Then he flew outside, the room becoming eerily silent as if much of its life had been sapped by the child's departure.

Shivering, Leila closed the door firmly against the brisk wind outside. She had never experienced such low temperatures in Damascus, even at the height of winter. Here, though it was only late fall, she always felt chilled, and on the numerous days when it rained she was miserable indeed.

Guy had told her that colder, wetter weather was yet to come, but she couldn't imagine it growing any worse. He had also said snow might fall, at least in the hills. The only snow she had ever seen was the year-round frost atop mighty Mount Kassioun, and that only from a distance.

Another first among many, Leila thought with a sense of resignation, donning her fur-lined mantle against the chill. She suspected she might very well see a winter at Warenne Castle unless her cache of coins grew at a faster rate.

Wondering how she might accomplish that, Leila picked up the large coal bucket near the door and went to each of the five braziers set about the room, replenishing them as needed. Straightening up from having filled the last one, she was suddenly assailed by dizziness and dropped the bucket. Coals rolled across the planked floor.

"Oh, no . . ." she groaned, sinking down on a bed flecked with coal dust. Resting her flushed face in her hands, she had the very real sensation that she was going to retch. She tried to swallow it down, but—

She upturned the bucket just in time.

When she was finished a few moments later, she knew that her worst suspicion was confirmed. There was another challenge she must face. She was pregnant.

She had hoped against hope that she was wrong when she missed her monthly flux two weeks ago, but the noticeable changes in her body all pointed to the same conclusion. She could have read them from one of her father's medical texts on childbearing—the swollen tenderness in her breasts, her unusual sluggishness, her pale complexion . . .

She glanced miserably at the bucket. Now this.

She rose shakily and walked over to the tall cupboard where she kept all her medicines, well out of Nicholas's reach, and searched through the vials and small crocks until she found the cardamom. Using a pestle and mortar, she crushed the seeds into an aromatic powder, then stirred in some cool water. She didn't bother to pour the mixture into a goblet. Lifting the pestle, she drank it down, hoping the antinauseant would act quickly.

It did. In minutes she felt better. She dampened a cloth and wiped her face and mouth, grateful that her lightheadedness had all but disappeared. After pulling clean linen from a low drawer and grabbing a broom, she went back to the bed, anxious to clean up the mess before Nicholas returned. She was so intent on changing the coal dust-blackened sheets that she wasn't aware that the door had opened until she felt a cool breeze on her back.

"Close the door, Nicholas," she said, "and sit down at the table. I'll be right there."

"What happened, Leila? There are coals all the way to the door."

She gasped, shoving the offensive bucket under the bed as she whirled around.

"Guy!" It still felt strange to call him by his first name, but he had insisted she do so when he gave her the ring. She glanced from the telltale coals at his feet to his concerned face. "I—I tripped, 'tis all," she stammered, trying to regain her composure. "While filling the braziers. But I'm fine. Really."

"The servants should be doing that for you," he said almost sternly, shutting the door and walking toward her. "Or did you dismiss them again?"

Leila managed a nonchalant shrug, though his unnerving presence made her feel anything but calm. He seemed to dwarf the room.

"It looked to be another slow day, so there was no sense in keeping them here. I thought they might have other things to do." That was true enough. During the first two weeks she had spent at the hospital, she and the three serving women Guy had chosen to help her had done a lot of staring at each other. Now she just sent them away in the morning, saying she'd call upon them if needed. Attempting to change the subject, she added, "Have you and your men finished training so soon?"

Guy nodded, his face grim as he surveyed the empty room. "Nicholas stopped to watch us on his way to the kitchen. When I asked him how your morning was going, do you know what he said? 'No sick people today, Papa.' I'm convinced my tenants have been warned away from your hospital, but I can't confront the man I believe to be the culprit until I've had a chance to find out if there's any truth in my suspicion."

"Philip?" she asked softly, though she already sensed it was he. He had avoided her as if she were a leper since they had all stood together in this room.

"Yes. I'm taking some of my men with me into the villages to ask questions. I should know by sunset if Philip has broken our agreement." Guy reached out and stroked the side of her face. "Are you sure you're all right? You're so pale."

It was all Leila could do to meet his eyes. "Yes." She was relieved when Guy drew her into his arms and couldn't read the truth in her eyes.

He must never know about the child, she vowed fervently, her cheek pressed to his heart. He must never know. Somehow she would have to leave before he ever found out . . .

"Ah, Leila, you've done such a wonderful job preparing this hospital," Guy said, hugging her tightly. His voice grew impassioned, his body tense. "No one shall take this from you. That I promise. No one."

She closed her eyes as he lifted her chin, his mouth moving over hers with such poignant intimacy and passion that she could not help but respond. He knew how to ply her, how to set her blood on fire, and he did so now, kissing her until she was breathless.

Her arms snaked around his neck and she leaned against him, her fingers threading through his sweat-damp hair.

The chain mail beneath his surcoat pressed into her tender breasts, but she didn't care, the sensation arousing a desire that ever burned for this man.

She felt his strong hands cup her bottom and she gasped, thinking wantonly of the night he had been so hot for her that he had not waited to remove all of his armor. His engorged shaft, when freed, had been as hard and relentless as the metal sheathing his body, their merging so intense that the memory of it filled her even now with the wildest yearning.

Would he take her now as he had that night? Oh, please. Please . . .

Her disappointment was painfully acute when he drew back from her, and she dazedly opened her eyes to find him smiling.

"You tempt me beyond all endurance, wife. My body longs for your sweet softness . . ." His short laugh was more a groan, and he captured her in his fierce embrace. "But I fear our passion must wait until my return. I think we would soon be interrupted by a young boy bringing spiced cider for his mother."

Leila froze in his arms. "Nicholas called me his mother?"

"Yes. You've won his heart. Hasn't he told you?"

She shook her head, stunned.

Guy chuckled as he played with an ebony tendril that had come loose from her braid. "Give him time. He is cautious with his emotions, as was his father until he met his own lady fair." He pushed her slightly away so he could look in her eyes, his expression serious. "But once the love is given, it is forever."

Dear God, why, why was he saying this to her? Leila thought wildly. It was one more band of iron around her heart. One more bond she must break to leave him.

She saw a flicker of pain cross his striking features—because she did not answer?—but it was quickly gone and he kissed her again. This time it was a kiss of farewell.

"I must go," Guy said, releasing her slowly and with obvious reluctance. "Langton, Burnell, and a few others are waiting for me by the gatehouse. Until tonight, my love."

He strode to the door, calling out to his son, who suddenly appeared on the threshold, "Ho! There you are, Nicholas. And where is the hot cider you promised the beautiful lady?"

"Cook is bringing it," Nicholas replied, flourishing what looked to be the last of a honey roll. "And more pastries, too!" Giggling, he popped the bit into his mouth and noisily licked his fingers.

Guy glanced wryly at Leila, who was smiling at the boy's antics despite her deep anguish.

"His manners leave much to be desired, but he's a good lad." His gaze trailed over her lingeringly. "And oh, how I envy him his company." Throwing her a roguish smile that hinted of their reunion later, he rumpled Nicholas's hair and was gone.

Leila walked to the door, unable to take her eyes from Guy as he crossed the bailey and mounted Griffin. She felt a small sticky hand clutch hers.

"Come on, Lady Leila. Let's make some more bandages until cook gets here."

She nodded, watching as the huge gates swung closed behind the small band of six knights, but still she did not move. It was only after she felt an impatient tug that she shut the door and followed Nicholas back into the room.

"I've heard enough," Guy said grimly to Henry Langton as they strode from the farmhouse back to where the rest of his men were waiting. "Damn Philip and his pious fervor! No wonder Leila's hospital has remained virtually empty. He's scared everyone away with his nonsensical warnings. Eastern witchery. The devil's magic. I'm going to throttle him!"

He got no response from Henry, nor did he expect one. His usually jovial knight had become more subdued with each farm and village they visited. There were no merry jests to lighten this situation. It was very grave indeed.

Guy swept up the reins dangling on the ground and mounted a restless Griffin. "Let's get back to the castle before it grows dark," he muttered, his five knights falling in behind him as he nudged the huge destrier into a thundering gallop.

How dare Philip jeopardize all the progress he had made with Leila? Guy raged inwardly, his gaze piercing the gray dusk settling over the surrounding woods. Just when he was beginning to catch glimpses of a new emotion in her eyes—not defiance, resentment, or simply desire, but something that set hope flaring in his heart—now he would see only disappointment and hurt as she withdrew from him again. Damn!

Half brother or no, Philip would pay for this gross indiscretion. Any man who would so wantonly disregard an agreement could no longer be trusted. On the morrow, there would be a new steward at Warenne Castle.

Burning to get home so that he might exact his retribution, Guy urged his war-horse into a fast canter as they rounded a curve in the road. He was so caught up in his angry thoughts that he did not hear the deadly zing of arrows until it was too late. As one struck him in the left thigh, cleanly piercing his chain mail, he roared out through his pain, "Ambush!"

Guy lifted his shield to fend off another barrage of arrows and, grabbing the wooden shaft, yanked it from his flesh. Blood spurted and he cursed, realizing the pointed iron head remained embedded in the wound.

There was nothing to be done about it here, and no time to staunch the bleeding. Drawing his sword, he plunged Griffin into the woods after the retreating attackers, who looked to be Welsh from their short leather jerkins and bare legs. God's bones, and he had thought they were done with these rebels!

Several quickly disappeared into the dense undergrowth, but Guy caught up with one man who was almost to his horse. With a single swipe from his sword, he decapitated him. Charging on through the gathering gloom, he heard shrill death screams behind him and hoped they weren't the cries of his own men.

Spying another Welshman already in the saddle and veering his horse hard about, Guy gave chase and easily caught up with him, having the advantage of momentum. Dodging a swinging mace, he struck sideways, and the dark-haired man shrieked horribly, falling from his mount and writhing upon the ground. Guy jumped down from his destrier to deal a death blow, but his sword stopped in midair when he saw his victim's bearded face. The dying man was no Welshman.

"You!" Guy cried, recognizing Baldwin D'Eyvill. He fell to his knees, wincing at the fiery pain in his thigh, and grabbed the knight's bloodied jerkin to shake him hard. "By God, man, what mad folly is this?" he demanded, drawing great ragged breaths.

"So . . . you still live," Baldwin rasped, his hate-filled eyes glittering deliriously in the twilight. They fell to the crimson stain spreading beneath Guy's chausses. "But not for long. You will not escape death again as you did in the Holy Land." He grimaced, his hands futilely gripping his gaping stomach wound. "At last. At last I have avenged . . . my beloved Christine."

Cold realization settled upon Guy. "You murdered the Syrian Governor's messenger." When Baldwin turned away, groaning, Guy shook him again fiercely, disregarding the knight's cries of pain. "You bastard! Your foul treachery almost cost me my head!"

He was greeted by a bubbling rattle from Baldwin's throat, and knew then the man had only moments to live.

"Tell me, damn you! Roger planned this ambush, didn't he? You and the others were sent to murder me, but you disguised yourselves as marauding Welshmen so the blame could not be traced."

"Revenge will be sweet . . . for both of us," the dying knight whispered cryptically, a macabre grin on his swarthy face. "See you in hell, de Warenne. The arrow . . . was poison . . ."

Baldwin jerked, gasping desperately for air as blood oozed from the corner of his mouth, then suddenly he exhaled in a wheezing gasp and fell still. Dead.

Guy released the jerkin, his hands stiff from clutching

it so tightly, and looked with horror at the wound in his leg.

A poison arrow. God help him. His own mortality was so glaring at that moment he could almost taste it. He could almost smell the stench of death creeping over him. One burning thought seized him.

He must get home. He must see Leila. If he was destined to die this night, let it be in her arms, the arms of the only woman he had ever loved.

"Langton! Burnell!" he shouted through the trees, rising shakily to his feet. He wiped the cold sweat from his face, knowing true fear for the first time in his life. Was it happening so swiftly?

Feeling strangely weak, he hoisted himself into the saddle as the sound of hooves pounded toward him. Relief flooded him at the sight of Langton and two other knights. They would help him get home.

"My lord!" Henry cried, reining in beside him. "We've been searching for you. We managed to cut down four of the rebels, but the rest escaped—"

"Not rebels," Guy cut him off. "Gervais's knights, sent to kill me." He gestured to the dead man lying on the ground, the eyes staring sightlessly at the darkening sky. "Baldwin D'Eyvill." He leaned upon the pommel, gritting his teeth against the pain. "Get me to Warenne Castle, Henry. Fast. I took an arrow in the leg. Just before he died, D'Eyvill said it was tipped with poison."

"Can you ride?" Henry asked, his face etched with shock and worry.

"I don't know . . ." In the next instant, the knight was taking the reins from Guy's trembling fingers and jumping up into the saddle in front of him.

"For God's sake, my lord, hold on to me," Henry pleaded, wrapping Guy's arms around his waist and securing them with his free hand. He turned to the other two knights. "Find Montgomery and Burnell and tell them what's happened. We'll meet you at the castle." Then, kicking the war-horse, he shouted, "On with you, Griffin, like the wind. Go!"

As they crashed through the woods to the road, Guy

rested his forehead against Henry's shoulder. The pain in his leg was becoming excruciating, unbearable.

"Leila. I must see her . . .."

"You will, my lord. We haven't far to go."

It was the last thing Guy heard.

Chapter 24

───────◦⟩⟨◦───────

"**O**h, my lady, come quick! Something terrible has happened!" Enid cried, rushing into the bedchamber.

Leila whirled from the window, where she had been admiring the tranquil view of the river, and was astonished to see tears streaming down the serving woman's face. Her heart leaped into her throat, her mind racing. "Nicholas?" He had gone to play in the garden after they closed up the hospital for the day—

"No, no, the boy is fine. 'Tis your husband."

"Guy?" Now it seemed her heart had stopped, everything growing eerily still around her.

"They've taken him to your hospital, my lady. I was near the gatehouse when Sir Henry rode in with him, and he sent me to fetch you. Your husband was wounded in the leg. A poison arrow." Enid wrung her hands miserably. "They said it was a surprise attack. Some of Lord Gervais's men."

Her brother? Horrified, Leila did not wait to hear more. She dashed past the serving woman and down the spiral stairs, one word boring into her brain.

Poison.

She knew from experience that time was of the essence. Perhaps it might already be too late. In all the cases of poisoning she had seen at the Hospital of Nureddine, whether from snakebites, scorpion stings, or a deliberate act of treachery, few sufferers survived unless they were brought in very quickly for treatment.

No, don't even think it! Leila told herself fiercely, tearing outside the keep. She lifted her skirts and raced across the bailey as fast as she could.

It seemed the entire castle was in an uproar, servants huddled here and there in nervous groups, extra guards manning the castle walls—perhaps fearing another attack by her brother?—and agitated knights pacing in front of the hospital. Yet the men cleared a path for her to the door. Leila entered in a rush, stopping short just beyond the threshold at the sight that greeted her.

She could have sworn she had been transported back in time to the night she first saw Guy in the governor's prison.

The room was brightly lit by a dozen or more oil lamps and braziers aglow with fresh coals. Guy was sprawled on two beds that had been drawn together to accommodate his size, and he was surrounded by several knights, Henry Langton among them, who worked feverishly to remove the last of his armor and under clothing. Philip was standing with his back to her at the side of the bed, directing the men.

Seeing the priest, Leila was filled with anger, but she knew she must keep her emotions in check. She did not have time to think or feel. She could only react. Guy's life depended upon it.

"Sir Henry, how long ago did this happen?" she asked in a tone laced with authority, hurrying toward the cupboard where she kept all of her supplies. She quickly piled a thin, sharp knife, linen bandages, and a vessel of olive oil in an earthenware bowl.

Henry glanced up, clearly relieved to see her. "A quarter hour, maybe a little more—"

"There is no need to trouble yourself, Lady Leila," Philip interjected. "I've already prepared a herb poultice to soothe my brother's pain, and St. Rochus, the patron saint of limbs, has been invoked against the vile poison."

Leila gave him little notice as she moved briskly to the bed, her eyes on Henry. "Sir Henry, it is my understanding that when a lord is indisposed or away at court, the wife takes temporary charge of the estate. So I recall being told by the good priest here during my tour of this castle. Am I correct?''

"Yes."

She skipped her gaze to Philip. "Then kindly remove Father D'Arcy from my husband's bedside so I may treat his injury. Unless of course, Father D'Arcy chooses to leave willingly. I believe in prayer, but his particular remedy of invoking the saints to heal my lord's wound will not be needed.''

Without waiting for a reply from either of them, she sat down on the bed and arranged her supplies in front of her. She noticed her hands were shaking and tried to keep calm despite her unease at the ashen pallor of Guy's face. Please, please may I not be too late . . .

That was the last such thought she indulged herself. Ignoring Philip's loud protests as he was escorted to a far side of the room, she tied a linen tourniquet just above the small, jagged hole in Guy's lower thigh.

"Hold him down," she directed the two knights who remained at the bedside as she began to feel gently around the wound. Recalling how Guy had struggled against the scorching irons, she added, "You might want to call a few others to help. The pain of this treatment may be enough to overcome his unconsciousness.''

As three more knights hastened forward from the hushed group standing just inside the door, Leila realized grimly that the arrowhead was still inside the wound, something Philip had obviously missed. She went to the cupboard and fetched wine vinegar to use as an antiseptic and some surgical tools. They weren't as finely made as the ones she had used in Damascus, but they would have to do.

She knelt by the bed this time, daubed around the swollen area with wine, and set to work. To her relief Guy did not even stir, a good thing because the procedure was delicate. In minutes she had removed the iron head, silently cursing whoever had shot the offending arrow, and tossed it with disgust into the bowl.

"Keep holding him," Leila ordered, smearing her lips and the inside of her mouth with olive oil to disinfect them.

She heard gasps as she began to lance the wound with

the razor-sharp knife and vigorously suck out the blood and poison. Probably no one present had ever seen this procedure done before. She immediately spat into the bowl, repeating the process until she judged she had cleansed the wound. Wiping her mouth, she decided to allow the bleeding to continue for a moment to flush the now slightly larger hole. Meanwhile, she would prepare the plaster needed to draw out any remaining poison.

Knowing all eyes were upon her, she worked quickly at the cupboard preparing a paste of sulphur, salt, and citron, the seed of which was known for its extraordinary power against all kinds of poison. After crushing and mixing the ingredients with vinegar and oil, she hurried back to the bed. She cleansed away the blood, then packed the wound with the plaster and covered it with bandages.

Still she was not finished. Guy must take some medicine internally. She prepared another concoction, this time crushing only the inner kernels of citrus seed. Stirring two drams of the powder in a cup of wine, she approached the two knights holding Guy's arms.

"Lift his shoulders and head. He must drink this medicine."

"It is blasphemy, I tell you!" Philip cried, able to remain silent no longer. "She'll only make him worse."

When the knights hesitated, regarding her doubtfully, Leila began to quake inside. Surely Philip would not sway them! She fought to keep her voice steady as she said with as much sternness as she could muster, "The plaster I applied to his wound will not save him if some of the poison has already spread into his body. Only with this medication will he have a chance."

"Dammit, you're wasting time, you fools!" Henry shouted, rushing to the bed and pushing the closest knight out of the way. "I'll help you, my lady." He lifted Guy from behind, but his head hung limply. "Hold up his head or you'll lose yours, I swear it!" he commanded the other knight, who hastily obliged.

Casting Henry a grateful glance, Leila concentrated on opening Guy's slack mouth and pouring in small amounts of the liquid. To her surprise he groaned, choking slightly, his eyes flickering open and then closing again. He was still far from conscious, but this slight change in his condition helped her give him the rest of the medication.

At last the cup was empty and she began to breathe a bit easier. Yes, now he had a chance.

"Lay him down, Sir Henry . . . gently." Leila rested the back of her hand upon Guy's cheek. He had a fever, but that was to be expected. His body was doing battle with the poison that had invaded him. Covering his nakedness with a blanket, she turned and faced the roomful of observers.

"I've done what I can for now," she said truthfully, looking from one concerned face to the next but avoiding Philip's eyes. "Only time will tell if any further treatment will be needed. I suggest you all retire to the hall, where I'm sure supper is waiting. There's nothing you can do here. I'll let you know at once if his condition improves"—she felt a catch in her throat—"or worsens."

"I have a better suggestion," Philip said, glaring at her. "I will be holding a vigil in the chapel for those of you who wish to join me. We shall pray that the lady's cure"—he spat caustically—"proves more than the eastern devilry I believe it to be. If it does not, she and her accursed brother will both share in the blame for my brother's death!"

As the knights filed from the hospital after Philip, talking furtively among themselves, Leila sat heavily on the bench Henry had placed for her near the bed. Her stoic facade was crumbling fast, and it took all her remaining self-restraint not to burst into tears at her helplessness. There was nothing else she could do now but wait.

"Is there anything I can get you, my lady?" Henry asked, lightly touching her shoulder.

She offered him a small smile, but shook her head.

"I'll stay here with you if you'd like."

"No, no, I'd like to be alone with him," she murmured. "There is something you can do, though."

"Name it."

"See to Nicholas. He's probably frightened and confused about all the commotion. Explain to him what has happened and tell him"—she had to swallow hard against the lump in her throat—"tell him I'm taking very good care of his papa. He'll believe that, even if no one else does."

"*I* believe it, my lady," Henry said fervently. "You saved Lord de Warenne's life once. Philip and his herb poultices be damned. I believe that if anyone can save his life now, it is you."

Touched by his faith in her, Leila turned back to Guy as the knight left the room.

She stared through her blinding tears at the rise and fall of his chest, so shallow it almost appeared that he was not breathing. But he was, and she clung to that knowledge, hoping his superb physical condition would help him again as it had in Damascus. If only it hadn't been a poison arrow . . .

No, she didn't want to think about Roger's treachery right now, Leila decided numbly, reaching out and clasping Guy's too warm hand.

She wanted only to think of this man lying so still before her. How she could help him. How she could make him more comfortable.

How much she loved him.

A few hours later, Leila was laying a damp cloth on Guy's feverish forehead when the hospital door creaked open. She glanced over her shoulder and stiffened when she saw Philip.

Now she wished she had not sent Henry away. She was in no frame of mind for another unpleasant encounter with the priest, and from his stony expression, she guessed that was exactly what he intended. She faced him as he approached the sickbed.

"How is my brother?" Philip demanded, glancing beyond her to Guy.

"He is breathing more easily, but otherwise he is much the same," she said honestly, though she hated to admit that her treatment was not acting as well or as quickly as she had hoped. "I've changed the plaster twice and just given him another dose of medicine, but I fear it will take a while longer to know—"

"By then he will be dead," Philip interrupted harshly, his narrowed eyes a volatile gray as he riveted them upon her. "I have no doubt the drugs you use are poisoning his body as much as that arrow, if not more so."

Leila turned away, offering no comment to such a preposterous statement, and missed his sudden movement. She was stunned when Philip rushed right up to the bed. Before she could stop him, he had flung back the blanket and ripped off the bandages covering the plastered wound. He pointed accusingly at the ugly red swelling radiating from Guy's knee to his upper thigh.

"You see! It grows worse. You're killing him!"

Leila tried to re-cover the area, but Philip caught her arm and pulled her back. She winced at his grip, which was astonishingly strong for a man so spare.

"The swelling is normal and would be the same for any such wound, regardless of the poison," she countered calmly, though she was deeply frightened. "Let me go, Philip."

He did not. Instead he twisted her arm until she was forced to sit down on the bench.

"I've had enough of your views, my lady. Now you will hear mine. It is because of you that my brother is lying here near death, and not just from your supposed cure. At the welcoming feast, I heard much from Guy about the events at King Edward's coronation—the fight in the abbey, the tournament. I sensed then that Lord Gervais might seek revenge for your marriage, and so he has. Your brother sent out a band of his men disguised as Welsh rebels to accomplish the foul deed."

Philip's angry words struck home, reinforcing Leila's own sense of blame. She already knew she lay at the heart of this calamity, but what could she do?

"While I still had Guy's confidence," Philip rushed on, his fingers biting cruelly into her flesh, "which has since been denied to me because of you, he also said that you refused his offer of marriage in Canterbury, believing Lord Gervais would allow you to return to Damascus. Is this not true?"

"Yes," Leila answered, trying to pull her arm away. It was no use. Philip held her fast.

"And it was only when you discovered your brother's true plans for you that you finally agreed to the marriage?"

Wondering where these strange questions were leading, she cried, "Yes, yes! Now let go of of me. You're hurting my arm!"

Philip only tightened his grip. "Guy admitted to me that he feared you might still nurture that same vain hope, but he wanted with all his heart to believe you had forsaken it." He lowered his face close to hers. "Tell me, Lady Leila. Is it possible you still harbor a desire to see Damascus again?"

Taken completely by surprise, she could only stammer, "Wh-why do you ask me such a question?"

"Because I would like nothing more than to be rid of you! You've been a curse to Guy since the day he married you and a plague upon this household since the moment you arrived here. You have caused great dissension where there was none before, and now you have brought this terrible misfortune down upon us."

Philip glanced at Guy as if checking to see that his brother was still unconscious, then he met her eyes again. "Leave Warenne Castle. Tonight, this very hour. Lord Gervais's attacks will cease only when you are gone from here. I'll give you as much money as you need to return to Syria, and I will arrange an escort to see you safely as far as Marseilles. I know you came to this land and this marriage unwillingly, and I am offering you a chance to leave it all behind you. What do you say, my lady?"

Leila's thoughts spun wildly. Dear God, if Philip's offer had come earlier that day she would surely have accepted it. Now the goal that had consumed her heart and mind for so long meant nothing to her. Nothing at all.

She didn't want to leave Guy! She had thought of little else since she had been left alone with him. She loved him. He was the father of her child. She wanted to stay with him. She wanted to try and make things work no matter what obstacles they faced. Even if it meant giving up her hospital. For Guy, she would do anything.

Leila was jolted by that sudden realization. Was that why another part of her was urging her to scream out yes, she would go back to Damascus? If there was the slightest chance that her leaving would protect Guy from any more of Roger's vengeful attacks, she would gladly go.

Yet she wasn't convinced that was the case. Maybe Roger would be so incensed to learn that she had gotten away from him that he would continue his bloodthirsty quest for revenge. And even if she was sure, she couldn't leave Guy tonight. His life was still in danger. He might die if left in Philip's care.

"No! You are mistaken," she said vehemently, this last terrible thought fueling her reply. "I have no wish to return to Damascus. Not now. My husband needs me. I have no intention of leaving him."

Yet even as she spoke the words, Leila knew she had not fully made up her mind. She could not bear the thought that Guy might suffer another attack because of her. Sick at heart, she glanced from Philip's face, mottled with rage, to Guy's. She was so lost in her private agony she did not see Philip raise his hand against her. Nor did she hear the door opening or Henry's incredulous cry just as she was struck hard across the face.

"Good God, man, have you lost your senses?"

Pressing the back of her hand to her stinging cheek, Leila watched wide-eyed as Henry rushed across the room with his sword drawn. Outraged, the blond knight pointed the blade at the startled priest's throat.

"Move away from the lady, Father D'Arcy. Now!"

Philip did so, bumping into beds as he inched his way backward to the door. "How dare you raise a weapon against me, Langton," he muttered. "I am the steward of this castle—"

"I daresay not for long," Henry interrupted him, his face reddened with anger. "Not when Lord de Warenne learns of what you have just done. He already knows how you've turned his tenants against Lady Leila with your ridiculous warnings. He was going to confront you when he returned . . ." He swallowed hard, unable to finish. Instead, he glanced at Leila. "Are you all right, my lady?"

"Yes," she murmured, though her ears still rang from the blow.

Henry shifted his gaze back to Philip. "Get out," he ordered. "If I see you near this hospital again, I'll have you thrown in the castle dungeon. Is that clear?"

Philip said nothing as he stormed from the room, his black robes fading quickly into the night.

Slamming the door behind him, Henry shook his head as he walked back to the bench. "I should never have left you alone in here," he berated himself as he sat down next to Leila. "I should have known he would try to harass you further."

Leila heaved a ragged sigh, compassion for the misguided priest welling inside her. She knew there was pain, frustration, and worry behind his anger.

"Philip was only trying to protect his brother from what he doesn't understand," she said quietly. "A brother he loves."

Henry looked bewildered. "You defend him after what he just did to you?"

"I would probably react much the same if I believed someone I loved was being threatened. I, too, would try to stop it."

Pondering the words that had come from some deep part of herself, Leila rose and gently placed the bandages back over Guy's plastered wound. As she covered him with the blanket, she noted that his color was somewhat better, and she pressed her fingers to the base of his throat to check his pulse. It was much stronger.

Relief swept through her. That last dose of medicine must have helped.

"How is he, my lady?"

Leila's hand was shaking as she swept the hair back from Guy's forehead. Her reply was hardly more than a whisper. "Improving."

"Thank God."

Yes, she thought, murmuring a fervent prayer. Thank God.

Dozing fitfully on the bed next to Guy's, Leila woke abruptly when she suddenly heard a noise, half sigh, half whisper. She propped herself up on one elbow and looked around the dimly lit room.

Guy was still flat on his back, his features masked by shadows. His breathing was slow and regular, just as it had been when she had finally lain down to get a little rest.

She glanced at Henry, who was lying on a bed pushed in front of the door, his drawn sword held crosswise upon his chest. Had he perhaps said something in his sleep?

After a long moment Leila lay back down and laced her fingers behind her head. She stared at the raftered ceiling, wondering if she had only dreamed the sound.

"Leila . . ."

She sat up, her gaze flying instinctively to Guy. Sweet Jesu, she hadn't dreamed it! She knew that voice.

She was at his bedside in an instant. She had never known such joy as when she saw his eyes flutter open. Her breath seemed to be stuck in her throat when he turned his head and looked at her. To her amazement, he smiled weakly.

"I knew . . . I knew you were here, my love. Your perfume . . . so sweet. Damask rose."

Hot tears stung her eyes. "Yes. I'm here."

Guy's smile faded to a grimace as he shifted on the mattress. "God, the pain," he murmured hoarsely.

"You must lie still," she admonished him, wiping away the tears on her face. "The pain is bad now, but it will pass. I promise you. Just lie still."

He found her damp hand and clutched it tightly. "Stay with me, Leila."

She could not speak. She still did not know if she should go or stay. Dying inside, she forced a faint smile and nodded.

Chapter 25

～・◯◯・～

"**Y**ou have a fine hospital, my love, but those straw-filled mattresses leave much to be desired," Guy said with some effort, wincing as Leila continued her light prodding. "If I must remain abed for the rest of the week, as you say, I'd rather be in here, in our bedchamber."

Leila did not readily reply, her concentration focused on his wound.

Considering that it had been less than two days since Guy had been injured, his leg was healing remarkably well. The swelling and redness were nearly gone, and already the flesh appeared to be mending. As for the rest of him, his healthy pallor had finally returned along with his appetite, both very good signs that the poison in his body had been defeated. His stubborn insistence that he be moved out of the hospital was also evidence of his rapid recovery.

"Yes, I'm sure you'll be more comfortable now," Leila agreed softly. Her heartache was painfully acute as she busied herself spreading ointment around the wound and applying fresh bandages.

She still had come no closer to deciding if she should leave him or stay. Every time that it was on the tip of her tongue to tell Guy how much she loved him, she had only to think of Roger's treachery, and the impulse was stilled. What use was there in revealing her true feelings to Guy if she might be gone on the morrow?

"Damn!"

She glanced anxiously at Guy. "Did I hurt you? Have I wound the bandages too tightly?"

"No, no, I was just thinking of Philip."

Reserving comment, Leila quietly resumed her task. She imagined he was recalling the unpleasant scene in the hospital yesterday morning.

Despite her plea to let the matter wait until he was feeling better, Guy had summoned Philip to his bedside and angrily relieved his half brother of all his duties at the castle. Then he had banished him to his private chambers in the chapel until he decided further what was to be done with him.

Surprisingly, Philip had said little. When he had looked at her just before leaving, his expression had been almost contrite. She could not forget how shocked he had appeared when he first walked into the hospital to find Guy sitting up in bed. Perhaps he thought he had been summoned to administer last rites.

"I've decided he must leave Warenne Castle," Guy said as she finished tying the last bandage. "I will not have him disrupting your work here any longer." He leaned his head against the brace of pillows propped behind him and sighed with exasperation. "I would forgive him everything if he admitted how wrong he was about you and your medical skills. Surely he can see that you saved my life. That's twice now, Leila."

As Guy reached out and clasped her hand, Leila met his eyes reluctantly, her heart thundering in her breast. Struck by the love she saw reflected in his unswerving gaze, it was all she could do not to throw herself in his arms.

"You should get some rest," she murmured, easing her hand from his grasp. "There will be many more well-wishers who will want to see you this evening."

Knowing he was watching her, and doing her best to ignore it, Leila moved quickly to each window and closed the wooden shutters against the early afternoon sunshine to darken the room. The only light came from the low-burning fire in the fireplace.

She poked at the logs to revive the flames, and froze

when she heard him say, "Perhaps I don't wish to rest, my love. We are blessedly alone. No visitors. Nicholas is at his nap. I would have the reunion promised by your kiss the other day. Did you think I had forgotten?"

Swept by intense longing, Leila felt her hand tremble as she set down the iron poker.

She wanted him. Oh, how she wanted him. She would give anything to feel his kiss upon her lips and his stirring touch. But she knew that if she went to him now, when she was feeling so weak, she would surely lay bare her heart. Lost in her passionate quandary, she was saved from making a reply by a loud knock on the door.

"Who is it?" Guy called out sharply, his irritation at being interrupted evident in his voice.

"Robert Burnell, my lord. I have a reply for you from Roger Gervais."

A reply from Roger? Leila wondered, her desirous thoughts receding as Guy bade him enter. About what?

She had heard several discussions in the hospital among Guy and his knights about the surprise attack—she still was in shock at the news of Baldwin D'Eyvill's unsettling connection with events in the Holy Land—but she did not recall hearing Burnell being charged to visit her brother. Perhaps Guy had done so during one of the few times she was not there. It was possible.

As Robert walked into the firelit room, he seemed nonplussed by the closed shutters. Glancing at her in some embarrassment, as if expecting to find her barely clothed, he mumbled a greeting and hastened to the bed. She followed, anxious to hear their exchange.

"So, how does Lord Gervais answer my charge of attempted murder?" Guy asked his knight tersely.

"He has denied it, just as you expected. He claimed Baldwin D'Eyvill acted only for himself, convincing other Gervais knights to participate in his plan for vengeance both here and in Acre. Gervais said those men have been punished."

"Lies. And has he agreed to meet me in a trial by combat?"

"Aye, my lord. To quote him exactly, 'Tell de Warenne

I look forward to that day with the greatest impatience. When I prove the victor, justice will have been served, and my innocence proclaimed.' ''

''Innocence,'' Guy scoffed. ''He will soon feel the sting of his guilt. Did the bastard sign the agreement?''

''Aye, and it has been dispatched by messenger to the king. The matter now awaits his decision.''

''Good. I have no doubt Edward will approve it. He will recognize that this time Roger has gone too far. We should receive the king's answer within two weeks. By then, I will be ready to fight.''

As they continued to converse in low tones, Leila gripped the bedpost, horrified.

A trial by combat.

She had never seen one, but she knew from the stories she had heard in the great hall after supper that these trials were a grisly business which often led to death. The lance and sword were used to determine guilt or innocence, the barbarous practice fueled by the supposition that God granted victory to the righteous. Yet how could Guy expect to prevail so soon after his injury? He could be struck down. Killed. And all because of her.

Suddenly it became very clear to Leila what she must do.

There was only one way to stop this madness. A devil's bargain must be struck with Roger, who for her had come to embody evil. She would rather lose Guy forever than see him fight her brother to the death.

When Guy learned what she had done, he would hate her for it—and that was exactly what she wanted. He would make no attempt to come after her because he would no longer care . . .

''My thanks for seeing to such an unsavory task, Robert,'' Guy said, drawing Leila back from her numbing reverie. ''Give the same to the men-at-arms who accompanied you. I can imagine Gervais was hardly hospitable to your visit.''

The burly knight snorted, shaking his head. ''He didn't trust us to find our way off his bloody land. We had a fully armed escort to the de Warenne border.''

Guy gave a dry laugh. "Go and refresh yourself, my friend. You look like you could use a good draft of ale."

"So I could, my lord." Robert turned to Leila. "Forgive the intrusion, Lady de Warenne." Then with a nod to Guy, he quit the room.

Leila watched the door close behind the knight, desperately wanting to leave as well. Now that she had made her decision, it was simply too painful to linger. What could she possibly say to Guy—

"Leila, did you hear me?"

She faced the bed with a start. "What? I-I'm sorry."

"I said, if it had been anyone else but Burnell, I would have made him wait," Guy repeated, noting the heightened color on her cheeks which made her appear all the more beautiful. "I've been anxious to hear what Rog—"

"If you don't mind, my lord, I'd rather not talk about my brother right now," she said sharply. "You really should rest, and there are a few things I must attend to in the hospital."

"Very well. We can discuss the matter later," Guy answered slowly, perplexed by her tone.

It was clear she was upset by this news, but why? He had already explained to her weeks ago that she need have no fear that Roger would become her guardian again if he himself was ever struck down in battle. King Edward himself had promised him as much the morning they had left for Wales.

"Is there anything I can get for you before I go?" she asked, her eyes bright in the soft firelight. "Another pillow? A goblet of water?"

"It is not rest my body craves, Leila," Guy said, his gaze falling to the tempting rise and fall of her breasts beneath her snugly fitting lilac tunic. Imagining their pink-crested fullness bared to his touch, he felt a flash of blistering heat race across his loins. "I thirst, but not for water."

His need to possess her was overwhelming. All-consuming. He had demanded to be moved into the privacy of their bedchamber for that very reason. After so narrowly thwarting death, he burned to hold her in his arms again and feel her panting breaths like life's sweet affirmation upon his lips.

Guy held out his hand to her. "Come, my love. Surely your tasks at the hospital can wait."

To his consternation, Leila took several steps backward and darted a glance at the door.

Whatever was the matter with her? he wondered, his hand falling to the mattress. He had never seen her so distracted. He didn't want to think that she was withdrawing from him again, but it seemed that might be the case. Now that he thought about it, her behavior had puzzled him from the moment he had been lucid enough to notice. She had seemed preoccupied and subdued, as if something was troubling her.

Damn Philip anyway! He could only imagine what his half brother must have said to her before Henry had thankfully intervened. Leila had refused to discuss the incident, and he had not pressed her. Now it seemed he should have insisted she tell him about it.

Guy was gripped by a familiar sense of frustration. When, when would Leila ever give him her heart? At times he could swear she had already done so—when he kissed her, when they made love. But when she acted like this he doubted his own instincts.

Enough! he berated himself. If he had to start over with her again, so be it. She meant everything to him. She was worth his every effort to capture her love. Let it begin anew with a kiss.

"Very well. If you will not come to me," he said, flinging aside the fur coverlet, "I will simply come to you."

"No!" Leila cried, rushing back to the foot of the bed. "You mustn't stand on that leg. Not yet."

Guy held out his hand, his startling blue eyes searing into hers. "Then what will it be, my love?"

Desire flooded her body, and Leila knew she had already succumbed to his challenge. There would be no hasty exit. Her heartrending plan would have to wait awhile longer. She only prayed that she would have the strength to leave him after . . .

She took his hand almost before she knew what she was

doing, her knees growing weak at the warm pressure of his palm against hers. He drew her slowly toward him, then his other hand was caressing her face as he looked deeply into her eyes.

"Ah, Leila. I feared I would never touch you like this again. Never hold you—" He seemed to choke, his eyes misting. "God, woman, how I love you. Love you . . ."

And I will always love you, Leila thought with an aching tightness in her breast. *You will be forever in my heart, Guy de Warenne.*

She inclined her head, her gaze straying to his sensuous mouth, and offered no resistance as he tunneled his fingers in her hair and gently pulled her down to him. She felt a warm whisper of breath and then their lips met, fervently, passionately . . . his kiss a joyous reunion, hers a poignant parting.

Yet she realized in that moment that this was what she wanted. This was how she wanted to say goodbye.

With a wantonness born of her overwhelming desire for him, she pulled away slightly and ran the moist tip of her tongue boldly across his lips. She felt a rush of pleasure, knowing she had pleased him, when he groaned against her mouth.

And, oh, how she wanted to please him! She wanted to share herself fully with him, to give him what was rightfully his, holding nothing back!

Leila deepened their kiss, her tongue darting and teasing as she cradled his stubbled jaw in her hands. She was not surprised when his strong arms flew around her and he crushed her to his chest, or when he took the lead. He ravaged her with his mouth until she was breathless and dizzy, and only then did he tear his lips away.

"This must go," Guy demanded hoarsely, tugging impatiently at her tunic. He wanted her so badly he was prepared to shred the cloth from her body.

"Then release me and it shall be done," she murmured, her violet eyes large and liquid with passion. "And in a way I think you will enjoy, my lord."

Guy let her go reluctantly and as she seemed to glide

away from him, he marveled at how little he understood her, this exquisite and baffling woman who was his wife.

He could not comprehend how one moment she could be so reluctant and wary while in the next she was teasing him to madness. But he was certain he would understand in time. If she could desire him like this, then surely one day she would love him as wildly. They had a lifetime to learn to understand each other.

Guy watched spellbound as Leila began to strip out of her clothing, not swiftly but in a languorous fashion that made his blood boil hotter with each passing second.

After removing the silver girdle from around her slender waist, she caught the embroidered hem of her tunic and dragged it over her head, exposing a nearly transparent chainse that did little to hide her bewitching curves. With a motion that was enticingly slow, she began to pull the linen shift up over her body.

Guy wet his lips as her shapely legs were revealed, slim calves and sleek white thighs, and he caught his breath when her ebony woman's hair came into view. The chainse drifted like a gossamer mist over a torso that was wondrous in its perfection, over upturned breasts with hardened, rosy nipples that seemed to plead for his touch.

Guy was in agony by the time she dropped the flimsy garment to the floor to stand naked before him. He began to work at the drawstring on his braies, the only thing he was wearing.

"No, my lord. Wait," Leila bade him when she saw his intent.

She could tell he was aroused from the hungry way he was looking at her and the provocative swelling beneath his short trousers, but she wasn't finished yet. She loosened her thick braid with trembling fingers. She was aroused herself just from the magnificent sight of him. With a light toss of her head, her long silken tresses rippled around her body like a crimped veil. She knew how much he loved her hair.

Leila approached the bed slowly, giving herself time to admire his masculine beauty, which earlier she had done her best to ignore. She never ceased to be amazed by the

massive breadth of his shoulders or the hard muscles which
bound him; she ached to feel their rippling strength beneath her fingers once more. "Let me, my lord," she
insisted when she finally reached the bed.

Guy did not protest when she pushed his hands away
from the drawstring at his waist and finished untying it for
him. Then she began to pull his braies from his hips; he
helped her by lifting his buttocks. She inhaled softly when
his manhood sprang free, but she concentrated for the moment on sliding the trousers carefully from his legs.

"You may sit against those pillows as you are now,"
Leila admonished him gently, climbing onto the bed as
she tossed away his braies, "or you may lie on your back.
But nothing else because of your wound." When he did
not move, his eyes devouring her, she straddled his hips
gracefully and rested her hands on his broad shoulders.
She gasped when he took an aroused nipple into his mouth,
but she shook her head and pushed him back. "No, my
lord. Allow me to pleasure you."

She leaned toward him and kissed him deeply then, her
heart thudding painfully. It was hard to forget that everything she was doing would be for the last time, but she
made a brave attempt. She didn't want him to sense that
anything was wrong.

As her lips strayed from his mouth to his throat, her
splayed fingers glided down his hard, ridged stomach. She
found what she was seeking, for his smooth shaft seemed
to jump into her hand. When she caressed away the wetness already on its tip with her thumb, he moaned softly.

"Leila, no. I don't think I can bear—"

"Shhh," she whispered, leaving a trail of tender kisses
along his scarred right shoulder.

Tears stung her eyes as memories crowded in upon her,
but she willed them away. She edged her knees backward
as she forged a passionate path down his furred chest, her
racing senses reveling in the familiar taste of his skin and
the musky, male scent of him.

Her tongue dipped into his navel and he groaned, his
hips arching slightly. She licked and nipped her way down
the dark line of his hair which she found so erotic and was

amazed to recall that she had once considered body hair offensive.

Even more seductive was the nest of brown curls between his legs. She enmeshed her fingers in them, her nails lightly grazing the thick base of his shaft. Guy arched again, more wildly this time, but it was nothing to when she kissed him up and down the silken length. He cried out her name, rearing and groaning as she took him fully into her mouth. Using her lips, tongue, and even her eyelashes, she plied him with all the special techniques she had been taught.

Leila derived immense satisfaction from his enjoyment and she intensified her caresses, encircling him with both hands and slowly pumping. She could taste him upon her tongue, his skin slippery wet, and she thought fleetingly of the many nights when his mouth had explored the sensitive recesses of her body until she had screamed with ecstasy. She knew he was close to climax, but she didn't want him to spurt his seed just yet. She longed to feel him deep inside her body one last time.

Leila raised her head just as Guy was reaching for her. His eyes were stormy with passion as he dragged her toward him, his mouth capturing hers. She gasped when he lifted her hips and impaled her upon his magnificent erection, and she was not surprised that she was slick and ready for him. His pleasure had already aroused her beyond measure.

"Now it's my turn, my beautiful, beautiful love," Guy whispered jaggedly against her lips. Holding her buttocks, he drove upward until she was full of him, his throbbing strength and power sheathed in her body's tight embrace.

Lifting her head, Leila clutched wildly at the pillows, her fingers digging into them as Guy effortlessly slid her back and forth on top of him in rhythm with his demanding thrusts.

Each time she moved forward, his tongue was a flicking flame at her breasts, and she whimpered incoherently at the delicious combination. It was all sweetness and fire and she closed her eyes tightly, moaning when the sensations grew too hot, too intense . . .

"Hold me, Guy!" she cried, hovering at the brink of rapture for the barest instant until she felt him shudder and explode deep within her, his release igniting her bliss. With lips fused and breaths merging, together they plummeted headlong into that incredible oblivion.

Long moments later, Leila very slowly relaxed her grip on the pillows.

Utterly sated, her head resting upon his shoulder and her body still trembling with echoes of their passion, she could see nothing through the tangled web of hair covering her face. But in one movement, Guy swept it from her cheek and gazed lovingly into her eyes.

"Now I know I am yet alive and this is not a dream," he whispered, tracing the soft curve of her cheekbone.

Leila could have cried out aloud as her false sense of peace and contentment shattered into sharp, glittering shards, his words bringing harsh reality crashing in around her.

And with it came pain. Terrible, heart-wrenching pain. She was being torn in two, her desire to tell him how dearly she loved him threatening to overwhelm her decision to leave. She knew that if she did not free herself from his arms quickly, her resolve would vanish. Reluctantly she began to pull away, but Guy only tightened his embrace.

"Why must you hasten from me, my love?" he asked, kissing the tip of her nose. "We have the whole afternoon—"

She silenced him with a finger to his lips and adopted her most physicianlike tone, though it was all she could do to keep her voice steady. "No, my lord. You must rest now. It is important that you regain your strength, for I doubt you wish to stay abed for more than a week."

"Indeed I do not." He loosened his hold a little, then seemed to reconsider. His hands moved caressingly up and down her slender back. "Stay with me awhile longer, Leila."

She shivered at his touch, recklessly tempted to linger. Somehow she managed to answer convincingly, "I cannot. I may have patients waiting for me in the hospital."

Guy frowned, but she knew it was feigned from the

amusement lighting his eyes. "I can see now that I have
a rival for your attentions, my lady." He squeezed her
bottom playfully, then suddenly sobered. "If it makes you
happy, I suppose I can bear it. We will have tonight."

"Yes," she lied, her heart breaking. "We will have
tonight."

Forcing a small smile, she lifted herself from him and
climbed from the bed. She felt his gaze upon her as she
dressed hurriedly, and was grateful for the room's darkness so he wouldn't see how her hands were shaking. She
took another moment to twist her hair into a loose braid,
tying off the end with a ribbon as she walked to the door.

"You are forgetting something, my love."

Leila spun, her breath catching as she met his eyes.

Guy smiled at her roguishly. "I would have a parting
kiss. Something to last me until you return."

Walking those few steps back to the bed was the hardest
task she had ever undertaken. His warm lips on hers rocked
her completely. After covering him to the waist with the
fur blanket, she hurried from the room without a backward
glance, the door shutting behind her with awful finality.

Don't think of it now, Leila told herself fiercely, running down the stairs. There will be plenty of time for tears
later. You must think only of your escape.

When she stepped outside the keep, she saw that the
sky had grown dark, the heavy clouds which masked the
sun portending a rainstorm. Wrapping her cloak tightly
about her and donning the fur-trimmed hood against the
chill wind, she hurried toward the hospital.

She was relieved to see that there were still some wagons and two-wheeled carts lined up in front of the grain
storehouse, and a group of de Warenne tenants were gathered just outside the open double doors. It was sowing
season for wheat and rye, and an everyday occurrence
for several weeks now to see wagons laden with sacks of
seed rumbling through the gates. If she managed to climb
into one of the wagons without anyone noticing her, she
might be thus able to leave the castle.

As Leila passed the large timbered building, her plan
began to look easier than she had imagined. She spied

two loaded wagons pulled up along the side wall which faced the adjacent storehouse. Even better, they were both covered with canvas—no doubt as a precaution against the threatening storm—and situated in such a way that they were protected from the view of anyone crossing the bailey or the castle guards strolling along the battlements.

Surmising that the drivers were still laughing and talking with the tenants whose wagons were yet to be filled with grain, Leila seized her chance.

Her heart thumping nervously, she cut in between the two storehouses and waited an interminable moment with her back pressed up against the logged wall to see if she was being followed. When boisterous laughter carried to her from the front of the building, she knew none of the tenants had seen her. She rushed to the nearest wagon and was just about to flip aside the canvas when three little boys dashed around the corner, playing a merry game of chase. Her hands fell, and she whirled around when she spied Nicholas at the lead.

"Lady Leila!"

She groaned inwardly at his cry of greeting, wondering what she was going to say to him as the boys came to a breathless halt in front of her, almost stumbling over one another. Eyeing her curiously, Nicholas swiped an errant lock of blond hair from his flushed forehead.

"I-I thought you were napping," she began lamely.

Nicholas shrugged. "I woke up." He glanced at the ground, then back at her. "Did you lose something? We could help you find it." He twisted to look at his friends. "Right?" The two boys bobbed their heads eagerly.

"Ah, no," she replied uncomfortably, hating the thought that she must lie to him. "I didn't lose anything. I was just going to peek under this canvas to see what was inside the wagon."

Nicholas laughed as if she'd said something silly. "It's just seeds. Papa's tenants are going to plant them in the fields."

"Ooohhh." She smiled self-mockingly. "All that curiosity just for seeds. Well, I guess I'll just go on to the hospital—''

"We'll walk you there!" Nicholas blurted, "I want to show my friends the bandages I've made."

"No, no, another time, Nicholas," Leila said, a hard lump in her throat. "The hospital is untidy from all the visitors who came to see your papa the past few days. I'm just going to clean it up." As his face fell, she chucked him gently under the chin. "How about tomorrow morning? You can bring your friends and we'll all make more bandages. Would you like that?"

As he brightened, Leila felt even more wretched.

"Good." She bent and whispered in his ear. "If you start running right now, Nicholas, you'll get a good lead on them and they'll never catch you."

He nodded, throwing his arms around her neck in a fierce hug, then just as quickly he released her and took off at a run toward the back of the storehouse. Startled, the two boys followed him, shouting his name and crying "No fair!" In an instant, all three had disappeared around the corner.

Heartsick, Leila wasted no more time. She threw back the canvas and hoisted herself over the side of the wagon. Taking a last deep breath of fresh air, she dragged the canvas back into place just as thunder crackled high overhead.

A light rain began to pelt the covering and the next thing she knew, a man's voice shouted out, "We'll have to leave now if we're going to beat the worst of this storm."

"Aye, let's be off."

Huddled between two large sacks of grain, Leila let her tears fall as the driver's seat creaked and the wagon lurched into motion.

It couldn't have been more than a half hour later when the wagon came to a final stop.

Wiping her damp face with a fold of her cloak, Leila discerned that they must be in some kind of shelter, for the rain had ceased to batter the canvas and she could hear

the two horses being unhitched. Fearfully she wondered if
the tenant might unload the wagon, but, to her relief, she
guessed he had decided not to when a door opened and
closed, and the building grew quiet. No doubt a warm fire
and a good hot meal awaited him.

She remained very still for a few more minutes just to
make sure he wasn't coming back, then she could stand
the close confines and stuffy air no longer. She cautiously
drew back the canvas and peered above the rim of the
wagon.

To her surprise and good fortune, she found herself in
a stable. And here she had thought she would have to walk
all the way to her brother's castle!

She clambered over the side, wrenching her cloak free
when it snagged on a nail. She immediately went to
the nearest stall and in great haste bridled and saddled the
roan palfrey she found there. She had no idea when the
tenant might return.

She led the nickering animal to the stable door, glad for
the storm raging outside. She hoped the rumbling thunder
and whistling wind would mask the horse's hoofbeats and
conceal her furtive escape.

As Leila pushed open the door, cold rain lashed her
face. Squinting against it, she mounted and nudged the
now agitated palfrey into a trot. The wind whipped the
hood from her head, but she didn't care. All that mattered
was that she reach her brother's castle before sunset. She
did not want to spend the night wandering blind in the
woods.

Once they had cleared the stableyard, she urged the
horse into a gallop across a muddy field. She threw an
anxious glance over her shoulder, thankful that no one was
running out of the small farmhouse. She turned her
thoughts to what lay ahead, trying to get her sense of direction.

She got her bearings a short while later when she
reached the River Usk, which flowed to the south. She
already knew that the Gervais fortress lay some ten miles
southward along the same river.

Leila looked to the north, but she couldn't see Warenne

Castle through the billowing gray mist and driving rain. It was just as well.

"On with you!" she cried hoarsely, veering the palfrey along the rolling bank as they headed south.

Chapter 26

Shivering, wet to the skin and exhausted, Leila sat silently on a bench, a small puddle of water forming at her feet. She watched as Roger paced in front of her, stopping now and again to stare incredulously at her.

He hadn't even given her a chance to change out of her sodden, mud-spattered clothes, which really didn't surprise her. She had no sooner arrived at Gervais Castle, formidably perched upon a cliff above the River Usk, than she was rushed into this private solar adjoining the great hall by the two silent knights who now guarded the entrance. That had been scarcely five minutes ago.

Leila's stomach grumbled noisily at the scent of food wafting through the closed door. The household was at their early evening supper, but she hadn't been offered any sustenance. It seemed Roger had no thought for any amenities, especially after what she had just told him.

"I want to know if I heard you correctly," Roger said, halting a few feet from the bench. His hard blue eyes searched her face. "You have left your husband."

Leila sighed wearily. "Yes."

"And you wish to obtain an annulment of your marriage because you were forced to consent to it against your will. Is that right?"

"Yes." Her low answer was like a death knell upon her heart.

Roger shook his head in disbelief and glanced at Maude, standing off to the side, her face composed as if chiseled in stone. She had said nothing yet, just listened with her hands clasped so tightly that her knuckles shone white.

Leila saw the look which passed between them, a strange mix of total amazement and shrewd cunning. She could sense their barely controlled excitement like a ripe fragrance hanging in the air. She imagined they were already counting the money her fortuitous appearance would soon bring them.

"Who told you marriages could be so annulled?" Maude queried, breaking her icy silence.

"We had overnight visitors a week ago at Warenne Castle, a Marcher lord traveling with his lady to north Wales," Leila explained dully. "At supper, the woman was quite free with her talk of the past, saying she had once been married against her will to a man three times her age. After she pressed her suit to King Henry, the unlawful union was dissolved." When Maude's expression did not change, Leila grew fearful that her efforts might have been wasted. "I can do this, can't I?"

"Oh, yes, you certainly can," Roger answered for his wife. "But what I want to know, dear sister, is how you managed to escape from a heavily guarded fortress."

When Leila told him, Roger threw back his head and laughed. The ringing sound gave her chills, for it held no humor, only scorn.

"Priceless. Absolutely priceless," he said to Maude. "De Warenne's recent misfortune gave her just the opportunity she needed. While he was lying abed convalescing, his wife eluded him in a grain wagon! God, how I would love to see his face when he discovers she's gone, and for good. When Guy finds out she's taken refuge here with us and wants an annulment . . ." His voice trailed into loud, mocking laughter.

He will hate me, Leila thought desolately, finishing her brother's sentence. She lowered her head and stared blindly at the floor.

She had never felt so sick at heart or so weary of spirit, yet she knew she would simply have to grow used to this wretched pain. It was the price she had to pay.

She wanted Guy to hate her, to curse her name, to wish

he had never met her, to wish she had never lived. If his hatred and sense of betrayal kept him away from Roger, her sacrifice would not be in vain. If her annulment kept Roger away from Guy, her loss would have gained her something. She would do anything to keep them apart.

She started when she saw two black boots plant themselves in front of her, and she cried out when Roger roughly forced up her chin. No longer laughing, his face was very grim.

"Something doesn't make sense to me, Leila, and I want you to tell me the truth. Why did you really come here? Why didn't you keep riding all the way to Dover and be rid of us all? You made no secret of your desire to return to Damascus, and you already know damn well what we will plan for you once your annulment becomes final." He squeezed her jaw cruelly. "Something drove you here. What?"

Her throat was so constricted with emotion, Leila could barely force out an answer. She lowered her lashes as tears filled her eyes. "I came here . . . to propose a trade. If you refuse to meet Lord de Warenne in a trial by combat and cease your acts of vengeance against him, I promise to willingly marry anyone you choose for me."

Roger's eyes narrowed and he snorted with disgust. "By God, I don't believe it." He released her so abruptly she almost fell backward off the bench. "She's in love with the bastard. She's doing this for him."

"Does Lord de Warenne know you love him?" Maude demanded, rushing forward to grip Roger's arm. "If he does, my husband, that will surely bring him down upon us—"

"No, of course not!" Leila cried. "He knows nothing. He thinks I despise him and he will surely believe it now that I have left him to seek an annulment. He doesn't even know I'm pregnant with his child!"

As her last words echoed in the room, she immediately wished she could retract them. Roger's face was red with anger.

"You're breeding?" he demanded, approaching her slowly.

"Y-yes, but why should that matter?" she replied, her voice sounding strangely shrill to her ears. "When I overheard you in your tent at Westminster, you said it would make no difference. Y-you said that whomever you married me to"—she almost choked—"would accept the child as his own."

"You little fool!" Roger cried. "What I said then has no bearing on our situation now. If we could marry you off quickly, it would be one thing. Any potential suitors would easily be deceived. But your annulment could take weeks to be approved by the Church, maybe longer."

"There might also be a royal inquiry," Maude interjected, staring coldly at Leila, "since you stated your consent to the king in Westminster Abbey."

"Yes, that could further delay the ruling," Roger continued harshly. "By then, you will be far gone with de Warenne's bastard, for that is what you will bear when your union is declared void. Your damnable pregnancy will only hinder our chances of arranging a marriage from which we can profit. Few will want to wed you, knowing you will soon have another man's bastard at your tit, and even if someone does, he'll hardly be willing to pay the full bride price I demand."

"What are you saying?" Leila asked, panic building inside her.

"You must rid yourself of the child."

"No," she breathed, horrified. "No!" Jumping up from the bench, she attempted to dart around it, but Roger caught her arm and wrenched her back to face him.

"Hear me well, my dearest sister. Your touching sacrifice will save Guy from any more unfortunate accidents in the future only if you do exactly as I say. And yes, I might even refuse to meet him in judicial combat if you rid yourself of his bastard spawn. You saw how he fell at the king's tournament. If I fight him, I promise you he will fall again, but this time with my lance buried deep in his heart. Now decide!"

Stricken with horror, Leila could only shake her head numbly, which infuriated Roger all the more.

"Perhaps you need some time to think," he muttered

through clenched teeth. "I believe a dark cell is just the place to encourage some serious reflection." As he began to drag her to a side door, he threw a terse command at Maude. "Send for the healer and have her prepare a potion. I want it to be ready when Leila comes to her senses. And you two"—he sharply addressed his somber-faced knights—"find the priest! If Anselm is not at supper, he's probably in the village visiting that Welsh mistress of his. If so, ride out and fetch him. I want him to prepare the annulment documents tonight so they may be sent by messenger to the archbishop first thing in the morning."

"Aye, my lord," they answered as one, following Maude from the solar.

Leila's eyes were so blinded by tears she could barely see as Roger yanked her through a dark corridor and into an adjoining building. She sensed it was the keep when her hand scraped against a rough stone wall, and she wiped her eyes so she might have some idea where she was being taken.

Roger had said a dark cell, she thought wildly. Did he mean to lock her inside . . . ?

Her worst fears were confirmed when Roger grabbed a hanging lantern and they began to descend a narrow flight of stairs. Deeper and deeper into the bowels of the keep he led her, down two more flights of worn stone steps until finally they reached the bottom. There was no floor, only hard-packed dirt, and a barred door fitted into each wall.

"You'll find this dungeon is quite unpleasant," Roger said tightly. He flung open one of the doors and thrust Leila so roughly inside the small cell that she tripped and went sprawling into the filthy straw. "I doubt you'll want to stay here very long. As soon as you agree to my demand, you will be released." He began to swing the door closed, then stopped, holding up the lantern in such a way that his eyes shone malevolently. "Just think well on everything I've said, Leila. There will be nothing else for you to do down here."

Leila flinched as the door slammed shut and the bar outside clanked into place. She was alone. In pitch darkness.

Great wrenching sobs began to tear at her throat and chest, and for a long moment she was too paralyzed with shock to move. It was only when she heard faint squeaking sounds that she gasped and fell quiet, choking on her tears.

Dear God. She was not alone.

Shrieking in terror, she scrambled through the straw, groping wildly for a corner. When she found one, she huddled there, hugging her knees to her chest and pressing her wet face to the cold wall.

She bit her clenched fist until blood came, listening as the straw rustled and seemed to come alive all around her. Something brushed her foot.

She began to scream and could not stop.

Furious, Guy burst into Philip's bedchamber. His eyes narrowed as his half brother rose in surprise from his writing desk.

"Dammit, man! What did you say to her?"

Philip looked confused. "Say to whom? What are you talking about?"

"Leila! She's gone, fled the castle, and I think it's because of something you said to her."

Philip stared at him in disbelief. "Lady Leila is gone?"

Grimacing from the pain in his leg, made all the more acute by his chausses rubbing against the bandages, Guy leaned on a chair for support. "Good God, man, haven't you heard the uproar outside? I've over a hundred men mounting up at this moment to go out and look for her."

"No. I've been so absorbed in my work . . ." Philip spread his hands. "Are you sure she's gone? Have you looked in the hospital?"

"Of course! That's where I thought she was all afternoon until I sent Enid a short while ago to fetch her. Enid found the hospital empty and the braziers cold. No one has been there for hours. As she came rushing back to tell me, she spied Nicholas playing in some mud puddles near the kitchen. Do you know what he said when she asked him if he'd seen Leila?"

Philip shook his head, his face pale.

Guy's gut twisted in torment, his anxiety eating him

alive. "Nicholas saw her by a wagon near the grain store-house. She must have hidden herself in it to get out of the castle."

"But have you looked everywhere else?" Philip blurted. "There are so many places she could be—"

"She's nowhere to be found. No one has seen her," Guy cut him off sharply. Limping, he approached his brother. "What the hell did you say to her the other night before Henry found you together in the hospital? Damn you, Philip, you struck her!" His voice rose to a shout. "Tell me!"

Clearly shaken, Philip sank onto the stool. "I-I told her she was a curse to you and this household. I blamed her for the dissension between us and for the assault that almost killed you, and I said that it was because of your marriage that Lord Gervais was seeking revenge against you. I said I wanted to be rid of her and I made her an offer. But she turned it down. I was so angry, I hit her . . ." Philip's shoulders slumped, and he fell silent.

Guy was assailed by dread. "What offer?"

"If she agreed to leave that night, I was prepared to give her enough money to see her way back to Damascus, with safe escort to Marseilles."

"You would have done this to me?" Guy asked incredulously, quiet rage building inside him. "You know Leila means more to me than my life, yet you would have helped her to leave me?"

"I thought she was killing you with her cure!" Philip exclaimed, his eyes heavy with remorse. "I didn't know what else to do to get her away from you. How could I have known her eastern medicine would save your life?" He lowered his head. "I'm sorry, Guy. Truly sorry. I was wrong about Leila, about her skills. I've thought of nothing else for two days. I was planning to talk to her tonight, to ask her forgiveness—"

"It seems you are too late," Guy said bitterly. "Since she found so little acceptance here, maybe she decided to take your words to heart after all. Or perhaps she planned to leave me all along, and in that wagon she finally found her opportunity. Oh, God . . ."

"I cannot believe that," Philip objected. "When she denied my offer, she said she had no wish to return to Damascus. I saw her eyes, Guy. I would swear she meant it."

Guy was so mired in his tormented thoughts that he barely heard him. He had never been at such a loss.

Ah, Leila, why have you done this? Why?

He simply could not bring himself to believe she had left him out of hatred. Not after what they had shared earlier that day. She had never made love to him so completely, so freely. It wasn't possible—or was it?

Had her impassioned kiss, her trembling touch fooled him so thoroughly? While he had exulted that he lived to hold her in his arms again, what had filled her heart? Loathing? Resentment? She had lied to him about going to the hospital. She had said she would return, that they would spend tonight together, when all the while she knew she was going to leave him!

Guy clenched his fists. Had she saved his life, then, not because she cared, but only because of her ingrained duty as a physician? And when he had recovered, had she felt that her obligation was fulfilled? Dear God, someone tell him it wasn't so!

"My lord. Griffin is saddled and waiting outside the chapel."

Guy glanced up at Henry Langton in the doorway. "Are the men ready to ride?"

"Yes. We await your orders."

"Surely you can't mean to join them, Guy," Philip said in disbelief, rising abruptly. "Your wound—"

"The hell with my wound! Do you think I could sit idly by while my wife is out there somewhere, alone and unprotected?" Guy ignored the burning pain in his leg as he moved with impatience to the door. "Enough talk. It's already growing dark. I have discovered what I needed to know."

As he and Henry hurried down the stone steps, Philip hastened after them.

"I want to ride with you, Guy. I want to help look for Leila."

Stepping outside the chapel into a light drizzle, Guy looked back at his half brother, his expression grim. "No. I want you to stay here and pray, Philip. Pray very, very hard that we find her. I promise you there will be hell to pay if we don't."

"Lord de Warenne!"

Guy turned as Robert Burnell rushed toward him, a stout, red-faced farmer puffing alongside the swarthy knight. He recognized the man as one of his tenants.

"What is it?" he demanded, growing increasingly impatient to begin their search while there was yet some daylight.

"My lord, this is one of the men who came to the castle today for grain. He has some news—"

"Aye, my lord, news indeed," the farmer blurted. "I only discovered an hour past, when I went to unload the wagon and feed the stock, that my fine roan mare was stolen from the stable. I found this"—he held out a piece of dove-gray fabric—"hanging from a nail on the sideboard. I've never known a Welsh rebel to dress in fine velvet, my lord. Then when I arrived here to report the crime, Sir Burnell told me about your lady . . ." He grew silent, looking extremely uncomfortable.

Guy's pounding heart seemed to fill his throat as he took the tattered fragment and rubbed it between his fingers. "It's from Leila's cloak," he said. "Were you able to find any tracks after the storm?"

"Aye, my lord, I followed what was left of the hoofprints for a good distance before I came here. They headed west for about a half mile, then turned sharply south at the River Usk."

West and south, Guy thought, puzzled. Leila should have ridden directly to the east if she was heading for London. Then where the hell . . . ?

His gut instinct suddenly gave him the startling answer. "She's gone to her brother," he stated with cold certainty. "I would swear it. There would have been no other reason for her to ride south."

"God's teeth, my lord, why would she have done that?" Henry exclaimed, shaking his head. Then he glanced sharply at Guy, incredulity in his eyes. "Does she know of the trial by combat?"

"Yes. We were together when Burnell gave me the news. What of it?"

"She said something to me, my lord, the night you were wounded. It might explain—"

"Speak up, man!" Guy demanded.

"Philip had just left the hospital, and Lady Leila pitied him, even though he had struck her. She said that Philip was only trying to protect you, and that if she believed someone she loved was being threatened, she would do the same. She would try to stop it."

Someone she loved . . .

Henry's words seemed to ring in Guy's brain, flooding his heart with bittersweet joy.

Had Leila left him out of love? She had acted so strangely after hearing that he would fight Roger. Had she gone to her brother in hopes of somehow preventing the trial by combat? Surely she knew Roger would not be swayed by tearful pleas. She would have to give him something, promise him something. But what? All she had to barter with was herself . . .

"Mount up," Guy ordered, his realization chilling him to the bone. "I have no illusions that Roger will release Leila if I make a formal demand for her return. Though she went of her own accord, she will be his prisoner now. And I have no patience to make preparations for a lengthy siege. By the time we reach the Gervais fortress, it will be dark, and there will be no moon tonight to betray our movements. We'll scale the walls and take them by surprise."

"And if Roger and his men already expect us, my lord?" Henry queried, his face clouded with doubt.

"Unlikely. After his mistreatment of Leila at Westminster, I'm sure Roger believes the last place I'd expect her to go would be to him. And he probably thinks I'm still too ill to get out of bed even if I did guess where she was, the bastard! I imagine that he and Maude are raising a goblet right now in honor of their unexpected good fortune." Infuriated by the thought, Guy seized Griffin's reins from his squire, adding grimly, "If the fortress does prove heavily guarded, we'll just have to fight all the harder."

As the two knights nodded in assent, Guy clenched his teeth against the pain and hoisted himself into the saddle. He pulled his restless war-horse hard about, then rode to the gatehouse, where he turned and faced the crowded bailey. Forty armored knights and almost a hundred men-at-arms stared back at him, silent and waiting.

"Prepare your hearts for battle," he roared. "We ride against Roger Gervais!"

Chapter 27

～◦◦◦～

Guy watched from the trees as a small force of thirty men-at-arms carrying hastily constructed scaling ladders crept stealthily across cleared ground toward the Gervais fortress. When they received his signal, their orders were to clamber over the curtain wall and open the massive gate to the remainder of his forces.

He took a deep breath and said another swift prayer of thanks that there was no moonlight. A cold drizzle continued to fall and a mist was rising from the river, but as yet it wasn't thick enough to grant them extra cover.

"My lord, someone approaches along the road from the village," came Henry's tense whisper.

"Damn!" Guy hid himself behind a huge tree trunk, signaling for the rest of his men to do the same. Their horses had been left a quarter mile to the north as an added precaution against discovery. When they got inside the castle, theirs would be a battle fought on foot and hand to hand.

Guy peered around the tree, his gaze keenly piercing the darkness. He counted three men on horseback. Excitement gripped him as he realized they were headed for the castle, offering his forces an unforeseen opportunity. If they could take down these men, three of his own knights could proceed in their place and, when the gate was opened for them, the rest of his men could rush inside . . .

Guy gestured for five knights to follow him. Swords drawn, they crouched in the ditch at the side of the road until the unsuspecting travelers were almost upon them,

358

then attacked with silent swiftness. The three men were yanked from their saddles so suddenly they had no chance to cry out, and their mounts were quickly calmed.

Only when the captives were dragged into the trees did Guy discover one of the men was dressed as a priest. As the two Gervais knights were mercilessly dispatched, their throats cut, the clergyman was propped up against a tree, a blade pressed beneath his fat double chin.

"Please do not kill me! I beg you—"

"Silence!" Guy hissed, towering over him. "Speak only to answer my questions. Is that understood?"

The priest bobbed his head, his wide eyes showing white in the darkness.

"Who are you?"

"I am Father Anselm, priest to Lord Gervais. My lord is expecting me at this very moment."

Guy's mind raced with this news. Obviously he would have to include this priest in his new plan if they wanted to get beyond the gate. "Do you always ride about with two armed knights as your escort?" he queried tersely, thinking it strange.

"No, no. They were sent out to find me," the man answered in a nervous rush. "I-I was in the village paying a call. My lord Gervais wants me to prepare some special documents which must be sent to the archbishop by morning. I tell you, he awaits me with great impatience! He is sure to send out more of his men if I don't arrive soon—"

"What kind of documents?" Guy cut in coldly, his intuition pricked.

"Annulment papers for his sister. She has left her husband, Lord de Warenne."

An annulment, Guy thought grimly. If not for what Henry had told him, he might have truly believed Leila hated him. Now he could see her actions for what they were, all part of a desperate plan to sway Roger against fighting him in a trial by combat. If the annulment was approved, she would be free to marry whomever that bastard chose for her.

His heart filled with anguish. Ah, my brave, sweet love,

did you so fear for my life that you would be willing to make such a sacrifice?

Guy lifted the priest's trembling chin with his sword. "Hear me well, Father Anselm. I am Lord Guy de Warenne. There will be no annulment papers drawn up this night, for I have come for my wife. You are going to help us get into the castle."

The rotund clergyman crossed himself several times, gulping air. "Wh-what do you want me to do?"

"I and one of my knights are going to ride with you to the gatehouse. You will act normally and say only enough to have the gate thrown open for us. When we are inside the bailey, get out of the way if you value your life." His voice fell to a fierce whisper. "I warn you, Father. I am willing to risk hell's eternal fire for my wife. If you give us away, your blood will stain my sword."

"You need have no fear," the priest blurted. "I will not betray you."

"A wise decision," Guy said, easing the blade slightly away from the man's throat. "Now, I take it you know the castle well. Where will I most likely find Lady de Warenne? In the keep, or are there private chambers in the great hall?"

"She . . . she's in the keep's dungeon, my lord."

Guy stared at the man incredulously. "In the dungeon?"

"Yes. Lord Gervais's men told me she will be held there until she agrees . . . Oh, it is a terrible, terrible business, but what can I do? I have no sway in such matters. I know little else but that my lord wishes his sister to rid herself of the babe she carries in her womb."

Guy's initial shock that Leila was pregnant with his child was quickly swept away by blinding rage. It was clear Roger's greed and cruelty knew no limits!

Sheathing his sword, Guy grabbed the priest by the cowl and shoved him toward the horses, calling over his shoulder, "Burnell! You will ride with us. Bring me one of the dead men's cloaks and you put on the other. Langton, see that the men are prepared to storm the gate as soon as it is opened. Montgomery, take a half dozen knights with you to the curtain wall and tell the men waiting there to forgo the ladders and rush the gate as well. Go!''

A round of whispered ''Ayes!'' sounded in the darkness as he heaved the fat priest into a saddle.

''Remember what I told you, Father,'' Guy hissed, throwing the proffered cloak around his shoulders. He mounted and drew his horse alongside the priest's. ''One wrong word—''

''I-I have not forgotten, my lord.''

Guy kept his head down as they left the cover of the trees and rode up the barren incline to the gatehouse, he and Robert flanking the frightened priest. His fury intensified as they drew closer, and when they were almost at the gate, he tightly gripped the rains. His every muscle was taut, his blood running hot in anticipation of battle.

''Name yourselves!'' a castle guard demanded from a lighted window in the gatehouse.

''Surely you can see who it is,'' the priest cried, his voice quavering slightly. ''Father Anselm! Open the gate. Lord Gervais has summoned me in great haste!''

Guy glanced at his knight as the immense timbered gate swung fully open, a look of grim understanding passing between them. Together they drew their swords and in the next instant, Guy's enraged battle cry shattered the night's stillness. He was answered by the fierce shouting of his men as they raced toward the gatehouse.

Spurring his horse forward, Guy cut down with mighty strokes the astonished guards who rushed at him while Burnell slew the men who frantically attempted to close the gate. Screaming in terror, the priest slid from his mount and took off running toward the great hall. He began to wave his arms hysterically and yell that the castle was under attack.

Guy decided not to waste his time on Father Anselm. The man's cries of warning came too late. Already his own knights and men-at-arms were streaming through the gate, trampling the fallen guards and almost slipping in the slick blood that covered the ground. It was clear from the meager forces upon the battlements that Roger had not prepared for a surprise assault. Blessed fool!

"Strike down any man who will not surrender!" Guy shouted as his men surged with brandished swords across the torchlit bailey to meet those Gervais knights who were just now running from the hall. Still other de Warenne men forged up the stone steps to the battlements, holding high their shields as arrows began to rain down upon the castle yard.

Guy chose a different path, riding hard for the towering rectangular keep. His only thought was to find Leila.

Jumping down from the horse, he cursed as pain shot like hot flames through his leg. He shoved open the arched door to the keep and stepped inside, his eyes quickly adjusting to the hazy light cast by a single hanging lantern. He was about to descend a flight of stone steps which he believed led to the dungeon when a side door crashed open and Roger Gervais rushed into the room. The sword he carried was dripping blood.

"So my priest saw fit to assist you and your men through the gatehouse," Roger said harshly, his narrowed gaze full of hatred. "My dead priest. He will not betray me again. Before I struck him down, he told me you had come for your wife, de Warenne. How did you know to find her with me?"

"Suffice it to say I know Leila's heart."

"And suffice it to say you will not be taking her with you. Stand away from those stairs!"

Guy held his ground, his back against the wall and his sword poised in front of him. "You would do well to surrender, Gervais. This battle has already been lost. Our sudden attack has overwhelmed your forces. Throw down your sword."

"Surrender is a word unknown to me, my lord." Roger's blade swiped menacingly at the air as he edged closer. "To fight to the death has always been my creed, and so it is for my men as well. I think you will find if you step outside the keep that the battle still rages."

"I will not leave this place as long as my wife is in your dungeon, Gervais."

"Then die here!"

Cold steel rang out against steel, Roger's enraged curses

echoing all around them. The ferocity of his attack forced Guy to retreat into the middle of the room and then onto the circular stairs which led to the keep's upper floors. He backed up step after excruciating step, pain ripping through his leg and sweat drenching him as he deflected Roger's vicious blows.

"You should be the one to surrender, my lord de War-enne," Roger sneered, his breath coming harder as he drove Guy relentlessly up the stairs, around and around. "You're weak. I can feel it. I can see it in your face. That poison must have sapped your strength. Give up now . . . while I might have a mind to let you live."

"And let you drive your sword through my heart when I lower my weapon?" Guy demanded, responding with a wild thrust that Roger barely managed to dodge. Swearing vehemently, Roger clutched his arm where Guy's blade had sliced into his flesh, although he continued to swing his sword in a wide, deadly arc.

"You were never the fool," Roger muttered through clenched teeth. "These stairs make as fitting a killing ground as any jousting field. My revenge . . . has been a long time in coming, de Warenne. Perhaps you would not have despoiled our friendship so readily . . . if you had known it would one day lead to your death."

"If by honoring Ranulf's dying wish I spawned your hatred, Gervais," Guy countered, grunting with exertion as he parried a fierce blow, "then ours was no true friend-ship. I think . . . it was not Christine you loved but her rich dower. My supposed betrayal has not ruled your ac-tions so much as your own jealousy and greed! You forget that I, too, have a score to settle!"

Roaring in fury, Roger attacked him with such a ven-geance that Guy was forced to retreat still higher up the stairs, passing the fourth floor. Fiery sparks flew as hard steel struck and scraped against rough stone walls. Guy's ears rang from the clamor of battle. Ducking a savage swipe, he swore loudly when he backed straight into a stout wooden barrier, and he realized that there were no more steps to climb. They had reached the roof.

Swinging his sword violently at Roger to buy himself a

few precious seconds, Guy slammed his full weight against what proved to be a door behind him. The wood splintered and gave away, and he tumbled onto a graveled surface. Groaning in pain, he rolled out of the way just as Roger's sword came down where his head had been only an instant before, and he hauled himself quickly to his feet.

It was dark, but Guy could faintly make out his opponent's massive silhouette from the light cast by torches far below in the bailey. As he bettered his stance, he dragged in great lungfuls of cool air and fought against the weakness that was plaguing his limbs. A warm wetness was oozing down his leg, and he knew that his wound had reopened, that blood was soaking through the bandages.

"Come on, de Warenne!" Roger shouted, his blade whistling as he swiped viciously. "So far this battle has been no contest but a game of cat and mouse. Strike like a man, damn you, or I shall feel I've killed a green youth and not a trained knight!"

Guy did just that, taking the offensive now that he had ample room with which to maneuver. Their swords met again and again in the darkness, grunts and curses and ragged inhalations of breath melding with the sharp ring of clashing blades and the dim sounds of battle still raging below in the castle yard.

Just when it seemed neither man could gain the advantage, both being so well matched in skill and size, Roger again took the upper hand, driving Guy almost to the battlement with his furious blows.

"Say a fast prayer, de Warenne! Death is upon you!"

As he fended off a mighty swing, Guy's sword was knocked from his grasp and clattered upon the stones a few feet away. He ducked and lunged for his weapon at the same moment Roger rushed at him with a bloodcurdling cry of victory. But with amazing swiftness Guy swept up his sword and rolled free just as Roger's arm descended in a brutal downward thrust. In an instant Guy was on his feet and smashing Roger's weapon from his grasp in a blow so powerful that his arm reverberated with the impact. Then, without thinking, bloodlust coursing through his veins, Guy clamped his massive hands around Roger's surcoat, lifted him bodily, and, as Roger's screams echoed in his ears, pitched him headlong over the battlement . . .

The abrupt silence seemed deafening to Guy.

Heaving for breath, he picked up his sword and went to the parapet, where he leaned on the cold, damp masonry for support. Sweat dripped onto his hands as he peered down into the bailey at Roger's broken body. He felt no great sense of triumph. He knew it could have easily been he lying still and lifeless upon the ground.

As Guy wiped the sweat from his face, his gaze swept the bailey. It appeared his men had subdued the bulk of Roger's forces. Many of his knights, Robert and Henry among them, were busy rounding up prisoners near the great hall.

His eyes were drawn to the slender figure of a woman running toward the keep, her long blond hair flying behind her, and he recognized Maude. She collapsed to her knees beside Roger and began to rock his body back and forth as if she sought to rouse him. Suddenly she shrieked in anguish at the realization that he was dead.

Staggering to her feet, Maude raised her clenched fists at the keep. Her face was twisted in crazed fury as she shouted at him, "Murderer! I curse you, de Warenne. Curse you! Your precious wife shall die for this deed!"

Oh, God. Leila.

Guy's stomach roiled as Maude grabbed a blazing torch from a bracket and disappeared into the keep. He rushed to the roof entrance, and in his desperate haste, he nearly tripped as he vaulted over what was left of the door. He began to run down the winding stairs, his blood pounding in his ears, his heart battering against his chest. The pain in his leg was so acute it felt as if sharp spikes were driving into his flesh with each step. But it didn't matter. Nothing mattered but Leila.

He was only to the second floor when he heard terrible screaming, shrill and high-pitched. The piercing sound sent chills down his spine and filled him with dread. By the time he reached the ground floor, acrid gray smoke was flooding up the narrow flight of stairs which led to the dungeon.

As Guy took the steps three at a time, the smoke grew thicker and he began to cough, his eyes stinging. The agonized screams grew louder, more horrible. At the bottom of the stairs, the smoke reflected the fiery orange of flames shooting out from an open cell. Terrified rats skittered and squeaked around his feet. He raced to the door but was pushed back by the intense heat. Then he saw a sight which flooded him with stark horror. He could have been staring straight into hell.

Maude was engulfed in flames and staggering around the cell, screaming . . . screaming . . .

God help him! Leila must be in there, too!

Twisting his damp cloak around his arm, Guy held it in front of his face like a shield and tried again to enter, but it was impossible. The flames were too hot, and now the floor of the cell was nothing but a boiling sea of fire. Choking from the billowing smoke, tears streaming down his cheeks, he backed away, shaking his head in horrified disbelief. He could no longer see Maude. Her hideous screams had ceased.

"Leila . . ." he rasped hoarsely, unable to tear his watery eyes from the blazing inferno. "Why? Why!" He knew he must escape the dungeon quickly or be overcome by smoke, but he couldn't bring himself to move. God in heaven, he did not want to live without her!

The sound of weeping somewhere behind him made Guy wheel around. Surely he hadn't imagined it! Then he saw that another cell door was partially open and he lurched crazily toward it, stumbling inside.

He couldn't believe his eyes. Huddled in the middle of the cell, rocking on her knees and sobbing uncontrollably, was Leila. Seeing Guy, she wept harder, her hands held out rigidly in front of her.

"Ooohhh, it burns . . . it burns!" she babbled through her tears, clearly in shock. "I tried to stop it . . . The fire caught her skirts. Her hair! Oh, the screaming! I tried to help her! I tried . . ."

Guy gathered her into his arms, his relief so immense, so overwhelming that he could not speak. Hugging her close, he reeled through the smoke-filled dungeon and up the stairs to the ground floor, where he threw open the door and lunged outside.

He did not stop until they were well away from the keep, then he sank to his knees, gasping for breath and cradling Leila against his chest. In the torchlight he could see that her hands were reddened, but thankfully not seriously burned. He kissed her blistered palms and tenderly stroked her hair.

"Shhh, love. The nightmare is over. Shhh."

Suddenly Leila went limp in his arms, the horror of what she had witnessed proving too much for her.

Guy was grateful for her unconscious state. He did not want her to see the bloody carnage strewn all across the bailey. He did not want her to think she was still living a nightmare. Not when she was finally safe in his arms.

The first thing Leila felt when she awoke was a stinging sensation in her hands. Dazed, she lifted them slowly, only to discover they were swathed in bandages. Then she felt someone softly stroking her cheek. She turned her head to find Guy lying beside her on top of the fur coverlet, propped up on an elbow. He smiled warmly.

"Guy . . ." Astonished, she tried to sit up, but he pushed her gently back against the pillows.

"Easy, love. Give yourself a moment. You've been asleep for hours. Take a look around you and get your bearings. You're back at Warenne Castle, in your own bedchamber."

Leila drew a deep breath, her gaze trailing around the familiar room. It was true. She was home.

"But how?" she asked, her thoughts gradually growing less muddled.

"It is a long story, my love. Don't trouble yourself with it now. There will be time enough to hear it when you're feeling better."

She gazed into his eyes, so very, very blue in the bright sunshine flooding the room. The love she saw reflected there was enough to chase away the terrible memories beginning to crowd in on her, but she had to ask him one question.

"Roger?"

Guy seemed uncertain of how to answer, then he sighed, shaking his head. "He is gone, Leila. He fell from the castle keep to his death."

Leila absorbed this news, saying nothing for a long moment. With her relief that Roger would plague them no more, she felt a sense of sadness. She had never wished such misfortune upon either him or Maude. They had brought it upon themselves, evil begetting evil.

Finally she said, "You fought him, then."

"Yes, we fought."

Suddenly afraid that he might have been wounded, her eyes swept him frantically, the great breadth of his bare shoulders, his powerful arms, his heavily muscled chest. Skipping past his braies, she noticed the fresh bandages around his thigh.

"I am whole, Leila," Guy said with a small laugh, reading her concerned scrutiny.

"Yes, thank God, but I should attend to your leg wound—"

"That will not be possible for several days, my love," Guy told her gently, drawing up her chin to face him. "You must wait until your hands heal. Philip has been ably caring for both of us by using some of your prepared ointments. When he returns in an hour or so, I'm sure you will find him most eager to hear your suggestions for our continued care."

Leila was incredulous. "Philip said that?"

"Yes. He has undergone a miraculous change of heart. He has already visited the surrounding villages and farms to admit to my tenants that he was wrong about your medical skills. I'm sure you will have patients aplenty when you return to your hospital."

"Surely this must all be a dream," Leila murmured, stunned by this news.

"No," Guy replied firmly. "It is no dream."

"But I cannot believe you came after me!" she blurted, staring into his eyes. Then her voice fell to a broken whisper. "I thought . . . you would hate me for leaving you."

"Never," he said fervently. "I love you, Leila. You are

everything to me. How could I ever hate you? You are my beloved wife. You carry our child—''

"How did you know . . . ?'' she asked, amazed.

"It doesn't matter. Just know that I am pleased beyond measure about the babe.'' As he ran one finger lightly down her cheek and across her lips, his expression grew serious. "In truth, Leila, when I discovered you had fled, I almost believed that you hated me—''

"Never.'' Leila felt him tense beside her, his gaze so full of hope and longing that it took her breath away. If there was ever a moment to share with him exactly how she felt, it was now. "I love you, Guy de Warenne. You have forever won my heart. I will never, never leave you.''

His hoarse cry was exultant and she welcomed his impassioned kiss with open arms. The warmth of his lips was the sweetest affirmation that this incredible moment was real. The fierce desire flaring within her was just as real, and she yearned to share it with him. To give herself freely and fully, as she had just given her undying love.

"My lord, how shall we fill these long hours as we both convalesce?'' she teased softly, delighting in his roguish smile when he drew away to gaze into her face. She shivered deliciously. It seemed their thoughts were one and the same.

"I can think of countless ways, my love.''

Epilogue

Damascus, Syria
Spring, 1274

Eve Gervais sat alone in her fragrant courtyard, staring
at the water-stained, travel-worn packet she held in
her trembling hands.

She was told it had passed through many other hands to
reach her: messengers, pilgrims, a native Christian who
had journeyed all the way from Acre to deliver it to Friar
Thomas, and finally Majida. Her faithful odalisque had
just returned from the church in the Christian quarter with
the precious missive, then she had retired to leave Eve in
solitude.

Now it was all Eve could do to tear open the stiff outer
parchment. As she did so, she could not help but wonder
if the letter inside bore good news or bad. Drawing a deep,
steadying breath, she pulled it out and began to read by
the soft golden light of a lantern.

It was from Leila, written almost eight months ago, and
to her astonishment, the beautifully flowing script was in
English.

Eve's eyes quickly filled with tears, and she sighed brokenly, reading about Roger's cruel treachery and his death.
Yet her sadness was far outweighed by quiet joy. The rest
of the letter expressed Leila's radiant happiness.

Leila had married a man of good and brave heart. Lord
Guy de Warenne had promised Eve that Leila would come
to no harm, and he had kept his word. She could not have

hoped or prayed for a more worthy husband for her beloved daughter. He had even given Leila a hospital so that she might fulfill her fondest dream.

Eve traced her finger over the last few lines, as if by touching the ink she could somehow come closer to the delicate hand that had written them.

Leila was the mother of healthy twins, Eve and William, born last summer. She also had an adopted son, Nicholas, whom she dearly loved. Her life was rich and full. She and Guy were happy together . . . so very, very happy.

"So God has willed," Eve said softly to herself, reading the letter one more time before tearing it and the parchment packet into small pieces. Then she rose from the marble couch and cast the fragments into the stream which tumbled through her courtyard and emptied into the Barada River flowing just beyond the high, vine-covered wall.

Plucking a pink damask rose, Eve inhaled its lush scent as she stood beside the stream. She was so lost in her joyous thoughts she did not hear footsteps behind her. She realized she was no longer alone when someone gently touched her shoulder.

"What has captured your mind so, Eve? Did you not hear me call your name?"

She turned and smiled into Sinjar's dark eyes. "I was only thinking how happy I am, my husband," she answered truthfully. Even now, after reading the letter, she felt no guilt that she harbored one secret from the man she loved so completely.

It was Sinjar's belief that Leila had taken pity upon Guy de Warenne and somehow aided him in his escape from Damascus. At least that was what he had always maintained. If he had any idea that Eve had had something to do with the escape, he had kept it to himself. He had never asked her about that night, and she didn't think he ever would. His silent protection only endeared him more fiercely to her heart.

"You are my happiness, my beloved Eve. Come. The night is falling."

As she took his hand, thrilling to the warmth of his touch and the desire smoldering in his eyes, the rose slipped from her fingers and fell into the stream. It spun and bobbed in the current, then drifted away . . .

If You've Enjoyed This Avon Romance— Be Sure to Read. . .

THE MAGIC OF YOU
by Johanna Lindsey
75629-3/$5.99 US/$6.99 Can

SHANNA
by Kathleen Woodiwiss
38588-0/$5.99 US/$6.99 Can

UNTAMED
by Elizabeth Lowell
76953-0/$5.99 US/$6.99 Can

EACH TIME WE LOVE
by Shirlee Busbee
75212-3/$5.99 US/$6.99 Can

The WONDER of WOODIWISS

continues with the publication of
her newest novel in trade paperback—

FOREVER IN YOUR EMBRACE
☐ #89818-7
$12.50 U.S. ($15.00 Canada)

**THE FLAME AND
THE FLOWER**
☐ #00525-5
$5.99 U.S. ($6.99 Canada)

**THE WOLF AND
THE DOVE**
☐ #00778-9
$5.99 U.S. ($6.99 Canada)

SHANNA
☐ #38588-0
$5.99 U.S. ($6.99 Canada)

ASHES IN THE WIND
☐ #76984-0
$5.99 U.S. ($6.99 Canada)

A ROSE IN WINTER
☐ #84400-1
$5.99 U.S. ($6.99 Canada)

**COME LOVE A
STRANGER**
☐ #89936-1
$5.99 U.S. ($6.99 Canada)

SO WORTHY MY LOVE
☐ #76148-3
$5.95 U.S. ($6.95 Canada)

America Loves Lindsey!

The Timeless Romances
of #1 Bestselling Author

GENTLE ROGUE	75302-2/$5.99 US/$6.99 Can
DEFY NOT THE HEART	75299-9/$5.50 US/$6.50 Can
SILVER ANGEL	75294-8/$5.50 US/$6.50 Can
TENDER REBEL	75086-4/$5.99 US/$6.99 Can
SECRET FIRE	75087-2/$5.50 US/$6.50 Can
HEARTS AFLAME	89982-5/$5.99 US/$6.99 Can
A HEART SO WILD	75084-8/$5.99 US/$6.99 Can
WHEN LOVE AWAITS	89739-3/$5.99 US/$6.99 Can
LOVE ONLY ONCE	89953-1/$5.99 US/$6.99 Can
BRAVE THE WILD WIND	89284-7/$5.50 US/$6.50 Can
A GENTLE FEUDING	87155-6/$5.99 US/$6.99 Can
HEART OF THUNDER	85118-0/$5.99 US/$6.99 Can
SO SPEAKS THE HEART	81471-4/$5.50 US/$6.50 Can
GLORIOUS ANGEL	84947-X/$5.50 US/$6.50 Can
PARADISE WILD	77651-0/$5.99 US/$6.99 Can
FIRES OF THE WINTER	75747-8/$5.99 US/$6.99 Can
A PIRATE'S LOVE	40048-0/$5.50 US/$6.50 Can
CAPTIVE BRIDE	01697-4/$4.95 US/$5.95 Can
TENDER IS THE STORM	89693-1/$5.99 US/$6.99 Can
SAVAGE THUNDER	75300-6/$5.50 US/$6.50 Can